STRIKE BACK

A MASON SHARPE THRILLER

LOGAN RYLES

INKUBATOR
BOOKS

Published by Inkubator Books
www.inkubatorbooks.com

ISBN (eBook): 978-1-83756-413-2
ISBN (Paperback): 978-1-83756-414-9
ISBN (Hardback): 978-1-83756-415-6

To Richard and Emma...
For all the support, and so much more for the friendship.

1

The first thing he hit wasn't the girl, it was the washing machine. One flat-palmed strike that rattled the entire row of industrial-grade laundry tumblers. He called her a dirty name, and she jumped in the way that battered women do.

All raw energy and immediate alarm, but a little indignation, also. A stubborn refusal to believe that this man that she loved—or had once loved—could actually be speaking to her in this way.

I sat at the back of the laundromat, an empty garbage bag crumpled next to me. I held a burner cell phone in one hand and a prepaid debit card from the local Western Union in the other. Three hundred and fifteen dollars were loaded on that card—my payment for the month, and it felt like a rip-off. Sure, I could breathe through my nose again, and it was no longer contorted and collapsed the way it had been only three weeks prior, but I would be paying those three hundred and fifteen dollars a month for a long time.

Maybe longer than the battered girl would live, by the

look of it. She was about twenty. Blonde and very cute, but a little malnourished also. Big green eyes all laced with fear as she backed away from her boyfriend. Or fiancé. Or husband.

Whatever he was, he worked outside. He had thick muscles and a good Alabama tan. His hands were worn after the fashion of road pavers and brick layers, and he wore work boots. I wasn't sure if he was a little drunk or just a little demon possessed, but he was clearly in a foul temper. He grumbled unintelligible darkness through his teeth as he fed coins into the washing machine.

I glanced toward the only other occupant of the small building. He was short, black, and a little stooped. In his late sixties, I thought, and the apparent owner of the establishment. He had a key to access the coin deposits of each machine, and he was busy rolling quarters.

I cocked an eyebrow. He pursed his lips. Neither of us spoke.

The guy in the work boots gestured to the door and snapped something about a soda. The girl scurried off, headed for a nearby convenience store. The guy returned to fiddling with the washing machine, now smashing the buttons and flat-palming the control panel whenever the hapless washer failed to respond quickly enough.

The owner observed, but he remained quiet. Probably because he was small, and his muscles outgunned. As yet, no real damage had been inflicted to the industrial machines.

I, on the other hand, was neither small nor outgunned. I also wasn't worried about the washing machines, but I was concerned with the girl's continued survival. Placing both the phone and the card on the seat next to me, I slumped my shoulders as I approached, trying to look as unthreatening as possible.

Just a guy with something to say.

"Can I have a word with you?"

His dark eyebrows furrowed, but he otherwise ignored me. I detected a slight blur in his bloodshot eyes. A lot of blinking, and an odd twitch of his nose.

No, he wasn't drunk, he was high. Or more likely he was coming down from a high, and not enjoying the ride.

"Find another," he growled. "Plenty of machines."

"No, I want to talk about that girl."

That got his attention. He pivoted toward me, teeth bared. I noticed his gaze catching on the white plastic nose brace I wore. It was a gaudy thing, affixed to my head by an elastic band, designed to keep my newly reconstructed snout in place long enough to heal.

It also, I imagined, served another purpose. It sent a subliminal message—there had been a fight, and regardless of the broken nose, I had been the one to walk away. Whether he was smart enough or sober enough to decipher that message was another matter.

"What about her?" he growled.

"She's got bruises on her arms. Another on her neck. Seems to be limping a little. I find myself concerned about her health."

Bloodshot eyes blinked rapidly. His tongue darted over dry lips, and his gaze passed across the laundromat behind me. I could no longer hear the sliding tap of quarters being counted. I figured the old man was watching. He was a witness.

The tweaking druggy was at least sober enough to understand the implications of a witness.

"Mind your own business," he said. "She's fine."

Then he turned away, suddenly relaxed. He drew a hand-held gaming device from his back pocket and headed for a row of chairs. I remained motionless, evaluating my options.

I had an instinct, and it was almost overwhelming. It involved his face and the curb outside. Maybe a need for another nose brace in the end, and not for me. But I've spent much of the past two years living that way—swinging first and asking questions later. It had earned me more than a broken nose, and even though it was effective, I was starting to question the justice in that sort of unfettered approach.

Maybe it was the little leather-bound Bible resting in the seat of my pickup truck that was getting to me. All those verses I'd been reading in the book of Proverbs about the patient man, and the violent one. The line in between.

Whatever the case, I decided on an alternative course of action. I approached the line of chairs my druggy target had absconded to and sat next to him with a quiet sigh.

He looked up from the gaming device. "*What?*"

"Look," I said. "We both know what's happening here, and we both know it's not acceptable. You're rough on that girl, and it needs to stop. She deserves your respect and protection. Men are meant to look out for women, not abuse them. So you're going to make a change. Understand?"

Something between disbelief and outrage contorted his face into a scowl. He seemed to be caught in a deadlock, like a CD skipping over a scratch. Trying to reach the next melody, but unable to move past this unthinkable roadblock now fallen across his path like a toppling tree.

The drugs certainly didn't help his mental faculties. In the end, he went with his basest instincts. Those same raw, animal impulses that drove him to throw that girl around like a rag doll.

"You better *split*, jackass, before I reverse that nose surgery."

I cocked an eyebrow and didn't blink.

He was the first to look away. His face dropped. Transparent shame overcame him like a thundercloud. He returned to the game without a comment, and I stood. I made it back to my dryer in time to shovel clean laundry into the garbage bag. My back was turned as the door opened with a ding and the soft footsteps of the girl returned. A paper bag crinkled—the guy snapped a curse.

"I said *diet*," he snapped.

"They didn't have it." Her voice was timid and shaky, underscored by an Alabama drawl.

Then his fist struck the seat next to him. I heard it as a meaty thud against plastic, and my shoulders dropped. I closed my eyes and sighed. The door dinged again, and they both went crashing outside. By the time I turned around, I could see them through the dirty windows standing next to a rusty Buick, him waving his arms and cursing. Her looking less afraid and more indignant. She gestured toward the convenience store, defending herself.

And then he hit her. One swift crack across the face that sent her tumbling against the Buick's trunk. I dropped the laundry bag and made a bee-line for the door. Dirty names were flying thick as I reached the parking lot. Base insults slurred together amid a shower of spittle.

He didn't even hear me as my boots crunched on gravel. I made it all the way to within reach of his shoulder before his dampened situational awareness finally alerted him to an incoming threat.

By then, it was far too late. I spun him around and drove a fist straight toward his face, dropping at the last moment to strike his windpipe instead of his nose. It's a cheap, dirty move, but it hurts the knuckles less than skull bone does, and the damage is instantaneous. He choked, lungs cut off from air, and stumbled back. I followed him up, left shin snapping up like a baseball bat to collide with his groin. A sickly shriek exploded from his busted throat, further emptying his already depleted lungs. He doubled over and I grabbed a fistful of his greasy hair with my left hand. I pivoted at the hips. I dragged him right, leveraging my body mass and driving his face full-force into the rear fender of the Buick. His nose collapsed on impact, bones shattering and teeth crunching. I reversed my hip twist and drove my right knee into his stomach—hard.

Then I finally let him go. Only four seconds had passed since I first made contact, but when I released him he was so winded and caught off balance that he couldn't break his own fall. His skull struck asphalt, and his eyes rolled back in his head.

Not dead, but very unconscious. I inhaled once, heart thumping, and shook my right hand. Windpipe or otherwise, my knuckles still burned.

A soft cry erupted to my right, and I turned to see the girl standing with a hand over her mouth, wide eyes fixated on her unconscious abuser. Then pivoting to me.

"This your car?" I asked.

She blinked. Then shook her head.

"Okay then. There's a bus stop two blocks that way. You got money?"

Another swallow. A split hesitation. Then a nod.

"Take the bus. You're done with him. Okay? You're never going back."

A swollen tear leaked from her right eye. Her hand

shook, and she turned back to the limp form of her abuser, seeming to hang for a moment between horror and disgust. I half expected her to sling herself at me. Domestic disputes are like that. Cops always respond in pairs for such things— one cop to manage the aggressor, and the other to hold back the victim.

But the girl didn't turn on me. The heat of indignation won out. Her jaw closed and her chin lifted. Then she looked back to me.

"Thank you," she whispered.

I nodded once, and then she was gone, fast-walking up the sidewalk toward the bus stop. I toed the unconscious jerk on the ground, but he was out cold.

Good riddance.

Back inside the laundromat I made eye contact with the owner. He was still standing over his pile of quarters, a half-loaded paper tube in one hand.

Looking out at the parking lot.

"He gonna walk again?" the owner said at last.

"Sure."

A soft grunt. A shake of his head. "Too bad."

He resumed counting, and I headed for my laundry. I had just slung it over my shoulder, pocketing the phone and prepaid card when the owner spoke again.

"Five-oh."

Looking over one shoulder I saw the Birmingham police cruiser rolling into the parking lot, slowing as the cop behind the wheel detected the feet sticking out from behind the Buick. Momentary indecision clouded my mind as I evaluated my options. My truck was parked fifty yards away, in front of a dollar store. I couldn't reach it without walking right past the police cruiser, unless—

"Door in back," the owner said, still shuffling quarters. "Leads into the parking lot. Think I'm gonna lock up today. Seems like some of these machines need maintenance."

He made eye contact again. There was something of a twinkle in his gaze. I nodded once.

"Thanks."

Another grunt. He shuffled toward the door, keys in hand, and I turned for the back. Thirty seconds later I was tossing the bag of laundry into my battered old 1967 GMC pickup. The suspension groaned and the door hinges creaked as I settled in, but the motor started right up. I looked into my rearview to check the position of the cops. They were interviewing the laundromat owner.

He was doing a lot of shrugging and head scratching.

Smiling, I withdrew my phone from my pocket, remembering the payment. The confirmation page had failed to load, so I pivoted over to my email account to check for a receipt. A conglomeration of a few thousand unread marketing messages, newsletters, and junk mail filled the screen. I never checked my email. I never needed it.

But as I scrolled past the first half dozen messages, searching for the receipt, my thumb stopped cold. There was one email address I recognized. One name that blasted out from the screen like a storm of hot fireworks. No subject line —no attachments. I smashed the message and found myself holding my breath as it loaded. The service attached to the burner phone was cheap and unreliable, and the loading icon spun. And spun.

When the screen finally blinked and displayed the contents of the message, I found no words. Only two collections of numbers, the first five-digits long, the second four-digits long, with a hyphen in the middle. It was incoherent. To almost anyone, it would have looked random.

But not to me.

72576.
10-78.

Throwing the truck in gear, I dumped the clutch and raced out of the parking lot.

2

It was late evening in Birmingham, and rush hour had set in. Upon reaching the highway I was mired in bumper-to-bumper traffic, everyone creeping along in the mass daily migration away from the business district and toward the suburbs.

I didn't bother to return to the seedy little motel near the UAB medical center where I had taken up residency during my nasal reconstruction surgery. My clothes were all in the trash bag, my personal effects stacked on the bench seat next to me. There was nothing to return to, and according to a quick Google search of the zip code provided in the email, I had a long ride ahead of me.

I shot off a quick reply, notifying the sender that her message had been received and that I was en route. I also provided my latest phone number and asked for a call, but after thirty minutes the phone still hadn't rung, and my cortisol levels were spiking.

Not only because the original message was already two days old, or because the sender was Jacquie Richardson, my former partner at the homicide division of the Phoenix Police Department. Most of what drove me to weave through traffic, searching for any advantage through the slog, were those last four digits. The numbers with the dash in between.

They constituted what cops called a *ten code*, which is a mostly retired radio messaging system that police departments used to use to conceal the meanings of their radio transmissions. These days, most cops just use plain English.

But not Jacquie. She liked the codes. She'd learned them and applied them religiously, forcing me to learn and apply them also. She enjoyed speaking in shorthand, leaving the ignorant masses oblivious to her meaning. Code *10-78* was a radio call I could only ever remember using on very rare occasion. Maybe twice in my entire policing career.

But those times were hallmark moments, because code 10-78 means emergency backup needed—*immediately.*

By the time I cleared the outskirts of Birmingham and reached Interstate 22 West, the GPS on my phone displayed an arrival time of four a.m., but that was based on traditional highway speeds, and the old GMC was really pushing it to reach sixty miles per hour. The destination I'd selected lay right at the heart of the 72576 zip code, in a little town called Whitford, Arkansas. Located in the heart of deeply rural Mullins County, Whitford was truly on the backside of nowhere, with empty farmland to its east and the rising bulk of the Boston Mountains to its west.

Total county population: under ten thousand. Total city population: twelve hundred.

But it wasn't the extreme remoteness of the county that threw me off, or even the cryptic nature of Jacquie's abrupt and unexplained email. It was the knowledge that Jacquie

Richardson, my former investigative partner, career nuisance, and longtime friend didn't *live* in Arkansas. She lived in Phoenix, where she still practiced the trade that I'd abandoned two years prior. Sure, her family was from Arkansas, and she'd occasionally mentioned rolling hills and abject poverty during her elementary years.

But she never went back. That chapter of her life had been firmly—and permanently—closed. Why, I never knew. I was smart enough not to ask.

What I did know was that Jacquie Richardson was a strong and competent cop, able to handle herself in the worst of circumstances without breaking a sweat. She'd saved my neck on multiple occasions, and talked her way out of sticky situations with greater ease than your average con artists.

She was independent. Smart. Quick on her feet and handy with a gun. Most importantly, she had never—not once—called a code 10-78. She'd never needed it.

At least not until fifty-two hours prior, amid some back-water town just forty miles south of the Missouri state line, when something had occurred which required immediate, emergency backup...and I was the person she needed.

I swerved into the left lane and gave the old truck every-thing it had.

3

I dialed Jacquie's cell phone five times during the drive. Every time it went directly to voicemail, and she never called back. She never replied to my email, either. I called the Phoenix Police Department and was informed that Detective Richardson was on leave. That was all the desk sergeant would say, and when I pressed for details he hung up.

I hit more traffic in Memphis—a nasty car accident. By the time I reached northern Arkansas it was after six a.m. and the sun rose behind tangled hardwoods. The landscape was semi-mountainous—foothills, navigated by narrow roads that wound through valleys and lost themselves between tree-covered ridges. Even without the population statistics I'd reviewed I would have known that Mullins County was not only rural, but also isolated. The last significant town I passed through was Jonesboro, which was where I left the interstate nearly three hours prior. Now it was all four-lane state highways, followed by two-lane county roads, many of them riddled by potholes and washed-out ruts, their double yellow lines so faded I could barely see them.

All the signs were weathered, and many of them were decorated by bullet holes, the peculiar tradition of rural people with firearms and too much time on their hands. Late summer grass grew high in the ditches, littered with aluminum cans and beer bottles, while what occasional driveways I passed were marked by homemade mailboxes welded to metal fence posts.

The air smelled of mountain brooks and pine needles as it blasted through my open windows, but even the luminous sunrise wasn't enough to ease the dull anxiety that had gnawed through my gut all night long. I wasn't tired. I wasn't even sleepy. My mind was alive with focus, some voice deep in my subconscious alerting me to the promise of unspoken danger.

Jacquie had never called code 10-78 before.

On the outskirts of Whitford the speed limit decreased, and I surveyed sagging old homes clad in faded—and often mildewy—lapboard siding. Most of the yards were as over-grown as the ditches behind me, the mailboxes leaning. There were rusted cars in the driveways, shirtless men smoking cigarettes and drinking coffee on the front porches. The first gas station I passed doubled as a feed and hardware store, with some kid fueling a tractor out front. There was a library built into an old schoolhouse, a school built into an old church, and a church built into a strip mall alongside a boarded-up grocery store.

There were no fast-food chains. No big-name box stores or car dealerships. I noticed only one motel, and that consisted merely of eight doors shedding dirty brown paint —four stacked on top of four, framed by moldy brick, with an office and a little red sign that proclaimed the word *vacancy*.

I rolled on, reaching downtown. I passed a city hall that shared a space with the Whitford police department and the Whitford volunteer fire department. Then came a square surrounded by tall brick buildings that looked to be older than my truck, many of them boarded up and long vacant. One populated by a tiny law firm, another occupied by a gun store, and three joined together to constitute a little diner marked by a rusted metal sign. There was a courthouse in the middle of the square—a very ugly thing that must have been tremendously sexy in about 1972—and in the back corner of the square, opposite the gun store, was the Mullins County Sheriff's Office. Another old brick building with dirty windows and a gold star pasted to the door.

There were maybe twenty vehicles parked around the square, most of which were concentrated around the diner. Everyone I saw looked as shabby as the rest of their town, dressed in worn jeans and stained shirts, gathered around pickup trucks to drink coffee or piled into booths next to the diner windows.

The overwhelming vibe of the place was sadness—perhaps loneliness. Whitford reminded me of the kind of Appalachian coal towns you see in old movies. Places that boomed during the early half of the twentieth century but were quickly forgotten thereafter, leaving their residents in a perpetual state of spiraling poverty while they stubbornly refused to pull up stakes and seek better fortunes elsewhere.

I could respect that. I'm a little stubborn myself. But I hadn't come to this place as a tourist, I'd come here because my old partner had asked for backup, and it was only logical to assume that I wouldn't be the first person she asked. If there was any trouble, a rational person would first consult the local police, and so I would do the same.

I pulled into a parking space in front of the Mullins County Sheriff's Office and piled out, smelling gasoline, dirt, and hardwoods. The concrete beneath my boots was so blackened by time that it looked like asphalt. I marched straight to the sheriff's office and pushed through the glass door, rattling a little bell as I did. A wash of propane heat assaulted my face, joined by the stench of sweat, burned coffee, and cigarette smoke. The floor was linoleum and stained, the walls sheetrock and scuffed by boots and furniture. There was a metal reception desk with a desk sergeant, an open door leading to a bullpen full of additional desks staffed by overweight cops in wrinkled uniforms, and a number of shelves lining every wall, each loaded with file folders, banker's boxes, and old newspapers. In fact, the entire place was cluttered, with every flat surface stacked high with paperwork, takeout cartons, and aged computers.

But what struck me most about the place was the waiting room. It sat to my immediate left—a large square equipped with sagging chairs. There was a water cooler, a coffee bar, and a dated television broadcasting a local news station. The story was about the crisis on America's southern border— thousands of migrants pouring over the Rio Grande and consuming American jobs. Or so the talking head said. About half a dozen old timers with long beards sat kicked back, sipping coffee and watching the news.

They all looked up when I entered, whatever conversation they'd been sharing instantly freezing over at the prospect of an outsider. I stood just inside the door, taking it all in and feeling as though the room I had entered had more in common with a barber shop than a law enforcement headquarters. The guys lounging in the waiting room were very clearly not waiting at all. They were just...*there.* Hanging out. Loitering.

And now watching me, many of their gazes fixating on that gaudy plastic nose brace as their eyes squinted in immediate suspicion.

I looked to the desk sergeant and cleared my throat. He sat leaned back in his chair, one boot on his desk, an inflated gut testing the integrity of his shirt buttons. Lazy eyes flickered toward me as he slowly lifted a coffee cup, taking a lethargic sip without any pretense of rushing. I noticed him fixating on the nose brace, same as the others.

"May I help you?"

His voice was slow, with an accent that was a little bit southern, a little bit mountain hick, and a lot apathetic.

"Who's in charge?" I demanded. There was no trace of apathy in my voice, and the directness seemed to offend him. He set the cup down.

"I'm the desk sergeant. Maybe you'd like to introduce yourself?"

There was an insolence to his nature that made me want to kick his boot right off the desk. After a long, hard drive out of Alabama I'd arrived in Whitford with very little in the way of patience. Whatever remained was now quickly evaporating.

"Get the sheriff," I said.

He raised an eyebrow. "Excuse me?"

"Did I stutter? Get off your butt and *get the sheriff.*"

That probably wasn't the correct tack. I could feel the tension spike in the room the moment the words left my lips. He flushed red, and his boot finally dropped off the desk. He looked as though he were coming out of the chair, but maybe not to get his boss. My right hand closed into a fist, ready for anything.

Then, as if by magic, the boss appeared anyway. A toilet flushed and a door opened, allowing passage for a skinny guy about two miles tall. He had to stoop to get his head through the door frame, still zipping his pants as he went.

Gray hair, but not an old guy. Mid-forties, perhaps, with three days of razor stubble and another wrinkled shirt. No tie. No gun belt. Not even a badge, but I knew he was the boss because of the yellow monogram over his chest pocket —*Sheriff Conroy*.

The newcomer must have heard my exchange with the desk sergeant from the bathroom, or else he could simply detect the tension. His eyes narrowed and he looked to me first, then he glanced sideways at the desk sergeant.

I expected the sergeant to interject, but he didn't. He simply tightened his lips and shook his head. Some kind of prearranged signal.

Conroy stepped across the room and extended a hand.

"Sheriff Jeb Conroy, Mullins County. And you are?"

I shook the hand once. It was still damp—hopefully from the bathroom sink. "Mason Sharpe. Do you have an office?"

Conroy cocked an eyebrow as though I'd just asked him to disclose the value of his retirement accounts. He sucked his teeth, then he nodded. I followed him into the bullpen, weaving our way through overloaded desks. Besides the cops, the only other person in the room was a young black kid, about seventeen or eighteen years old, muscular and handsome. He worked a mop across the stained tile floor, fighting a losing battle against the overall decay of the place.

The only office in the room lay in the back. Conroy's

name was printed on a name plate pasted to the door, and the letters were faded and starting to peel. He'd been sheriff for some time.

Inside there was a desk, two chairs, and a lot of paper-work. A lot of dust. Conroy settled behind his desk and slurped coffee from a mug printed with the Mullins County seal. He didn't offer me a seat. The second chair was over-flowing with case files.

High over our heads, a single ceiling fan squeaked. One groaning rotation after another, not nearly strong enough to be felt. Conroy smacked his lips.

"All right, Mr. Sharpe. What brings you to my county?"

4

_____

It was a strange question. Not because it was passive aggressive—I'd earned that, at this point. More because of the assumption the question made. What *brings you* to my county?

As though I'd never been here before, and certainly wasn't a resident. I squinted.

"Who says I'm visiting?"

Conroy shook a toothpick out of a canister and worked it between his lips. He studied me. Then:

"For a start, there's the North Carolina antique license plate mounted to that rust bucket of a truck you're driving. Already ran that. Registration comes back under *Marley Grier*. I'm guessing you bought the truck from her and saw no need to register it under your own name, given that North Carolina antique license plates don't expire."

It was a good guess, and as it happened, completely accurate. I hadn't registered the truck in my name, but that wasn't out of laziness. I simply didn't have a permanent address to register it *to,* and regardless, I was much more interested in the question of how Conroy could have already run my plate. I'd been in town for all of ten minutes.

"Beyond that, though," Conroy continued, "I been sheriff of this county for going on twenty years. Ain't but about nine thousand people who live here, and I know every one of 'em. If anybody moves in, I get a report from the landlord who leased to them, or the realtor who sold to them. We're real personal like that. Real close-knit."

"Awesome," I said. "So you should recognize the name *Jacquie Richardson*."

Conroy didn't blink. He didn't so much as budge, but a trace of tension shot through his face like a flash of lightning. Come and gone in an instant, but there nonetheless.

"Who now?"

"Jacquie Richardson. She's a detective from Phoenix, Arizona. She has family here."

Conroy sucked on the toothpick. He cocked his head and pondered—or pretended to ponder.

"No...no Jacquie Richardson 'round here. You said she has family?"

"That's right."

"Who are they?"

I rolled back my mental records of all the conversations Jacquie and I had shared about our pasts. There weren't many. When I had joined the Phoenix Police Department, I'd been months out of the United States Army's 75th Ranger Regiment. Multiple deployments, all of them to nasty places, mostly Afghanistan. I wasn't interested in talking about it. My patrol partner was petite, abrupt, and a little standoffish. Truth be told, I didn't like her at first.

We started to click when she saved my neck from an excessive force investigation—some incident involving a pimp that I caught getting rough with one of his girls. I returned the favor, and an inquiry was launched. Jacquie was the only witness, and she had no memory of the matter. Apparently, she'd suffered from a headache that night.

From then on our relationship blossomed, and when I made detective Jacquie promoted also, remaining my partner. We worked well together. We busted a lot of homicide cases. We locked up a lot of murderers, talked a lot of basketball and football over beers after work. When Mia came along and I fell head over heels in love, Jacquie was the first to hear about it.

When Mia was murdered only a few months later, Jacquie was the one who kept me from toppling over the edge.

But for all that—for all that camaraderie, loyalty, and friendship—we never really talked about our respective pasts. I didn't talk about the Army, and she didn't talk about Arkansas. Those topics were mutually respected as off limits.

"I don't know who her family is," I said. "Maybe some more Richardsons. You know everybody in the county, right? Who would her family be?"

My tone carried an edge, but Conroy didn't take the bait. He withdrew the toothpick from his lips.

"You got a picture?"

I scooped my phone from my pocket. There were no photos on it. I didn't have social media. But there was a news story that ran after the so-called Sundevil Killer case—the case that rocketed Jacquie and me into the homicide division. Our picture was in it, and the article was easy enough to find on Google. I rotated the phone and Conroy took it. He squinted.

"Ah. She's a colored girl."

There was something in his tone that rankled me. More than just his use of an outdated and generally derogatory racial descriptor, it was the way he said it. With condescension, and amusement.

"She's black," I said. "You seen her?"

Conroy returned the phone. "Naw. Truth be told we ain't got many of them around these parts. I'd have noticed."

"Many of *what?*"

Conroy grinned. "Coloreds."

I wanted to punch him. Blood boiled just beneath my skin. I could feel it in my face, and I knew that he noticed. He was getting to me, and there wasn't a thing I could do about it. I was in a police station, after all. The cops in the bullpen were watching us. The janitor kid had stopped mopping.

My only choice was to press ahead with the questions.

"What about her family? Anybody around here named Richardson?"

Conroy flicked the toothpick into the trash. He sat up, suddenly looking impatient.

"You know, I gotta tell ya. We don't take too kindly to folks coming around asking about our neighbors. I don't think you've properly explained your business here, Mr. Sharpe."

My business here.

No. I hadn't explained, and I wasn't sure that I wanted to. As hostile as this place felt, I could only imagine that Jacquie —"*one of them*"—hadn't been welcome. The fact that Conroy was now probing didn't encourage me to take any chances.

"I'm looking for my friend," I said. "Is that against the law?"

Conroy sipped coffee. Wrinkled his nose and tossed the remainder of the drink into the trash can.

"Hey, boy!" he shouted into the bullpen.

Over my shoulder feet scuffled on the floor, then the janitor appeared. He glowered at Conroy, but he didn't say anything. Conroy extended the cup.

"Fresh coffee. No sugar."

The janitor took the cup without comment. He turned back for the door.

As he did our gazes locked. I saw something searching there—something very suspicious. Then he was gone.

"I don't know nothing about any family of hers," Conroy said. "You can ask around town if you want. Now, if you'll excuse me."

He turned to the computer and went to work with the mouse. I wasn't sure if he knew about the reflection of the computer screen in the glass face of a cabinet behind him, but I could see what he was doing.

It was Solitaire. A card game.

I gritted my teeth and headed for the door. Conroy called after me.

"Hey, Sharpe?"

"What?"

He looked up from the computer. Skinny lips stretched over teeth stained by tobacco juice. "We're real traditional around here. Don't care too much for brash outsiders. You might try a little honey before dumping on the vinegar."

My jaw remained clenched. "I'll remember that," I said.

Then I headed for the town square.

5

I tried the diner first. It was by far the most populous location in town, even though the occupancy had thinned a little as the clock ticked toward eight a.m. The patrons packed around those tables were more of the same sorts I'd witnessed smoking on front porches and lounging in the waiting room at the sheriff's office. All a little shabby, their hands rough and dirty, their plates loaded with carbohydrates to fuel the long, hard day ahead.

But it was the look in their cold eyes that snagged my attention. After spending more than a year in the Deep South, slowly bumming my way through Georgia, Alabama, Florida, Mississippi, and Louisiana, I'd become familiar with stereotypical southern hospitality. It was a stereotype for a reason. I found southern people to be warm and welcoming —a little too eager to gossip, maybe, and occasionally two-faced in their generosity. But even if they secretly hated you, they at least made the pretense of warmth. I expected Arkansas to be the same, and maybe it was, but the town of

Whitford most certainly *wasn't*. The overwhelming vibe of the diner, much as the sheriff's station, was cool to the point of being hostile.

I passed from table to table, displaying Jacquie's picture and asking if anybody had seen her. Most of the diners simply grunted and shook their heads, not even bothering to make eye contact. Some took a second glance at the photo and muttered a short "Naw."

Mostly it was the sober silence of the place that caught my attention. The diner became as still as a graveyard when I first entered, and even as the clink of forks against plates resumed, the conversation did not. It was as though I were a priest walking into a whorehouse. The tension was transparent.

I didn't care. I completed my circuit of the room and went back outside, inhaling that cocktail of gasoline fumes and mountain air as I surveyed the square. Many of the loiterers I had observed when first arriving had departed, but even with their absence considered, the town somehow felt...too quiet. What locals remained avoided my gaze, and yet I felt their eyes on me the moment I turned my back.

It was disconcerting. Infuriating. My blood pressure spiked as I withdrew my burner phone and checked my email for the fifteenth time since departing Birmingham. The message from Jacquie was still there, joined by my reply.

But Jacquie had yet to email back. She hadn't returned my phone calls or texts. It was complete radio silence, and in my very gut I knew that was a bad sign.

Marching back to my truck, I fired up the engine and screamed out of the parking slot, headed back the way I'd first arrived. The grimy motel sat with weathered bricks baking in the morning sun, dust from the gravel parking lot erupting over my windshield as I ground to a stop and cut the motor. I wasn't altogether sure if I was thinking rationally or simply acting on instinct, but the obstinance and unhelpfulness of the population downtown had done nothing to dampen my resolve.

I was being lied to. I could feel it. I didn't know why, but if the aim of Whitford's collective hostility was to drive me out of town, it was going to fail. I wasn't leaving Mullins County until I found some answers, and they might as well know it.

Marching to the little office built into the end of the building, I fished my wallet out and rapped on a window. The glass was filthy, and I could barely see, but what I did see reminded me of the sheriff's office. Disorder and disrepair. Paperwork and trash piled everywhere. There was no clerk seated in the sagging desk chair, but another heavy rap of my knuckles finally produced one. She was middle-aged and overweight, dressed in sweatpants and an overworked t-shirt. Dark eyes peered at me through smudged glasses, and she took her seat before unlocking the window.

"What'dya want?"

"A room," I said. "How much?"

Those dark eyes narrowed. Her hand remained on the window, lips pursed. A long moment dragged by, and still she made no acknowledgment of my request or my question.

"Well?" I pressed.

"We're all booked. Sorry."

I squinted, looking impulsively back to the parking lot. My truck was the only vehicle parked there. Nobody stood in the breezeway outside the row of rooms. No air conditioners ran.

But when I looked to the vacancy sign mounted over my head, the neon tubes that had flickered as I first rolled into town were now dark, the sign switched off.

I turned back to the clerk. "Are you kidding me?"

She shrugged. "Contractors coming in tonight. Got the place booked up."

"Contractors, huh? I guess they just called."

Lips stretched into a smile, revealing stained and crooked teeth. "That's right."

I snapped my wallet closed, replacing it with my phone. "You ever see this woman? Did she rent a room from you?"

The clerk barely glanced at the screen.

"Never seen her."

"You sure about that?"

"That's what I said."

Frustration finally overwhelmed the bounds of my better judgement as I returned to my truck. I slammed the door, unable to tell whether outrage at the obstinance of everyone I'd met since entering Whitford, or simply a growing premonition of doom on Jacquie's behalf was driving the feeling of desperation rising in my chest. Nothing I'd seen or experienced since rolling into Mullins County had served to assuage the anxiety I felt the first moment I opened Jacquie's email.

Something was wrong here. Very wrong, and not just in the way things normally go wrong, like a car sliding off the road or a tornado blowing over a barn. There was an active, sort of intentionally sinister vibe that permeated the very asphalt beneath my tires and spoke to something more insidiously corrupt than mere bad luck or happenstance.

It wasn't an accident. It wasn't a mistake. Whatever had generated the 10-78 code was a sincere, malicious problem, and these people were lying to me. Whether about Jacquie or about something else, I wasn't sure, but I was done playing nice. I was going to get some answers, or I was going to start burning buildings down.

Roaring back onto the main drag, I made directly for the town hall that shared space with the Whitford police department and the volunteer fire station. The parking lot was more gravel. The cars outside were dusty and worn—most of them, anyway. The exception was a late model Cadillac CT5. It sat parked in front of a little blue sign that read:

RESERVED PARKING: MAYOR.

Perfect.

I routed for the town hall's entrance. From the fire department wing of the building another dirty loiterer called toward me, asking my business. I ignored him and rammed through the door, stepping into air-conditioned staleness that tasted exactly like the sheriff's office. There was a receptionist's desk, a long hall paved in carpet, and a series of offices opening on either side. The receptionist herself was a scrawny old woman in a flower-print dress, cat-eye glasses perched on an eagle nose. She glared at me as I barged in, but I looked right past her to the pair of men standing in the hallway.

One was short and fat, dressed in slacks and a golf shirt. The other tall and muscular, with hair clipped so close to his skull that I could clearly see the veins running through his scalp. I seemed to have caught the two men in some manner of conference, because they both looked up quickly as the door exploded open.

The fat guy flushed, then forced a quick smile. The

muscular guy's face remained perfectly blank, hollow blue eyes so pale they almost looked like ice. A jagged scar ran along his left cheek—it reminded me of the signature an IED leaves across unprotected skin. His stance spoke to military training, his demeanor feeling like a mirror that reflected the hostility of this entire town.

"Well hello there, stranger," the fat guy said, stepping quickly toward the lobby. Flabby cheeks jiggled as he walked, thin blonde hair combed over a growing bald spot atop his round head. He wasn't more than five foot six, with little feet planted into leather boat shoes. Mid-forties, maybe three hundred pounds.

Everything about him looked soft, like a blob of lard. His gaze caught on my nose brace, just the way everybody else's had, but the smile never wavered. It was forced—produced.

"You the mayor?" I demanded.

"That's right." He extended a hand. From the hallway I noticed that the muscular guy with the scarred face had disappeared.

"Mayor Andrew Kiddle, at your service. And you are?"

I ignored his extended hand, thrusting my phone into his face instead. "I'm looking for this woman. You seen her?"

Kiddle seemed perturbed by my abruptness, his thick lips constricted into focused pucker. He withdrew reading glasses from his breast pocket and slid them over thick red ears. His inspection of the phone was prolonged.

Eventually he shook his head. "Can't say that I have. Who is she?"

"Jacquie Richardson. Her family lives here. You know any Richardsons?"

Another frown of concentration, lips working. I couldn't

tell if Kiddle was actually reviewing a mental catalog of constituents, or if he were mentally inhibited.

At last, he held up a chunky finger. "Hold on a moment. I may know somebody."

He turned and shuffled down the hallway, hitching his pants up along the way and disappearing into his office. I was left alone with the old crow behind reception. I glanced her way and found that eagle stare still fixed on me behind the cat glasses, perfectly stiff and unblinking, as though her wrinkled face were made of stone.

What was happening here? It felt like I was on a movie set, and all the extras had been instructed not to interact with the lead actors. People were all around me...and yet they weren't.

Cat-Eyes made no attempt to initiate conversation, but from down the hall I could hear Kiddle talking. His voice was a murmur, and I got the impression that he was on the phone. My suspicions were confirmed a moment later when the familiar plastic clack of a handset resting on a receiver echoed down the hallway.

Kiddle reappeared, waddling again, smiling again, a sticky note in one hand.

"Cyrus Richardson?" he asked.

"Does he live here?"

Kiddle nodded. "Outside of town, along County Road 19. Here's the address."

He handed me the note. I examined it, finding a street number written in handwriting so sloppy I could barely read it. I squinted, sudden uneasiness edging into my gut to join the frustration.

Something felt wrong. I couldn't pinpoint what it was,

but the sudden production of the address after so much resistance felt...too easy, almost.

I looked back to Kiddle. He smiled, hands now jammed into tight khaki pockets. Not blinking.

Not asking any additional questions, either.

I folded the note and turned for the door.

6

The address on Mullins County Road 19 lay five miles outside of Whitford, northwest of town amid the foothills. The route was technically a two-lane but in many places the grass on either side had encroached so much toward the faint double yellow lines that I was forced to straddle them with my GMC as the busted road rose and fell.

What driveways I did pass disappeared directly amid the trees, the houses they led to concealed from view. The air was crisp as it blew through my truck windows, the sun now risen over the hilltops and blazing down on me. I kept my foot on the gas, pushing the old inline six to its limits as the GPS on my burner phone guided me onward.

I still couldn't pinpoint the discomfort in the back of my mind, but every instinct born out of my Army and police careers alerted me that something about this situation simply wasn't right. I'd been ramming my head against a brick wall all morning, and when that wall finally collapsed it didn't feel like I had won. It felt like I had been let in.

Two miles before I reached the turnoff for my destination, I was convinced. It was a setup. I couldn't be sure exactly why, or what the nature of the scheme would be, but I knew Kiddle had made a call before giving me the address. Somebody had fed him the information—somebody who held Kiddle on the end of puppet strings. Brand new Cadillac CT5s aren't cheap, after all, and nothing about Whitford felt like the kind of place where an elected official drew a generous salary.

He'd sent me here because I'd made it clear to the fine folks of Whitford that I wasn't going to be brushed aside. For whatever reason, that was a problem. My questions about Jacquie were a problem. My entire presence was a problem.

So now they—whoever *they* were—had to erase that problem.

Well, fine then. If they wanted to play rough, I could play rougher. An ambush can be turned into a counter-ambush. I would reach the property, scope out the terrain, identify the belligerents, and—

My thoughts were cut short as I topped the next hill and immediately slammed on the brake. The front tires of the GMC locked and the back end fishtailed as I dove into the next valley, sliding straight toward a one-ton Dodge pickup truck that sat parked right across the middle of the road. It was jet black, a little jacked up, and almost brand new.

I finally reached a stop with barely ten yards to spare, the Dodge resting motionless ahead of me. Its windows were dark, and I couldn't hear an engine. I thought it was shut off. My own truck continued to hum as my heart thundered, both hands wrapped tight around the steering wheel. I looked instinctively into both ditches and the tree-covered hillsides beyond but saw nobody.

All was quiet. Only the hum of the GMC's inline six and the thunder of my own heart broke the silence.

I cut the motor off, leaving the truck in gear. From behind the Dodge's window tint I thought I saw a shadow move, but I couldn't be sure. Reaching beneath my seat, I felt past the little metal cashbox that served as my bank account and touched cold, hard steel.

A tire iron. A favorite weapon of mine.

I stepped out onto the blacktop but remained behind the shelter of my open door, the tire iron within easy reach. Waiting.

The driver's door of the pickup opened without a sound, and a black combat boot appeared, followed by a black pants leg. The guy who dropped out of the pickup was handsome —blond headed, blue eyed, but not like the scar-faced man at the town hall. This fellow had an almost movie star quality about him. Very calm and self-assured. Mid-thirties. Perfectly relaxed for having nearly been T-boned by an oncoming block of steel. He even smiled.

"Sorry to surprise you this way. I thought we should talk."

The voice was strikingly clear and articulate, in contrast with the locals in Whitford. Almost pleasant. I remained behind the door of my truck, hand within reach of the tire iron.

"Where's Jacquie Richardson?" I said.

Movie Star's smile remained unbroken. He pocketed his hands and took a step closer toward my truck, as relaxed as ever.

"You seem pretty fixated on that question, bud," he said. "You really don't take *I don't know* as an answer, do you?"

"Not when it's a lie."

Movie Star stopped, still five yards removed from my front bumper. His shoulders lifted in a shrug.

"Well. It's not a lie. I don't know what else to tell you. There's no Jacquie Richardson here, and to be honest with you, our community takes issue with outsiders crashing around. Especially those with a clear history of rabble rousing."

He tilted his head, and I knew he was looking at my nose brace. Even so, the smile hadn't faltered, and that was starting to really get under my skin.

"Let me tell you what I take issue with," I said. "I take issue with anybody I've ever called a brother in arms, or a partner, or even just a friend being up the creek without a paddle. I take issue with ignorant hillbillies in dumpy towns obstructing my efforts to render assistance. And I *really* take issue with smug rodents in shiny pickup trucks parking in the middle of the road when I've got somewhere to be."

I reached beneath the seat and wrapped my hand around the tire iron. I stepped out from behind the GMC's door and slammed it, iron swinging at my side. I gritted my teeth.

"So get your slimy ass back in that truck and *move* before I leave you here like roadkill."

It was a blunt approach. The message was crystal clear. I vaguely recalled Sheriff Conroy's admonition for honey over vinegar, and the rational part of me knew he was right, but the rational part of me had succumbed to the frustrated part of me.

The anxiety had taken over. The urgency. I was resorting to those methods of brute force and violence of action that had served me so well in the Army.

Movie Star's smile faded, his gaze switching down to the tire iron. He sighed, very theatrically.

"Man. That's a mistake."

Then the doors of the Dodge popped open. From the back seat three men piled out. A fourth dropped out of the front passenger seat. They all wore black jeans and tight shirts, were muscled and tall, with tattoos running the length of their arms and short haircuts. Icy-cold hatred radiated off them like the invisible waves of a nuclear reactor.

There were no guns but there were plenty of weapons. A baseball bat, two pairs of brass knuckles, and a nightstick. Movie Star held out a hand and one of his compatriots pitched him a telescoping metal baton. He flicked it open with a snap, and the smile returned.

"Second thoughts?" he asked.

From behind me a stick snapped. I looked over my shoulder to see three more dudes emerge from the trees. More baseball bats and close-cropped haircuts. They circled in behind me, cutting off any option of retreat. In a split second, I was encircled.

I turned back to Movie Star. This time I smiled.

"Thanks," I said.

He cocked an eyebrow. "Thanks?"

"For confirming what I already knew—this whole town is rotten to the core. And also for making what happens next easy."

Movie Star's grin melted. He jerked his head, and the goons closed in. I stepped quickly left, moving away from the GMC. Opening up my right side. I waited until the first guy —the guy with the nightstick—closed within five feet. Then I rushed him, easily ducking his first blow and landing a strike of my own against his left knee. The tire iron landed with a crack, and he shrieked. Then his buddy with brass knuckles circled in from my right. Boots thundered on the pavement behind me. Nightstick fell, clutching his knee, and I brought the sharp end of the tire iron down over his shoulder blade. The pry tip sank into unprotected flesh, and I shot a knee toward the groin of Brass Knuckles.

That was my last good hit. It landed with force, and I ducked the whistle of a baseball bat rocketing in from behind. All around me a field of black legs, leather jackets, and glinting metal flooded my vision. Their first successful strike landed in the form of Movie Star's baton over my right calf. I stumbled and caught a brass-knuckled blow to my sternum. The air raced from my lungs, and I flailed with the tire iron.

Then the first strike to my skull landed. It came in the form of a tap from a baseball bat, not nearly hard enough to kill me, but hard enough to stun me. The world spun and I pitched to the ground, landing on my back. The blows kept falling, raining over my stomach and legs. Movie Star's handsome face appeared, his teeth set in a sneer.

"Lights out, blackie lover."

Then his baton fell right between my eyes—just an inch over that bulky plastic nose brace—and the world disappeared.

7

Consciousness returned slowly and painfully. The first thing I became aware of was a fiery sensation radiating from my ribcage. Then my thighs, and right calf. Pretty soon my entire body was alive with the burning sensation of bruised muscles, pounded flesh, and a thundering head.

I couldn't see a thing. Everything was pitch black, and I had the vague sensation of dampness draining off my forehead and down my face. I tasted cold water, and adrenaline flooded my veins as panic took over.

Water boarding.

It was the first thought that entered my mind. Memories of Afghanistan surged my system, images of black-site prisons and interrogation facilities populated by terrorists and those suspected of being terrorists. All the wooden beds. The straps. The buckets of water.

I surged upright, jerking my arms away from invisible, perceived bonds. My hand struck my face and fresh pain radiated through my body. I yanked a wet towel away and blinked back the water as I gasped for breath. The darkness around me persisted, but voices now joined it. A dull cry of *"Jeremiah! Jeremiah, get in here!"*

A hand closed around my shoulder, pressing me down. I fought, shoving back. Water drained into my mouth, and I choked.

Then a light flashed on, temporarily blinding me. Footsteps thumped across carpet, and a male voice barked.

"Get yo hands off her!"

The next set of fingers that closed around my arm thrust me back onto the bed with a forceful shove. Black skin gleamed in the overhead light as my vision returned. A face appeared over mine, skin taught and young, eyes sharp and bright. I recognized the face, but my mind took a moment to place it.

Then the sheriff's station returned to me. The black kid pushing the mop.

The janitor.

"Calm down," the kid barked, holding me down. "Ain't nobody hurtin' you."

My body remained rigid but my brain took control of the fight-or-flight responses the panic had induced. I blinked hard and the tidal waves of pain returned. I saw the light hanging from the ceiling as a bright orb of orange, like the sun. A ceiling fan squeaked, and the kid kept pressure on my shoulders. From somewhere behind him soft feet padded on the carpet. The gentle feminine voice returned.

"Ease up now, Jeremiah. He don't mean no harm. I just startled him, is all."

The kid—Jeremiah, I guessed—narrowed his eyes, but he relaxed a little pressure off my shoulders as a second face appeared next to his. It was a woman, also black, and much older than the kid. Maybe early fifties, with the gentlest smile I'd seen in forever. She laid a hand on my arm and nodded reassurance.

"Easy now, big fella. You're all good. You're with friends."

Calm overcame my body, dampening the surge of adrenaline. I breathed a little slower and relaxed into the bedding. The mattress sagged under my weight, but it was still a great deal more comfortable than...

Where was I last? I could barely remember. There had been a road...a truck.

Skinny.

The memories returned and my jaw clenched. I looked instinctively to Jeremiah.

"Where am I?" I demanded.

It was the woman who answered. Jeremiah only stared in transparent suspicion.

"You're in Creedmore. Little community outside of Whitford. Where us poor folk live."

She chuckled at her own joke, and water trickled into a pan. She was wringing a towel out, and presently she replaced it across my forehead. It was cool and soothed a little of the headache.

It did nothing for the burning sensation ripping up my legs and across my chest. I dipped my chin to gain a view of my body and saw nothing but a sheet. I did see my pants, shirt, and boots piled on the floor next to me. The carpet was worn and orange. Very nineteen seventies in style.

I looked back to the woman.

"Who are you?"

"I'm sorry, dear," the lady said. "My manners clear left me. My name is Lucile. Lucile Richardson."

Richardson.

The name landed with a bang in my mind, and I tried to sit up again. Jeremiah shoved me down.

"You be still now!" he barked. "You just lie down."

The force of his bunched muscles caught me off guard, and I landed with a grunt. Pain raced through my chest, and I bit back a scream. Lucile's hand struck like a snake, swatting Jeremiah in the arm.

"You now! Get off him. Ain't no call for that."

"He's violent!" Jeremiah objected. "He tried to shove you!"

"He didn't know what he was doing. He got panicked. Now go and fetch him one of those sports drinks you be sucking on. He'll need the sugar."

Jeremiah opened his mouth in another objection, and Lucile's eyes bulged. She came halfway out of her chair, and that did it. Jeremiah withdrew his hand, shot me another glare, and then he was gone. Across the carpet and out the door.

I lay still, a long way from shoving anybody. It hurt just to breathe, let alone sit up. Now that full consciousness had returned, I wished that I could pass out again. The riddle of my misery wasn't a difficult one to solve. I remembered Movie Star and his baton, knocking me out. It was reasonable to assume that the blows from brass knuckles, baseball bats, and nightsticks had proceeded for some time after that. And then...

I rotated to Lucile, surveying her kindly face. Searching for any distinct characteristics or familiar features. The image of another Richardson I knew so well.

I didn't see it, but maybe she was a Richardson by marriage.

Jeremiah returned to the room with a Gatorade and

Lucile twisted it open. She poured a little into a cup with a straw and offered it to me with another one of her reassuring nods.

"Here now. Get you some electrolytes. They say they help."

I suddenly felt desperately thirsty, and I sucked hard on the straw. Four swallows later, the cup ran dry. I collapsed back against the bed, gasping a little.

Jeremiah stood over me, glaring down. I estimated the mass of his toned biceps—the obvious product of considerable gym time—and did the math. It was another easy riddle. There was no way Lucile had lifted my two-hundred-pound frame, anyway.

"You found me?" I asked.

"About half dead," Jeremiah said.

"Out by the road?"

A nod.

"Jeremiah drives that way to get home," Lucile says. "He's got a good eye. Saw you right amongst the leaves. A good thing, too. You're banged up good, child."

No joke. I could feel the handiwork of Movie Star and his army of goons all over my body. The memory almost brought a smile to my face as a strange hint of irony joined it. Since abandoning my career as a cop and becoming a full-time vagrant, I'd encountered a number of thick-headed bullies, many of whom made the dramatic mistake of placing themselves into the crosshairs of my distaste for injustice. The consequences they suffered were both swift and absolute.

But for all those fist fights and street brawls where I'd learned the brutal effectiveness of a tire iron against unprotected flesh and bone, I had never encountered anyone who had—straight from the start—assaulted me with a full mob of equally armed thugs. For all his bravado and disgusting condescension, Movie Star had paid me the respect of bringing reinforcements.

A *lot* of reinforcements.

"Why didn't you take me to a hospital?" I asked.

"Hospital's fifty miles away," Jeremiah said. "And you don't wanna go there, no way. Ain't but a bunch of meth heads and crack hoes."

That brought another swat from Lucile. "Watch your language, child!"

He pulled easily away and shot her a mischievous grin. Lucile turned back to me.

"We did the best we could with you. Truth is...well..." She trailed off.

"You didn't want to be seen taking me in," I finished.

Lucile looked both apologetic and ashamed.

"Don't be sorry," I said. "I understand. The guys who jumped me would hardly take responsibility, and I've already seen how the sheriff's department treats Jeremiah. They'd be only too happy to pin this on him."

"Bunch of racist pigs," Jeremiah snarled.

Lucile scowled, but this time she spared him the swat. I inhaled as deeply as I could manage with my bruised ribcage. I wasn't sure if it might be a fractured ribcage. The thought of broken bones reminded me of my nose, and I lifted a hand to my face. The plastic brace was gone, but as my fingertips probed I felt no collapsed bones nor fresh inflammation. Everything felt generally in place, signaling that Movie Star's band of merry skinheads had spared me the brutality of yet another smashed nose.

A small miracle.

Reassured about the status of my very expensive facial reconstruction surgery, my mind proceeded backwards from the fight on the county road. Back to Whitford, the mayor's office, the hotel...the sheriff's station.

I pivoted to Lucile. "Do you know Jacquie Richardson?"

Lucile nodded. "She's my niece."

"She's here?" I asked, barely concealing the hope that rushed my tone.

Lucile's gaze dropped, and my stomach dropped with it. Pressing one hand against the mattress, I forced myself up with a creaking of aged springs. This time, neither Jeremiah nor Lucile stopped me. I rotated on the bed and put two feet on the orange carpet.

Every part of me hurt. My arms trembled as I sank my fingers into the mattress. I caught Jeremiah and Lucile sharing a look.

Mother to son. Uncertain and conflicted.

"Where is she?" I asked. "Where's Jacquie?"

Another prolonged hesitation from them both. Jeremiah's lips parted, but it was Lucile who spoke first.

"We don't know," she said, her voice barely above a whisper. "She's missing."

8

Whatever minor relief I felt at the absence of Jacquie's death being announced was short lived as a vaguer reality set in. The reality of *not knowing*.

I sat on the edge of the bed, head spinning, and forced an even breath. I gathered my thoughts, organizing them into an investigative grid of priorities, and backtracked to the most foundational questions. The ones I needed to ask first.

Before I could speak Jeremiah cut back in, tone brash and demanding.

"You better tell us who you are, man."

I half expected Lucile to interject again, but this time she didn't. I thought back to my interaction with the cops at the sheriff's office, and how Jeremiah had brushed up against me while fetching coffee for Conroy. I recalled the look in his eyes, that gleam of suspicion.

It made sense, now. He'd heard me asking about Jacquie. He knew Jacquie. He knew that she was missing.

And so did the cops. They must have, which confirmed what I already knew to be true. They were lying.

"My name is Mason Sharpe," I said. "I was a cop back in Phoenix. Jacquie was my partner."

"Nah." Jeremiah shook his head. "Her partner's name is Dallas. I know, cuz Jacquie called him while she was here. She never mentioned no Mason Sharpe."

"I was her partner before, Sherlock." I couldn't resist the sarcasm in my tone. "I quit the department two years ago."

"So why are you here now?"

There was an undertone of aggression to Jeremiah's voice that didn't really seem justified given the context of our conversation. I was in his house, yes. Poking around and asking intrusive questions about his missing cousin. But only because he'd picked me up out of a ditch and brought me here in the first place.

"Jacquie sent me an email requesting backup," I said. "I thought she was in trouble. So I drove here, met your delightful neighbors, got the run-around from the sheriff's department, and then got jumped by a truckload of thugs with baseball bats and brass knuckles. End scene. Happy?"

I shot him a nastier look than he deserved. Jeremiah just glowered. Running a hand through my hair, I clamped my eyes closed to endure a crushing wave of my headache before refocusing on the problem at hand—the *actual* problem.

Then I looked up.

"Why was Jacquie here?"

The moment the question left my lips the entire atmosphere of the room seemed to change. It felt colder and somehow very heavy. Lucile's gaze dropped and her eyes watered. Jeremiah turned away, looking out through the bedroom window. I followed his line of sight over a sunbathed front lawn, freshly cut and clean, to a pickup truck parked against the curb. It was an old truck—mid-eighties, Ford F-150. There was a camper shell covering the bed, just like the camper shell that covered the bed on my old GMC.

A magnetic sign stuck to the door of the truck. I couldn't read the entire thing, but the top letters were clear.

Richardson Janitorial Service.

Jeremiah just stared, and I looked back to Lucile. I noticed her fiddling with a ring on her left hand. Just a simple gold band, spinning it slowly. Her whole body visibly crushed under the weight of invisible grief.

And then I understood—better than Lucile or Jeremiah could ever know. My own head bowed and I uttered a mental prayer for strength. Not just for me, but for Lucile and her son. Because I know what that pain feels like. I'd been carrying around my own invisible load for nearly two years.

"I'm so sorry," I said.

Jeremiah turned back from the window, eyes bulging. They were rimmed red now, and moist.

"Yeah? You're *so sorry?* Man, what do you know?"

The anger in his voice was no longer a mystery, and it didn't even bother me.

"Jeremiah, please." Lucile's voice cracked. Jeremiah gritted his teeth and hurried out of the room. I gave time for Lucile to collect herself. When at last she looked up she appeared older...more tired.

"My Cyrus died two weeks ago. Jacquie came here for the funeral. She was real close to Cyrus growing up. Her own daddy—Cyrus's brother—died when Jacquie was little. Drunk driver. Cyrus weren't old enough to be raising no kid back then. He and I were still in high school. But you know, he did what he could. We both did."

Lucile swallowed. A faint hint of a smile crossed her lips. "Lawd knows I love that child. She's got hellfire for blood, but there's a heart of gold pumping it."

It was perhaps the most accurate description of my old partner that I'd ever heard. I knew exactly what Lucile meant, on both points.

I also knew I had a question to ask. I didn't want to, but it was unavoidable.

"How did Cyrus die?"

Lucile pursed her lips. I could see her struggling to hold herself together, and I had to remind myself how very fresh her wounds were. In time, she would find peace. She would learn to bury or manage the pain. Maybe even accept it. But for the moment, she was likely overwhelmed.

Still, I had to know.

"Cyrus was murdered," Lucile whispered.

I winced despite myself. The words resurrected my own internal pain, and I almost regretted asking the question. There was nothing to say except what I'd already said.

"I'm so sorry."

Lucile ducked her head. I wanted to reach out and touch her hand, offering some semblance of comfort, but I wasn't sure if it would be appropriate. Instead, I just sat while she sobbed, waiting until Jeremiah reappeared in the doorway with a cup of tea in one hand. He passed it to his mother. He glowered at me.

Lucile sipped the drink, still quaking with the emotional agony. Already my mind was unpacking what she'd told me, my thoughts orbiting around a possible connection between Jacquie's disappearance and Cyrus's death. The link was obvious.

"Jacquie was investigating the murder," I said.

Lucile nodded.

I turned my attention to Jeremiah. "Why?"

The kid's teeth gritted. He looked so angry I thought he might punch me. Instead, he stood with folded arms, like a statue.

"Pigs wouldn't do it," he said. "They said Pop was mugged by some rambling thugs. City bangers from Memphis. Pow-pow, random thing, throw his ass in the woods."

"Jeremiah!"

"That's what they said!" the boy protested. He was crying again, shaking with constrained emotion. I took a chance that he had reached the zenith of his instability and would be most likely to speak the truth. I pressed a little harder.

"Jacquie didn't believe that?"

Jeremiah scoffed. "Heck naw, she didn't believe it. Jacquie's a good cop. She said she was gonna do her own investigation. That's what she was working on."

"She stuck around town?" I asked.

"Yeah. Making phone calls, visiting places. Harassing the cops."

"And then she went missing," I finished.

Lucile flinched. She'd stopped crying. She sat very still. Jeremiah stopped quaking also. The first hint of uncertainty crossed his stony face. He managed a nod.

"When?" I said. "When did she go missing?"

The boy exchanged a look with is mother. Then:

"I saw her two days ago. In town. She came by the sheriff's office while I was cleaning."

"Two days? You're sure?"

"Positive." He curled his lip. "It was toilet day."

Reaching down from the bed, I fished for my pants. They were muddy. My wallet fell out of the left front pocket, and I dug my hand into its righthand twin. I fished past my Macro-Stream flashlight and my Victorinox Swiss Army knife to find my burner phone. There was still a little battery left. I tapped the web browser and loaded my email account.

It took some time. The signal wasn't good in Lucile's house. Jeremiah and his mother waited patiently, one glaring, the other holding back tears.

At last the email server loaded, producing the message thread with Jacquie. One email from her, followed by my unanswered reply. I checked the date and time on her message.

"What time was Jacquie at the sheriff's office?"

Jeremiah pondered. "Afternoon. Maybe...four p.m.?"

My gaze fell back to the email. Sent on a Tuesday, two days prior. The time?

Six seventeen p.m. Code 10-78.

Emergency backup needed.

9

I didn't push Lucile or Jeremiah for details about Cyrus's death, or Jacquie's subsequent disappearance. Already I had enough information to make some assumptions, chief of which was that Cyrus's death was likely not as simple or as random as the local sheriff's department declared it to be. That fact was proven not only by Jacquie's instincts and her missing status, but also by the hostility of the Whitford locals and the brutality of the thugs who had jumped me.

People don't resort so quickly to force when they don't have something to hide. What perplexed me most was how the entire town seemed bent against me from the moment I arrived—right down to the motel clerk who had denied me a room in a building full of empty rooms. They wanted me gone. They didn't want me asking questions. It was logical to assume that they felt the same about Jacquie, which in turn meant that the thing they didn't want to discuss must be Cyrus's death.

And yet, even as provocative as that conclusion was, it

wasn't the thought that most angered me, or the fact that glared most prominently from my line of mental investigation. No, what *really* angered me was the certain knowledge that every one of the Whitfordites I had interviewed, from the cops to the breakfast diners to the motel clerk, had lied straight through their teeth.

They recognized Jacquie. They knew her well. She would have made sure of that, what with her hellfire blood and all. But they had denied it.

Why?

It was a question I would find the answer to one way or the other. But not right away. For the moment I needed to recover. I was so badly banged up that I didn't think I could walk straight until the meds kicked in and I regained some sense of physical equilibrium. Fortunately, no bones seemed to be broken, but that was only logical. The guys in the pickup truck didn't want me dead, and they didn't want me incapacitated, either. They wanted me *scared*, enough so that I got back in my truck and left town, never to return. That was also why they had left my personal effects in my pockets, and simply recognizing their strategy gave me a little hope for Jacquie's survival.

A little. Not a lot.

Lucile retreated to her kitchen to fix me some "feel better food", and Jeremiah collected my clothes to wash. Then he went outside and I watched through the window while he carefully washed and hand-dried the pickup truck, taking care with the chrome and the windows. He even got out a little brush to clean the bullet hole rims. The entire process reflected a studious dedication that I felt must have been inherited, and likely explained why the old truck was in such good shape.

It made me sad to watch. I couldn't help but assume that the cleaning ritual was something Jeremiah had practiced with his old man. Maybe a weekend habit. Clearly, he'd worked with his father in the family business, and now he'd assumed the role of chief operating officer, keeping up with the losing battle of cleaning the sheriff's station.

Mocked by the locals. Disparaged by a racist sheriff. Crushed by the weight of his grief but stepping up to the plate to take care of his mother, all the same. I couldn't really overstate how much I respected Jeremiah for that, and yet I had questions. Several of them, beginning with why he had lied to Lucile.

As if on cue, Jeremiah's mother appeared with a hot plate of steaming food—collard greens, corn bread, pot roast, and English peas. Plenty of everything. I couldn't fathom how she had whipped together such a feast so quickly, but I wasn't about to question her. Seated on the edge of the bed with the sheet wrapped around my body in place of my clothes, I wolfed the meal down while Lucile looked on and smiled.

The meal was something beyond delicious in the way only home-cooked meals can be. It wasn't a luxury I'd grown up with, but on occasion I'd enjoyed Jacquie's cooking...or the cooking of my late fiancée. Both women were talented in a kitchen. Both "cooked with love", as Mia used to say.

I paused over the plate, the stub of cornbread crumbling between my fingers. My eyes misted and I thought of Mia in a way I hadn't in some months. Not just as the girl I loved and lost, but as a woman I could have grown old with. My retirement friend. The mother of my son, whom I taught to wash cars and work hard.

Suddenly, I thought I understood something about

Cyrus, also, and the reality of that mental picture landed hard. I set the cornbread down and offered Lucile a smile.

"I think I'm packed."

She beamed. "Go down okay?"

"Amazing. Best meal I've had in years."

She blushed and swatted a hand. "Hush now, child. You want some nanner puddin'?"

"I don't think I could swallow another bite. Maybe after a while."

She gathered my dishes and headed for the door. "Clothes are almost dry. I'll bring them in a minute."

Lucile was as good as her word, and she left me to grit my teeth through the stiffness and tug my jeans and t-shirt back on. The mud had been washed away, but there was a crimson stain on the tail of my t-shirt that displayed a spray pattern of little droplets—the product of a successful nose strike, I thought. One of my own.

At least I'd given an account of myself.

Sliding my feet back into my boots, I staggered down the hallway and found the front door. The house was small and simply decorated. Old furniture, clean but worn. No TV in the living room. The gentle sounds of dishes clinked as Lucile worked in the kitchen. There were family photographs hanging on the walls, many of them displaying a trio of people standing in their Sunday best in front of an old white church. Jeremiah was there, as was Lucile.

Cyrus Richardson looked a lot like his son. Or better put, his son looked a lot like him. They were both tall and broad, muscular and proud. Handsome men. Hard workers.

I left the photographs and slipped into the front yard. It was late afternoon and the air hung thick with the rich scent of pine trees. Jeremiah had the pickup's camper shell open and was organizing janitorial supplies. The truck's front bumper gleamed in the sunlight, chrome freshly polished and reminding me of my own truck.

Which was...where? No telling. Maybe Movie Star's thugs had taken it. I would deal with that later.

I worked my way around to the back of the truck, catching side eyes from Jeremiah. His hands moved with practiced efficiency, refilling spray bottles with liquid cleaners without spilling a drop. Repacking freshly washed rags in a bin. Replacing the head of a string mop.

Maybe it was the mop he'd used at the sheriff's station. That brought the questions back to my mind.

"I wanted to thank you," I said. "For picking me up. You might have saved my life."

Jeremiah grunted, spinning the top back onto a spray bottle. I leaned against the back of the truck and he looked up abruptly. I straightened.

"Sorry," I said. "Force of habit. Your truck is a lot cleaner than mine."

He resumed his work and I waited, hoping for him to offer me a bridge into conversation. After another two minutes, I accepted the fact that it wasn't happening. The kid was angry. Deeply so, in a way no kid should ever experience. He was shutting down.

I know something about how that feels. I know how long it takes to recover, if a person recovers at all. Regrettably, I didn't have that kind of time—not with Jacquie missing. I would have to go for the throat.

"So you saw me in the ditch, huh?"

Another grunt.

"Passing along County Road 19," I said.

"That's right."

"That's west of town, isn't it? Headed out into the county."

Jeremiah paused, just for a moment. He didn't look at me, but I could tell he wanted to. He knew where I was headed.

"Sure," he said.

I cocked my head, feigning confusion. "But you told Lucile that you saw me on your way home. I looked up our location on my phone. Creedmore is southeast of town..."

Jeremiah finally faced me. His hands stopped over his work, and his mouth closed into a tight line. From the house behind us the screen door creaked and Lucile called out. Something about lemonade. Jeremiah dismissed her with a gentle refusal, not breaking eye contact.

As soon as she was gone he said, "You got something to say, man?"

I raised both eyebrows but I didn't speak. The implication was clear enough.

Jeremiah gritted his teeth. He shoved the freshly folded towels out of the way and took a seat on the pickup's tailgate. Sweeping his ball cap off, he ran a hand through short-cropped hair, mopping sweat away. He looked at the ground.

"Okay. So I followed you."

"From Whitford?"

"Yeah."

"Why?"

Pause. He sucked his teeth, then looked up. "Cuz I heard you asking them pigs about Jacquie."

"Officers," I said.

"What?"

"They're called police officers. Or sheriff's deputies, technically. Cops, if you like. *Pig* is an offensive term."

Jeremiah snorted. "Bruh, if the shoe fits."

The disgust in Jeremiah's eyes was something close to hate. I chose to bypass the argument and return to the subject at hand.

"So you heard me asking about Jacquie and decided to follow. Why?"

"Cuz she's missing."

"Maybe she went back to Phoenix."

I knew it wasn't true, but it was evident that Jeremiah wouldn't be volunteering any information. I had to manipulate it out of him.

"No chance," Jeremiah said. "She woulda called. Jacquie's good about communication. Always has been."

He spoke like somebody who knew her well, and what he said was true. Jacquie was good about communication, which was one reason I was so concerned. Not just because of the 10-78 code, but because she hadn't replied to my email or my many phone calls.

"So you think she's in trouble," I said.

"I know she's in trouble. Them pigs—"

He stopped as my eyebrows shot up again. He resumed through gritted teeth.

"Them *cops* know it, too. She went there asking about Pop, several times."

"But now they're denying it," I said. "Why?"

Jeremiah breathed a curse. "Man, why you think? They *hates us*, bro. Every one of them. If it were up to them, folks like me wouldn't exist."

"Folks like you?"

"Black folks, dude. Are you stupid? This ain't no big city police force with a diversity department. This is back water, bro. Big time. You seen the way they talk to me. These dudes don't want nothing to do with me except keeping their toilets clean."

"Funny you mentioned that. I've been wondering."

"Wondering what?"

"Wondering why you're pushing a mop at the sheriff's station. It's not like you're making any headway. That's just about the filthiest police department I've ever seen. I'm guessing they don't even care about keeping it clean. They just like bossing you around—demeaning you. And you're taking it on the chin. Why?"

Jeremiah's jaw closed. His chin lifted, and suddenly I was reminded of the older man in the photograph. Cyrus Richardson, the father. The owner of the janitorial service and the faithful patriarch of his little family. A hard-working, rock-steady anchor for a hot-blooded son.

I looked over my shoulder toward the house, just to make sure Lucile wasn't around. I didn't see her. I took a step forward and lowered my voice.

"You know what I think?" I said. "I think you're pushing that mop at the police station because you don't believe the cops did their job in investigating your father's murder. Clearly, Jacquie agreed, which is why she took up the case. Now she's missing. The cops are playing dumb, and there's a pack of thugs rumbling around in a big Dodge pounding anybody who asks questions. That's more than a kid like you can handle...unless he plays the slow game. Keeps his ears open. Runs a background investigation. Collects potential witnesses out of ditches..."

I trailed off. Jeremiah didn't say a thing, his mouth still pressed into that tight line, but deep in his dark eyes I saw a trace of respect. A keen light of interest.

"You gonna investigate?" he said at last.

"Absolutely."

"And you're going after whoever's responsible?"

"You better believe it."

"You know something about that? About dealing with these kinda thugs?"

I snorted. It was an impulsive reaction—not because I was condescending, but merely because I felt like I'd been dealing with *these kinda thugs* my whole life.

"I know plenty," I said.

Jeremiah slid off the tailgate and shut it with a crash of metal. He turned to me.

"Okay then. Where do we start?"

"With a list of priorities," I said. "Emergencies first. We've got to find Jacquie."

"How do we do that?"

"Simple. We trace her steps. We start with your father's murder."

10

J eremiah had questions. He was understandably anxious to get started, and predictably impulsive in the way only teenagers can be. He was also worried about Jacquie, whom he was close to. He wanted to know why I was starting with the question of Cyrus's murder instead of launching a search party.

I didn't have a lot of time to explain to Jeremiah the origins of my rationale, or to win him over to my strategy. In truth, I was every bit as worried about Jacquie as anybody. Thoughts of her safety and the slow grind of time weighed on my mind like an anchor. As an experienced former cop, I knew that every hour that ticked by lessened the chances not only of her survival, but also of the truth of her disappearance ever being discovered. Based on the timestamp printed to her email, we were now sixty-four hours past her last known communication.

We could already be too late, but that was a horror I wouldn't yet allow myself to accept, no matter the statistical odds. At the same time I couldn't just go charging around the county ramming my head through doors hoping to locate her. Clearly, there were some menacing forces at play in Mullins County. Whether the sheriff's department was a part of that menace or simply accomplice to it remained to be seen. Regardless, Jeremiah's original tack was the correct one. We had to play this smart. I had to put myself in Jacquie's shoes and think the way she would think. I had to follow her trail.

And to do that I needed to start where she would have started—with the murder of Cyrus Richardson.

"They found Pop in the woods," Jeremiah told me. "Way out in the county, someplace he never went. All torn up, with a bad blow to his head. They said gangbangers done it, maybe from Memphis. But Memphis is two hundred miles away. Them city thugs never come up this way. Why should they?"

It was a reasonable argument, if a little naive. City criminals, especially gangs, journey into the sticks all the time. Usually to collect narcotics grown and manufactured in lonely trailers and hidden cabins way off the beaten path. At least, that's the way it was in Phoenix. Regardless, I shared Jeremiah's suspicions that Memphis gangbangers sounded like an unlikely explanation for Cyrus's death. It sounded more like the dismissive conclusion of a corrupt police force.

"Your father have any enemies?" I asked.

"Nah, man. Not him. All he ever did was work. 'Keep your head down', that's what he was always saying. 'Mind your business and take care of your own.' He didn't drink, didn't smoke, didn't play cards. Worst thing I ever seen him do is bet five dollars on a horseshoe game. Then he got to feeling so bad about it he gave me a long lecture on the evils of gambling."

Tears had returned to Jeremiah's eyes. I wanted to ease up on my questioning, but I didn't have the option. It was getting dark outside. I was formulating a plan—not for that evening, but for the next morning. It was bold, maybe even a little rash. But given the hand I'd been dealt, it felt like the most logical play.

"Are you cleaning the sheriff's department tomorrow?"

Jeremiah shook his head. "Tomorrow's the town hall."

"But you could go back to the sheriff's department. Maybe if you forgot something. You could get inside."

He hesitated. Then nodded. "Yeah...I guess."

"You got sticky fingers?" I asked.

Jeremiah squinted, still not following. Then a gleam of understanding passed across his eyes.

"They can be if you need them to be."

"Perfect. We leave first thing in the morning."

11

I figured that Lucile wouldn't be too enthusiastic about the idea of her only child being swept up in what had already become a violent investigation, so I didn't say anything about my intentions in Whitford. I only asked Jeremiah at the breakfast table the next morning if he could give me a ride into town to find my truck. He said that was no problem, he had to clean the town hall anyway.

I felt Lucile's eyes on me, but she didn't interject. Five minutes after shoveling down fried liver with eggs and two cups of black coffee, I heaved my aching body across the yard and clambered into the passenger seat of Jeremiah's—or Cyrus's—old Ford. The interior of the truck was as immaculately maintained as the exterior, and it made me feel a little guilty for the slipshod way I cared for my '67 GMC. The old truck deserved better.

We were halfway to town rumbling along more winding county roads before Jeremiah spoke. He looked sharp in a fresh button-down shirt with the Richardson Janitorial Services logo stitched over the left pocket, his face freshly shaved and his boots clean of any dirt. In fact, he looked a lot sharper than any of the cops at the sheriff's station. He looked like he cared.

"What exactly am I looking for?"

"Case file," I said. "Normally it would be on a computer, but by the look of that police station they haven't updated their filing system since I was in preschool. So maybe it's a manila folder. Could be three pages long, could be a hundred pages long." I hesitated. Softened my voice. "It'll have your father's name on it."

Jeremiah chewed his lip. He drove the old pickup with a lot of care, using his turn signals at every intersection and braking and accelerating smoothly. The motor ran with an even *tick tick tick*, reflecting perfect tuning. More marks of intentionality and a working man's pride.

"This your dad's truck?" I asked.

Jeremiah swallowed. "Bought it new in '87. Got a second engine in it. The first one lasted three hundred thousand."

"They don't make them like that anymore," I said.

That brought the hint of a smile to Jeremiah's face, and it confirmed my suspicions that it was a statement Cyrus had made. That tracked. Nobody who takes care of a vehicle so well for so long thinks much of new production.

"How...how am I gonna not get caught?" There was no fear in Jeremiah's voice, just uncertainty. I remembered the harsh disgust with which Conroy addressed him. Maybe he had reason to be uncertain.

"Well, Jeremiah. You're not gonna get caught because there's not going to be anybody there to catch you."

He shot me a sideways look. "How you figure? Where they gonna be?"

I indulged in a humorless smile. "They're gonna be dealing with me."

I HAD Jeremiah drop me half a mile outside of town. I would walk the rest of the way. I knew he could handle himself, but I didn't think there was any advantage in letting the locals see us together. We might as well keep our little alliance concealed.

Jeremiah drove on toward the sheriff's station, and I walked with my hands in my pockets right past the gas station/hardware store, past the dumpy motel—the vacancy sign switched off as I approached—past the town hall/police station/volunteer fire department, and right onto the main drag. I whistled a little as I walked, monitoring the locals that I passed and making certain that they were monitoring me. By the time I reached the diner no less than two dozen people must have spotted me. I figured phones would be ringing. The appropriate authorities would be notified.

And if not, well. They would be soon enough.

It was just past eight a.m., and the morning rush had begun to thin at the diner. The booths were about half empty as I sauntered in, glass door smacking shut behind me. The instant silence I had experienced during my first visit was replicated perfectly—dead stillness closed over the room like a cloak, forks hanging in the air, wide and angry eyes locked onto me. From overhead a radio played the same news story I had seen in the police station—all about Central American migrants flocking to the US southern border. The feds were moving nearly fifteen thousand of them to a temporary asylum camp at Fort Smith. The commentator didn't sound happy about it. Maybe the locals weren't, either. They certainly appeared angry.

I ignored them and acknowledged the cook with a cheerful nod. She was black, middle aged, and heavy set. Her brow wrinkled into a frown when she saw me, but I didn't think it was alarm. Just surprise. She didn't recognize me.

"Have a seat wherever you like, honey."

I obliged, selecting a booth at the rear of the room where I could sit with my back against the wall. I walked heavily as I went, boots thumping. I whistled a tune I'd been practicing on my violin back in Birmingham—"The Sound of Silence", by Simon and Garfunkel. It's an overtly sad, semi-menacing melody. I was in a semi-sad, overtly menacing mood. Close enough.

Seated in the booth, my next opportunity for confrontation came in the form of the waitress. She was white, skinny, somewhat cute, maybe thirty years old. She orbited out of the kitchen beaming a smile, a menu under one arm.

Then she saw me, and she stopped. Her mouth opened. She didn't blink. Her mouth closed as her mind slowly computed my unfamiliar face, matched it with whatever sort of public notice the powers that be had distributed, and then fought toward a conclusion. As in for confirmation, she looked to one of the greasy locals seated next to her. He was a beefy guy with food on his face. He shook his head once but didn't speak. The waitress didn't speak either.

Eventually, she did the only thing she could do. She advanced, approaching my table and forcing a tight smile. It was a lot less genuine than it had looked five seconds prior.

"Good morning, sir. Can I help you?"

It was a weird question coming from a waitress in a

diner. It only served to confirm my initial suspicions. Everybody was in on this—or subjected to it. Whatever *it* was.

"Yes, actually. I think I'd like some pancakes. Are they good here? Blueberry syrup if you have it. Milk, cold as it comes. Oh, and bacon. Nice and crispy."

Her mouth closed again. A tight line. She looked once out a dirty window toward the street. Looking at what, I didn't know. I didn't look away. I just smiled, daring her to refuse my order.

She didn't. She took it down on a notepad, then disappeared behind the bar. I caught the cook looking at me again, and the temperature in the room rose a notch. Three or four minutes had passed since I first entered, and still the dining locals had yet to resume their conversations. Every eye in the room was on me, and unlike the day before, nobody bothered to hide it.

What on earth happened to this place?

I'd never visited a community quite so universally unfriendly in my life, and that includes Afghanistan. At least the liberated locals in Kabul offered me warm smiles and cold water. I thought I'd be doing good at the diner to be served anything that wasn't poisoned.

Relaxing in the booth, I pretended not to monitor the windows while I resumed whistling. Not loudly, but louder than a normally polite member of society might in an enclosed space. The cook was dropping pancake batter on the flattop and looking more edgy by the moment. The waitress returned with a glass of milk and set it down hard enough to splash droplets on the table top. I smiled warmly at her, still relaxed in my booth.

Then I flicked my hand and sent the glass hurtling across the room, shattering on the floor. Milk splashed against the wall in a white shower, and glass exploded over the tile. The waitress jumped and yelped. Several of the locals sat up—surprised, yes, but also bristling. The cook's gaze snapped in my direction. I chuckled.

"Whoops. Better get me another one of those."

The waitress's eyes bulged. I couldn't tell if she was angry or terrified. As it turned out, she never had the chance to fetch another glass. The front door of the diner exploded open, and none other than the distinguished Sheriff Conroy appeared, wrinkled shirt and all. I could have spared the milk glass—he'd brought two deputies with him, and outside the diner several more were visible, gathered on the street. There were additional locals, also. Everybody was watching the diner.

Just because I'd turned up back in town. I hadn't even reached the opening salvo of my prepared disturbance. I was almost disappointed.

Conroy stopped at the edge of the milk puddle, looking to the broken glass. Then to me. His jaw locked.

"He giving you trouble, Meredith?"

The waitress—Meredith, it seemed—stood ramrod straight, gaze fixed on the sheriff. She didn't answer. She swallowed.

"Well?" Conroy barked.

"Yes, sir."

So it's like that, is it.

Conroy advanced, boots crunching on the glass. He might have put his hand on his sidearm, but he still wasn't wearing a gun belt.

His deputies were—and they were already unsnapped.

"I thought I made it clear to you yesterday," Conroy said. "We don't know nothing about that dumb n—"

He caught himself. I raised both eyebrows. Conroy bunched his lips.

"We don't know nothing about that woman," he finished. "You'd best be leaving."

"Funny you should suggest that," I said. "I was on my way out of town when a bunch of dudes in a pickup truck jumped me. Beat the tar out of me, actually. I woke up in a ditch about half alive. Took me all morning to hike my way in here for some breakfast. Where's your hospitality, anyway? I thought this was the south."

That got to him. His teeth crunched. He leaned and placed one palm against the tabletop, hard enough to rattle the napkin dispenser.

"Let me boil it down for you," he said, barely above a whisper. "We don't like outsiders here. We ain't got no use for them. You're a troublemaker, quite obviously. So you can either split, or I'll split you. Understand?"

I just stared, long and expressionless, forcing Conroy to make the next move.

"Did you *hear me?*"

"Oh, I heard you," I said. "I just don't give a flying crap what you have to say."

Conroy blustered. His back straightened. He turned for his deputies and snapped his fingers. I wasn't sure what act of police brutality that signal was supposed to initiate—by the look of them, neither were they. Regardless, I took control again.

"Tough for me to leave town without my truck, Sheriff. I don't suppose you know where it is?"

Conroy's bluster morphed into sudden smugness. "As a matter of fact, I do. Seems it was found abandoned out on

County Road 19. Run into a ditch, actually. The county towed it for you. It's at the impound lot."

"Impound?"

"We have an ordinance about abandoned vehicles. You can get it out after you pay the fee."

A tinge of restrained outrage edged into my blood stream. My aching body stiffened a little more. But I didn't grab Conroy by the collar and rattle his teeth out the way I wanted to. I remained calm, not even getting up from the booth.

Buying Jeremiah just a little more time.

"You know why I was headed out County Road 19?" I asked.

Conroy snorted. "Couldn't care less."

"I imagine you couldn't. Bad cops never do. But you ought to take a look out there, sometime. You ought to check your vehicle registries for a late model Dodge 3500, driven by some handsome dude with a real annoying smile. Ask him what he knows about tire irons and brass knuckles. Are brass knuckles legal in Arkansas, Sheriff?"

As I spoke the last question the impact of my words reflected back at me in Conroy's posture. He grew still, and a vein in his temple twitched. His breath became just a little shallow.

The tongue can lie, but the body never does. I smiled.

"Friend of yours? You keep bad company, Sheriff. You know what the Proverbs say about that?"

Conroy gritted his teeth. "The impound lot is on Elm Street, behind the town hall. You get down there and get that junker on the road. I want you out of my county by lunchtime—or else."

I almost laughed. It was such a pointless thing to say.

There would be an *else*, all right. But not the *else* Conroy had in mind.

I held his gaze until something caught my peripheral vision through the diner window. The flash of a royal blue uniform shirt. A dark silhouette moving on the sidewalk. I glanced that way and saw Jeremiah walking toward his truck.

He made eye contact. He nodded once. He looked away.

I relaxed. "Okay, Sheriff. So what do I owe you?"

12

The fee was a hundred bucks, and the "impound lot" was just an abandoned square of gravel overgrown by weeds and littered by junked cars. There wasn't even a fence, but my truck was there, just as Conroy promised.

What he neglected to mention was the *status* of my truck. It had been wrecked—literally. The front bumper was smashed in, the antique grill contorted by the blows of baseball bats. The windshield was completely shattered, as were both windows. Dents ran the length of the front fender and down the side of the truck bed. My camping gear had been ransacked, and much of it was missing. Half the windows of the camper shell were knocked out, and the head and taillights were all busted. One tire was flat.

Hot outrage surged my bloodstream and I rushed to the driver's door, heart pounding. This wasn't the first time my truck had become the hapless target of bullying thugs, and the last time it happened the cost was a lot more personal than some shattered glass or dented fenders. Yanking the door open, I found the interior of the truck as wrecked as the exterior. The seat was shredded by knife slashes, the plexi-glass of one gauge was busted, and the radio was missing. I didn't care about any of that. I dove immediately beneath the seat, fishing across the hard metal floor, reaching all the way back for that little plastic box I'd bought at a sporting goods store.

A *waterproof* box. I'd learned my lesson. But if it wasn't there...

I touched it and overwhelming relief coursed through my body. Tugging the box out, I found my late fiancée's worn Bible housed safely inside, the faded script of her name gleaming up at me through the thick plastic—*Mia Hayes*. I flipped the latches and lifted the Bible out, running a thumb over the smooth leather cover. Suddenly, my hands were trembling, and my gaze fogged over. Something between resurrected grief and freshly birthed rage overcame me, and I looked instinctively back down Elm Street toward the main drag.

A Mullins County patrol car sat there, its aged body sagging over worn tires, one window rolled down to allow me a view inside. The two deputies who had accompanied Conroy to the diner sat there, both watching me. Both looking a little smug.

I returned the Bible to the box, blocking out the emotion and returning to the present. There would be time to confront the injustice of my vandalized truck later. For the moment, I was still alive, I still had Mia's Bible, and my violin seemed to have survived, also. It remained in its soft case, tucked way back under the passenger's side of the bench seat. Maybe they had missed it—all well and good, regardless.

Returning the waterproof box to its hiding place, I was sweeping broken glass out of the floorboard when another thought clicked in my mind. Not what I had found inside my truck, but what was missing.

Ducking quickly back beneath the seat, I shot my hand toward another space concealed closer to the door. I searched left and right but found nothing. I leaned farther down and dug again.

And then I touched the broken bicycle cable still wrapped around the bolted frame of the bench seat—the bicycle cable I'd used to secure the little metal lock box that served as my bank account. The box was gone, the bicycle cable pinched through by bolt cutters. I yanked it out and slammed my fist into the cab of the truck, shouting a curse.

There had been almost fifteen thousand dollars in that box—all that remained of the retirement account that Mia left me. My life savings. What I lived on. My only source of income between whatever odd jobs I picked up on the road.

It was gone, every dime of it. I glared back at Main Street, but the Mullins County patrol car was gone. The street was empty. The town perfectly silent.

And yet I could feel evil eyes bent on me. Defying me to push back.

13

Replacing my flattened tire should have been easy. I kept a spare suspended beneath the truck bed, and a jack in one of the plastic bins housed beneath the camper shell. The problem was the lack of my tire iron, which doubled as a lug wrench. That was missing —probably slung into the woods at the site of my beatdown. I had to scavenge through the junky cars scattered across the impound lot before I found a lug wrench that fit. After changing my tire I kicked the busted windshield out to allow myself an unobstructed view of the road, and fired up the engine.

Despite the extensive cosmetic and exterior damage, Movie Star and his thugs had been kind enough to leave the essential components beneath the hood unharmed—likely because they wanted me to leave town. It would have been easier for me to leave, of course, without a flat tire, and with my money.

Greed and intended intimidation could be blamed for those afflictions. Both were critical mistakes. I could get along without the money and I could pull the dents out of my fenders. Glass is replaceable. Paint re-paintable.

But it was the foundational essence of Movie Star's bullying that couldn't be undone or ignored. I don't tolerate bullies. Not in Afghanistan, not in Phoenix, and certainly not in some backwater hick town where my homicide partner was missing and cops were refusing to do their jobs. Movie Star was about to get more than he bargained for.

Driving with the late summer wind blasting through the open cab of the truck, I worked to calm my mind and body as I followed Jeremiah's written directions to the rendezvous point he and I had agreed on prior to embarking on our reconnaissance mission. It was an abandoned elementary school outside of town. Some Whitford city facility that had been closed as the town population shrank and the county took over the educational responsibilities of the region's elementary populace. Now the brick building sat alone beneath the sun, walls covered in vines and graffiti, windows blown out and parking lot riddled with weeds. I circled behind the main building as instructed by Jeremiah and found his truck parked next to an empty playground—also overgrown by weeds.

Jeremiah stood next to the Ford, tugging on a cigarette, and shifting on his feet. When he saw me circle the building he flicked the smoke away. Even before I cut my engine off, he was barking questions.

"Man, what took you so long? You tryin' let me get popped out here? You—dude." He broke short, gaze sweeping the truck as I piled out. "What happened to your wheels?"

"Thugs," I said. "You got the file?"

Jeremiah nodded, still wide eyed. He returned to his

pickup and produced a manila folder printed in black permanent marker—*Richardson, C.*

The ink was original. I flipped the file open and found an original police report housed inside, all details recorded in messy handwriting. I looked up.

"You didn't copy it?"

"Copy it?"

"*Photocopy.*"

"Nah, bro. Why would I do that?"

"So they wouldn't miss the original." I constrained my frustration as I said it.

"Man, them rednecks ain't got no photocopy machine."

I sighed and looked back to the report. Jeremiah was back to shifting on his feet, and as I swept down the first page he lit up another cigarette.

The document spread out across the hood of Cyrus Richardson's Ford wasn't what I would have called a *police report*. At least, not what the Phoenix Police Department would have accepted as official documentation of a homicide investigation. For one thing, it was only four pages long, and all those pages were filled out by hand. Blue ink, one of those cheap pens that slides and blurs, intensifying the sloppiness of already sloppy handwriting. I could barely read most of it. Critical details such as Cyrus's date of death, his demographics, and the nature of the investigation into his murder were decipherable only with effort.

Cyrus Delloy Richardson was fifty-six years old when he died, two weeks prior, on the seventh of September. He was six feet, one inch tall, one hundred and eighty pounds. "African", according to the ethnicity scrawled by the investigator—Detective L. Hornsby.

Cyrus's body was discovered off County Road 22, "two

miles down from the Carter filling station, in the woods".
That was as detailed as the location of the crime was
recorded. The discovering party was one Edwin Schwartz, a
local resident. He was hunting. He saw the vultures and
smelled the death.

He found Cyrus stretched out on the forest floor, his
body already half-consumed by scavengers. Cops responded.
Cause of death was ruled as blunt force trauma to the back
of Cyrus's skull, as confirmed by the coroner. Apparently,
Mullins County had no medical examiner. In fact, they didn't
even have a coroner. They borrowed the services of Sage
Fuller, an elected coroner from Arnold County...wherever
that was.

The guilty party in Cyrus's death was concluded to be
traveling gangs out of Memphis, based on reports from
Schwartz and other locals about recent petty crime. Busted
mailboxes, missing mail, and one case of a looted garage.

That was it. The file contained nothing more regarding
the investigation into *who* killed Cyrus Richardson—or why.
It was so thin I wanted to laugh, but it wasn't a laughing
matter, and sadly it wasn't so difficult to believe, either. The
most crucial thing I'd learned as a homicide detective
working in Phoenix was that initial conclusions, once
allowed to cement themselves into the minds of even competent investigators, are almost *impossible* to displace. Once a
bad guy is selected for a given crime, and enough logical
evidence is assembled to validate the assumption, alternate
theories have a way of being disregarded or actively *discarded*
in favor of the selected narrative.

It's not always corruption, or even incompetence. It's
simply human nature. Whatever the case, everything I'd
witnessed about the illustrious deputies at the Mullins

County Sheriff's Department was indicative of something a lot less excusable than overwork, or even incompetence. I smelled absolute corruption. Willful, designed concealment of the truth.

That was something that *could not* be allowed to stand.

"You see anything?" Jeremiah's voice rattled a little as he exhaled smoke. I wrinkled my nose and shifted through the pages, examining the handwriting to see how many different persons may have contributed to the report. I detected at least two.

"Does your mother know you smoke?" I asked.

No answer. I glanced sideways.

"Man, what do you care?"

"Smoking kills," I said, looking back to the paperwork. "You should quit."

Jeremiah grew still, and when I looked up again I detected tears in his eyes. His hand shook. Suddenly, I felt very stupid.

"I'm sorry. Poor choice of words."

He flicked the cigarette away. I looked back into the folder and saw three more sheets of paper tucked inside. By their size and thickness alone, I knew what they were without drawing them out.

"Turn away," I said.

"Huh?"

"Turn away. You don't need to see this."

Jeremiah's jaw locked. I held his gaze. He broke first and turned his back. I drew the photographs out...and almost puked.

It was worse than I imagined. The full-color prints of Cyrus's body, as discovered in the woods, depicted a human torso that was almost half consumed by wildlife. Both birds and beasts had had their way with his bowels and most of his organs. His legs were gnawed. His face was…

Well. It wasn't good. Anger bubbled up inside of me again. I shuffled through the pictures, holding them up to the sunlight for a better look. Forcing myself to ignore the gore and to focus in on the details. The things Detective Hornsby had missed, or perhaps ignored.

There wasn't much to see. Cyrus looked so bad he was barely recognizable, which raised questions in my mind about how the department had identified the body at all. I couldn't imagine they had run a DNA test. Maybe his wallet was found. Maybe Lucile had been forced to confirm somehow. There could be a scar, or…

My thoughts trailed off, my vision catching on Cyrus's left forearm. It was torn by the beaks of vultures, but a sizable patch of skin remained, wrinkled as the body decayed, baked by the sun…but there was a mark there. It looked like a deep gouge at first. The claw marks of birds or the teeth marks of a coyote. But no, the lines were too straight. In fact, they were geometrical.

I shifted the photo to remove glare from the sun and squinted. Then my blood ran cold, my stomach falling into a pit.

It was geometric, all right. It was perfectly clear, and impossible to misidentify.

The mark carved into Cyrus's arm was a swastika.

14

I lowered the photo, my heart pounding in my chest like a kick drum. I looked to Jeremiah, but he still had his back turned. Dropping the photographs into the folder, I snapped it closed and stood staring at the hood of Cyrus's old truck.

Thinking. Spinning, a little. Blood pressure spiking... because this changed everything. All my assumptions about corruption, all my suspicions about collusion between Conroy's sheriff's department and whoever the real killers might be—if they had missed *this*, or ignored it...

"Did you find anything?" Jeremiah turned around. I met his gaze and saw absolute heartbreak. Tombstones for eyes, and sagging shoulders that stood beneath a crushing weight far, far too heavy for any kid to bear. It added to the fury burning in my gut.

"Where's Arnold County?" I said, ignoring his question. Jeremiah frowned.

"South. Down forty-two."

"County seat?"

"Huh?"

"Biggest city," I clarified, guessing that to be a safe bet for where Sage Fuller would be headquartered.

"Evergreen. Also down forty-two."

I collected the remainder of the police report and headed for my pickup. Jeremiah called after me.

"Wait. Where you going?"

"I need to talk to the coroner," I said. "Go back to work, then go home. Keep your head down. I'll call you."

Boots crunched on the gravel behind me. Jeremiah caught up with long, powerful legs. He put a hand on my shoulder and yanked me back.

"*Hey.* Wait, man."

I looked back. He saw the rage in my face, and it cooled his youthful zeal. He paused. His mouth opened, and his lip trembled. Suddenly, he didn't look like a man at all, young or otherwise. He looked like a kid—a very overwhelmed kid, suddenly shoved into an adult's worst nightmare.

"You...you find something?" Jeremiah managed.

"I don't know. Maybe."

"I'm coming with you."

I shook my head. "Can't do that."

"Why not?"

"Because you've got to look after your mother. If whoever killed Cyrus finds out that you're helping me, the first thing they'll do is go after Lucile. You gotta be there."

He opened his mouth. Then closed it. He looked confused, but the call of duty grounded him, just the way I knew it would. Cyrus had taught him well.

"You got a gun?" I asked.

"Pop kept an old pistol. It's in a closet."

"You know how to use it?"

"Sure."

"Get it. Don't let her know. Keep it close. *Do not* pull it out unless somebody is kicking your door down. Understand? That's very important."

"Okay."

"You look after her and leave the investigating to me."

"You ain't gonna split?"

"Not a chance."

The bravado in my voice was enough to reassure him. He reached out a hand. I pulled him into a one-armed hug instead.

"Look after her," I said. "We're gonna get to the bottom of this. I swear it."

I LEFT Jeremiah in the parking lot and piled back into my semi-wrecked GMC for the drive into Arnold County. According to my burner phone, Evergreen Arkansas was a veritable metropolis compared to Whitford. With a population of thirty thousand, all the conveniences and essentials which Mullins County couldn't support were available at the cost of a forty-minute drive. I passed the car dealers I hadn't seen in Whitford, plus chain motels, grocery stores, and nicer homes. It was still rural. Still very quiet and slow, but somehow so much less depressed. With the Boston Mountain foothills rising in the background, Evergreen was downright quaint.

I found the office of Sage Fuller, medical doctor and

coroner for the "greater Arnold County region", situated near the heart of downtown across from a city park. There were ample parking spaces available, and my GMC rattled into one with a squeal of brakes and a shudder of recently misaligned tires. I cut the engine and swept my gaze up and down the sidewalks, inspecting for the presence of any beefy Dodge pickups or shady characters with cropped haircuts watching from park benches. There were trees, obscuring my view of a duck pond and offering ample concealments for anybody stationed on surveillance, but I really didn't think Skinny or any of his thugs had trailed me here. If they knew I was headed this way at all they would have cut me off somewhere along the long stretch of desolate two-lane highway, the way they had the previous day. No need to wait until I was surrounded by the good people of Evergreen.

Or else, not so good. At this point I wouldn't have trusted a priest if he offered me a glass of cool water.

Taking the Cyrus Richardson police report, I stepped out of the truck and winced as fresh surges of soreness ripped through my body. Every part of me hurt, to the point where none of me hurt. It was just a constant, dull sensation, like the whir of an air conditioner that nobody hears after a few minutes. Not to say I would be jumping any tall buildings any time soon. I made a mental note to find Tylenol, and I headed for the office's front entrance.

Dr. Fuller's name was printed on the door, and in the stale waiting room beyond I found her photograph framed on the wall alongside a trio of diplomas. Associate's degree from NorthWest Arkansas Community College, pre-med at the University of Arkansas, and then medical at the University of Mississippi. An educated professional, it seemed.

Yet she had forgone a profitable career in private medicine in favor of unprofitable public service. Based on the dates of the diplomas, matched with the photograph of a middle-aged woman with brown hair just beginning to turn gray at the temples, I guessed Sage Fuller to be about forty, maybe forty-five. A little chubby. A nice smile.

"Can I help you, sir?"

The voice came from behind a receptionist desk. It was one of those medical style desks—just a hole in the wall with a sliding glass door. The receptionist beyond looked positively sour.

"I'm here to see the coroner," I said.

"You have an appointment?"

"Nope. But I won't need one. She'll want to talk to me."

It was a bold strategy, and it bounced right off the receptionist as though she were a block wall.

"Sorry, sir. You need an appointment. What's your name?"

I briefly considered a pseudonym before deciding to return to my original strategy—bull right through.

Pivoting for the door to the right of the receptionist's desk, I reached for the handle. It wasn't locked. She exploded out of her chair and rushed into the hallway to block my path, all swinging arms and flushed cheeks.

"Hey! You can't come back here!"

"I need to see the coroner. Move."

"Sir, you *can't* see her! She's not even in. She's at lunch."

"Is that right?"

The receptionist realized she'd made a mistake. She flushed darker and her mouth opened. I didn't give her a chance to object further. Back outside I made a quick sweep of the street, marking the absence of any nearby diners or fast-food joints before turning back to check the parking lot. Two vehicles sat next to mine—a battered Toyota Camry with peeling clear coat, and a late model Lexus with a University of Mississippi sticker. Fuller's, no doubt. So she'd gone to lunch, but she'd walked...

Park.

I jogged across the street and found Sage Fuller within three minutes of entering the shady umbrella of towering oak trees. The coroner sat at a picnic table next to the duck pond, a lunch box open in front of her, a cell phone pressed to her ear. She saw me coming and frowned, then said something into the phone and hung up.

The receptionist, no doubt. Calling to alert her of a big guy with blood-stained clothes looking for her. Fuller made as if to stand, but I held up a calming hand and took a seat across from her without waiting for an invitation.

"Take a seat, Doctor. I'm not here for any trouble."

She remained half standing, suspicious eyes fixed on me, a bit of American cheese stuck to her lip. Before resuming her seat she cast a long look around the park, searching amid the trees almost as though she expected to see somebody else.

At last she settled down, but I made note of her jumpiness. She was awfully suspicious for a public servant with a presumably boring job.

"My office called. Whatever you want, you need to book an appointment. This is my lunch—"

"Oh, but I do have an appointment. Here's my confirmation."

I tossed the police file on the table. It landed with a smack, the cover flipping open in the wind. Cyrus Richardson's name was printed in that heavy black marker, and

resting on top of the report was a photograph of his mutilated body.

Sage Fuller saw it, and in a millisecond she turned rigid.
Her face drained of color.

And I knew...I'd hit pay dirt.

15

"Who are you?"

Fuller flipped the folder closed and kept her hand on the cover, the cheese still sticking to her lip. I motioned to my face with one hand, miming a wiping motion. She flushed and reached for a napkin.

"It doesn't matter who I am," I said. "For the sake of conversation, just call me Archie."

"Archie?"

"Yeah, like the quarterback. He played at UM. You should know."

It was a snotty comment, but the strategy was a good one. Knowing more about a person than a person knows about you is always a reliable tactic in knocking them off balance.

Fuller's mouth closed. She shoved the folder back at me.

"What do you want?"

"I want to talk about Cyrus Richardson. I understand that you were the coroner who examined his body."

"I'm not at liberty to discuss such matters, *Archie*."

"You sure? Because I'm headed to the media next."

It was another calculated guess, but a reasonable one. I was still curious as to why a woman in the prime of a lucrative career would shift into public service. My guess was that Fuller had been a medical doctor at some point, and had surrendered that career for her own reasons. I'd seen something similar back in Phoenix, when a surgeon suddenly and inexplicably took an ME's position for the county.

It turned out that the surgeon had a drug problem—specifically, a problem with raiding his hospital's supply of opioid painkillers. They busted him and were going to fire him. He resigned, saving himself a scar on his medical record, and then took a public service job to lie low for a few years before returning to private practice. He probably would have been successful in that endeavor, had he not converted his opioid habit into an embalming fluid habit, at which point the PPD got involved and his medical career reached a permanent terminus.

I wasn't necessarily convinced that Sage Fuller had an opioid addiction, or that she was hiding from a past life by taking quiet work in a quiet town. Some people actually care about public service, after all. But the pay gap was only the first half of my clues. The second half involved leverage. Assuming Cyrus Richardson had been murdered by individuals powerful enough to keep the entire city of Mullins under their thumb—which seemed to be the case—then the next question was how they managed to silence a coroner from the next county.

The obvious answer? They knew something she desperately wanted to keep hidden.

It was a good theory, and the moment I used the word *media*, the theory became proven fact. I could see the panic on Fuller's face. She had an odd lip-twitch, which I'd learned could be a lasting tic generated by substance abuse.

If I wasn't so fixated on finding Jacquie, I might have felt sorry for her. Given the pressures of the moment, I had something in common with Conroy—I couldn't care less.

"Are you a reporter?" Fuller's voice lowered in volume, but the strained redoubled.

"What if I am?"

"Then I'd give you a nickel's worth of advice for free and tell you to find something else to report on."

"Reporters hate being told that."

"Well, I'm serious. You don't want any part of this."

"I'm not a reporter."

"PI?"

"No."

Her gaze swept my torso, catching on the blood stains. The tears in my clothes. My shaggy, uncut hair. My nose that still had visible marks from surgery.

"You under cover?" she asked.

"Not even a little. Now it's my turn to ask questions, starting with the day Mullins County called you for an autopsy. When was that?"

She looked to the folder. "Isn't that a police report?"

"You'd think, wouldn't you? There's hardly anything in that file."

Fuller closed her lunch box and moved to stand. "I'm sorry. I can't talk about this."

Even with my sore and constricted muscles I made it out of my side of the table quicker than her, placing one hand on her shoulder and pressing her back into her seat. It wasn't a lot of force—certainly not enough to hurt her—but plenty to startle her.

"Doc, I'm gonna make this as clear as I can, because I'm short on time. I don't care what you're hiding, and I care even less about what happens to your career. The only thing I care about is *Jacquie Richardson*. My *partner*. Okay? She was looking into Cyrus's death, and she went missing. Now I'm here to find her, and I won't be leaving Arkansas until the job is done. You understand me? One way or the other."

I leaned over the table, still standing. Fuller sat frozen. She glanced to either side in search of a savior, but the nearest jogger was a hundred yards away.

"I need your help," I said. "And I'm not asking."

"You're a cop?" Fuller asked. Her voice faltered a little, like the tremors of a dam ready to break under pressure. It was a good sign.

"I was. Now I'm nobody, and I'll be out of here the moment you tell me what you know."

Fuller fixated on the folder. I sat down and waited. It took a moment longer, but my patience was rewarded in the end.

"They'll *kill me*," Fuller whispered.

"Who?"

She shook her head. She was crying. I leaned closer.

"Start with the autopsy. When was that?"

Easy question. Easy answer. Fuller capitulated.

"Two weeks ago."

"In Whitford?"

A nod.

"You determined a cause of death?"

I knew that answer, but I wanted to test her honesty.

"Blunt force trauma. Back of the head."

"And the crime scene?"

"I didn't see it. That's not part of my job."

"What was the condition of the body?"

"It...it was bad. Decayed. In pieces."

"In pieces?" I squinted. "What does that mean?"

"He was missing an arm."

An arm.

"The left arm?" I pressed. Fuller tensed, lips pressed closed. I reached into the folder and produced the photographs from the crime scene, specifically the one with Cyrus's left arm stretched out over the forest floor, mutilated by that geometric shape. It was lost in the carnage at first, but was impossible to unsee once you saw it. I tapped the photo.

"This arm?"

Fuller looked down. Momentary focus overtook her face. Her brows wrinkled into a frown, and she picked up the photo, holding it into the light. She squinted, eyes moving in little twitches as she passed from detail to detail.

Then she stopped cold.

"You see it?" I asked.

Fuller's face drained of blood. Her lips parted. Then her gaze passed over my right shoulder, behind me. Across the park. Her body went suddenly rigid, and the photograph fell out of her grasp.

"God save me," she whispered. Then she was up, scraping the lunchbox off the table, exploding out of the bench. I twisted, throwing one leg out from under the table, gaze sweeping the park. I saw the car only a moment before it took off. Jet black and long, lined with chrome and accented by a modified exhaust system that crackled and popped when the driver applied the gas. It was an old muscle car—something from the late sixties or early seventies, and long before I reached my feet it was racing toward the exit of the park's parking lot, nose swinging toward oncoming traffic.

I sprinted, stretching out hard and breaking between a pair of oak trees. Abandoning Sage Fuller and hurtling straight toward the car. I had no prayer of catching it—I didn't even need to catch it. I only needed to see a face, or a license plate. An identifying sticker. Something I could leverage into a lead.

I reached the edge of the parking lot just as the traffic cleared. The car was a Pontiac GTO—about a 1970 model, with wide tires and heavily tinted glass. A tall silver antenna was mounted to the rear bumper, and it bent as the Pontiac accelerated. I couldn't see inside. Afternoon sun blazing down from overhead obscured my view, forcing me to squint as the GTO hurtled into traffic. I traced its direction of travel and my stomach plummeted.

Sage Fuller had reached the sidewalk. She stood inches from the outside lane the GTO was hurtling down. She saw the car and stumbled back, turning the other way, ready to run.

She barely made it ten feet. The GTO passed alongside her as the righthand window buzzed down. A glint of sunlight reflected off polished gun metal. The pistol cracked.

Sage Fuller collapsed in a spray of blood, and long before I could break through the glare of the sun, the GTO was gone. It vanished over a hilltop, leaving the Arnold County Coroner lying in a pool of blood.

16

For the first time since reaching Arkansas, real panic overcame me. It wasn't because Sage Fuller was mortally wounded—I could tell long before reaching her body that if she wasn't dead, she would be soon. She'd already lost too much blood, the bullet cutting right through her chest and blasting out of her back. Truth be told, I didn't even feel sorry for her. Not because she deserved to die, but because I simply didn't have room in my overworked mind to mourn yet another tragedy.

No, the panic I felt was for Jacquie, because in the moment that handgun cracked and Fuller toppled to the ground, I knew two things with absolute clarity. First, I was right about everything. About the conspiracy. About murderous thugs hiding in the hills. About a greater darkness overhanging this lonely corner of Arkansas like a storm cloud.

And second, my best chance of snatching Jacquie out of that darkness—if she hadn't already been swallowed by it—was now bleeding out right in front of me.

I stumbled to a stop alongside the body, but didn't kneel. I could see the death in Sage Fuller's eyes, covering them in a mist. The crimson deluge draining across the sidewalk had slowed as her heart stopped beating, but the sheer mass of it was enough to tell the story. The doctor was dead, beyond any hope of resuscitation, and already my brain was grinding ahead to the next reality.

There was nothing I could do. Lingering now to talk to the cops wouldn't be helpful, and assuming those cops placed a phone call into neighboring Mullins County to confirm any part of my story—which they most certainly would—I couldn't predict what drama would result. At this stage I had to assume every member of the Mullins County Sheriff's Department—and the whole of Whitford, for that matter—were as crooked as scoliosis.

No. There was no win in staying. I had to move.

"Call an ambulance," I shouted to a nearby jogger. She fumbled for her phone, and I was gone. Into the park to retrieve Cyrus's murder file, and then back across the street to the little parking lot. Firing up my old GMC and turning down Main Street as cool afternoon breeze blew through my vacant windshield.

I wanted to punch something, but I focused on my driving until I was all the way across town, pulling into the parking lot of a Piggly Wiggly grocery store. I left the transmission in gear and cut the engine, one hand still wrapped around the wheel and the other clenching the keys. Eyes closed.

Seeing the Pontiac again...but not seeing a face or a license plate. Not seeing *anything* that offered a crack in the block wall obstructing my path.

Jacquie. I thought of my old partner, now edging closer to seventy-two hours missing, and the panic drew closer to raw desperation. I knew the math of recovered kidnaps. How every hour that drips by tilts the scales against you not in a linear exchange, but in an exponential one. I was *literally* slashing Jacquie's hopes of survival in half with every day I wasted flailing around. Even then she could be bloody and alone in some hole, tormented by the inevitable, crying out my name while I sat stupidly in my truck, clueless as to which way to turn...

"Get it together, jackass."

Jacquie's voice split through my head like a gunshot, and my eyes snapped open. I caught my breath, realizing that something wet and sticky was dripping off my right palm. I looked down to see the key of my truck jammed into my hand, breaking the skin. I hadn't even felt it, but I felt it now. I shook the key free and planted my hand against the leg of my jeans, the voice echoing in my mind again.

It wasn't one memory, it was several. *Jackass* was Jacquie's favorite nickname for me whenever she needed me to focus. I'd heard it when I'd cried at our first child homicide case. Heard it again when I lost my temper on the perpetrator we eventually tracked down. Heard it a third time after I met Mia and suddenly forgot the basic radio codes Jacquie prized.

And now I heard it in the truck, so crystal clear that I looked to the passenger seat, half expecting to see her there.

She wasn't, but the effect was the same. My breathing calmed. I refocused, reminding myself of the fundamentals. The essential practices that had never failed in me in any investigation—not ever.

Slow down. Back up. Start from the beginning.

What was the beginning?

I closed my eyes again, shoulders loose this time. I backed up, behind Jacquie's disappearance. Behind Cyrus's murder, even. Right to the heart of the matter, the origin of all the violence. The *trigger*, I used to call it. The first domino to fall. The thing that left Cyrus Richardson rotting in the woods.

What was it?

Jacquie would have asked.

I opened my eyes, and I saw it. The crime scene. Of course. Jacquie would have visited the site of Cyrus's murder. She would have taken notes, poked around. Maybe found something.

I had to do the same—I had to stay on Jacquie's trail by staying on the trail of Cyrus's murder.

Tugging the Mullins County police file out from under my backpack, I inspected the location of Cyrus's homicide. "*Off of County Road 22, two miles down from the Carter filling station, in the woods.*" A terrible description, but the best I had to go on. I would start there, map out the scene, search for clues the corrupt Mullins County cops had missed or ignored.

And then I would run this investigation right down the throat of whoever sat behind the wheel of that Pontiac. Bring justice not only for Cyrus, and for Sage Fuller...but if needs be, for Jacquie.

I jammed my key into the ignition and fired up the truck.

17

Before returning to Mullins County I took advantage of the larger shopping options in Evergreen to outfit myself for the investigation to come. The first challenge was to replace my pickup truck with a more subtle—and less smashed—form of transportation. The GMC would be recognized anywhere in Mullins County at this point. I needed something that would blend in and could accelerate more quickly than the speed of maple syrup dripping off a pancake. That meant a rental company, which could be challenging to find in a small town. In fact, none of the usual brand names were available in Evergreen, but there was a used car lot that offered rentals as a side business—Tally's Auto World.

The owner, Tally himself, wore boots, camouflage pants, and an easygoing smile. He set me up with a 2012 Chevrolet Traverse that had seen some millage but featured plenty of headroom and excellent ground clearance. The rate was a hundred bucks a day, and I paid him out of the backup cash

I kept in my boot—all the money I had left in the world. Tally didn't offer rental insurance.

"What happens if there's an accident?" I asked.

He shrugged. "Then you buy it."

Noted.

I left my battered GMC parked on Tally's lot and navigated back to the Piggly Wiggly, where I swapped the Traverse's generic dealer plate for a University of Arkansas plate I found on a random minivan. I purchased bottled water and dry foods, then I cruised farther down the road until I located a hardware store.

I asked the clerk for his flashlight section. He led me to a rack overloaded with all the usual household models. After a moment of searching, I found the kind I wanted buried near the back—a pocket-sized model with a blacklight bulb.

By the time I hit the highway it was late afternoon and I drove slowly. I didn't want to reach the crime scene during the daylight hours. Whatever I could see under the sun I could see under the light of the Streamlight MacroStream in my pocket, and much more importantly, I'd learned through careful experience that the blacklight would tell the most interesting story. Under its ultraviolet glow, dried body fluids would light up like neon signs, helping me to locate not only the spot where Cyrus's body may have been found, but also any trail leading up to it. Assuming he'd been killed elsewhere and dragged into the woods, I might be able to backtrack that path to another location with as-yet undiscovered evidence.

I'd look for tread marks. Abandoned trash. Forgotten receipts. Boot prints. Game cameras that might have captured the passage of killers dragging a dead janitor into the woods.

You never could be sure what you might find. Setting the GPS on my phone for a pinpoint on the map—the Carter Stop-n-Go gas station on County Road 22—I leaned back and breathed deep. I focused.

And drove.

18

I reached the Carter filling station an hour after sunset, and it was already closed for the night. The lights were turned out and nobody was around. I set the trip odometer on the Traverse as I cruised by, watching carefully as tenths stacked gradually closer to two full miles.

The compass built into the Traverse's rearview mirror read south. The two-lane was bathed in near-perfect darkness, broken only by my high beams as I crept along, sweeping both sides of the road for any sign of a police investigation now two weeks old.

There could be any number of indicators—a mass of fresh ruts on the shoulder from a small army of gathered patrol cars, a sign alerting the public to keep out of an active crime scene, or spray paint on the grass marking key locations. What gave it away in the end was the crime scene tape. Most of it had been torn away, but the staples used to pin bright yellow tape to various trees held a little of the plastic behind even after the rest was ripped away. I pulled the Traverse off the road and cut the engine.

The ditch was steep, the shoulder narrow. Empty beer cans and torn potato chip bags drifted in knee-high grass, with thick brambles tangling right up to the tree line. The torn bits of crime scene tape were stapled to a pair of trees just beyond those brambles, standing about four feet apart like the door posts of a house.

All was dark beyond—perfectly so, the thick branches of hardwoods tangled into a canopy that obscured any trace of starlight. The ground rose on the far side of the ditch and maintained that climb for a few hundred yards. I could measure the incline by the tops of the trees growing steadily taller, but it wasn't a mountainside. A man could walk it with ease.

The greater question was—why would he? Why had Cyrus Richardson come here?

I tapped the Traverse's key against my knee, measuring my options and sensing something deep in my gut that put me on edge. I couldn't pinpoint it, but the feeling was persistent. Almost enough to make me head back into Whitford.

But what waited there? Nothing. I needed a break. I needed some tangible handhold to dig into and pull myself forward. The crime scene would be a good start.

I shut the door quietly as I stepped out. A beaten path worn by the cops led me through the ditch and into the trees, where I clicked my MacroStream into its dimmest setting—just fifty lumens, enough to see but not enough to make a beacon out of myself.

It wasn't difficult to follow the trail left by the Mullins County Sheriff's Department. Whether by incompetence or sheer disregard, they had taken almost no care to coordinate their movements in any sort of evidence-protection pattern. Boot prints crushed sticks and grass in a tangled web of trails, kicking leaves aside and leading invariably to the same point—a trio of narrow oak trees standing like the points of a triangle, with additional scraps of crime scene tape still stapled to each. The ground between them was swept, the dirt fully exposed to the gentle glow of my MacroStream. Additional boot prints marred the soil, and a candy bar wrapper lay wrapped around a bramble. Five yards farther on a pair of paper coffee cups lay in the leaves, the logo of the gas station/hardware store back in Whitford printed on their sides.

Unbelievable.

I returned to the triangle of trees and cut the Macro-Stream off, replacing it with the blacklight. I thought I was ready for anything, but the moment that purple beam of ultraviolet cast its glow across the space between the trees, the breath froze in my lungs.

The spot lit up like Rockefeller Center on Christmas Eve —a mottled pattern of so many hot spots that it looked as though the ground itself was made of illuminated neon. Pools of dried body fluids stained the dirt in disorganized puddles, while splatters coated the tree trunks. I noted the vague outline of a body stretched across the ground, its feet joined together and pointed toward the singular tip of the triangle, while the arms were stretched apart, pointed at the corners of the triangle's base...

My spine tingled with a sudden shiver. Switching back to the MacroStream, I resumed the dim mode and knelt at the base of the nearest tree. Examining the bark, I found no disturbance on the face of the trunk pointed toward the triangle's interior, but as I orbited around the trunk, I found a worn spot. About an inch wide, tearing into the bark on the back side. Tiny fibers of white stuck to the bark, like the fuzz of a teddy bear.

No way.

I moved to the second tree, then the third. The pattern was reflected perfectly on all three—a worn spot exclusively on the back side of the trunks, each of them infested with tiny white fibers. *Nylon* fibers, I thought. Rope fibers.

The brutal reality of what lay before me descended like the crushing weight of an avalanche. I wasn't looking at the site of a body dumping at all. I was looking at a *torture site*. Cyrus Richardson had been stretched between the trees with arms and legs tied.

Had he been left that way? Had he been eaten alive by scavengers, helpless to defend himself? Or had he simply been carved apart, laid open by whoever had brought him here? Killed...then abandoned.

Whatever the case, only an absolute fool of an investigator—or else, a deliberately blind one—could have missed the evidence. It was blatantly obvious.

I returned to the blacklight and swept it over the leaves. I mapped out the pools of dry body fluids. The trails of runoff. The splatter over nearby brambles. And...what was that?

A narrow highway of gleaming blue reflected beneath the blacklight, leading away from the triangle of trees, farther up the hill. I followed it, creeping along, at times losing the trail but always regaining it. Another fifty yards away from the road I reached a narrow plateau that ran perpendicular to the rise of the hillside. I had to fight through a tangle of brush, working to keep the noise down. Reaching a giant sycamore tree, I placed one hand against its rough bark to steady myself. I orbited its outside edge. I pulled the light from my mouth and shone it down on the ground.

Two things were illuminated under the purple glow. The first was the carcass of a midsized dog—some sort of retriever—lying twisted on the ground, a long bloody gash ripped through its stomach and a puddle of dry blood pooled on the ground next to it. The dog was stiff, but I couldn't yet smell the stench of rotting flesh. A bullet hole was drilled through its skull.

The second item was a boot print. Deep in the soft soil. Crisp and clear, undisturbed by rain or wind. It was fresh.

My brow wrinkled in momentary confusion—a split second of hesitation. Not quite long enough for even a veteran investigator to put the pieces together, but *plenty* long enough for a war veteran to smell imminent danger.

Hurling myself backward, I dove to the ground behind the tree, throwing my legs out from under me and simply dropping. I struck the ground and adrenaline spiked. The investigator in me caught up with the soldier, and the pieces fit together. I saw the trap.

And then the first gunshot split the night like a thunderclap.

y first thought was *bomb*. That made the most sense, initially. The Taliban loved to plant IED's inside dead animals. It was an easy way to hide them in plain sight, and a rotting dog carcass generated the added benefit of blasting fresh wounds with infectious bacteria. It was a crude sort of biological weapon.

But this wasn't Afghanistan, this was Arkansas, and while bombs are simple to construct, they require knowhow. Pulling a trigger, on the other hand, requires almost no expertise, especially in a place like Arkansas where babies learned to pull triggers before they learned to chew solid food. In that case, the dead dog on the far side of the tree wasn't the weapon itself, but simply the trap. The weapon lay in the hands of my would-be killer, a hundred yards farther up the hill, raining bullets down on my helpless position like artillery shells.

The next gunshot blasted through the outer bark of the sycamore and raced so close to my leg that I could feel the shockwave. The report sounded like a DMR—a designated sniper's weapon. Possibly a 7.62 NATO round or else the civilian equivalent, a .308 Winchester. Whatever the case, the rifle fired much too quickly to be anything other than a semi-automatic. I yanked my leg closer to the tree and gasped for breath as the rounds came in thick, not really aimed but all flying within inches of my position. I was crouched at the base of the trunk, scrambling with my boots to keep from sliding down the hillside. There was nothing to cling to and nowhere to run. The plateau behind me offered level ground, but fleeing there would leave me fully exposed to incoming fire. It was a death channel, exactly what the shooter wanted.

I needed another option, and only two presented themselves— either I could move sideways beneath the plateau, fighting through brambles and between trees toward the shooter, or else I could head back the way I'd come, potentially exposing my back to a killer shot. It was a brutal catch twenty-two, worsened by the fact that I couldn't remain where I was. The gunshots had fallen silent. A soft breeze creeping amid the trees obscured my hearing. I couldn't tell if the shooter had moved—if even now he were circling toward me.

Think, Mason.

My heart hammered. I wasn't afraid, but the biological reactions of being shot at are difficult to ignore, even for an experienced veteran. The same instincts that had ordered me to throw myself to the ground now alerted me that it was time to move.

I chose a lateral path across the hillside. There was no point in attempting a retreat. I might escape but I would escape with empty hands. Whoever stood behind that rifle wasn't here by accident. He'd predicted the path of my investigative efforts, maybe because he'd already witnessed Jacquie taking similar steps. He knew I would turn up at the crime scene eventually, and he'd planted the dead dog blood trail to lead me into a trap. He might have waited here all day —he was a dedicated part in this mess, and that made him as valuable a target for me as I was for him.

I had to make the hunter the hunted.

Shoving both flashlights into my pockets, I was halfway back to my feet when my fingers touched something jammed alongside my wallet. It was thin and enclosed in paper. A little folder.

Tugging it free, I turned it over in my hand to expose the logo of a camping supply store in Florida. They'd thrown half a dozen books of matches into a bag alongside my order of a camp stove, and I still had most of a book remaining. A moment's deliberation crossed my mind as I considered the possibility of collateral damage, and then I committed.

These fools had pushed me into a corner. Collateral damage would be their problem.

I tore a match off and flicked it across the striker pad. Yellow flame erupted from the tip, and I dropped the match to the forest floor before the phosphorus could burn out. A split second later the first dry, crinkling leaf erupted into flame. Two seconds further on, and a campfire-sized blaze was growing toward the sycamore.

I didn't give it time to reach me. I sprinted through the darkness, carrying the matchbook with me. The next report cut the night with an earsplitting crack. I actually heard the bullet as it ricocheted off a hickory tree and whizzed overhead. The shot had been rushed, reflecting an inexperienced shooter. I skidded to cover behind a rotting log and flicked the next match.

Smoke carried from the previous fire. Flames were spreading up the hillside, gobbling up dry leaves and sticks, providing dull illumination of the forest. That glow might expose me if I stepped out of the shadows, but the benefits of the fire were worth the risk. There were basically only two ways the shooter could see me in the darkness—either by night vision, or by infrared. The first would be defeated by the glare of the fire, and the second by the heat of the flames.

With two flicks of a match book, I'd leveled the playing field considerably, but I was still armed with nothing more than a Swiss Army knife, while my adversary maintained the rifle. As I tossed the second match from behind the log, another trio of angry shots ripped amid the trees and blasted bark into my face. The shooter still knew my general position, and he wasn't concerned about precision—just effectiveness.

I leaned low and snatched my t-shirt over my face. The smoke was getting to me. My head grew light. I had to move again.

Launching from behind the log, I kept the flames between myself and the shooter and hurtled myself through the next thicket. The shots came just as I expected, but this time the misses were by yards instead of feet. My theory about night vision and infrared was working—he couldn't precisely see me.

I remained on my feet and tracked quickly to the right, dropping a third match on my way up the hillside. The fire had spread to consume a hundred yards of the forest, lapping against tree trunks and bursting into mini bonfires at every cluster of brambles. I had underestimated the dryness of the forest floor. Nothing would stop this blaze. It might carry clear into Missouri.

Problems for later. At present, only one objective mattered—catching the shooter before he caught me.

Drawing the Victorinox Locksmith from my pocket, I deployed the primary blade with the edge of my thumb. Three inches of razor-sharp steel locked open just as I reached another plateau about fifty yards above the site of the dead dog. The entire hillside beneath me was lost in orange and gray, flames dancing taller by the second.

I couldn't see the shooter. I choked on the smog and sheltered behind another hickory. The trees were smaller near the top of the ridge, the brambles thinner. There were fewer places to hide. I held the knife close to my chest and measured my breaths, listening.

I couldn't hear anything over the roar of the fire. The inferno had closed to within thirty yards of my position, the heat so strong against my bare skin that it stung. I was alive with animal focus, the obsessive instinct that drowns fear and fuels a soldier to charge into battle.

I thought about the rifle, picturing the extended barrel of a DMR propped across a shooting rest. A formidable weapon, at distance, but not easily maneuvered when things got close and personal—which was my plan.

I only needed a split second.

Swinging out from behind the tree, I leaned close to the ground and stalked forward. The smoke shrouded me like a curtain, obscuring my view and burning my eyes. Every breath stung. I crossed behind another felled log and nearly tripped over an abandoned backpack. Boot prints and disturbed leaves marked an abandoned sniper's nest. I looked left and thought I saw the plateau where the dog carcass now burned.

Then the rifle thundered again, a trio of rounds that

thudded into trees all around me. I dove and scrambled, rolling away from the log as bark exploded over my head. The next shot zipped barely a foot over my head. A third landed several yards away.

He couldn't see me, but he was content to dump on the fire and hope for luck. It was time I shattered the status quo.

"Hey!" I shouted at the same moment I threw a stick against a tree. The response was immediate, crazed rifle fire flying as fast as he could pull the trigger. Bullets exploded through a cluster of brambles only two yards to my left, and I rushed to my feet. Sticks snapped and leaves crunched as I hurtled through the smoke, rushing between the trees. His next shot zipped just over my head, and then I was certain of his position. I saw the muzzle flash as a blink of yellow forty yards ahead and to my left. He was shooting low to the ground, likely from behind cover, staying beneath the smoke.

Bullseye.

I accelerated, shrouded by smoke and concealed by flame. At any moment he might see me, or a random shot could find its mark. It was a risk I had to take. I cleared another twenty yards, flinching as a ricochet whined near my ear. He was losing me, and now the rifle fell silent. He must be reloading.

I swung left, hurtling amid a trio of tall spruces. I saw him as a vague gray bulk lying behind a fallen log, rifle rolled sideways as he fought with a fresh magazine. He coughed on the smoke, retching and wrestling with the mag. He couldn't see.

At ten yards away my boot crushed a stick, unleashing a loud crack. His head snapped toward me. White skin gleamed in dull firelight. Blue eyes widened with panic. He smacked the magazine and fumbled with the bolt release. His palm missed it and he struck again, frantically snatching the muzzle toward me.

Then I was on him. Our bodies collided with a fleshy thud, and my momentum easily overcame him. The rifle fell out of his hands and we hit the hillside, slipping and tumbling, leaves and sticks kicked up amid the smoke. I held the knife away from my body to avoid impaling myself, and neither of us stopped until we collided with the next tangle of brambles. Thorns shredded my arms and dug into my back. I thrashed to break my legs free, tracking his movements to my right.

He was faster—he wasn't as tangled in the brush as I was. He reached his feet just as I was tearing free of the thorns. His hand flailed at his side, tearing his jacket away. I could barely see him in the smoke. My eyes burned so badly it was difficult to keep them open. Flames danced at my peripherals, crackling closer. He got the jacket open, exposing the grip of a handgun. His fingers closed around it.

I lunged sideways and drove with the Victorinox. The blade found purchase in his calf, sinking up to the grip as an agonized shriek ripped from his throat. The gun cleared his waistband just as he stumbled backward. I twisted the knife and yanked it toward me, digging the blade deeper into unprotected flesh. He toppled. The pistol cracked, spitting a bullet into the ground only inches from my face. His shoulder blades struck the dirt, his leg jerking. The knife tore out of my hands, still rammed into his calf.

I rolled onto my knees, kicking my way out of burning leaves and clawing upward. He writhed, still screaming. I reached his legs and he swung upward with the pistol. My left fist made impact with the weapon just as he pressed the trigger. A shockwave erupted over my left shoulder, and my right hand found the Victorinox. I ripped it out of his leg and fell onto his chest, driving his gun arm to the ground.

Wide blue eyes gazed up at me, pure terror consuming them. The bloody knife trembled in my hand as I swept it upward. Flames encircled us on every side, and our gazes locked.

He gritted his teeth and twisted, snatching the pistol back toward me.

I drove the knife into his throat.

20

I first heard the sirens as I lay slumped over the body, gasping for air and trembling from head to foot. The blade of my knife sank all the way into his spinal cord, flicking off his lights before the grip even reached his windpipe. His body went limp and breath gurgled out of the hole in his neck.

The sirens sounded like fire trucks, and they were racing toward my position from someplace down County Road 22. I couldn't see their lights. I could barely see at all. The fire was hot on my skin, encircling me in the promise of brutal death if I didn't move quickly.

I forced myself into a kneeling position, now straddling the dead man. Pulling the knife free, I closed it without bothering to clean it and quickly scrubbed my hands on his shirt. Then I was pulling the pistol from his dead grasp—a Ruger American chambered in 9mm. I flicked the safety back on and jammed it into my waistband. Then I was going through his pockets, tearing out truck keys and a dirty pocketknife, fingernail clippers and chewing gum.

At last I found his wallet in his hip pocket. It was filthy and worn, containing only three cards. A community bank debit card, a rewards club card from some sporting goods store, and a driver's license.

Edwin Schwartz—Whitford, Arkansas.

No freaking way.

It was a name I'd heard before. Or *read*, rather, on the police report. Edwin Schwartz was the hunter who had supposedly discovered Cyrus Richardson's animal-torn body.

Fat chance.

A wad of cash packed the back of the wallet. I took the money, wiped my prints off the leather, then returned the wallet to his pocket for the firemen to find. I was halfway to my feet when something caught my eye—something printed on Schwartz's left arm, barely visible beneath the edge of his sleeve. I thought I'd imagined it at first, a product of my burning eyes and smoke-drunk mind. I decided to check anyway, and descending to one knee alongside Schwartz I ripped his sleeve up to expose his left bicep. Then my blood ran cold.

It was a tattoo. Black and red in color, etched into his pale skin in perfectly clear geometric lines. Not a swastika —at least, not *just* a swastika. The symbol was an eagle with wings spread and head turned sideways, beak razor sharp, eyes filled in with blood red. In its claws the eagle clutched a cross turned sideways. Each leg of that cross was linked to a limb that stuck out from its tip, converting the familiar Christian symbol into a sort of elongated swastika.

Beneath it all, three words curved from wingtip to wingtip:

Aryan Brotherhood Army.

From down the hill the chug of a diesel water pump was joined by shouting voices. I looked that way but couldn't see through the smoke. With a forest fire now consuming the bulk of half a dozen acres, they had their work cut out for them. It was time for me to go.

But still, I looked back at the tattoo, my mind descending into temporary deadlock. Maybe it was the words, or the horrific impact of the eagle/cross/swastika symbol. Whatever the case, it was instantly clarifying, instantly sinister and odious. The kind of symbol that sends a message a man can either submit to or defy but cannot possibly ignore.

It changed nothing, and at the same time it changed everything. All in the blink of an eye.

I used my phone to snap a quick photo of the tattoo, then at last pulled myself away from Schwartz's body. My lungs burned as I fought my way back up the hill, retrieving Schwartz's fallen rifle and spare magazines along the way. The shouts of the firemen dimmed in the background. I reached the crest of the ridge and broke out of the smoke, eyes still streaming with defensive tears as I turned westward and fought through the woods.

I worked a wide circle around the firemen fighting the blaze, returning to the Traverse just as another engine arrived on the scene. Starting the engine, I kept the head-lights off. I cranked the AC to max power and glided away around the bend, lost in Arkansas wilderness in mere seconds.

It wasn't until I had driven a full five miles deeper into the county that I pulled off at an intersection of two county roads and allowed myself a moment to clear my mind. I drained two bottles of water and splashed a third on my face and hands, scrubbing away the sweat, soot, and blood. Every time I blinked, I saw Edwin Schwartz stretched out across the leaves and sticks, eyes wide, chest convulsing.

My knife rammed up to the grip in his windpipe.

He had it coming. He was there to murder me, and the mark on his arm spoke to even darker intentions. I'm no expert on right-wing extremism, but it doesn't take a genius to understand the basic tenants of white supremacist, neo-Nazi teachings.

White people—good. Everybody else—not good. And maybe should be killed.

That was a simplification, but I wasn't interested in the nuances of hatred. The fact remained that I had one dead janitor and one missing cop on my hands, both of whom happened to be black. Now I had a dead Aryan, with presumably more Aryans linked to Cyrus's murder.

This situation was far worse than I initially imagined.

Shifting back into gear I programmed my phone for Evergreen, deliberately routing miles out of my way to avoid Whitford. It was a fifty-minute ride, but I had the time. I set the cruise, kept the radio off, and fought to calm my hyper-stressed body.

It takes time to come down from intense physical strain, especially the mortal combat kind. I was hyper alert, my vision darting to either side of the road and both mirrors, my skin tingling as though the heat of the flames were still only inches away.

I thought about Cyrus. About the triangle of trees, and the rope marks. I thought about Edwin Schwartz and the rifle resting in the back seat. It was some kind of custom AR-10 style DMR—chambered in 7.62 NATO, just as I suspected, with a very nice Pulsar night vision optic. A fancy setup for a casual night hunter, and yet Schwartz hadn't seemed to know what he was doing with it, which made me think he was nothing more than a paramilitary wannabe with too much money on his hands.

Money.

I dug Schwartz's cash from my pocket and dumped it into my lap. I couldn't count it all, not while driving. It was a couple thousand dollars, all in crisp hundred-dollar bills. Blood money, perhaps? The value of my head?

Or maybe Schwartz was motivated by something more intrinsic, something more ideological. Maybe the money came to him as part of his integration into an organism much larger and much more dangerous than himself alone.

Aryan Brotherhood Army.

The name rang in my head again as an ominous warning. The rumble of distant thunder.

I mashed the gas and hurtled on toward Evergreen.

21

By the time I reached a ragged little motel just outside the city, I'd managed to calm my body and clear my head. I wasn't relaxed—a long way from it—but I was back in control. I had forced the rising panic concerning Jacquie's survival into a mental pit. I'd memorized that hideous tattoo and shelved it for future evaluation once I obtained additional intelligence.

I'd even decided on a plan for the next eight hours—check in with Jeremiah and Lucile, then shower and sleep. Recharge. Refit.

It would be easy to hurtle on, driven by desperation to locate Jacquie, but I resisted the temptation with a dose of rational clarity. No amount of brute force would drag my enemy into the sunlight. As lethal as I could be, I couldn't afford to declare war on the whole of Mullins County—which seemed like the reality I would face if I crashed back into Whitford.

No. I had to play this smart, catch my breath, and stay sharp.

It was a stroke of good fortune that Edwin Schwartz had money on him, because the emergency stash drawn from my boot was nearly exhausted. Edwin bought me one night's stay at the motel, which I figured was the least he could do considering how he'd tried to blow my brains out. The clerk never asked for ID, and I provided a fake name. Then I parked the Traverse in a separate parking lot across the street—just in case—and locked myself into a second-floor room. The AR-10 I left in the SUV, hidden beneath the back seat, but the Ruger American I took with me. Fifteen rounds remained in the seventeen-round magazine.

I would dump every one of them through my motel door if somebody tried to kick it down.

Sitting down on the bed, I kicked off my boots and dialed Lucile. Cyrus Richardson's widow answered quickly, indicating that she was still awake. Maybe she'd heard the fire engines roaring by and suspected disaster.

"Hello?"

"Lucile, it's Mason. Are you alone?"

Brief pause. "Jeremiah's here."

"That's fine. Nobody else? If somebody's there, ask me why I'm calling."

"Nobody's here, Mason. It's just us."

I breathed an unconscious sigh. I hadn't realized it, but there had been a tension hanging in the back of my mind from the moment I left Jeremiah behind that abandoned elementary school. I wondered if our association had somehow been detected. If Lucile had suffered the consequences.

"I want to talk about Cyrus," I said. "I need to ask some questions."

"Okay." Lucile sounded tired, but willing.

I dug into my backpack and produced a notebook. I tore past campsite cooking recipes, addresses and short notations of my own lonely thoughts before finding a clean page. I clicked a pen open.

"I need to know about the week before Cyrus died," I said. "Everything you can remember."

It took some time for Lucile to gather her thoughts. It was very clearly difficult for her to talk about Cyrus. She mumbled and stumbled. I guided her to the relevant details.

She spoke about his work. Cyrus had opened his janitorial service some years earlier and developed it into a respectable enterprise. He maintained contracts with most of the government agencies across Mullins County, including all the civic buildings in Whitford. He cleaned schools, churches, office buildings, even motels. Cyrus worked hard and stayed on the road a lot. Sometimes he would be across the county working late and wouldn't come home. He'd sleep in his truck. Lucile might only see him a few nights a week. When Jeremiah graduated from high school the previous May, he shared the workload with his father.

"Cyrus worked so hard," Lucile said, choking a little. "He wanted the best for me. The best for Jeremiah."

"Where was he just before he passed?" I didn't want to be abrupt. I needed Lucile to focus.

"He...he'd been up in Missouri a few days. He had a big client up there. Fort Crowder."

I squinted. "A military base?"

"That's right. Army, I think. Just across the state line. He been cleaning a lot of their office facilities. Went up there twice a month, starting last year. He was really excited about it. The Army paid better than local jobs."

I made a note of the military base. It wasn't one I recognized, but the Army maintains literally hundreds of bases, and not all of them are very large. It might be a relevant detail.

"Cyrus was working up there before he died?"

Another hesitation. Lucile's voice sounded wet when she resumed. "He'd slept up there that night. He was headed back when...he went missing."

Bingo.

I circled the name of the base, then spent a few minutes longer quizzing Lucile about Cyrus's habits. His associations. His recreations.

It was a short list. Cyrus Richardson was a quiet man who associated almost exclusively with a small circle of friends and family. He was passionate about his local church. His only recreation was wood carving. He had a set of knives and liked to sit on the back porch, carving little animals and various ornate crosses. He didn't like technology. His cell phone was years out of date, and he often forgot to carry it.

He liked things simple. He was subdued. Gentle. Friendly to his neighbors and kind to anybody he met. He had a servant's heart. He was non-confrontational.

And yet he was also dead. Which meant he'd collided with somebody, and I knew in my very bones that it hadn't been a traveling gang out of Memphis.

No chance.

"Thank you, Lucile. I'll keep you posted."

I moved to hang up.

"Mason?"

"Yeah?"

"Jeremiah wants to speak with you."

I waited. Jeremiah came onto the line. Shoes thumped and a screen door groaned on its hinges. When Jeremiah spoke his voice was abrupt.

"You find anything?"

"Still working on it," I said, unwilling to divulge any specifics to a teenage loose cannon.

"You talk to that coroner down in Evergreen?"

"Yes..."

"You kill her?"

I sighed. "No. I didn't."

"I seen the news. They say she was shot, right on the street. You seen who did it? You gonna do something?"

"Let me worry about that. Are you looking after your mother?"

"Yeah. I found that heater. Got it in my waistband. She ain't seen it. I'm ready."

I'm ready. It wasn't the sort of comment I wanted to hear from a kid with a handgun, and it made me question my directions for him to arm himself. Maybe that had been a mistake.

Then again, Jeremiah Richardson had as much right to defend his hearth and home as any man. It was my job to make sure the "heater" never left his waistband.

"Keep it hidden. *Do not pull it out* unless the door is coming down. I'm dead serious."

"Yeah, yeah. I got you."

His tone wasn't convincing. He didn't hang up the phone.

"You good?" I asked.

Jeremiah swallowed. "They're killin' people, man."

"Yep. And they're going to live just long enough to regret it. Keep your head down, Jeremiah."

I hung up and tossed the phone onto the bed next to me.

The Ruger lay on my nightstand, chambered and ready. The safety already disengaged.

Across the room the bolted door stared at me like a paper curtain, barely holding back the roving evil just outside. A sheer barrier that one of us—myself or the enemy —would rip down in the coming days.

Not a doubt in my mind.

Tugging my shirt off, I rolled on top of the bed covers and flicked the lamp out. I gave my exhausted body time to relax while I stared at the ceiling, planning my next move. A drive into Missouri. A visit to Fort Crowder. An interview with the commanding staff. Questions to answer.

But when I closed my eyes, I didn't picture any of that. I only saw Jacquie, alone in a pit.

Reaching for me.

22

Three Years Prior

I arrived at the truck stop at 2:47 a.m. and clambered out of my unmarked, department-issued sedan. Even hours after the desert sun had faded, the asphalt beneath my boots was noticeably hot, and sweat ran down my back. Neon lights blinked atop tall signs, I-10 roaring in my ears from only a half mile away.

It was the middle of the night, but nobody had told south Phoenix. Traffic, commerce, and night life were in full swing. So, apparently, was murder.

I found my partner standing next to a pair of Phoenix patrol cars, their spotlights trained on a location sandwiched between the back of the truck stop and the side of a metal dumpster. Jacquie held a coffee in one hand and a jelly donut from the truck stop in the other. Her cheeks were puffed out and she looked like a chipmunk with acorns in its mouth. She chewed and slurped, shouting through the donut when a patrol officer dragged his shoe over the victim's arm while stretching crime scene tape.

"Hey! Watch it."

I rubbed sleep from my eyes and accepted the coffee from Jacquie. It was too sweet, but I sucked it down anyway, hoping for the caffeine to kick in.

"Donut?" Jacquie asked.

I handed the coffee back. "I don't know how you can eat staring at a brutalized body."

Brutalized was the right word. The victim was young. Maybe twenty, but likely in her late teens. Caucasian. Skinny. Red haired, but it looked dyed to me. Blue eyes stared lifelessly at the chocolate-brown side of the dumpster next to her.

Her clothes were torn. Her exposed thighs and stomach covered in purple bruises. Her right hand was coated in dried blood from where she'd fought the gushing tear ripped through her throat. It was a deep yet very precise cut, perfectly executed to leave her choking to death on her own blood.

Just like the first two.

"Seems we've got ourselves a serial killer," Jacquie murmured.

I made no reply, drawing the Streamlight MacroStream from my pocket instead. Bright white light illuminated the body, and I began my search at her toes. When I reached her eyes, my stomach descended into knots.

She was just a kid.

"Who called it in?" I said.

"I did, sir." A skinny beat cop with pale gray eyes answered me. He looked to be eight or ten years my junior, probably just out of the academy. The little brass name plate on his chest read *J. Pink.*

"You found the body?"

"That's right. Well. Not exactly. I was on patrol and stopped to pee. One of the truck stop cashiers took out some trash. She found the body."

"Where is she?" I said.

"Uhm...back inside. She had to work."

"Did you get her ID and contact information?"

"Uh. I didn't."

I waited. Raised both eyebrows. Pink seemed deadlocked in confusion.

At last I said, "*Then go get them.*"

That snapped him out of it. Pink fumbled for a pencil and hurried off. I restrained a curse. Jacquie chuckled.

"Kids are getting dumber."

"And younger," I said. I returned to the body, inspecting the bruises on her thighs. They were extensive, stretching as low as her knees. I tugged on a pair of rubber gloves. Using a thumb and forefinger, I applied pressure.

The skin faded from purple to light blue as I pressed. I grunted.

"Antemortem bruises," Jacquie said. "She was abused prior to death."

"Well prior," I said. "Just like the others."

I clicked the light off and bowed my head. I wasn't sure why. It was a habit that started in Afghanistan whenever I encountered dead noncombatants—which was often. They were nameless victims. Just numbers on a spreadsheet...or worse still, not a number at all. A life so perfectly erased it was as though it never existed.

Nobody would remember them, just like nobody would

remember this prostitute. A moment of silence for the memory of their life seemed like the least I could do.

Jacquie joined me in the silence. When I lifted my head I could see the hatred in her dark eyes. It boiled like lava spilling slowly out of a volcano.

"It's the same guy," I said.

"Yep."

"He's not stopping."

"No," Jacquie said. "And neither will we."

23

Present Day

I arose before dawn and showered away the sleepiness. The Traverse was low on gas. I filled the tank with Edwin Schwartz's money, then programed my phone's GPS for the fort. It was a two-hour drive, up through Mullins County and across the state line into southern Missouri. My early-morning research told me the fort was relatively small, with only one gate town—a dot on the map called *Gates*.

How inventive.

I stopped for coffee on my way out of Evergreen, but I couldn't eat. Thoughts of my dream from the night before still hung heavy in my mind, the circulating images as clear as the day they were formed.

It was a strange dream to have—a random, unrelated memory. There was nothing particularly striking about the case of three dead prostitutes, each surgically throat-cut before being left to drown in their own blood. Certainly, there had been some interesting twists and turns near the end of that investigation, but the case in no way related to my present predicament.

Maybe that was why my exhausted mind had resurrected it. It was another day in the life...with *Jacquie*. The ordinary sort of grind that developed the deepest of camaraderie over the course of years. The minor decisions and minuscule courtesies that birthed such lasting loyalty.

The kind of friendship that would drive a man to do unspeakable things when his partner's life came into jeopardy.

I waited until I'd crossed the state line to make my first phone call. Not because I minded dialing from Mullins County, but because I didn't have any reliable cell service in Mullins County. Amid the rapidly leveling farmlands of southern Missouri, my signal was strong, and the FBI answered the phone with predictable curtness.

"Federal Bureau of Investigation. How may I direct your call?"

"PAO, please."

"One moment."

The hold was brief. The FBI's Public Affairs Office picked up with no more enthusiasm than the operator.

"PAO. This is Special Agent Rich Bankers. How may I assist you?"

I blinked, momentarily disoriented by the unfortunate name. I wanted to crack a joke about cruel parents but didn't think it would grease the wheels any. He'd no doubt heard all the jokes before.

"I'm calling from the University of Arkansas. I'm a student in the criminal justice program, and I'm writing a paper on radical right wing extremist groups in the United States. Specifically, neo-Nazi organizations. I was hoping you could answer a few questions for me."

Special Agent Bankers sighed, not bothering to contain his irritation. Maybe I should have cracked a joke after all.

"That's not really what we do here—"

"I'm most interested in active white supremacist groups in northern Arkansas," I said, cutting him off. "My research uncovered a group called the Aryan Brotherhood Army. I was hoping you could tell me a little about the FBI's awareness of them."

Brief pause. "The Aryan what now?"

"Aryan Brotherhood Army. I believe they're active in the Mullins County region?"

A keyboard clacked. Bankers seemed to be indulging me out of forced patience, likely because I was a student. Everybody wants to help students. He would have already hung up if I'd claimed to be an investigative reporter.

"We don't have an Aryan Brotherhood Army. Do you mean the Aryan Brotherhood?"

"Maybe," I said, willing to see where the conversation led.

Banker's chair groaned. He slurped coffee. "So the Aryan Brotherhood, or *Brand*, is a prison gang. Estimated fifteen to twenty thousand members, mostly incarcerated or formerly incarcerated."

"Do they have a symbol?"

"Symbol?"

"Like a logo."

"Sure. It's a clover leaf with a swastika printed over it. It's a common prison tattoo."

No dice.

"What about an eagle holding a cross? Except the ends of the cross legs are twisted into the arms of a swastika."

"Where did you see that?"

"In my research."

It was literally true.

"I've never encountered that symbol. You may have bad information."

Yeah...I don't.

"What can you tell me about active supremacist groups in Arkansas?" I pressed. "Specifically militant, rural groups."

A long sigh. "I'm not sure where you're getting your information. Militant white supremacist groups are prevalent, but they aren't nearly as common nor as organized as the media would have you believe."

"So, there aren't any active groups in Arkansas?"

"I didn't say that. In fact, there are several. I'm only suggesting that you should double-check your facts. Hyperbole fuels the spread of hate as much as any other form of misinformation."

Thanks for the PSA.

"To be clear," I said, "the FBI has no record of an Aryan Brotherhood Army active in northern Arkansas? Specifically, in and around the town of Whitford."

The phone shifted. "Who did you say you were?"

"A student."

"From Arkansas?"

"That's right."

"And where did you come by the name *Aryan Brotherhood Army?*"

I thought quickly. "Locals."

"Well, they're pulling your leg, kid. The FBI has no

public record of any such group, and trust me when I tell you that we keep a careful eye on *all* such groups."

"You said public record. Could there be a classified investigation?"

"If there was, I couldn't tell you about it, now, could I?"

Right.

"Thank you for your time."

I hung up twice as frustrated as when I'd dialed. I should have known that calling the PAO wouldn't get me anywhere. These people were programed to hem and haw, to beat around the bush and to supply the public only with the type of information that the public could have found online. It was part of their job.

But no public record? How was that possible? I'd dealt with three-letter agencies of all sorts during my tenure both as an Army Ranger and as a Phoenix cop, and had generally developed a bad taste for them. Not because they're bad at their jobs, but because they tend to become tunnel visioned —to run over anything and *anybody* in the hunt for "their man".

The FBI was no different, and Special Agent Bankers certainly wasn't exaggerating when he said that the bureau kept a close eye on extremist groups. From the KKK to ISIS to whackos out in the woods, it was the FBI's job to prevent another Oklahoma City, or 9/11. They were good at it. They were effective.

So why were they ignorant to the presence of a highly militant sect of neo-Nazi extremists with their thumb crushing down over an entire town?

Maybe I was making too many assumptions. Maybe the tattoo was a one-off, something Edwin Schwartz came up with on his own. There could be a different, darker force at play behind the curtains. I wouldn't know without more information, and I was already rolling up on the site of my next investigation.

The sign was brick, and in desperate need of a power washing. Uncut shrubs grew high on either side, obscuring the face. I could still read it.

Welcome to Gates — Proud Home of Fort Crowder.

24

In my experience, Army gate towns are nearly all the same. Gates, Missouri, did nothing to challenge that stereotype. Cruising into the outskirts, I was greeted with all the usual accouterments of a dot on the map riding high off federal payroll dollars.

Apartment complexes and scores of rental homes, surrounded by a litany of restaurants, motorcycle shops, gun dealers and sporting goods stores. There was a paintball field and a few poorly managed city parks. A dozen or more bars. A pool hall. All the industries that converted an enlisted man's boredom into cold hard cash, one grinding week at a time. Those blinking neon signs and shiny show-room floors felt like a second home to me—I'd fallen for all their tricks, at one point or other. My favorite had always been a pool hall.

I was never any good, but beer is cheap in a pool hall, and there's usually a handful of girls around. Back when I had heart for that kind of thing.

The gate itself consisted of a tall metal pavilion with a split lane running either side of a guard shack. An Army MP stood outside, an AGSU hat pulled low around his ears. It was darker than the ACU cap I wore in Afghanistan. More traditional looking.

The MP himself appeared traditionally pissed off, like most MPs do. You dream of high crime and action, and what do you get? Guard shack duty, and a lot of drunk privates.

I eased to a stop, flashing my best smile. The Ruger American and the AR-10 I had taken off Schwartz were both concealed beneath the back seat—a major no-no for any visit to a military installation. But I didn't have any other place to hide the weapons, and it was unlikely that the MP would actually search my vehicle.

"Can I help you, sir?"

"I'm here to visit the PX."

"Can I see your ID?"

I produced my Arizona driver's license and a military ID nearly six years expired. I looked nothing like the stiff-faced soldier depicted in the black and white photograph. I'd rounded out a little. Softened somewhat.

And hardened, at the same time.

The MP examined each, squinting in the morning sun. He looked bored.

"What brings you to Missouri, Mr. Sharpe?"

"Visiting friends."

A grunt. "Your ID is out of date. You'll need to visit the Visitor Control Center and obtain a visitor's pass. That way."

I turned up a short drive to the VCC. It was a squat block building with a metal roof, faded by the sun and littered with the needles of an overhanging pine tree. The process to obtain my visitor's pass was brutally slow, but only because the E5 running the desk was about half awake. He cleared my IDs through whatever background check process the Army had migrated to since my retirement, then handed me a paper guest pass. It was good for twenty-four hours.

I cycled back through the gate, and the MP scanned the guest pass.

"Can I direct you anywhere?"

"MP post," I said. He cocked an eyebrow, but pointed.

"Left at the light. Half a mile. Building seven-oh-four."

I lifted two fingers in salute. "Thank you for your service, Corporal."

"Likewise."

The base was laid out like most Army facilities, with a lot of narrow, winding roads. Irregular clusters of brick and metal buildings. Architecture that may have dated from the fifties, the eighties, or the previous year, but looked the same regardless. The government's imagination was nonexistent, but I gauged the overall age of the fort to be no older than I was, and its mission to be something along administrative lines, not combat. I saw only a few military vehicles, and they were all generic trucks. No tanks. No helicopters. About half the buildings were office structures, another quarter were barracks or on-base family housing.

The last quarter consisted of very large metal structures. A little like aircraft hangars, but the doors were much too small to admit aircraft. Crowds of POVs—personally owned vehicles—sat outside. What civilians I saw wore work clothes. Military personnel were dressed in the new AGSUs, and they were all sweaty despite the mild weather.

I found Building 704 right where the MP promised it

would be. The two patrol Humvees parked out front were aged, and their tires appeared to be dry-rotting. Clearly not in any sort of regular use.

Quiet place.

I parked near the door and glanced over my shoulder to ensure that both firearms were well out of sight. Then I locked the Traverse and took my IDs along with the guest pass. I expected resistance.

The interior of the building smelled of cheap cleaners. The floor was tile, and well scrubbed. I wondered if Jeremiah Richardson had pushed the mop. Behind the receptionist desk a sergeant sat with MP patches on her arms. She had a crossword book spread across her desk, and glanced up when I entered but didn't rush to lay down the pencil.

"Can I help you?"

"Sergeant M. Sharpe to see your commanding officer, please."

Another glance once over my shabby clothes and uncut hair, then she extended a hand and I passed her the ID cards. She examined them. I expected some objection over my use of a military rank despite being discharged.

No objection came. She returned the cards back and pointed to a chair in the lobby. Then she made a phone call. It lasted four seconds. She hung up. She resumed the crossword.

I stood in the lobby, tapping the ID cards against my leg and surveying the room. Something about it was...*off*, somehow. Not necessarily wrong. But different. From the laidback MP at the gate to the half-awake E5 at the VCC to this checked-out, cross-wording sergeant. It was like...

My thoughts were cut short as a new figure stepped into

the room. He was tall—taller than me—but slimmer. AGCUs bore major's patches. His name tape read *Sotomeyer*.

"Sergeant?" He extended a hand. I shook once.

"Retired."

"I know. I pulled your file from the VCC. Seventy-fifth, right? Afghanistan."

Quick reading.

I nodded. Sotomeyer got down to business.

"So what can I do for you?"

"I'd like to ask you a few questions, if you have the time. It concerns a local crime."

That piqued the major's interest. I could see the gleam in his eye, but he didn't question me. He simply gestured and I followed him through the door and down a sterile hall, past multiple open offices stocked by men and women in AGCUs, most with their jackets taken off, none of them appearing very busy. One was actually asleep.

Sotomeyer's office lay at the end of the hall. It was cramped, with a metal desk and a lot of paperwork stacked on the file cabinets that surrounded him. Comic books, also. Maybe two dozen of them, well-thumbed and wrinkled. One lay open on his desk.

"Not a lot of action around here, I take it," I said. Sotomeyer grunted and tossed the book aside, taking his seat and gesturing for me to do the same. He reached into a cooler parked next to the desk and produced a ginger ale in a glass bottle. He offered me one. I accepted.

"Crowder is a small fort," Sotomeyer said. "Actually, smallest I ever served at. Pretty sleepy, too. Our garrison is barely two thousand strong, and most of those are late career infantry running out the clock until they can process out. Young parents with small children. Median age is thirty-one.

Well past the hooligan phase, so no. We don't get much action."

He took a long gulp of the ginger ale. I joined him. It was tangy and sweet. I felt a sugar buzz almost immediately.

"What's the mission?" I asked.

Sotomeyer restrained a burp. He thumped his chest. "Huh?"

"For the fort," I clarified.

"Oh. Decommission depot. Arms out processing."

I squinted. Sotomeyer held up a finger. He rattled a password into his computer—the common access card was already stuck into the card reader, presumably left behind when he went to greet me. A major infraction of cyber security.

Spinning the monitor around, Sotomeyer gestured as though he were revealing a five-course banquet.

"Behold the future...coming to you at seven-hundred-fifty rounds per minute."

I leaned across the desk to gain a view of the computer screen past the privacy tint. A photograph was displayed there, depicting what looked like an M4 rifle, but upon further inspection there were notable differences. The mag well was thicker. In place of a solid buffer tube jutting out of the rear of the receiver, there was a metal hinge mechanism to allow for a folding stock. The rifle was painted desert tan. There was no A-frame front sight, just a free-floating hand guard.

"Recognize it?" Sotomeyer asked.

I shook my head. He turned the monitor back.

"It's the SIG Sauer XM7 SPEAR. The Army's new standard issue rifle... or it will be, anyway, once we finish the transition. Takes a lot of time when you've got over a hundred thousand weapons to replace. The M4 will be phased out altogether. So is the old SAW. We're getting everything new from SIG, chambered in six-point-four millimeter instead of the old five-five-six. Heavier bullet, hits harder. More effective when shooting through obstructions. But you should know all about that."

I did. The standard issue M4 rifle chambered in 5.56 NATO ammunition that I'd carried in Afghanistan had a lot of virtues, but blowing through obstructions wasn't one of them. The bullet was too light to effectively penetrate such common impediments as block walls, or even very thick wooden ones.

The standard 7.62 AK-47 round, however—a favorite of the Taliban—never struggled with such minor annoyances. That meant that if Taliban fighters took shelter behind block walls, they could easily be safe from us, but we wouldn't necessarily be safe from them. As a result, many of the guys in my platoon carried captured AK's whenever they could get away with it.

"It looks expensive," I said, referring to the new rifle.

"Over four-point-five billion, but hey. So long as we're printing money like maniacs, who cares?"

"So what's Fort Crowder's part in all this?" I asked, dodging the question of economics.

"We're decommissioning the old M4s," Sotomeyer said, leaning back in his chair and hooking his hands behind his head. "They truck them in. We break them down, destroy key components, pack them back up and ship them to recycle facilities. Churn and burn...day in and day out."

"Sounds thrilling," I said, failing to hide the sarcasm in my voice.

Sotomeyer cocked an eyebrow, surveying my wrinkled

shirt and the bruises on my arms. They were starting to turn purple. I could only imagine what he was thinking.

"What exactly can I do for you, Mr. Sharpe?"

That was my cue. Down to business.

"It's about a murder," I said. "I want to talk about your janitor."

25

Major Sotomeyer's body language changed the moment I asked the question, assuming a guarded undertone. He no longer looked away from me. He didn't blink as he took a swallow of ginger ale.

I thought I understood why. Sotomeyer was a cop, after all. A cop dressed in camouflage, but still a cop. Any mention of a criminal case would put him on edge with the warnings of lawyers echoing in his ears.

For all that, he didn't evade. He cut right to the chase. "Cyrus Richardson."

"Right."

"What's your angle?"

I settled into my chair. I had my story ready. It was generally true.

"I'm a friend of the family. After I got out of the Army, I was a detective for a while. You may have heard that Cyrus's death remains unsolved. They asked me to look around. It's just a favor."

"You a PI?"

"No."

"But not a cop."

"I'm unemployed."

He pinched his lips together. Then he shrugged.

"Well, I don't see what harm it would do to discuss it, but frankly I don't know much. Cyrus was here, and the next day he wasn't. The day after that we called looking for him—or the admins did. That's what they told me. They couldn't find him. Then we heard he was killed down in Arkansas. Some business about roving gangs. That's all I know."

"He was found in the woods," I clarified. "The gang thing is more of a theory."

Sotomeyer finished his ginger ale. He was still guarded, but I detected disinterest seeping into his gaze, also. Boredom. Maybe he was thinking about his comic books, eager for me to leave.

"What exactly did Cyrus do for the fort?" I asked.

"He cleaned it. That's what janitors do."

"Right. But I thought he might have a specialty. Windows, or something."

"Nah. Not that I know of. I mean, he cleaned this building. Floors, windows, bathrooms. Everything. Did a real nice job, too. You could always tell the difference when they finished."

"They?"

"Him and his kid."

"Oh, right. Jeremiah."

Sotomeyer only shrugged.

"So you never had any memorable conversation with him? Can you remember anything about the day before he went missing?"

"Nope. He was working someplace else on post that day. I

didn't know he was missing until the bathroom started smelling. That's when somebody said he hadn't shown up."

"You never talked to him?"

"Why would I? He was the janitor."

Dry dismissal slipped into Sotomeyer's tone, as though he were speaking about disposable dinnerware or blown lightbulbs. Expendable things. It made me realize how invisible a guy like Cyrus must be in a place like this. Always there, but never really noticed. Come to think of it, I couldn't ever recall encountering a janitor on any of the military installations I'd been posted to. They must have been there... but I never noticed.

Sotomeyer must have seen something in my face. He became suddenly apologetic.

"I didn't mean it that way. I just mean...we had different jobs. We didn't really cross paths."

"Sure."

Sotomeyer set the empty bottle down and sat up. His posture had a very definite "we're finished here" tone about it. I didn't argue. I stood and thanked him for the drink. Sotomeyer didn't offer to walk me out. He returned to his comic book as I approached the door.

I turned back. "Hey, one other thing."

"Huh?" He didn't look up.

"What other building was Cyrus cleaning that day?"

He squinted.

"You said he was cleaning another building the day before he went missing. What other buildings did Cyrus clean?"

"Oh." Sotomeyer wrinkled his nose. Then shrugged. "Some admin building, probably."

"Not barracks? Warehouse?"

A shake of his head. "Grunts clean the barracks. Contractors maintain the warehouses. We don't let anybody else in there...too sensitive."

I nodded and lifted a hand. Sotomeyer didn't look up, and neither did the desk sergeant as I exited the building. The fresh air outside was a welcome relief to the burn of overused chemicals inside. Whoever had replaced Cyrus enjoyed bleach.

I was halfway to the Traverse before I heard the door open behind me. The familiar thump of Army-issued combat boots—a sound I'll never forget—struck the asphalt.

"Hey, buddy!"

I looked over my shoulder. Another Army officer fast-walked toward me. He wore AGCU pants, but no jacket. Just a tucked-in brown undershirt. The patch on his cap denoted him as a captain. The stretch of the shirt displayed thick gym muscles. He was handsome, a few years my junior. He offered his hand.

"Captain Thornton. I overhead some of your conversation with Sotomeyer. I just wanted to offer my condolences... to the family."

"You knew Cyrus?" I asked.

"We both liked baseball. Used to swap hot takes and talk stats. He was a good guy."

I simply nodded. Thornton shifted on his feet.

"You said you're looking into the case?"

"Trying to. You know something?"

He shook his head. "No. It's just like Sotomeyer said, he was here one day and then he wasn't. I read the story online. Details were scarce."

"Blunt force trauma," I said. "That's what the coroner ruled. The local cops think it was a Memphis gang."

Thornton frowned. "Memphis?"

"That's what they say."

"You buy that?"

I squinted. Cocked my head. Thornton held up a hand.

"No offense to the investigators. I just heard you say you were a cop. Thought you might have an opinion."

"I don't know what I buy. Seems to be a lot of unanswered questions. You know anything about Cyrus's activities before his death? Where he was cleaning? What he was up to?"

Thornton shook his head. "Sorry. No idea. We only talked when he came to clean the MP station."

"Any chance you could check around for me?"

A slight pause. Thornton nodded. "Yeah. Okay. Sure."

He wrote my number on the back of a business card. We shook hands again, and then I was back in the Traverse. I started the engine to get the air pumping but took my time leaving. I drove slowly. I surveyed the base, returning my attention to those long metal buildings with doors too small to admit aircraft, but not too small to admit semi-trucks.

They would be the demolition centers, I figured. The breakdown warehouses where old M4s were converted into scrap metal, barrels bent and bolts busted, receivers smashed, and trigger units crushed. It seemed such a waste of taxpayer dollars, but then, I hadn't filed taxes in nearly two years.

What did I care?

Outside the gate I surveyed the lineup of fast food restaurants, contemplating lunch as the nervous anxiety returned to my gut. Unless Captain Thornton called me with some relevant piece of information, my trip to Missouri had been generally fruitless. I had ground away another six hours and come no closer to locating Jacquie. The clock of her disappearance ticked inside my head, reminding me that the odds were now dramatically tilted against her survival.

But I still couldn't think about that. I had to remain calm. Fuel up, focus, start from the beginning again, and...

My thoughts broke short. I sat at a red light, my gaze flicking between a McDonalds and a Burger King, my appetite aroused by neither, when my vision snagged on a glint of polished chrome from the intersection between the two restaurants. It gleamed in the midday sunlight like a beacon. I squinted and dropped my foot off the brake as the light turned green. I rolled through the intersection, still not sure why my subconscious mind had fixated on this glint. I reached the McDonalds. The glint dampened as my angle changed. My vision clarified.

And then my heart rate surged. Adrenaline dumped into my bloodstream. My foot slammed against the accelerator just as a throaty rumble broke from the intersection, and a jet-black silhouette streaked from behind a stop sign.

It was a 1970 Pontiac GTO. Chrome bumper, tinted windows.

And it was headed straight for me.

26

The GTO crossed the outside lane without turning, its nose pointed across the street as though it were headed for the auto parts store directly ahead. As though the driver hadn't seen me.

But I knew he had, and I knew he fully expected a collision. The angry snarl of Detroit muscle broke through the air as he laid on the gas, likely expecting me to slam on the brakes.

I didn't hit the brakes—I hit the gas, hard. The Traverse surged and I yanked the wheel left, racing out of my lane, crossing the turn median, and heading straight into the path of oncoming traffic. Horns blared and I clipped the nose of the GTO with my passenger side rear fender. Metal crunched but the Traverse didn't stop. I swerved right again, narrowly missing a GI on a sport bike. He turned sideways and crashed to the ground, sliding on his butt and flailing, but escaping the oncoming tires of my SUV.

Behind me the GTO nosed down in the turn median as horns blared. I raced back onto the righthand side of the road, monitoring my mirrors. Just as I expected, the GTO was backing. Turning. Pointed toward me. There were half a dozen cars between us, but I could hear the Pontiac's throaty roar as the driver accelerated.

That pissed me off. *Majorly.* Baseball bats and brass knuckles in the woods are bad enough, but pulling an idiotic stunt like this with service members on motorcycles zipping around was absolute lunacy—lunacy I wouldn't tolerate.

Approaching the next intersection, I made no pretense of braking as the light flicked to yellow. I laid on the horn instead and blazed right through, knowing the GTO would follow. Hoping he wouldn't T-bone an Army mom in a mini-van, but unwilling to stop and find out what would happen if he pulled alongside me.

I made it to the far side of the intersection and hurtled past the "Welcome to Gates" sign just as the GTO screamed through the intersection. The sleek black car swerved around the minivan I had feared, but the two vehicles avoided collision by inches. Beefy tires caught the pavement and the Pontiac surged onward, the nose lifting and sunlight gleaming against the windshield. I accelerated to eighty miles per hour, more than double the posted speed limit, and prayed that no cops were parked nearby.

I needed to get this fool out of town. Someplace into the sticks, where I could either lose him or corner him. Maybe gain half a mile and prop that AR-10 across my hood. Let him eat lead for lunch.

Outside of town.

The four-lane opened into a highway as car dealerships faded into fields of dead corn. The asphalt was smooth and the lanes wide, but what had served as a comfort on the ride up now felt like a death trap. The GTO was big and heavy—

without significant modification, it was no sort of cornering car. But on a flat, straight highway? It was unbeatable. The overworked six-cylinder shaking beneath the Traverse's hood couldn't possibly compete, and the three-hundred-yard gap I'd built coming out of Gates was evaporating.

So I stopped trying to run. I simply relaxed off the accelerator, watching as three hundred yards became two. I monitored a stop sign planted alongside the four-lane, sucking toward me as though I were reeling it in on a fishing line. I looked back to the mirror to find the GTO closing to within a hundred yards, still roaring at full speed.

Then I slammed on the brakes. The nose of the Traverse dove toward the ground. The quad headlights of the GTO flashed in the sun as the driver panicked and struck his own brakes.

But he wasn't stopping as fast as I was—not with a car that heavy, and brakes that primitive. Clouds of tire smoke erupted on both sides of the Pontiac and the car began to fishtail. The driver was losing control. I kept my foot on the brake, daring him to flinch.

He did. He relaxed off the brake and swerved left at the same moment I pulled a hard right, toward the stop sign. The Traverse crossed off the highway and onto a gravel track that streaked into a field, vanishing between tall rows of dead corn.

The GTO couldn't have made that turn it if were driving at half the speed limit, and it was still well over. In a split second I was gone, gray dust erupting behind me as the highway vanished from sight. The road was rough and rutted, forcing me to wrestle the steering wheel to keep from sliding into the ditch. All I could see was corn—dense forests of it on either side as dust clogged my rear window. I slowed and looked over my shoulder, but the highway was lost to view. I rolled my window down, but I couldn't hear the snarl of the GTO's exhaust.

I looked ahead again, breathing hard despite myself. The road I ran on was some sort of farm track—an access path for tractors and combines. It intersected at regular intervals with similar tracks that formed a giant grid of access points to the field. The ruts were deep and wide, too aggressive for a low-slung muscle car.

At least, I hoped they were. The problem was the dust. The Traverse was kicking it up in tall clouds, carried by the wind over the tops of the corn stalks and exposing my position. I might be safe in the field, at least for the time being, but that safety would evaporate as soon as my enemy recruited an ally with a pickup truck.

No, I had to get out of the field. I had to get back onto the blacktop, losing him amid the traffic.

Keeping my foot in the gas, I accessed the GPS on my burner phone and switched the display to satellite mode. It wasn't a perfect picture—a far cry from the CIA satellite feeds I used to hunt Al-Qaeda terrorists in the mountains of Afghanistan. But as the visual loaded I obtained a clear enough picture to mark my quickest route back to the blacktop. It was a left turn. Three thousand yards down another tractor trail, and then there was a county road. Two lanes, running east to west.

A turn west would carry me farthest away from Gates, from Fort Crowder, and from innocent civilians. Someplace where I could match madness with madness.

I dropped the phone and planted my foot into the gas, roaring through the turn. The new road was so rough it sent my head slamming up into the ceiling. I had to wrestle the steering wheel to keep the ruts from driving me into the corn.

I wondered if my enemy in the GTO was tracking my dust cloud. If even now he had decoded my strategy and was rushing to cut me off, aided by the over-bored power of Detroit muscle.

I wasn't going to give him the chance. I pushed the SUV to its max and marked the stop sign at the end of the trail. It faded in and out of view as wind swept dead corn stalks across it. My knuckles whitened around the wheel. My heart hammered. With every passing second, I envisioned the GTO appearing across my path of travel, blocking my exit.

I already knew what I would do if it did. I would ram it, full speed. See how the airbags worked on a fifty-year-old vehicle.

The GTO didn't appear, and I slid to a stop at the intersection. Wide-open two-lane stretched to either side, as straight as an arrow, and totally empty. I caught a quick glimpse before my dust cloud caught up with me and enveloped the Traverse.

I pulled a hard right and hit the gas again. Up on the asphalt the SUV gained speed, the transmission crunching through gears as I monitored my mirrors. I didn't see the Pontiac, and a glint of hope rose in my chest as every passing second added distance between myself and the beacon of dust I'd left behind.

Then that hope vanished. In my rearview mirror I caught the glint of sunlight on chrome. Four familiar headlights, flashing a little as the heavy car behind them raced across an imperfection in the road.

It was the GTO—a thousand yards behind me and closing like a rocket.

27

The smart play would have been to floor the Traverse and race for the next intersection. Make another sharp turn and try to lose myself in the corn fields. But the thing about midwestern corn fields is, they're huge. The roads are square, flat, and long.

The absolute perfect conditions for a muscle car.

Looking into my mirror I saw that the GTO had closed a hundred yards despite my speedometer hopping around the seventy-mile-per-hour mark. I blazed through an intersection before I even saw the stop sign, my attention dominated by that black spec growing into a hulk. I could hear the exhaust. I could see the frame of the Pontiac pressing low against the road as V8 power drove the speedometer to much greater performance than I could hope to match. Ahead, it was nothing but flat road surrounded by more dead corn. No more intersections.

I was trapped in a tube, and the hounds were on my heels. So once again, I stopped fighting. I slammed on the brakes, screaming to a full stop. I yanked the shifter into reverse and cut the wheel hard to the right. The SUV spun backward, the driver side rotating as I came to a stop across double yellow lines. I looked left and I saw the GTO at five hundred yards, slowing a little and swerving to the middle of the road. Ready to cut me off from completing a three-point-turn and attempting to slide past him.

But I wasn't trying to escape. I was no longer interested in running. I shifted into park and threw my seatbelt off. I twisted and reached into the rear, my fingers finding the smooth aluminum of the AR-10's free-floating forend.

I pulled the charging handle as I brought the rifle across my chest, locking a fresh round into the chamber. I wound the window down. The polymer stock rose into my shoulder, my left elbow propped on the door. Black muzzle protruded from the Traverse. The Pulsar optic nested in front of my eye, and I rotated the forward dial control from the moon symbol to the sun symbol—daytime mode.

The Pulsar was crystal clear, projecting a precise red dot similar to a holographic sight. I found the GTO at three hundred yards and increased magnification to 14x. The car wasn't stopping. Maybe the glare of the sun obscured his view of the rifle. Maybe he was still confused by my sudden halt in the middle of the road.

Or maybe he was just stupid. Whatever the case, the consequences would be the same. I flicked the safety off and dropped my finger over the trigger. I inhaled a long, deep breath, calming the thunder of my heart. I lowered the dot over the driver's side of the windshield as the GTO drew within two hundred yards. At that distance, I wouldn't need hold over or click adjustments. The rifle was likely zeroed at one hundred yards, but even if it wasn't, the margin of error would be inches, not feet. He was a goner, and he didn't even know it.

I could tell the moment he identified my rifle by the sudden application of brakes. Tires screamed on the pavement, and the nose of the GTO plummeted. I adjusted my aim and took the slack out of the trigger. I held my breath. I approached that breaking point, ready for the crack of the bullet and the slam of the buttstock into my shoulder.

Then I heard another sound. A howl of sirens from someplace amid the corn. I squinted as the GTO completed its stop and shifted into reverse. I saw the flash of blue from a mile behind the muscle car—not one but two police cruisers, both rushing in. Probably answering the reports of a reckless driver in a black Pontiac. They would be here in seconds.

Would they find a dead body? An unidentified driver in a brown Chevrolet SUV racing away?

No good.

I made a split-second adjustment to my initial strategy and dropped my point of aim. The red dot found its mark, I held my breath, and pulled. One long, smooth squeeze. The AR-10 snapped, slamming into my shoulder and spitting a heavy chunk of lead just as the back tires of the GTO howled. The Pontiac snatched backwards, away from the threat of imminent death.

But not quickly enough. The driver survived—the front left tire did not. It blew with a snap, and the GTO collapsed in that direction. I flicked the safety back on and drew the rifle into the SUV. The cops were now only half a mile away, still racing in with lights and sirens going. I rolled up the window and ratcheted the shifter into drive. The GTO nearly slid into the ditch as the driver fought for control. He ground to a stop.

He was no longer trying to flee—he couldn't. The cops would eat him for lunch.

I punched the gas. The Traverse whined and hauled me back into the righthand lane, my nose pointed away from the GTO. I watched the patrol cars in my mirror, fanning into a protective semi-circle, doors popping open. Handguns appearing from behind A-pillars.

Not because they'd heard my gunshot—their sirens were too loud. They were drawing on that GTO because they were good and ticked off.

My problem was being solved for me.

28

The satisfaction of checkmating my enemy did little to elevate my overall mood. Maybe it was the car chase, or the fruitlessness of my trip to Fort Crowder. More than likely, it was the rising frustration of a grinding clock. Another day, another hour, and no results. Desperation was setting in at the back of my mind, a fiendish voice of fear whispering that I was already too late. Jacquie was already dead, and it was my fault.

I should have checked my email sooner. I should have struck a match in downtown Whitford, not way out in the sticks at the site of Cyrus's murder. Maybe it was a mistake to pursue his murder at all—it might have been better to treat this like a missing person's investigation and to focus on Jacquie's specific movements.

Whatever the case, I had now initiated a war between myself and an invisible enemy. I'd kicked a hornet's nest and there were hornets swirling all around me...and yet I couldn't put my thumb on any of them. I couldn't pin them down. Who sat behind the wheel of that GTO? Who had jumped me outside Whitford?

Most importantly—what did they know about Jacquie? And where could I find them?

It was time to turn things on their head. It was time to hit this thing straight in the teeth.

Digging out my phone I dialed Lucile as I crossed the state line back into Arkansas. It was midafternoon and shadows were lengthening. I had maybe three hours until full dark, and that was perfect. It gave me just enough time to complete some reconnaissance, sketch out a basic plan, and trigger a trap.

"Mason?" Lucile sounded as though she hadn't slept in days.

"It's me," I said. "Listen, I've got a question about the county."

"What about it?"

"I need to know where the rabble hangs out. The white rabble, specifically."

"Huh?"

I realized I was moving too quickly for Lucile. As a cop, I'd learned long ago that every town, no matter how small or how quiet, has a rowdy spot. It might be a dozen blocks wide or might consist of a single dilapidated building way out in the sticks where ruffians gather and hooligans get wasted.

But it exists, and in a county like Mullins, it was a logical assumption that there might actually be two such spots—one for blacks and one for whites. Not by law or the enforcement of men in white robes, but simply by tradition, comfort, and mutual mistrust. The same way I'd learned that southern churches were often segregated.

"I don't know about no rabble, Mason."

"I'm talking about bars," I clarified. "Clubs. Places where black people aren't welcome, or don't feel safe. Maybe someplace outside of town."

"You mean like that rat hole out on Forty?"

"Maybe. What's it like?"

"Little bar beside the road, 'bout three miles outside of Whitford on County Road Forty. Always lots of bikers and flag people hanging out round there."

"Flag people?"

"Yeah, you know. The folks that fly flags. White folks. Confederate flags, military flags. That yellow snake flag. Them folk."

I knew exactly the kind of people she was talking about. It was a broad spectrum, ranging from patriotic military veterans with POW flags on their Harleys, to considerably less patriotic but just as passionate extremists displaying symbols of division. The block building Lucile described could be a pleasant little dive—a place where veterans gathered to swap war stories, lament the decline of the old republic, and drink good American beer until their wives called them home. The kind of place I could happily spend a weekend, betting fivers on pool games.

Alternatively, it could be something else. Something a lot less savory. There are all kinds of flag people.

"Three miles out Forty?" I asked.

"Yeah. I think so. You ain't lookin' for trouble, are you?"

"Don't need to. Already found some."

Lucile's voice softened. "Mason...I don't want you gettin' in no trouble over Cyrus. He...he could be stubborn. Defy the wrong people, sometimes."

White hot anger flashed in my stomach. My fingers tightened around the phone. "Never apologize for Cyrus, Lucile. Whatever he did, he didn't deserve what he got."

Quiet. I thought I heard her crying, and my temper softened. I hadn't meant to be so harsh.

"Keep your head down," I said. "Keep Jeremiah close. This will be over soon."

I hung up. I pulled up the GPS on my phone and located County Road 40 streaking southwest out of Whitford. There was a little dot on the map marked by a fork and a knife—it was labeled as a bar and grill.

Bingo.

I set the cruise control and settled in for the ride. I would make one stop along the way—a sporting goods store if I could find it. I was looking for a very specific sort of conversation piece.

Then I would be back in Mullins County. It was time to get some answers.

29

Lucile was right about the bar three miles outside of Whitford—it was chock-full of flag people, and not the good kind. In place of military banners, POW flags, or even Old Glory, I found nothing but Confederate stars and bars, black flags printed with skulls and unintelligible lines of Latin, and even a modified Betsy Ross style American flag with three letter I's printed inside the circle of stars. It was a Three Percenter Flag—the symbol of a rambunctious and troublesome right-wing militia group I'd encountered on multiple occasions while working as a cop in Phoenix.

Clearly, this place was a hive for a certain sort of ideology. Specifically, the anti-government, anti-minority, alt-right sort of ideology. It might even be the headquarters of a militia...or maybe just a room full of drunken morons who spent too much time in the radicalized corners of the internet. Regardless, I could smell the hostility of the place from two hundred yards away, stretched out on my stomach with the AR-10 resting next to me. I had left my binoculars in my pickup, but I didn't need them. The Pulsar optic provided all the magnification I required, and gaps between the trees opened a view of the squat block building situated on the far side of the road, about thirty yards beneath my current elevation.

The roof was metal and rusted. The neon sign only partially worked. There were no windows. A Confederate battle flag flapped over a gravel lot occupied by motorcycles, jacked up pickup trucks...and classic muscle cars. Five of them, to be precise. Two sixty-nine Camaros, a seventy Boss Mustang, a seventy Oldsmobile 4-4-2, and a sixty-nine Mercury Cougar Eliminator—all of them sporting the same sorts of backwoods, extremist symbolism as the motorcycles and pickups parked around them.

It was a regular little classic car club. The only thing missing was a 1970 Pontiac GTO, jet black, with one blown tire. Even without the GTO, the presence of the other cars was a good sign. Birds of a feather flock together. I didn't need the guy who had chased me through Missouri corn- fields, I only needed one of his buddies, a quiet spot in the woods...and ten minutes with my brand-new aluminum baseball bat. One heck of a conversation piece.

I watched the bar as the sun slipped behind the foothills and the forest darkened. A few additional bikes and one very clean '68 Cutlass rolled up. All their drivers went inside, and nobody came out.

That was a good thing. It offered me privacy, assuming I could draw my target outside the building. There were no visible security cameras on the property, and whenever a newcomer entered, a cacophony of heavy metal music blared out, reinforcing my confidence that nobody inside the bar would be aware of what was happening outside.

Perfect.

Departing the hillside, I returned to where I had hidden the Traverse, just off the road beneath an oak tree. Firing up the engine, I drove down the road and past the bar, stopping just twenty yards around the bend and once more sliding the Chevy as far off the road as I could risk without getting stuck.

I stuck the Ruger in my waistband, and took a coil of rope and the baseball bat from the rear cargo compartment. I left the hatch open and tugged on a pair of golf gloves and a knit ski mask as I approached the bar, crouching at the edge of the tree line just outside the gravel parking lot. I still couldn't see any security cameras, but that didn't surprise me.

Guys like these don't need cameras. They're real tough. They can handle anything.

Looking behind the bar I found stacks of empty kegs, cardboard boxes, and used fryer oil. I knew it was fryer oil, because I could smell it. Matched with the ventilation pipe rising out of the back of the building, it wasn't a difficult riddle to solve. There must be a small kitchen inside, fed from the propane tank resting on blocks beyond the boxes and kegs.

Target acquired.

Navigating the field of trash by the dull glow of a parking lot light, I circled the end of the windowless building and reached the rear. A single metal door stood there, opening to a grimy patio occupied by a plastic table. The table was laden with bloody fish intestines and severed trout heads. The air reeked of rotting flesh, and when I looked to the ventilation stack I could see the heat waves wafting out.

The fryers were going. A fish fry was underway. I'd found my opening.

Circling behind the propane tank, I traced a half-inch copper pipe out of the rocky Arkansas soil, beneath a metal dome cover, and to the regulator dispensing pressurized fuel. There was a valve, which was padlocked open, but there was also an emergency cut-off lever. Standard regulation for propane dispensers, I guessed.

I cut the valve off and looked to the roof vent. The ripples of exhaust fumes dissipated almost immediately. I hefted the bat and descended into a crouch behind the tank—waiting.

Barely sixty seconds passed. Kitchen diagnostics were efficient, it seemed. The problem was traced to the supply line. A bolt snapped open from the back door, and heavy metal music blared through the stillness.

Then a flashlight beam flitted across the tank. A voice called a question from inside the bar. A louder voice answered from the door. Then boots crunched across the gravel. Hiccups preceded a soppy wet stream of spit. I saw it from beneath the tank, and my fingers tightened around the bat.

Not too hard. He can't be braindead.

The flashlight danced across the ground, and my muscles tensed. I only needed to hear the groan of hinges as the dome cover was lifted. Two seconds dragged by in slow motion.

Then: "What tha—hey!"

I sprang out of the darkness. My target stood on the far side of the tank, flashlight pointed at my gut, a weathered white face grimy with dirt. He was bald. He wore a leather biker vest, no shirt beneath it. His belly stuck out. His eyes went wide.

The bat found him right over the crown of his head, arcing down like a missile and breaking speed at the last possible moment. Aluminum rapped against his skull, and the flashlight fell out of his hand. His jaw fell slack, and then he toppled.

Just like that.

I knelt alongside him, keeping my face up to survey my surroundings as I checked his body for weapons. I found a dirty Charter revolver and slung it aside. Then I tucked the bat beneath my left arm and grabbed him by the vest for the long drag back to the Chevy.

The dude was heavy—over two hundred pounds, and totally limp. It was more meat than I wanted to deal with, but I didn't have the luxury of selecting who would be sent to inspect the propane problem. Hopefully, this guy knew something.

I made it halfway across the back yard, weaving between empty beer kegs, before the back door of the bar opened again. There was no chance to hide. No use in ducking to the ground and scrambling for cover. My prisoner still lay sprawled across the ground, fully exposed to the back door. A skinny guy in a similar leather jacket appeared, sticking his head out and squinting into the dark.

"Bucky?"

I didn't give the newcomer a chance to see the unconscious body. Launching out from the shadows, I closed the ten feet between myself and the back door just as he was pivoting to face me, eyes growing wide, mouth opening.

The bat caught him in the side of the head and he collapsed, as quick as the first. I caught him on the way down and yanked him free of the door, allowing it to smack shut under spring tension. The pair of us fell to the gravel, his skinny body landing on top of me, smelling of sweat and beer. I threw him off and drew the Ruger, all my senses locked on the bar and the undefined number of combatants inside.

I waited. My heart hammered. But nothing happened. The door remained closed. Through the block wall I could barely hear the pound of music. I couldn't hear voices. Everything outside was perfectly still.

I lowered the pistol and looked to my left, sweeping the yard.

Not one prisoner, but two.

The more the merrier.

I shoved the Ruger back into my belt and started with the skinny guy.

30

L oading the skinny guy was easy. He weighed maybe a hundred and forty pounds and folded neatly into the rear of the SUV.

The fat one—Bucky, I guessed—was a lot more trouble. I almost left him behind, estimating that the risks of being caught dragging his limp carcass to the Chevy were greater than the benefits of having two men to interrogate. But the problem with baseball bat-induced comas is that you can never be sure how long they will last. Maybe two hours, maybe two minutes. It's an imprecise science, and if he came to behind that bar and reported to the others, there would be a manhunt underway within the hour.

I could weather that, but I'd rather not. I'd rather take my time. So I wrestled his blubbery body through the ditch and heaved him alongside his companion with effort. I tied them both with rope and stuffed their own socks into their mouths. I emptied their pockets of knives and wallets, then I shut the hatch and circled to the driver's seat.

The entire escapade consumed eleven minutes and

significant quantities of energy. My battered body burned from every extremity, but I had my prisoners. I finally had a tangible lead. Ratcheting the Chevy into drive, I powered away from the bar and turned deeper into the county.

I drove for half an hour. There was no destination in mind. I trusted my instincts, flicking the headlights off and waiting until it was so dark outside that the moon itself was bright enough to cast a clear shadow of my vehicle. Taking turns at random, I found myself on a lonely asphalt road so deteriorated that it felt like gravel. Tall pines leaned overhead, with the nearest foothills a hundred yards beyond.

I had found the bottom of a valley, and I parked the Traverse at the edge of the road. Sitting quietly for five minutes, I listened for the growl of engines. The call of voices.

I heard nothing but nocturnal animals. Certainly no humanity—at least not until a pained grunt and the thrash of legs heralded the resurrection of my prisoners.

Donning the ski mask again, I circled to the back and lifted the hatch to find both men staring wide eyed. Panic rushed their faces as I yanked the skinny one out first. He fought as I dragged him into the woods, shouting through the sock. A swift kick to his rib cage was enough to silence the effort. I slung him down at the base of a pine and returned for his companion.

And the baseball bat.

By the time I had them both on their feet, restrained to the tree and facing me, I was exhausted, breathing hard through the mask. I clicked my MacroStream on and jammed it into the crook of a nearby tree, the beam pointed into their faces. They jerked against their bonds, but I had tied them well. They weren't going anywhere. I stood framed by the flashlight beam and cradled the bat, catching my breath and wondering...

Could I really do this?

It had been years. It had never happened in the United States. I had shot some men and beaten others. I'd killed more than a few. But I'd never tortured. Not since Afghanistan. Not since my unit was in jeopardy.

Was this really any different?

I approached the skinny guy and raised the bat, jamming it beneath his chin and forcing his face up.

"I'm going to remove the sock. You scream, and I break your leg. Understand?"

He shook. He mumbled something. I ripped the sock out.

And he screamed.

Closing my eyes I breathed a silent curse and stepped back from the tree. He saw me cocking the bat and he howled louder, pleading.

It was too late. I'd made a deal with him. I had to hold up my end of the bargain if there was any hope for the remainder of this conversation to produce reliable results.

The bat landed across his left shinbone, and the scream was so loud I almost regretted it. I heard the bone snap. His head slammed back against the trunk of the tree and he jerked against the ropes. I cocked the bat again, but I didn't swing. There was no need to. He'd clenched his jaw and now stood shaking, moans of agony bursting through his lips but no longer erupting from an open throat.

He was doing his best. He didn't require further motivation. I circled to the fat one and repeated my promise. The guy nodded enthusiastically. I removed the sock. He gasped for air but didn't scream. I stepped back into the glare of the MacroStream.

"What's your name?"

"B-Bucky." The fat guy almost choked on the word.

"And him?"

"Sid," Bucky said.

I rested the bat over one shoulder.

"Do you know who I am, Bucky?"

Bucky did know. I could tell by the way he instantly avoided my gaze. It was more than fear. It was guilt.

So much for the mask.

I tugged it off and spat into the pine needles.

"You were there, weren't you? On the road. One of the guys who came from behind. I never saw your face. Did you slash my tire, Bucky? Did you bust my windshield?"

Bucky trembled. Tears slipped down his cheeks. That was more than I could handle. I swung the bat hard. It whistled through the air like a missile and struck the pine tree only inches above his head. Bark exploded in a shower and I roared into his ear.

"Answer me!"

"Yes! Yes!" Bucky almost choked on the words. "I was there, but I didn't do nothing, I swear. I had no choice. I had to go. I—"

"*Why?*"

"Don't tell 'im nothing!"

It was Sid. He'd recovered enough of his gumption to interject himself into the conversation, and his statement of resistance didn't surprise me. It highlighted the problem with torture. Raw pain is terrifying, but it's the terror itself which is most useful. Bucky was drowned in that terror, forced to watch Sid suffer and dreading the moment when that suffering visited him as well. Bucky was well motivated.

Sid, on the other hand, had already experienced a tidal wave of pain, and now his body was hard at work suppressing the misery. Numbing the pain with adrenaline and lending him artificial strength when he needed it most. Forcing me to escalate.

I broke his second shin with a backhanded crack of the bat. Bone shattered, but I didn't quit. I wanted to—desperately. But I knew how the game worked. So long as Sid believed in his own power to overcome whatever suffering I had hitherto unleashed, he would never break.

I had to keep going. He'd left me no choice.

When I finished, Sid's wails had morphed into one constant howl of abject suffering. It was brutal. Consistent. Never ending. It echoed in my mind and threatened to snap my psyche like an overloaded dam. Bucky's psyche did snap. I could see it in his face. As I jammed the bloody bat beneath his chin, the terror in his eyes was so sincere that I no longer had to question the veracity of his answers.

He would tell the truth. His very soul demanded it.

"Who are the people at the bar?" I demanded.

Bucky shook. His gaze snapped sideways to Sid, but Sid was nearly unconscious. Bucky was on his own.

"We're the Brotherhood."

I reached across Bucky's body and caught his left sleeve. The t-shirt ripped with ease, exposing a tattoo that gleamed with sweat. The lines matched those of Edwin Schwartz's tattoo perfectly—an eagle clutching a deformed cross.

"You're Nazis?" I demanded.

Bucky's face hardened. He nodded once.

"Who's in charge?"

A brief hesitation. I flexed my bat arm and Bucky cowered.

"Hoffman! Hoffman is in charge. Please don't hit me!"

I closed the distance between us, silhouetting myself in the beam of the flashlight.

"The guy in the black Dodge? The one with the sunglasses?"

Bucky nodded. *Rock Star*, I thought.

"What about the Pontiac?"

"Huh?"

"Black Pontiac GTO. About a nineteen-seventy model. Who drives it? Hoffman?"

Bucky looked away, and I saw new terror in his face, unlike the first wave of raw animal fear that consumed him at the sound of Sid's snapping bones. This was more intellectual.

It was a learned fear.

"Please," Bucky sobbed. "They'll kill me. They'll kill my family!"

"Like you killed Cyrus Richardson?"

"That wasn't me!" The desperation in Bucky's voice was overwhelming. I flicked the bat and he didn't even notice. He was fixated on me, eyes pleading.

"I swear, man. I don't know nothing about that. I just run the bar, okay? I'm just a guy—"

"No." I shoved the bat into his stomach. "*I'm* just a guy. A guy you're gonna wish you'd never met if you don't start answering my questions. *Who drives the Pontiac?*"

Bucky's lips parted but he didn't answer. I rammed with the bat.

"Shiver!" Bucky howled. "His name is Shiver! Big killer from Little Rock. That's all I know, I swear!"

"Is he part of your Brotherhood?"

"He's the enforcer. He works for Hoffman. You don't want to meet him. He's bad news."

"*I'm* bad news," I growled. "Why did they kill Richardson?"

"I don't know." He said it, but he looked sideways when he did. It was a lie, and once again I had no choice but to honor my side of our contract.

I struck him in the left thigh, just hard enough to unleash panic in his mind. More psychological warfare. Bucky yelped and then Bucky spilled.

"He knew something! Something Hoffman was up to. They don't give me details. I'm just a cook!"

"What did Richardson know?"

"I don't know! Okay? I don't know! I don't know nothing!"

He was screaming now. His voice turned raw. There was no lie in his tone.

"What about Jacquie Richardson?" I pressed. "The black cop from Arizona. You know about her?"

A hesitation. I shook him. He folded.

"I saw her. She was here."

"*Where is she?*"

Fear of my own raced my bloodstream. My fingers dug into the bat's grip. I waited for the answer and every second felt like an eternity. Bucky was sobbing...but he met my gaze.

"They don't know, man. They can't find her anywhere."

31

I wanted to break every bone in Bucky's body, but it wouldn't have done any good. Another ten minutes of questioning resulted in only a repeat of the same facts. He didn't know why Cyrus Richardson had been killed. He didn't know where Jacquie was. He didn't know what Hoffman was up to or why Shiver was roaring across two states, gunning people down.

Bucky was just the cook. Sid had descended into unconsciousness. I knew little more than when I started.

Eventually I put Bucky to sleep with a tap of the bat, then crashed away from my prisoners, my body suddenly racked by vicious chills and stomach convulsions. I reached a tree and leaned against it, dry-heaving over the ground. Begging for something to come up.

Nothing did. My body had already consumed the last meal I'd eaten...whenever that was. Now I was left to shake and gasp. I couldn't close my eyes. If I did, I was transported to another mountain valley on the far side of the world. Another cluster of trees, another group of men tied to them.

Except that time, I wasn't alone. There were fellow Rangers around me. We weren't using baseball bats, we used knives. And the screams...

I closed my eyes and forced myself to see their faces. It had been years since I'd allowed myself to acknowledge those memories. I had buried them. But the shocking speed with which I had resorted to animal violence against Sid and Bucky terrified me. It left me feeling cold, and lifeless. Like a monster.

Forcing myself away from the tree, I looked into the sky. The light of the moon overshone the forest, so bright it reminded me of the glaring sun overhanging Afghanistan. When I looked to my trembling knuckles, I found the splashes of blood from the compound fractures I had inflicted on Sid's legs.

He would never walk the same way again. Maybe he didn't deserve to walk. But what did that mean? How was that my choice?

It took another ten long minutes for my body to calm down. I was left to stare at Sid and Bucky and contemplate my options while the dry heaves subsided. The uncomfortable truth was that I had backed myself into a pretty tight corner. Emotions had overtaken me when I decided on this rash plan of kidnap and interrogation. I really believed it would result in some meaningful intelligence.

It hadn't. So now what? Did I *kill them?*

No. No chance. I was violent, but I wasn't a murderer.

Returning to the trees, I flicked my knife open and slashed the rope holding their limp bodies to the tree. Both men fell like rotten logs. I grabbed Sid first and dragged him back to the road. Bucky was harder, but he reached the ditch eventually. Both men breathed, even though Sid looked like he'd been run over by a bulldozer.

I left them there beside the road and returned to the Traverse. Three hundred yards down the road I located a road sign and a mile marker. I made note of each, then drove until my burner phone generated enough signal for me to use the GPS and make a pair of phone calls.

The first was to Lucile. She was still awake and didn't hesitate when I asked to come over. She would put some coffee on. I would see her in forty-five minutes.

The second phone call was to the Mullins County Sheriff's Department. I recognized the sullen, nasal voice of the desk sergeant who answered. I distorted my own voice into a growl, hoping to disguise it.

"Two bodies on County Road Thirteen, mile post twenty-two. Righthand ditch."

I hung up without waiting for an answer. I set the phone on the dash and sat stopped at an intersection. There were no streetlights. Only my headlights drove back the darkness ahead.

I clenched my fingers around the wheel, forcing out memories of Afghanistan and focusing on one thought over and over. The most critical thing Bucky had said. The thing I didn't want to believe and couldn't make sense of.

Yet he had said it with absolute conviction. No hint of deceit in his eyes.

Where was Jacquie Richardson?

"They don't know. They can't find her anywhere."

I shifted into gear and spun the wheel left, headed for Lucile's house.

32

Lucile Richardson greeted me with a gentle smile. Her dark gaze swept across my dirty, blood-splattered clothes, but she didn't ask questions. She simply led me through the living room to the kitchen, where a fresh pot of coffee steamed next to the stove.

The house was quiet. I saw no sign of Jeremiah.

"I'm sorry it's so late," I said.

Lucile gestured to me to sit at the kitchen table while she fixed two cups of coffee. Each was treated to a generous measure of milk and sugar, a worn silver spoon stirring them in. Lucile sat across from me.

I couldn't look her in the eye. It was all I could do to stop my right hand from trembling as I sipped. Every psychological groove carved into my brain had my mind careening along the tracks of open warfare. Of blood spraying across walls and battle buddies screaming as they died.

I'd never thought I had PTSD. At least, not from the Army. Now I wasn't so sure.

"You look tired." Lucile's voice was like the water of a lethargic brook. So calming I couldn't help but respond.

"I'm sorry I came this way. It's...been a long day."

She nodded. Didn't pry.

"Did I wake you?" I asked.

"No, child. I don't sleep much these days. Actually, when you called, I was reading."

"Anything good?"

Lucile sighed. "The book of Job. One of Cyrus's favorites. I'm not sure why...it's so devastating. Have you read it?"

"No. It's in the Bible?"

A nod. "It's all about a man what lost everything. He was rich, and God let the Devil take it all away. Brought him right to ashes. Kilt his family and everything."

Lucile's eyes watered, and suddenly I thought I saw a battle raging behind them. A tug-of-war between grief, her own gentleness...and something darker. Something angry.

"Job was a man of God. A righteous man. But he was crushed like the wicked...like Cyrus."

It was the last of her words that struck hardest. I was reminded of all her glowing description of her husband. What a strong man he was. How he loved his family and worked so hard. Kept his head down. Honored his community.

"Was Cyrus a man of God?" I asked. I wasn't exactly sure what I meant by the question. I left the interpretation to Lucile, and apparently the interpretation was a good one. She smiled.

"Oh yes. A true man of God, long as I known him. Weren't nothing he did but serve the Lord. When he wasn't toiling at work, he would be toiling up at the church. Fixing stuff, painting stuff. Trying to keep the thing standing. If we had ten dollars and only needed six, the other four went into the offering plate. Never saw him buy a thing for himself. Never saw him raise his voice in anger. He—"

She broke off. The coffee trembled in her hand. She forced a sip as a single tear slid down her cheek. She set the cup down.

"Yes, child. My Cyrus were a man of God. As much as Job. But I'm more like Job...I'm the one asking why."

I lost myself in the surface of my coffee, impulsively thinking about Mia. About loss. I understood something of the pain in Lucile's voice. Something about asking *why*. It was the most wretched emptiness I'd ever experienced...and two years in, it hadn't faded. I'd only learned to endure it.

"Are you a man of God, Mason?"

Lucile's question came out of left field. I looked up, my lips parting, but I didn't answer. I didn't know how to answer.

"Better a hesitation than a no," Lucile said. "That's how He works, sometimes. Slow, like. He's a patient God."

I swallowed, seeing Sid and Bucky again in the woods. Listening to their screams, their pleas for mercy. God might be patient, but I wasn't. I never had been.

"I'm not sure God has much use for a man like me," I said. "I'm nothing like Cyrus."

Lucile didn't answer, and the moment lingered until I felt obliged to look up. I was surprised to see her smiling. It was that same gentle expression as before, but somehow steadier.

"Not yet," Lucile said. Another tear slipped down her cheek, and she buried her face in the coffee. I did the same and we sat in silence. When Lucile next spoke, her tone had flattened again.

"Did you find anything about Jacquie?"

"No."

"And Cyrus?"

"I'm still working on it."

She nodded. "Can I help?"

I hesitated, retracing the logic that had led me back to Whitford. The questions behind the questions—the heart of this problem.

Why had Cyrus Richardson been murdered?

"I was hoping you could tell me more about Cyrus. Specifically, the days leading up to...his passing."

Lucile wiped her lips on a napkin. She took her time in answering.

"Cyrus was a creature of habit. Lots of routine. Up at the same time, in bed at the same time. Same three eggs and toast for breakfast, every day for thirty years. But...that last week before we lost him..."

She trailed off.

"The routine changed?" I prompted.

"No. But Cyrus did. I couldn't put my finger on it. He was...quieter, I suppose. Seemed sort of tense and distracted."

"Can you pinpoint when that change happened?"

"Not really. There was a lot going on. Jeremiah was...well."

"In trouble?" I asked. It was an easy guess, given his temperament.

"No, not trouble. Just growing up hard. Jeremiah isn't as patient as his father was. He takes offense more easily. He fights back."

"You mean the locals. The racism."

Lucile shrugged. "Everything changes...and everything stays the same. Just the way of the world."

"So Cyrus was distracted about Jeremiah?"

"I thought so, but he kept saying it was just a phase. Jeremiah would grow out of it, learn to settle down. Pick his battles. Cyrus wouldn't talk about it much. That's when I started to think something else was bothering him."

"Like what?"

"He wouldn't say, but he started spending more time off by himself. After work. Lots of time at the church, working on the restoration. I don't think he was sleeping too good, either. I woke up a few times and found him out of bed, out on the porch, just...sitting. Praying, maybe. He prayed a lot when he was stressed."

"Out loud?"

"No. Not out loud. I don't know what he was praying about."

I picked at the edge of the tablecloth, sorting through the pieces in my mind. I could sense that something was there. That I was staring right at it. Cyrus had discovered something, so they—Hoffman and his crew—killed him.

But what? And more importantly, what had Jacquie found when she retraced his steps? Had she discovered the same evidence? Had Shiver, the enforcer, put her into an early grave without Bucky or Sid hearing anything about it?

No. That didn't add up. Bucky indicated that the Brotherhood was still looking for Jacquie—actively. Maybe even desperately. She was still missing, and she knew something, also.

That made the intel—whatever secret that the Brotherhood so desperately needed to protect—the linchpin of this entire case. The hinge that everything else turned on.

So what was it?

I rubbed my eyes, sudden exhaustion descending on me

in a cloud. My mind collided with a brick wall, my body crumpling into temporary defeat in a way it never had when I was a young, lithe Ranger. Maybe it was the age. More likely, it was the mileage.

Whatever the case, my own desperation to locate Jacquie was blanketed by a more pressing necessity—the demand for rest.

"Thanks for the coffee." I rose from the chair, and Lucile wrapped me in a hug. I turned for the door.

"Mason?"

"Yeah?"

Lucile stood behind her chair, both hands on its back. Looking somehow more broken than she had before. A lot older.

"It ain't worth it. Whatever happened to Cyrus...whatever happened to Jacquie. You can't wash it away with more blood. God calls us to forgive our enemies."

I squinted. "And what if she's still alive, Lucile?"

"You really think that?" There was no faith in Lucile's voice. It angered me, somehow. My back stiffened.

"Absolutely. And I'm not stopping until I find her."

33

Three Years Prior

I t was midnight, and the Phoenix Police Department bullpen was all but empty. Desk lamps were turned out, computers locked. Cops were either at home or out on patrol, embracing the night shift over sour cups of coffee. Ten hours into my shift, I felt ready to drop.

It had been a desk day. Just working my phone, running down digital leads, and interviewing one potential witness whom the patrol cops brought in. He was a weed dealer they picked up on possession charges. Sober, but not exactly lucid. His known territory included the area around the truck stop where Jane Doe #3 had been found—we still didn't know the girl's name.

There was a plea deal on the table for the drug dealer if he could tell me something useful. He wasn't even smart enough to make something up. He knew nothing about the girl, nothing about that hot July night when her young life ran headlong into the jaws of death.

We were back to square one.

I trashed the rest of my cold coffee before weaving through the desks to the back of the room. I found Jacquie by the murder board, right where she'd stood for most of the last hour. A collection of photographs, sketch artist portraits, and printouts were connected by lines and dry erase notes.

An open box of donuts sat on the counter next to Jacquie, but she hadn't touched them. She just stood with her arms crossed, staring at the board.

"Anything?" I asked.

Jacquie simply shook her head. I surveyed the three names written across the top of the board—Ashely Morris, LaToya Carter, and Jane Doe #3. All confirmed prostitutes. All ranging from eighteen to about twenty-four years of age. All very pretty, but otherwise in no way similar. Morris was brunette and heavy set. LaToya was tall and rail thin. Jane Doe was a classic baby doll blonde.

"It's random," Jacquie whispered. "It's so freaking random."

"Nothing is random," I said. "There's a common denominator. We just haven't seen it yet."

Jacquie didn't answer. I leaned against the edge of the desk and rubbed my eyes. Three weeks had passed since Jane Doe's death, and the trail was about as cold as a block of ice. Pressure from up the chain had pivoted toward more "pressing" matters of investigation—issues like the murder of a white jogger at South Mountain Park, or multiple recent break-ins across nice neighborhoods. Things that jeopardized the mayor's reelection campaign.

"I'm gonna speak to the captain," I said. "If they're going to breathe down our necks about the media headlines, they've got to take something off our plate. Might as well be this."

The defeat in my voice pained even me. Again, Jacquie shook her head.

"No."

"You're exhausted, Jac. I'm exhausted. We can only handle so much."

She remained fixated on the murder board. She looked like a limp dishrag.

But her chin lifted.

"I requested this case, Mason."

"You what?" I squinted.

"I should have told you. Given you an option. I asked for us to be put on it."

"Why?"

Jacquie shrugged. Stared at the photograph of Jane Doe. Then she looked at me.

"Because if we don't care...who does?"

The words landed like a sledgehammer. I winced, instantly ashamed of myself. I couldn't blame it on the weariness. On the long hours or the political distractions pouring down from the police commissioner.

Jacquie was right. One hundred percent.

"We're gonna nail this guy," Jacquie said. "No matter what it takes."

34

Present Day

I awoke with a start, gasping for air. My Evergreen motel room smelled vaguely of marijuana smoke, the sheets glued to my body by sweat stained with...well. Other people's sweat, most likely.

I tore the bedclothes aside and placed both feet on a sticky floor. When I closed my eyes the visions of Jacquie standing in front of the murder board were as crystal clear as the day they'd occurred. Every little detail, right down to the arrangement of photographs, the hurried handwriting Jacquie had used to spell out each name. The Phoenix Suns coffee mug resting cold next to her donuts.

And her voice: *"Whatever it takes."*

I pushed my hair back and stared across the room at the peeling wallpaper. Outside I heard voices calling across the parking lot. A child screaming. An engine running. Light leaked between the curtains, matching the time displayed on the nightstand clock—eight fifteen. I'd overslept.

Why the prostitute case?

I couldn't make sense of the dream. It was the second installment in a seemingly random investigation Jacquie and I had pursued midway through our partnership. A bloody case, yes. An exhausting one.

But nothing special in the context of the dozens of homicides we unpacked over the years. Nothing related to my present predicament.

Just a memory of Jacquie, keeping my body from sleep.

I dug a fresh pair of underwear from my backpack and showered off the sweat. I didn't bother with a shave. A clean t-shirt and a sort-of-clean pair of jeans completed my ensemble, and I was just reaching for my backpack when a calm settled over the parking lot outside. It was as sudden and defined as when dark clouds pass over the midday sun. Tires ground on concrete, and a door closed, but the voices were gone.

I moved to my window and parted the curtain, peering out across the parking lot. It was scarred by potholes and mostly empty. Only a few motel guests were visible outside their rooms, and none caught my eye.

What dominated my attention—what was dominating everybody's attention, apparently—was the Mullins County patrol car parked right in the middle of the lot. Both front doors were open. One cop was moving slowly down the breezeway, knocking on doors and holding brief conferences with anybody who would talk.

The second cop I recognized from my visit to Conroy's sheriff's department. He was short, disheveled, and overweight. He approached the motel's office and rapped on the glass security panel. The clerk approached. The cop raised a clipboard.

I didn't have to wonder what was clipped to it. I only had to wonder if the clerk would rat me out. It turned out the answer was *yes*. The clerk nodded once. Then she pointed right at my motel room.

Great.

I stepped back from the window, allowing the curtain to fall back. Looking over my shoulder, I saw only a blank wall behind the bathroom sink. There was a closet, also, and sheetrock. But no auxiliary exit.

Outside, one cop called to the other. I imagined them drawing their weapons and closing on my position, eager to apprehend a kidnapper. Calling in the evidence of my own crime, it seemed, wasn't paying any dividends. Clearly, the two Aryans had no difficulty in squealing about me the moment they were saved.

Footsteps neared the door and I weighed the merits of fight or flight. I was in a corner, but gunning down cops was no sort of solution. I had to get creative.

Scanning the room once more, my eyes stopped over the ceiling. It wasn't sheetrock, but suspended tiles. Cheap, like a hospital, with stainless steel ribs holding each tile up in neat two-foot squares.

Good enough.

Rushing to the bathroom, I used the sink as a stepping stool. My head struck the underside of a ceiling tile just as a fist landed on the door outside.

"Sheriff's department! Open up. We have a warrant."

I shifted the tile aside, rising up to my shoulders in the attic beyond. It was dark and smelled of mildew. Eighteen inches to my right ran the top of the wall barricading my room from the next in line. It looked solid enough to support my weight. I grabbed the overhead rafters and heaved, every brutalized muscle in my body screaming in protest.

I almost fell. My fingers slipped. A fingernail tore.

I clung on by sheer willpower and wrenched my body up through the ceiling tile hole. Outside, the cop beat on the door again. I pulled myself up to my waist into the attic, then twisted to drag a boot through. Ceiling tiles rattled in their frames and the aluminum ribs groaned. My fingers were slipping. I got one boot through and placed it atop the dividing wall. That took some weight off my shoulders and I was able to draw my second leg through. I hung suspended from the roof, my butt swinging over the hole in the ceiling, both feet planted atop the wall. Releasing the rafter with my left hand, I shoved the ceiling tile back into place just as the motel door lock clicked beneath me. Boots struck the floor, and voices barked.

I held my breath, still clinging to one rafter with my body bunched up like a contortionist. From beneath me a heavy body reached the motel closet and tore the door open. A hillbilly voice barked across the room.

"He ain't here!"

"Whatcha mean he ain't here? The bed's still warm!"

"Whall, check under it!"

Check under it. Real Sherlocks at work.

More thumping of boots. Furniture shifted. The motel clerk objected and was advised to shut up. My hand began to slip, and I pivoted my weight more directly over the dividing wall. There was no easy way for me to proceed any farther. A field of suspended ceiling tiles offered no footing sure enough to support my body weight.

My best hope was to drop straight through into the next room.

The nearest ceiling tile lifted with ease, exposing darkness beneath. I had to use my MacroStream to see anything at all. The beam revealed a bathroom sink directly beneath me, this one cracked and covered in dust. I couldn't see deeper in the room, but with my fingers burning I knew I didn't have a choice. I dropped straight through the hole, landing on the sink with a soft thud.

With the flashlight held between my teeth I surveyed the room. It wasn't a room at all, but a makeshift janitorial closet stocked with towels and cleaning supplies. There wasn't even a bed. Sliding off the sink, I hurried to the window and parted the curtain.

The patrol car remained in the parking lot, and voices continued to my left. The door to my room was still open, blocking my view—and theirs.

I flipped the lock and eased the door open. I passed onto the breezeway only a yard removed from the still-objecting motel clerk. She was arguing on the other side of the open door to my room. The cop was arguing back, his hillbilly voice escalated into a nasal howl.

"You *told me* he was in here! Where is he?"

I didn't wait for the answer. I fast-walked to the outside of the property and pivoted around the end of the building. Thirty seconds later I had cleared the vacant lot next door and reached the sprawling parking lot of a strip mall. I'd left the Traverse parked next to some donation bins for two reasons. In case the cops identified the vehicle, I didn't want them to connect it to the motel. In case they identified the motel, I didn't want to lose access to my only set of wheels.

That was now feeling like a solid strategy. I fired up the engine and looked back to the motel. I couldn't see the patrol car. The cops must still be searching the property. They would be searching for some time—enough time for me to slip out of Evergreen and back into Mullins county.

I already knew my next step. It came to me as my mind unpacked the dream. I pictured Jacquie's elaborate murder board, and how she used to use it to organize her thoughts. To keep track of the details.

It was a natural strategy—to keep notes. To document observations. And maybe Jacquie wasn't the only one who had used it. If Cyrus Richardson knew something, maybe he had documented it.

I dialed Lucile. She answered with no hint of surprise.

"Mason?"

"You told me before that Cyrus didn't use technology. Didn't have a smartphone."

"That's right. He was old fashioned that way."

"Did he used a computer?"

"No...never."

I thought quickly, stripping technology out of the mix and asking myself what options that would have left Cyrus. There weren't many. He wouldn't have had an elaborate board covered in photographs and notes. Maybe just a notebook.

And where would he have kept it? At his house?

No. Too near to his family. Too much risk for them. So where?

"You said Cyrus was working on a church?" I asked.

"Yes. Our church. He had been for months."

"But he was there more often just before he died."

Brief pause. "Yes...he was."

"I need the address."

35

Pleasant Hill Baptist Church didn't sit on a hill at all. It sat in a valley, with foothills rising in the distance and about three acres of rolling green meadowland surrounding it. The architectural style was late nineteenth century. The lapboard siding was painted in faded white, the primary sanctuary set atop stone pillars with a bell tower rising above a grass parking lot.

There was a steeple atop the bell tower. A lonely wooden cross faded by the sun stood atop it. The windows of the church reflected the morning sunlight in a rippled pattern, a signature of lead-based glass that had lost its clarity over time. A single pickup truck sat parked in front of the church with a utility trailer hitched behind it.

The tailgate of the trailer was lowered. A lawn mower rumbled from the far side of the church, slicing down the late summer grass in the last cut of the season. The man operating the mower was black, and he wore a dust mask. I didn't recognize him, but he looked directly at me as I stopped the Traverse on the two-lane.

I didn't see anyone else. Certainly, no Nazis skulking behind the wheels of classic muscle cars. No cops either, but something in my gut warned me not to park in the church's lot. I proceeded down the road instead, around the bend to another turnoff. Maybe the entrance of a personal driveway, or a mountain distillery for all I knew. I slid the Traverse far into the trees to conceal it from view of the road, then I walked back to the church.

The lawn mower's engine rattled and clacked as I approached the property from the rear. A neat little picnic field had already been cut. There was a tether ball stand and a couple of concrete picnic benches. Two tire swings dangled from an oak tree, and a fresh coat of paint adorned a mini picket fence enclosing a playground. The playground was simple—one see-saw and a couple of plastic rocking horses—but everything about it looked fresh and orderly.

I met the lawnmower on the sheltered side of the church, and its operator cut the engine. He lifted his mask but didn't rise from the battered old machine as I raised a hand in greeting.

"Good morning, sir. Sorry to disturb you. Is the pastor around?"

The man removed his work gloves and clambered off the lawn mower with a little grunt. He could have been fifty or seventy-five. I couldn't tell, but he was certainly older than me. The mileage had left its mark in his dark eyes.

"That would be me," he said, offering a hand. "Reverend Arthur Polk. Junior, if anybody's asking. You must be Mr. Sharpe."

I cocked an eyebrow, taking his hand. The grip was firm, but not overbearing.

"Lucile telephoned me that you were stopping by," Polk clarified. "She didn't say why..."

He trailed off. I inhaled a deep breath of fresh grass clippings. It was a comforting smell. Very domestic. It reminded me of my little house in south Phoenix...that sliver of paradise that for such a brief period had been my own.

"It's a beautiful church," I said, lifting my chin toward the old building. Now that I had drawn closer, I could see the age. Many of the lapboards were split and rotting. Paint peeled. Shingles were broken, exposing patches of roofing covered over with bits of tarp. The bell tower seemed to lean, and some of the window panes had been replaced with plywood.

It was battered. Like everything else in Mullins County.

"That it is." There was pride in Polk's voice. "Built by the brethren not long after the war. Lots of sharecroppin' dollars went into the construction. Lots of deep sacrifice."

He regarded the church with a proud but semi-sad smile. For a moment he seemed lost in whimsey, as though he'd forgotten I was present.

Then he caught himself and blinked out of it.

"Would you like a glass of water, Mr. Sharpe?"

"Very much."

Polk led me to a set of concrete steps at the church's front entrance. There was a little anteroom just inside. A worn wooden floor, slouching tables laden with freshly cut flowers, and a ladder leading up to the bell tower. A rope dangled there, and when I lifted my head I could see the bell hanging high above.

It was bronze and corroded. I imagined what it might sound like, calling parishioners to morning worship in a bygone era. Suddenly, I felt a little sad myself.

"That bell is the pride of the church," Polk said, guiding me into the sanctuary. It filled the remainder of the building—just a few rows of wooden pews with a tiny choir loft and a pulpit. High ceilings. A small, weathered piano.

Nothing else.

"Cost nearly two hundred dollars, way back in nineteen thirteen. A pretty penny, I can tell you. Especially back then. Folks around here always been poor."

Polk dug into an ice chest and produced two bottles of water. We drank quietly while I surveyed the interior of the sanctuary. It was much like the exterior. The floors were so worn they looked raw, and the window frames seemed to slouch.

"Been a rough couple of decades," Polk murmured.

He was watching me, and I felt a sudden flash of embarrassment. I hadn't meant to call attention to the imperfections of his church.

"I'm sorry," I said.

Polk smiled. "The buildings fade. The faith remains. I've still got a flock, the Lord be praised. None truer than Cyrus Richardson."

I cocked my head. There was a keen light in Polk's eyes—a knowing light.

"I guess you know why I'm here," I said.

"Lucile says you been looking into Cyrus's death. Says you been asking questions."

"That's right."

"Been rustling some feathers, too. Upsetting the locals."

"Only the bad ones."

A smirk. Polk folded his arms. He seemed to be considering. I decided to influence him in my favor.

"I'm not here to burn down your county, Reverend. I just want my partner back."

"Miss Jacquie, you mean."

"That's right. She's in trouble."

He pursed his lips. I knew what he was thinking.

"She's not dead, Reverend. I'm getting her back."

He pondered that. I let him. At last Polk finished his water.

"Okay, Mr. Sharpe. I reckon if Lucile trusts you, I can trust you. What do you want to know?"

"Nothing that should endanger you. I just want to know about Cyrus. Lucile said he was acting strangely just before he was murdered. He seemed preoccupied. She said he spent a lot of time here at the church."

"That he did. Cyrus was real handy with a hammer. He was trying to fix the place up. We hardly got two pennies to rub together, as you can imagine. I myself work two jobs, aside from pastoring. Cyrus donated a lot to this flock."

"Were you ever here with him while he was working?"

"Sure, plenty of times. He tried his best to teach me a thing or two. Never had much luck." Polk laughed, but there were tears in his eyes.

"Did he ever confide in you? Was anything on his mind?"

"Nothing that should have got him killed. Cyrus was like any man. He had his demons. Had his worries. Mostly about his family, and about this church. Nothing about himself. He was a servant like that...a real man of God."

Man of God. There was that phrase again.

"He never said anything about something he found? Something he learned?"

Polk squinted. "What you fishing for, Mr. Sharpe?"

"I'm not fishing. I'm just trying to understand. I..." I hesitated. Measured my words carefully. I didn't want to say anything that might endanger Polk. Nothing that he didn't need to know.

"I have reason to believe that Cyrus crossed some dangerous people. That he learned something about them... something they needed to protect."

"Some people here?"

"Some people," I said.

A soft nod. Polk chewed his lip, then he shrugged. "Cyrus was here a lot just before he died. But not talking to me. He was up in the tower." Polk lifted a thumb toward the bell.

"How come?"

"Wood was decaying, same as everything else. He was reinforcing the bell scaffolding. Trying to keep it from dropping with a good puff of wind."

"He was remodeling up there?"

"Yep. All of the week before he died. Funny, too, because he said he was gonna be adding a sandbox to the playground for the chilluns. Then all of a sudden he gets fixated on that bell tower." Polk shrugged. "That was Cyrus."

"You mind if I have a look?"

"A look at what?"

"His work."

Polk scratched his neck, then shrugged. "I guess it can't hurt. You see where the ladder is. Imma climb back on that tractor if you don't need me."

I offered my thanks and headed for the ladder, thinking again of Jacquie's murder board. Of her obsession with documentation.

Had Cyrus taught her that obsession? Had he himself kept notes, hidden away in the last place anyone would look?

I shinnied up the ladder, body aching as I hauled myself

through a trap door onto a cramped landing. The bell hung from the tower's rafters, its bronze shell rippling with cast marks. A rope disappeared through the floorboards, which were all new. The beam suspending the bell itself was also new, and Cyrus had replaced several of the wall planks as well. There was fresh wire mesh stapled over an open window to keep the birds out.

I clicked on my MacroStream and shone it up through the rafters and around the floor, admiring the careful handiwork of a skilled craftsman. Tapping with my boots, I felt for loose floorboards or hollow compartments. Everything sounded the same. I edged around the perimeter and ran my hand along the wall, tugging at seems and corners. Tapping with my palm. Pressing on smooth spots.

"Come on, Cyrus. I know you had something..."

I reached the back side of the tower and placed the flashlight in my mouth. The floorboards groaned under my weight. I squatted and felt along a baseboard. It was the only baseboard in the tower which was new, and I couldn't see any hammer marks or nail heads affixing it in place. I thought it gave a little when I pressed on it, but it was too tightly jammed against each corner to be sure.

I drew my Victorinox. The locking blade snapped open, and I pressed it into the crack at the top of the board. It flexed a little. It moved. I pried, and then two things happened at once.

First, the board fell out, exposing a dark compartment behind. Second, tires ground against the gravel outside, matched with a surging engine. I darted up and looked out the wire-covered window. Even with a partial view of the parking lot, I easily recognized the silhouette and markings of a Mullins County police cruiser, the tail end of the motto "protect and serve" visible on the rear fender.

A door popped open. A voice called across the lawn.

"Howdy, preacher!"

I turned back to the cavity at the back of the bell tower. I shone the light into the compartment, and stopped.

There was something inside.

36

Polk's lawn tractor cut off as the deputy repeated his shout. I hit my knees and slipped my hand into the gap. The object inside was about the size of a cell phone, but softer. Covered in leather. It was a notebook, held closed by a rubber band. I tore the band off and used the flashlight to illuminate the first page.

Outside, the voice of the deputy mingled with that of Reverend Polk. I didn't recognize the cop. It wasn't one of those who had searched my motel in Evergreen, which meant multiple units had been deployed across the region to track me down. In a way, that was a good thing. It drew a clear and undeniable connection between the Aryan Brotherhood Army and Conroy's sheriff's department.

Bones to pick later.

"Sorry to bother you, preacher man. I just been lookin' for a fella. Thought you might have seen him."

The cop's voice dripped with condescension, as though he were speaking to a child. I looked toward the window and held my breath. The Ruger American was hidden in the back of my waistband, but from the top of a bell tower a handgun would be useless. Not because I couldn't make a killing shot at fifty feet, but because I would be a sitting duck trapped inside a tower with nothing but lapboard siding as a shield.

Shooting at a cop—even a dirty one—was an ill-advised plan anyway.

"Who you lookin' for?" Polk asked. It wasn't the answer I had hoped for, but maybe it was the most logical.

"White guy. 'Bout six foot, maybe six foot two inches. Good build. Goes by the name *Mason Sharpe.*"

The cop said it as though my name were a pseudonym. I waited.

"You got a picture?" Polk asked. There was a brief pause. Then Polk spoke again.

"Yeah, I seen him. He was in town the other day, wasn't he? At the diner."

My heart almost stopped. I slid the notebook into my pocket and backed up against the wall, twisting my face to look out the window. I could see the top of the car. I could see the deputy's hat. I couldn't see Polk.

"That's right," the deputy said. "Been causing an awful lot of trouble."

"What you want him for?" Polk asked.

My chest tightened. *Don't do it, Reverend. Don't put me in this position.*

"He beat a couple fellas," the deputy said. "Near killed them both. Busted up one of their legs with a baseball bat. They said he was all strung out, maybe on drugs."

"Oh geez," Polk said. "What did they do to him?"

From my vantage point atop the steeple, I saw the cop stiffen.

"What did they do to him? You trying to get cute with me, preacher man?"

"Easy does it, deputy. Easy does it. I was just curious."

"Yeah, well, let me ask the questions. You seen this dude or not?"

"Like I said, I saw him in the diner."

"*Have you seen him since?*"

"You know, sonny," Polk said. "I don't enjoy your tone. You may be a badge-carrying official, but I been tending to this community since you was in diapers. You might like to remember that before you accuse an old man of lying."

"I didn't—"

"I said I seen him at the diner and that's the truth of it. What's become of you young folks? Does your mama know you're out here sassing preachers? I oughta call Ms. Belle right now. Boy, I got grass to cut, and I can't get a moment's peace with you out here stomping around like I'm some kinda common criminal. Just wait until Ms. Belle hears—"

"All right, all right!" the cop blustered. "Wind it down, old man. I'm just doing my job."

"Sassing me," Polk snorted. "I'd call your grandma too, if she was still with us. Lord knows Ms. Margie wouldn't tolerate no sass. Salt of the earth, that woman. My pappy used to tend to her garden beds. He was always good with flowers and—"

The deputy wasn't listening. His car door slammed. His engine roared. He was gone...and I smiled.

Returning down the ladder, I met Polk at the church's front door. He shot me a sideways look.

"What he said true?"

"Do you really want to know?" I asked.

Polk didn't answer. He pinched his lips, and I could tell

he was wrestling with something, maybe trying to decide whether or not to say it.

"I'll go now," I said. "Thank you for your help. It means a lot."

I was halfway back to the road when Polk called after me. "Make sure I don't regret it, son."

BACK INSIDE THE Traverse I fired up the engine before I finally opened the notebook. I didn't see any sign of the deputy or his car, but I wanted to be ready in case he made a sudden reappearance. Under the light of a midday sun it was easy enough to read Cyrus's notes. Most of the pages were blank. The first five were filled with personal items—a grocery list, a few to-do lists. A section of bills, most of them marked off as paid. A few not.

I didn't hit pay dirt until I reached a sixth page, and even then I wasn't immediately sure what I was looking at. It was a sort of table, with a line scrawled down the middle. On the lefthand side was a column of dates, ranging back to around two weeks before Cyrus died. In the righthand column were numbers—whole numbers, with no identifying symbols to indicate whether they represented dollars or gallons or light years. Most were two-digits long, a few three-digits long. Some odd, some even. Some ending in a five or a zero. Some appearing abjectly random.

There was no discernible pattern to the values represented. They didn't seem to relate to each other in any particular way. One number doubled—first it was ten, and the next day was twenty. But the day after that it was twenty-seven and the day after that fourteen. The doubling seemed to be a coincidence.

What wasn't a coincidence was the total. It was perfectly round, and it was written in harsh pencil lines, then circled. One thousand, with a little notation etched next to it. I had to squint to make out the handwriting, but I thought the notation read "units".

I ran a thumb over the page, checking for imperfections or any kind of wrinkled paper that could indicate invisible ink. Not that I really expected such a thing. Flipping to the next page—page seven—I found it to be the last page marked in any way. The remainder of the notebook was blank.

The seventh page contained two notations. At the top was a phone number—ten full digits beginning with an area code of 501. I didn't recognize that code, and I didn't recognize the rest of the number, either. There was no name associated with it. No explanation of whom the number belonged to.

But beneath the number was another circled note. It was a street address, complete with a number, a road name, a city, and even a zip code. The city was Little Rock. Beneath the city was written a date and a time. The time was eight thirty p.m.

The date was September 17th, which felt significant to me. It took me a moment to discern why, and then it was only by chance. I glanced to the dash where the Chevy's built-in clock glowed against the sunlight. The date was displayed there.

September 17th.

I looked back to the notebook and again inspected the page for water damage. Nothing. Digging my burner phone from my pocket, I dialed the 501 number and listened to it ring while I studied the address. I wasn't sure how far Little Rock lay from Mullins County, but it couldn't be more than a few hours. The Traverse's clock displayed one fifteen, which meant I had plenty of time to ride south—

"ATF Little Rock, Agent Feldon's office. How may I help you?"

My mind ground to an abrupt stop. It wasn't the three-letter agency that surprised me. It was the *name*. Feldon—a very familiar name, and a somewhat unusual one. But surely it couldn't belong to the same person I immediately thought of when I heard it.

"Agent Mark Feldon?" I asked, just to be sure.

"That's right. How can I help you?"

I squinted. *No way.*

Mark Feldon was a federal agent I'd met before, about eighteen months prior, in Atlanta. Our meeting had been explosive, and eventually resulted in a mass drug bust of Mexican fentanyl shipments into the city.

A drug bust because Mark Feldon was a *drug agent.* He worked for the DEA, not the ATF.

"This is the ATF?" I questioned.

"*Yes.*" Now the man sounded irritated. "Can I help you, sir?"

I hung up and tossed the phone into the passenger seat. I ran a hand over my face, brushing a growing beard. My gaze drifted back to the open notebook, and I flipped the page to the scrawled pencil table.

One thousand units, spread across two weeks of dates. A number connecting Cyrus Richardson to the ATF—the bureau of alcohol, tobacco...and *firearms.*

Suddenly I saw it. It was blatantly clear. The connection

between Cyrus's work and the Aryan Brotherhood Army. That critical bit of intelligence he had uncovered and must have been in the process of reporting to the ATF, but his investigation had been cut short because the Aryans caught him first.

The key factor was Fort Crowder, that small Army installation just across the border where a humble janitor had cleaned bathrooms and office space. What was Crowder's mission?

Destroying phased-out M4 rifles. Thousands of them. But not all of them.

Not the one thousand that had been smuggled off base and sold to the Aryan Brotherhood Army.

I breathed a curse and slammed the shifter into gear. I spun back onto the two-lane and turned for Whitford. But I wasn't heading for the corrupt sheriff's office, and I wasn't heading back to the bar to confront more half-rate supremacist thugs.

I was headed south, to Little Rock. Because I had to assume that whatever arms-dealing plot Cyrus had stumbled into, Jacquie would have uncovered it also. She would have run it right to the ground.

And then been swallowed by it.

37

L ittle Rock lay exactly one-hundred fifty miles south of Whitford, situated along the north and south banks of the Arkansas River, surrounded by a nest of freeways. Long before I reached the city the foothills of the Boston Mountains melted into expansive farmland. It was much like southern Missouri, but in place of corn fields I found cotton, soybeans, and cow pastures. Traffic was light, and I made good time in the fast lane. Tally called to inquire about his rental car, which was now overdue to be returned. I expected outrage, but he sounded more bemused than irate.

"You know I've got a tracker on that car," he said.

"I'm not stealing it. Just give me a couple more days. I'll make it worth your while."

I hung up, a little unsure *how* I would make it worth his while. Edwin Schwartz's cash was running out.

Problems for later.

The address recorded in Cyrus's notebooks carried me across the river and through the heart of downtown Little

Rock before eventually reaching a neighborhood called Meadowcliff. The street was University Avenue, and it was a four-lane populated by all the usual businesses you find on the economically slumping side of any town—muffler shops, mixed martial arts studios, adult stores, cheap motels. Lots of thrift stores.

The address in question lay off University Avenue. It was a gravel road barricaded by a chain-link gate, tall trees growing out of the ditch and obscuring my view of what lay beyond. I thought it might be a dump at first, or some kind of scrap yard. It had that kind of look. But then I ducked deeper beneath the roofline of the Chevy to see the outline of what looked like a billboard rising above leafy tree tops. Only, it was much too big to a billboard. It wasn't a sign at all, it was a movie screen. The place beyond the chain-link gate was an old drive-in movie theatre, now long abandoned by the decay of time and the progress of streaming services and iPads.

I double-checked the street number in Cyrus's notebook, then swept the ditch on either side of the drive-in entrance, noting the blackened concrete base of what must have once been a large sign. The sign was long gone, but printed into the concrete surface was a five-digit number.

It matched the street number in Cyrus's notebook.

I shifted back into gear and pulled onto the four-lane. I proceeded south until I found a fast food restaurant specializing in Italian food. I ordered a lasagna in a cardboard bowl and ate in Tally's SUV. The food was mediocre at best, but it allowed me time to contemplate my next move.

It was nearly four o'clock. The time listed next to the address in Cyrus's notebook was eight fifteen. I had over four hours to kill, but I was no longer in a hurry. I could feel myself closing in on the heart of this problem, drawing nearer to the truth.

Sid and Bucky were nothing more than common henchmen. Foot soldiers, at best. But if my theory about the one thousand "units" recorded in the notebook was accurate—if the appointment recorded and circled beneath was some sort of sale of illegally obtained military surplus—then there would be much higher-ranking members of the ABA present at tonight's rendezvous. An abandoned drive-in movie theater was an intelligent spot. Drive-ins are designed to be sheltered from view of the passing highway. An abandoned one would be quiet, with ample room to work.

And the ABA wouldn't send the likes of Sid and Bucky, they would send their best. Hoffman, maybe. Or the man in the black Pontiac. The so-called *enforcer*—Shiver.

I was willing to bet that the likes of Shiver and Hoffman would know a lot more about Cyrus's death and Jacquie's disappearance than Sid or Bucky, but there was one thing all four men held in common.

They would talk under the application of a baseball bat.

38

I opted not to conduct a full, on-foot recon of the movie theater property prior to the eight thirty appointment time. It would have been helpful to scope out every entrance and exit, every potential hiding place, and the nuances of the terrain. However, there was a chance that because this property was pre-ordained to be a rendezvous point, the Aryans would have installed surveillance. Game cameras, or even an in-person sentry. If I caught their attention during a recon, they would call their operation off altogether. Then where would I be? Back at square one.

So in place of the recon I passed the next four hours doing something I'd learned to specialize in as both a soldier and a cop—waiting. Leaned back in the front seat of the Chevy, I donned dollar-store sunglasses and watched the cars pass on University Avenue, keeping an eye out for any vintage muscle cars and trying to stay alert.

I was exhausted. No, something worse than exhausted. I was weary in my very bones. It wasn't just that I had missed out on sleep over the past few days. What sleep I had managed was plagued by the dreams of Jacquie and the prostitute case. A random memory that I still couldn't make sense of. Out of all the cases we had worked together, all the murderers we put behind bars—or into early graves—why had this one oddball case resurrected itself amid all this chaos?

I wondered, and as the warmth of the afternoon sun loosened my muscles it grew harder to keep my eyes open. My lids felt like they were weighed down by bricks. My muscles relaxed, my breaths slowed. Each car that whizzed past on the four-lane sounded like the soothing wash of waves on a beach.

My head rolled back against the seat. The sunlight outside the car faded.

And then the prostitute case returned.

Three Years Earlier

I AWOKE with a start at ten minutes past midnight. I'd been asleep for maybe two hours, and I sat up in bed with a sweaty gasp for breath.

The dream about Afghanistan—a nightly occurrence for me during the early years of my military retirement. The place was outside Kandahar, and the mission was to recover an Afghani informant whose name had been leaked to the Taliban. He lived in a little village on the backside of nowhere. My Ranger unit arrived on site only minutes before the Taliban fighters.

What happened next was the stuff out of nightmares...literally.

I rubbed my eyes and swabbed sweat off my forehead. My studio apartment was dark and still, smelling of sour clothes and unwashed dishes. I hadn't eaten dinner and still wasn't hungry. I knew I wouldn't sleep again, either. Not that night. The memories had taken over.

When I closed my eyes I saw Afghanistan. The firefight broke out on the outskirts of a village, and it was one of the worst I ever experienced. The Taliban deployed nearly sixty fighters. We dug in and returned fire, screaming into our radios for QRF.

The guns roared. RPGs screamed into houses and turned concrete to dust. The screams of mortally wounded civilians rang like nails on a chalkboard. And my buddies...

I opened my eyes, staring mindlessly at the nightstand next to me. My department-issued iPad lay there, stocked mostly with crime scene photographs from the prostitute case. Ashley. LaToya. Jane Doe. Their bodies cold and lifeless. Brutalized and left to rot. I'd viewed these pictures a few hundred times. I'd scrutinized every detail.

But there was always a chance I'd missed something, and as bad as those photographs were, they were less painful than the nightmares.

I studied the images individually. Zooming and tilting the screen. Tuning out the horror of what I was looking at and treating it like a case study in a textbook.

What was different? What was the same? What stood out?

After ten minutes I thought I had something. It was small, but something I hadn't noticed before. It was the picture of Jane Doe—a minuscule detail that likely didn't matter, but it was unique to her. It was her right hand, the one coated in blood. I'd noted the blood at the time of arriving on her crime scene, but hadn't attached any special significance to it. Maybe she had been trying to stem her own bleeding.

Now I studied the hand and noticed that much of the blood had been scrubbed away from the tip of her index finger...almost as though she had been rubbing it against something.

I squinted. I scrolled. Then I stopped. My heart slammed once in my chest. I noted the side of the dumpster she'd died next to. The dumpster was dark brown. The lighting was poor. But I thought I saw a bloody line only a foot from where her hand fell.

Had Jane left it there? How had I missed it?

I searched for a better image of the dumpster. There was only one, and the line I thought I saw was nearly invisible. Blood blends well with brown paint. It could have been dismissed as spatter.

Very likely, it was. The mark was nothing. But I wasn't sleeping, anyway. I might as well stretch my legs.

It was a seven-mile drive to the truck stop, easily made in the middle of the night with no traffic. I didn't call Jacquie. We'd both been off duty the previous day, and I knew she was planning to attend a Suns game. She usually drank at ball games, and she deserved a chance to unwind. I could handle this myself.

At the truck stop I parked outside the glaring pavilion lights and stepped onto pothole-infested gravel. The crime scene lay directly ahead, sheltered by darkness, the crime scene tape long since removed. But the dumpster was still there.

I clicked on my MacroStream and advanced methodically, scanning the spot where the body had been found.

The blood was gone. Trash blew across the concrete. I thought the dumpster had shifted a few feet since the day of Jane's death...likely during garbage collection.

I moved around the dumpster's corner and swept the light up its side. I hadn't meant to be holding my breath, but I realized I was. The LED illuminated the brown side of the dumpster...

And revealed nothing. Dirt. Mud. Some unidentified slime. Certainly nothing that looked like a last-minute, desperate message written in blood.

My shoulders slumped and the light drooped. My head bowed, and I thought again of Jane. The girl that time itself would swallow without anything left behind. Not so much as a name.

And it was my fault.

I was starting back toward the car when I thought of something else. I felt it as I pocketed the MacroStream. It was another flashlight, a smaller one. Something Jacquie had given me. Built of plastic with relatively low output, it wasn't the illumination that made the light special, it was the bulb.

It was a blacklight. A tool for deeper inspection.

Worth a shot.

I turned back to the dumpster. The button clicked and ultraviolet spilled across the concrete, revealing a myriad of neon splatter marks from God only knew what sort of substances. I reached the spot where Jane lay and lifted the light up the side of the dumpster.

I didn't see anything at first. Just meaningless reflective grime.

And then...a curve. Wide and unsteady, scratched as

though left with a trembling fingertip. I squatted, adjusting the light angle.

The curve clarified. Then there was another curve next to it—a complete one. A circle, followed by a stick. A final curve. A complete word. My heart slammed into my throat.

The word was COP.

Adrenaline rushed my system as I lunged to my feet. Dizziness swamped me and I stumbled back, thoughts racing. All the data from the investigation, all the people involved, and evidence collected. The common denominator I so desperately wanted to find.

Cop?

I had to get Jacquie. I had to get the forensic techs out of bed. I had—

I spun toward my car and froze, my body instantly rigid. I was no longer alone. Standing ten feet behind me, sheltered by the shadow of the truck stop with his pale face glued to mine was a Phoenix patrol officer. Dressed in blue, eyes wide. A coffee branded with the truck stop's logo in one hand...and in his other?

A duty pistol, pointed right at me. I recognized the officer. I'd seen him before, in this same place, some weeks earlier. His name was Pink.

"You called in the body," I whispered.

Pink's eyes flicked. He swallowed. Then he jerked the Glock. "Back! Behind the building."

I didn't resist. I walked backwards, conscious of my service pistol riding in the passenger seat of my sedan. My backup was strapped to my right ankle—a Smith and Wesson 340PD, but it was hopelessly out of reach.

We circled behind the building and what little light I'd

enjoyed from the fuel pumps faded. Pink twitched his gun hand again.

"Drop the flashlight. Easy, now."

I complied. He motioned for me to lift my hands. I put them at shoulder level and shook my head.

"You killed all three of them, didn't you? A beat cop patrolling the bad side of town. Calling in his own crimes to cover his tracks."

Pink's tongue zipped across his lips. He was breathing hard. I knew his mind was racing. He was struggling to select a next step.

But it wasn't a complex problem. He'd killed before, after all, and succeeded in covering it up. I was a cop, but what did that matter? So was he.

"Before you kill me," I said, "you should know that I've already texted my partner. She knows everything. You won't get away, and one more body only brings you closer to the death penalty."

Pink gritted his teeth. The coffee trembled so badly that it overtopped the cup and seared his hand. He didn't even notice.

"You're bluffing," he snapped. "Nobody knows."

I shrugged, forcing calm. Hoping my posture and tone would soften his own.

"I figured it out, didn't I? Somebody else will. Then what?"

"I'll wash the dumpster!" he sneered.

"You should have done that already. It was a mistake. Mistakes have a way of stacking. You need to turn yourself in, Pink. I have some pull. I'll help you."

"Liar!" Pink closed on me. The gun trembled. "Turn around."

Not good.

"You don't want to do this."

He dropped the coffee. It splashed over filthy concrete. The muzzle of the Glock rose to point at my face. His finger dropped over the trigger.

"*Turn around.*"

My heart hammered. I kept my hands up and turned slowly. His boots splashed through the spilt coffee as he pivoted, placing the block wall of the truck stop as a backstop to his point of aim.

I closed my eyes, mind racing. Cursing myself for my own mistakes.

Now they would cost me.

"I'm sorry," Pink whispered, voice hoarse.

I gritted my teeth, disgust overcoming the fear. I wasn't going to die like this. I began to turn.

Then the gunshots rained in. Not one, not two, not even three. A whole storm of them in rapid succession. I hit the ground and covered my head. I couldn't tell who was shooting. Blood sprayed across my face, and beneath my arms I saw Pink's gun strike the pavement. My ears rang. Perfect stillness consumed the truck stop for a split second...

Then Pink's body struck the concrete with a meaty thud, riddled with bullet holes, his eyes wide and lifeless.

My breath caught in my lungs and my head snapped up. From ten feet away Jacquie advanced, handgun riding at eye level, a white Phoenix Suns jersey stained with blood spatter. She reached the body and toed it with one sandaled foot. Pink didn't move and Jacquie shook her head, lip lifted in disgust.

I slumped against the wall as I fought to catch my breath.

I'd stopped breathing the moment the gunshots started. Now my stressed body felt starved for oxygen.

Jacquie knelt beside me, squeezing my shoulder. "Hey. You hurt?"

I shook my head, slowly starting to calm. I closed my eyes and focused on each breath. "How...how did you know?"

"Common denominator, like you said. It came to me during the game. Pink reported every murder...heck of a coincidence, huh? Then I looked up your car's beacon and saw that you were back at the truck stop. I thought I'd join you."

I nodded. Rubbed my eyes. Looked at the body.

Then I squinted. "Wait. The game finished hours ago."

"Yeah..."

I pivoted to face her. "So what took you so long?"

Jacquie grinned. "After-party, dude. We won."

39

I awoke with a start, heart hammering in my chest. Sitting upright in the SUV, I let my gaze dart across the four-lane. Little Rock had grown dark—the sun was gone. My wrist snapped around to reveal the face of my watch, maddened panic temporarily overwhelming me.

It was seven forty-five, and I exhaled a long breath. I hadn't missed the appointment—but I had allowed myself to drift off.

After-party, dude. We won.

Jacquie's cheerful remark echoed in my mind, carrying a double meaning that night. It wasn't only the Suns who won —the Phoenix PD won, also. Jane, Ashley, and LaToya won. Jacquie's quick thinking—and quick trigger finger—had saved my life. She'd been late, yes. But she'd turned up when I needed her most.

What was I doing? Arriving too late? Stalling too long, thinking too slowly?

Jacquie needed me. She needed me *now*.

The thought was enough to drive away any lingering sleepiness. I was fully awake. I was wired. I was ready to get into position.

I turned north up the avenue and headed for the drive-in. I passed right by it, inspecting the chain-link gate under the glow of streetlights and finding it closed. Then I made a U-turn and passed by it again, taking a closer look.

All was quiet. Abandoned. Dark.

Heading half a mile down the street I found a tire shop closed for the night, the parking lot empty. I parked the Traverse near the back and surveyed the streets again for any sign of a 1970 Pontiac GTO. Then I circled to the back of the Traverse, lifted the hatch, and found the AR-10 waiting for me beneath one of my jackets. It was fully loaded with twenty-five rounds of full metal jackets. I chambered one but kept the safety on. Then I wrapped the rifle in the jacket again, closed the hatch, and started into the woods behind the mechanic's shop.

The walk to the edge of the drive-in property was arduous, tangled underbrush scattered with beer bottles and crumpled cigarette packs from a thousand clandestine meetings of teenagers hell-bent on developing lifelong vices. The traffic continued to surge along nearby University Avenue, clearly audible amid the trees but not at all visible. Sheltered by tangled hardwoods and pine trees, it was so dark that I needed my MacroStream just to keep from face-planting into the dirt. I kept the light switched to its lowest setting, the rifle held under my left arm while my right hand remained free to deploy the Ruger should anything spring out from the shadows.

I found the outskirts of the drive-in marked by an eight-foot privacy fence, and my suspicions about rogue teenagers were confirmed by missing planks and a lot of names carved into the boards, some of them surrounded by hearts.

Hunter loves Dannie.
Sam and Trish 4ever.
Josh got the hots for Josie.

The carvings made me smile. Not because I'd ever been a normal, happy teenager sneaking off into the woods to drink beer and carve my girlfriend's name into a fence, but because I had been in love. I knew what that magic felt like.

I flicked the flashlight off and ducked through the hole in the fence. The cold ashes of an old camp fire and an abandoned beach chair greeted me beyond. More signs of miscreants at work. The grass rose up to my waist and the trees faded. A hundred yards distant the movie theater sign blocked out the sky. The parking lot beneath it spread out in a wide semi-circle, with little metal poles jutting out of the ground where audio speakers used to hang.

I bent into a crouch and wove amid the grass, advancing right to the edge of the parking lot before descending onto my stomach. I withdrew the AR-10 and folded the jacket into a makeshift shooting rest. With the Pulsar scope powered on and the selector dial switched to the moon symbol, I gained a clear view of three hundred yards of open pavement, dotted only by those speaker poles. To my right lay the gate, hidden behind trees and additional grass. Dead ahead stood the movie screen and abandoned concession stands.

I reached ahead with my thumb and flipped the rifle's safety off. I kept my finger high above the trigger guard and settled in for the wait, breathing easily. Not bothering to count the minutes. Patient, and relaxed. Willing to wait.

I didn't have to wait long. My watch displayed eight fifteen exactly, and just like clockwork, the first headlights appeared.

There were four of them. They were mounted to the front grill of a 1970 Pontiac GTO.

40

The Pontiac arrived accompanied by its trademark growl. It rolled in not by the front gate, but by a hitherto invisible rear access point. Jet-black paint and jet-black windows melded with the shadows as the car wove amongst the speaker poles and completed a careful sweep of the entire property. I could tell while it was still a hundred yards off that it would pass within feet of my position, and I preemptively shrank into the grass.

As the GTO neared, the air around me turned sour with the stench of gasoline fumes. Gravel popped beneath wide tires, then the Pontiac was gone, headed back toward the hidden secondary entrance. It parked at the edge of the lot and the engine cut off, as did the lights.

I wormed my way back to the edge of the parking lot and settled behind the scope. I swung the AR-10 in line with the Pontiac and measured my breaths as both doors popped open. Two men climbed out, both clad in dark jeans and tight t-shirts. I didn't recognize the passenger, but I did recognize the tattoo on his exposed left shoulder. At max zoom, the Pulsar provided just enough clarity to make out the disfigured cross and the black eagle. Another member of the Brotherhood.

I swept the gun left, over the roof of the Pontiac, to the second man. He was taller and broader. About my size. Clothed in a black jacket despite the late summer heat. He flicked a lighter and the spark of an orange flame gleamed in my scope, followed shortly by a cloud of cigarette smoke. He turned to say something to his companion, and his face squared with the muzzle of my rifle.

As soon as it did, my chest tightened. I'd seen this man before, back in Whitford. Not at the sheriff's office or the diner, but at the town hall. He was the ice-eyed man Mayor Kiddle had been talking to when I barged in—the one with the ugly white scars on his face. I recognized the familiar mark of exploding shrapnel shredding flesh with the kiss of a hundred white-hot razor blades. The signature of an IED, of a soldier wounded in action.

He was *military*, or better put, he had been military. Now he was something else. Something far less honorable, but just as deadly.

Was this Shiver? Hoffman's enforcer?

Presumably. Which likely made him Sage Fuller's killer, and possibly Cyrus's, also. That put him near the top of my hit list. I could take him out right then with a flick of my trigger finger.

I wouldn't. There were more headlights coming—first the LED glow of a modern pickup truck. A big one, also black, and a little jacked up. It was Hoffman's Dodge 3500, and it pulled to the side of the Pontiac. The engine cut off, but nobody got out. Shiver continued smoking while his companion paced.

Another ten minutes passed. Then the final vehicle appeared. It was a sedan, some kind of generic, American model without any identifiable personalization. The color was soft gray, and the front license plate was white with black letters.

Texas, I thought, even though I couldn't fully read the plate. Texas had black and white front license plates. The car felt like a rental. It emerged from the trees and Shiver pointed, directing it to park next to the Dodge. The rental obliged. Three doors popped open, and three men emerged.

They were not like Shiver and his companions. They were shorter, slighter of build, with brown skin. I recognized the smooth features of Hispanic heritage even in the darkness, and again my stomach tightened.

Not because I'm prejudiced against Hispanics, but because this whole charade was starting to feel like a previous experience of mine back in Atlanta. That experience with Feldon, and a Mexican cartel.

The doors of the Dodge opened, and two men got out. The passenger was nobody I recognized. The driver was Hoffman—that handsome POS I first met just before having my skull pounded into darkness. No sunglasses this time, but he somehow looked just as smug.

The Aryans greeted the Hispanics with warm smiles, which I thought was ironic given Nazi teachings concerning minorities. Handshakes were exchanged. Some kind of joke. Hoffman laughed, as did his companion. The Hispanics did not. They gestured to the pickup. Hoffman led the way to the tailgate. The bed was covered with one of those hard, folding tops. The pickup's taillights flashed as Hoffman unlocked the tailgate. He was talking, a broad smile still plastered across his face.

Just the way it had been when he confronted me on that lonely county road. *Thug.*

While Hoffman worked, Shiver remained by his Pontiac. The enforcer was still smoking, but I could now see the outline of a handgun strapped to his hip. He managed the cigarette with his left hand, keeping his right hand free. Ready for action.

Hoffman tugged something long and black from beneath the bed cover. He flipped latches and lifted a lid. I held my breath, already knowing what I would see. I wasn't wrong.

From inside the case Hoffman withdrew a standard issue US Army M4A1 rifle. All the familiar markings were present —an A-frame front sight post, a telescoping stock, and a fourteen-and-a-half-inch barrel. There was even an M203 grenade launcher mounted beneath the forend. The weapon looked ready for deployment straight to Afghanistan, albeit a little worn by age and use. Just the sight of it escalated the cortisol already flooding my brain. I steadied the Pulsar's red dot over the rear of the truck and watched as Hoffman passed the weapon off to one of the Hispanics. He produced three more rifles, each equipped in various ways. One had the grenade launcher. One featured a bipod and an Aimpoint optic. The last was an Mk 18 CQBR model—the close-quarters battle option, which modified the standard M4A1 by replacing the fourteen-point-five-inch barrel with a ten-point-three-inch barrel. I'd seen them before and used them in multiple missions as an Army Ranger. The Mk 18 was a favorite of SOCOM personnel—members of the United States Special Operations Command. It was a spec ops weapon.

What.

Hoffman passed the rifles around like demo items at a

trade show. The Hispanics examined each, lifting them into their shoulders and testing the charging handles. One was broken open and the bolt carrier group inspected. Hoffman stood by and answered questions.

Then the negotiations began. I could sense the change in tone of the interaction. Nobody was looking at the rifles anymore. The Hispanic point man spoke. Hoffman shook his head and waved a hand, feigning offense. Alongside the Pontiac the remaining Aryans stood by and watched, like sentries.

The negotiations continued. There was a lot of give and take. At last, a bargain was struck. Hoffman extended a hand. The point man shook it. The rifle cases were closed and the tailgate closed behind them. The Hispanics returned to their rental car and headed for the exit. I followed them with the rifle, but I couldn't get a clear view of their license plate. The distance was too great.

Snapping back to the pair of black vehicles, I found Hoffman meeting Shiver at the nose of the Pontiac. The smile was gone. Both men looked cold as ice. A brief conference was held. Shiver dropped his cigarette and stamped it out. Each man turned back for his vehicle and I lifted my head from behind the scope, heart rate spiking.

The meeting was over. Everyone was headed out. So what came next? Delivery of one thousand units?

So many rifles would consume a lot of space. Hoffman would need an enclosed trailer to drag behind his truck. Would he head back to Mullins County, back to a hidden warehouse deep in the mountains to retrieve the goods? I could follow him and find out. Maybe capture the weapons stash before it was delivered.

But I didn't care about one thousand missing rifles. I only

cared about Jacquie. I would capture Hoffman long before he returned to his stash, and once I was finished with him, the so-called Brotherhood wouldn't be in the business of stealing phased-out weaponry. They wouldn't be in any business at all.

From the far side of the theater the Dodge started up. The Pontiac followed suit. Cradling the rifle, I hurried to my feet.

I turned back through the weeds and sprinted for my SUV.

41

I reached the Traverse and blasted out of the mechanic's parking lot, struggling with my phone to call up the GPS map that would provide me a view of the far side of the drive-in property. My decision to not conduct a full recon upon arriving at the movie theatre was now costing me. I was blind to Hoffman and Shiver's possible routes of departure—but there was no use fretting about that. I simply had to catch up.

Taking the first right I came to off University Avenue, I followed back streets amid battered old houses with moss-covered roofs. I estimated distances and when I thought I'd driven far enough to eclipse the drive-in, I hauled another right at the next intersection. A horn blared and I saw another highway up ahead—no, not a highway. Just a major city street. Two wide lanes with a yellow-marked turn lane in the middle. The map on my phone had finally loaded and I could see that this path led along the backside of the drive-in property. The auxiliary entrance should connect with the street someplace to my right.

I didn't have to wonder long. I reached the next intersection and slammed on my brakes just as a roar of Detroit thunder ripped from behind the trees, and then Shiver's Pontiac appeared. It was headed south, moving from my right to my left. It blazed past with a howl of exhaust and then it was lost around the next bend.

He hadn't seen me. I had seen him. But I didn't turn left. I leaned out over the dash of the Traverse and looked both ways down the street. It was Hoffman's pickup truck that I was looking for—a vehicle I was much more interested in than the Pontiac for two reasons.

First, I couldn't catch that Pontiac even if I got a jump start. I'd already learned that lesson, and I didn't relish the idea of whipping out the AR-10 in the middle of a major city.

And second, interrogating Shiver would be better than interrogating Sid and Bucky, but it would still be a step down the chain of command. Why work my way up the ladder when I could jump straight to the top?

A half mile to my right lay an intersection. I thought I saw a bulky vehicle leading the pack of personal vehicles across it. Maybe that bulky vehicle was a one-ton Dodge—I couldn't be sure.

I took a chance and punched the gas. I shot through the next intersection just as the traffic light turned from yellow to red. The column of cars ground to a halt. I threw my door open and leaned out around the A-pillar, looking down the line of traffic. I could make out only one taillight of the hulking lead vehicle, but there was no doubt that vehicle was a Dodge. The taillight was covered over by a black plastic plate cut in the shape of a ram with lowered horns. The paint was black and shiny clean. There was a bedcover.

Gotcha.

Red turned to green. The truck surged ahead. I slammed the door and hit my horn. The cars moved out slowly. I slid into the middle turn lane, ready to rush ahead. I was forced to swerve back in to avoid colliding with a minivan waiting to access a grocery store. The car ahead of me was an old beater, its rear bumper wired in place, a sticker pasted to the back window that read:

HIT ME – I NEED THE INSURANCE MONEY.

I stepped on the brake to avoid a rear-end collision. The beater's driver flashed me a toothy smile in his sideview mirror. His brake lights were dead. I was forced to slow to barely thirty miles an hour while the traffic ahead began to spread. We were turning west. The Dodge still led the pack, guiding us through sprawling neighborhoods. I kept my eyes on the ram taillights, forcing myself to remain calm. I lost the beater and was able to accelerate, but I didn't want to close too quickly. I couldn't afford to.

I needed the Dodge outside the city, away from innocent civilians. Someplace where I could take out the tires, then manage the rest of my business up close and personal.

But as it turned out, I would never have that chance. I first noticed the cop out of the left corner of my eye. The Ford Taurus was unmarked, but the aggressive brush guard rising from its front bumper gave it away as a police vehicle. A split second after I blazed past it, blue lights flashed and the Taurus raced onto the four-lane, sliding in behind me.

What?

My gaze dropped instinctively to my speedometer. I was running hard, but not much over the speed limit. Not enough to draw a ticket in most jurisdictions. I looked back into the mirror but couldn't see the cop behind his windshield—it was tinted. The nose of the Taurus raced in close and I swerved into the slow lane, offering him an opportunity to pass.

Maybe he's after somebody else.

But he wasn't. Again, he swerved in behind me, and adrenaline spiked in my bloodstream. I looked for the Dodge and found it half a mile ahead, gaining speed. A dozen cars filled the gap between us, and a sign to my right advertised the on ramp for I-430 coming up fast. Hoffman was slipping away—in mere moments I would lose him. Back to square one yet again, leaving Jacquie in a pit. Maximizing the odds that she never made it out.

Failing her.

No. It wasn't happening. I was in a rented vehicle with a stolen license plate. The cop behind me had no idea who I was, and I knew his tricks. I'd learned them at the same sort of school where he studied.

I wasn't pulling over.

Flooring the Traverse, I pulled a quick left back into the fast lane and put a bread truck between myself and the Taurus. That was enough to trigger a police siren, and the driver of the bread truck scrambled to get out of the way. I drove hard, weaving between cars with inches to spare, keeping one eye on my mirror and one eye on the Dodge ahead. I'd lost another hundred yards on Hoffman. I couldn't predict his next move. I needed to get off the four-lane and onto smaller streets where I could lose the cop before additional units arrived. I had to do that *without* losing my quarry.

But again, I never had the chance. The next intersection arrived, and out of nowhere two more cops appeared. Both in jet-black, unmarked cars, slicing in from opposite sides. The windshields were tinted. Brush guards stuck from their bumpers like buck teeth. One laid on the gas and blazed down the turn lane, swinging in ahead of me. The original car stayed on my bumper, and the final car swung into my four o'clock position.

I knew what was happening long before the brake lights of the cop in front of me flashed to life. There was simply nothing I could do about it, short of swerving into a head-on collision with an oncoming bus. Sure enough, the cop ahead of me hit his brakes, forcing me to hit mine. The cop behind accelerated, closing the gap.

And then the four o'clock cop—the shark awaiting the kill—rushed in for the PIT maneuver. It was so graceful and smooth I was almost impressed. That bucktooth brush guard swung left and caught the back right corner of the Traverse, wrenching my rear tires sideways and breaking traction. I lost complete control a millisecond later as the SUV first fishtailed, then descended into a complete spin. I rocketed clockwise across the righthand lanes, tires screaming and world flashing. The Traverse was pointed back the way I'd come by the time I reached the curb. My wheels struck it sidelong at fully thirty miles per hour, and there was no stopping the roll.

Off the street. Onto the sidewalk. Tumbling, glass shattering, roof crunching. It was a mindless din, slamming me back in my seat. Lights flashed and dirt exploded through my busted window. I caught a glimpse into the night and saw the tree racing toward me like a rocket.

I closed my eyes and braced for impact.

42

The Traverse came to a stop on its roof. All the airbags had deployed, and I hung awkwardly from my seatbelt. My head spun and my ears rang. I thought I tasted blood, likely from a busted lip. I blinked through the airbag dust, still clinging to the wheel with both hands.

I heard sirens—the unmarked cars, no doubt, encircling me. I fought with my belt, trying to break myself free. Through my shattered driver's side window I saw nothing save the scarred bark of the hickory tree I'd rammed into.

The belt broke free and I slammed into the ceiling of the SUV, head spinning again. I was too dazed to hurt. Too disoriented to know which way to run. It wouldn't have mattered if I somehow extracted myself from the overturned vehicle. I was trapped in a ring of cops. All I could do was claw the Ruger out of my waistband and toss it away from my body before raising both hands toward the busted windshield. Shouts blended with the accelerated thud of heavy boots. Somebody reached the

Traverse and shone a light into my eyes. I turned my face away.

"Keep your hands where I can see 'em!" A cop barked. "You got any weapons?"

I didn't answer. There was no point. They would know soon enough.

———

THE ARREST PROCESS was quick and merciless. I never got the chance to use the handcuff key hidden in a compartment of my nylon belt. They took my belt. They took my shoes. They took the Ruger and the AR-10 and they loaded me into the back of a Taurus without any pretense of a medical exam or Miranda rights.

All of that would come at the station, I thought. These guys were angry, and a little too jubilant at the same time. I absently wondered if Tally had reported his Chevy as stolen, but most likely I had the Mullins County Sheriff's Office to blame. They must have put out an APB on me, possibly with a warrant for my arrest under kidnapping charges.

I was in trouble, and yet something didn't add up. It wasn't only the fact that all the men who arrested me wore suits instead of uniforms, or that they had ambushed me so suddenly, or even that they had resorted to a PIT maneuver so quickly. The core of my confusion orbited back to the moment that first cop switched on his blue lights.

Why? I wasn't speeding. I wasn't breaking any laws. There was a chance he ran my license plate and found it to be stolen, but that didn't explain his two buddies lurking just up ahead, ready to corner me.

No. This wasn't the work of Little Rock PD, even though

my captors were driving me to the Little Rock police station. This had *feds* written all over it. And that meant my best option—my only option—was to keep silent and wait.

The black suits plunked me into an interview room at the Little Rock Police Department, still handcuffed, and read me my rights. No water was offered. A medical exam would happen "soon". There was likely a lawsuit buried in that, but I would never get the chance to sue, and the medical exam was the least of my worries.

Regardless of who had arrested me or why, things were worse, now. Much worse. I couldn't justify my kidnapping of Sid and Bucky. Not legally, anyway. There was no way to prove my side of the story if Sheriff Conroy lobbed accusations against me—and he most certainly would.

Worst of all, Hoffman had yet again escaped my grasp. Jacquie was *still* missing. And I knew in my very bones that I was running out of time.

A miserable hour crept by, then two. Then three. Still, nobody entered the interview room. Nobody spoke to me. No one so much as acknowledged my existence. It must have been past midnight when I finally heard voices outside the metal door to my little prison. One was energetic and inquisitive. The other was gruff and demanding.

Demanding...and vaguely familiar.

I looked toward the door and waited. Feet tapped. A lock rotated with a snap. Hinges groaned and the dapper little Little Rock police sergeant stepped in, gesturing.

Then, just behind him, another man followed. He was tall and well built. Dark haired, but with a substantial amount of gray creeping in around his temples. A clean suit, pressed and crisp. But not as expensive looking as I remembered. Dark eyes glaring hellfire.

That much hadn't changed.

The man in the suit stared me down, not speaking. The police sergeant looked ready to burst with questions, but he kept silent. Waiting, just like me.

At last the man in the suit jerked his head toward the door.

"Out. Cut the cameras and recording devices."

"We're not—"

The man in the suit turned blazing eyes on the cop. The sergeant wilted in place, then scurried out. The door shut. I looked to the camera in the corner of the room and observed the red light blink off.

The man in the suit pulled back a chair. He sat down without breaking eye contact.

I relaxed in my chair, almost wanting to smile despite everything. Instead, I simply said, "Hello, Feldon."

43

Agent Mark Feldon—I assumed he was still an agent, although I was so confused I wouldn't have bet on anything—sat motionless, just staring. At last he reached into his jacket and produced a pack of cigarettes. He shook one out. He didn't offer me one. He lit up and took a long drag. The doorknob twisted and the dapper police sergeant stuck his head in, probably to complain about the smoke.

He took one look at Feldon's lethal glare and changed his mind. He shut the door. Feldon lowered the cigarette.

"I swore if I ever saw your mangy ass again, it would be too soon."

"I can't say I'm thrilled to see you either."

Feldon snorted, a humorless smile stretching his lips.

"Something funny?" I asked.

"It's funny that you aren't happy to see me."

"Should I be?"

"You should be on your knees begging right about now.

You're so far up the creek without a paddle you might not see the outside of a jail cell unless you're in a court room."

"What, you're a lawyer now? Career change?"

Feldon tensed, and I knew I'd hit pay dirt. He reached back into his jacket. This time he came out with a wallet. It fell open on the table, and I scanned the ID. It was ATF, just as I expected. I was more interested in the accompanying business card.

"Mark Feldon...Special Agent in Charge of the Little Rock Field Division. South Region. Bureau of Alcohol, Tobacco, Firearms, and Explosives." I looked up. "Well, congratulations. You've got your own little kingdom."

Feldon's lips lifted in a snarl. He looked suddenly like a dog—but not a very big one. More like one of those little dogs that become so nasty over the slightest provocations.

I tossed the ID case back. "Okay, Feldon. So what's the story? Why are you here?"

"I could ask you the same."

"But you haven't, which leads me to think you already know. I'll bet you know about the arms-smuggling operation up in Mullins County, also. I mean...that's why the ATF ambushed me, right?"

"What makes you think I know about any of that?"

"Two words. *Cyrus Richardson.*"

He should have flinched. He didn't. He didn't so much as blink. He just dragged on the smoke, thumping cigarette ash straight onto the tabletop.

I imagined the dapper little sergeant was having a conniption.

"You made a mess," Feldon said. "A *real* mess."

"Actually, it was your goons who did that. A PIT maneuver that aggressive? I should call an attorney."

"I'm not talking about tonight, dumbass. I'm talking about Atlanta. About that drug bust and all the bodies you stacked."

I noted a tremor in Feldon's jaw. More anger it seemed, rippling just beneath the surface.

I remembered Atlanta, of course. There was a drug gang with their sights bent against a helpless kid caught in the wrong place at the wrong time. I'd stepped in. I'd taken certain direct actions. Feldon had been there, also. Not as an ATF agent but as a DEA agent. A ranking one. He'd lost a man undercover to that drug gang and wanted revenge.

So we partnered up. There had been fireworks. A lot of bloodshed. I left Feldon to clean it all up, and he didn't have much of a choice, because he'd colored outside the lines himself. I hadn't really considered what might have become of him after I left Atlanta.

Clearly, things hadn't gone his way.

"You were fired," I said.

"I was offered an opportunity to resign," Feldon spoke through his teeth.

"You should have been promoted."

"You figure?"

"It was a big bust. The only people who died were justified kills."

"Yeah, well, turns out the guys upstairs don't take too kindly to a bust that big that they know nothing about. They would prefer advance notice. You know, so they get to arrange a news conference and take credit. The bodies didn't help."

"I'm sorry."

I wasn't, but it seemed like the only thing to say. Feldon mashed out the cigarette against the tabletop.

"It was suggested to me that I interview for the Little Rock ATF job. A...parking place. A small consolation to appease me before additional news stories broke."

"Sounds like a deal to me. You're the big cheese now, right?"

"The big cheese in Little Rock is a small, moldy slice. And I never wanted to *be* in the ATF. I wanted to be in the DEA."

Now the anger was boiling over, and I really didn't have time for it. Left to my own accord, I could have been breaking bones by then. Smashing the truth out of Hoffman.

Saving Jacquie.

"Get to the point, Feldon. What do you want?"

"You're awfully fresh for the man who cost me my job."

"That's because I know you still need me. I'm not sure why, but you wouldn't be here if you didn't. So let's skip ahead to that part, because I don't enjoy your company any more than you enjoy mine."

Feldon thumped one finger against the table top, seeming to evaluate something. I could guess what.

At last he said, "You came to Arkansas because of Cyrus Richardson?"

"No. I came to Arkansas because of Jacquie Richardson, his niece."

"Girlfriend?"

"No. My old partner at the PPD. She sent me an email. She needed help."

"Help with what?"

"Email didn't say."

"So you just scurried up here and threw yourself into the soup?"

"It's becoming a habit."

A soft snort. More table thumping.

"Spit it out, Feldon."

He leaned across the table. His voice lowered to a growl. "Okay. So here it is, then. You're right about the arms trafficking. We got a tip two weeks ago from a civilian informant."

"Cyrus Richardson."

"Maybe."

"He discovered retired M4 rifles leaking out of Fort Crowder," I said.

"Correct. At least, that was his claim. We were waiting for evidence."

"Why haven't you contacted the Army?"

A snort. No answer. I narrowed my eyes.

"You're going cowboy again, aren't you? Like you did in Atlanta."

"It's a long way back to the top," Feldon growled. "A boost wouldn't hurt."

"And a massive arms bust would be a heck of a boost."

Feldon rocked his head. Suddenly, I wanted to break his nose. I wanted to grab him by the hair and smash his ugly face right into the tabletop.

"Cyrus Richardson is *dead*, you prick. Jacquie Richardson is missing. While you're playing career games, people are bleeding."

"Don't you dare pin that on me! You spilt enough blood in Atlanta to choke a whale. You want to find your partner? This is your chance. Alternatively, I can leave you to rot with the Little Rock PD. Turns out there's a warrant for your arrest up in Mullins County...seems you've been busy busting shin bones. It could be *years* before you see the sunshine."

So that was it. Feldon's diabolical plot snapped into focus

the moment he mentioned the shin bones. He knew a lot about me—more than he should have, and I thought I knew how.

"You've been following me, haven't you?"

Feldon didn't answer, but I saw the truth in his face. I thought back to all the unknown faces in downtown Whitford. The diner. The background check run at Fort Crowder. There were a myriad of ways Feldon could have put his thumb on me.

Then he had kept tabs one me, and when the moment was right, he sprang the trap.

"You're an idiot," I snapped. "A raging moron. I could have busted this thing tonight if your henchmen had stayed out of the way."

"Exactly," Feldon snapped. "*You* could have busted it. That doesn't do a heck of a lot for my career, does it?"

Incredible.

I shook my head in something between disgust at Feldon and disgust at myself for falling into his trap. Nothing he said really surprised me. I already knew what a savage Mark Feldon could be.

Now I had to devise a way out of this mess. A way that saved Jacquie.

"I'm waiting." Feldon shot me a smug little smile. I gritted my teeth.

"What do you want?"

"We know there are rifles missing," Feldon said. "Somebody is pulling them out of Crowder just before they hit the shredder. The serial numbers are already scrubbed from the DOD database, so they're effectively invisible. I need to find them."

"You could have found them tonight," I said. "Four of

them were riding around in the back of a one-ton Dodge pickup."

"Driven by Michael Hoffman," Feldon said. "I know. We've been tracking him for nearly a week. We think he may be the head of a smuggling operation. Some kind of black-market program."

"He is. He's also the head honcho of an upstart white extremist group. They call themselves the Aryan Brother-hood Army. So why didn't you bust him?"

"You said it yourself. He only had four rifles."

I shook my head. "You're unbelievable, Feldon."

"Four rifles is hardly enough to catapult my career back to the top. Especially when nobody knows for sure exactly how many rifles are missing. I need the whole stash. As many as a thousand, according to our informant."

"*Cyrus Richardson*," I snarled. "Say his name, you coward."

"Fine. *Cyrus Richardson*. The dumb mop pusher who let himself get caught. Now he's dead. You want to make that right or what?"

I took a moment to recount what Feldon had just admitted to. It was tantamount to insanity. Gross law enforcement malpractice, at the least. No doubt laws were being broken.

But did I really care? I wasn't here to eradicate bureau-cratic corruption. I was here for Jacquie. Feldon was ready to use me, and that street ran both ways.

"Just so we're clear," I said, "you have your thumb on a black-market weapons operation bleeding fully automatic rifles directly from a military base. You have one murder and one missing person on your hands. You have a chief suspect and a working theory on what he's up to. But you're not going to the FBI, you're not contacting the Army, and you're not even conducting a direct raid of Hoffman's property... because you want the whole pie. All to yourself."

A lifeless smile stretched Feldon's lips. "Couldn't have said it better."

Incredible.

I inhaled. Looked to the watch on Feldon's wrist. It was grinding near to one a.m. I was burning time.

There was only one thing left to say.

"What's your plan?"

Feldon lowered his voice to barely a whisper. "I'm going to have Little Rock PD release you. I've already fabricated records listing you as an undercover ATF asset. A misunderstanding. I'll take you back to Mullins County."

"And then?"

"And then I want you to do what you do best, Sharpe. I want you to put your nose to the ground and *bring me the pie.*"

44

"Take me to Evergreen."

The Little Rock PD released me upon Feldon's demand, surrendering my personal effects but not the firearms I'd been found with. I followed him to a dingy little sedan permanently odorized by cheap coffee and cheaper fast food. The floor mats were worn. The suspension sagged.

I was starting to see why Special Agent in Charge of the Little Rock Field Division was no dream job.

"Why Evergreen?" Feldon demanded. He drove with angry aggression, cutting off a Little Rock cop as we exited the police station.

"I like the name," I said. "Reminds me of a scented candle. You could use a candle in this rattletrap."

Feldon glared, but he turned northeast anyway. I leaned back and watched the lights flash by, not really focusing on anything. My brain was already three or four steps ahead of my current situation, and I didn't like what lay ahead. Not any of it.

I didn't believe for one millisecond that Feldon was acting in any sort of good faith. Whether he admitted it or not, his decision to stall the investigation until the jackpot could be located had cost Cyrus Richardson his life. It had cost Jacquie her freedom at the least.

Also, Feldon had made it abundantly clear that he held a grudge for the events in Atlanta. They had cost him his job, and potentially his career. In my mind those penalties were entirely his own fault, but so long as he blamed me, I couldn't expect him to shake hands and part ways when all this was over. He was using me, just the way he'd used me in Atlanta. But unlike Atlanta, there was no way he'd let me walk away a second time.

No. He was going to burn me. Guaranteed. He would do whatever it took to claw his way back on top. Whatever it took to restore his career.

Three-letter agencies—they're all the same.

"What's in Evergreen?" Feldon pressed.

"My truck," I said. It was true, but it wasn't why I wanted to be there. My truck was no better an option for transportation now than it had been when I ditched it for Tally's Traverse. I would need something better. Something off the books.

But there was another reason I wanted to be in Evergreen. Something that had been nagging at the back of my mind for most of that day and was finally beginning to take shape. A basic premise, a logical question. Something I should have seen from the moment I was refused service at the rat-hole motel in Whitford.

The Whitfordites didn't want me around—likely because the Brotherhood had made it known that I was unwelcome. Jacquie would have been unwelcome also, for the same reasons. Lucile had already stated that Jacquie wasn't staying with her and Jeremiah out of concern for endangering them.

So where was Jacquie staying? It had to be Evergreen, the only other place around. I wanted to find her motel because Cyrus's notebook had unlocked a thought in my mind. Memories of Jacquie's obsession with mind maps—with her murder board.

She might have left notes behind, possibly in her room. It was a thin lead, but until either myself or Feldon could locate Hoffman, it was my best option.

Feldon didn't say another word for the rest of the ninety-three-minute ride, and I enjoyed the silence. I turned every piece of the puzzle over in my mind, assembling it like a three-dimensional model. More than a picture. More like a spiderweb. Each thread ran toward the middle, toward the heart of the matter.

Where was Jacquie?

I didn't really care who the Hispanic guys were, or what fiendish things Hoffman planned to do with his money. I only wanted my partner back, and I was going to find her. Even if I had to rip this entire state to pieces.

"Pull over here." I motioned to an empty parking lot at the edge of the Evergreen motel district. Feldon stepped on his brakes and peered to either side.

"I don't see your truck."

I ignored him and reached for the door handle. Feldon put a hand on my arm.

"Sharpe."

"What?"

"I got you off the hook. I can put you back."

I held his gaze. Neither of us blinked.

"Get your hands off me, Feldon."

Feldon released me and I climbed out. The window buzzed down.

"Find my pie, Sharpe. Or you'll wish you had."

Feldon yanked the sedan into an illegal U-turn and roared off. I turned for the street. There were eight motels in total, and none of them looked like the kinds of places Jacquie's refined tastes would tolerate. I started down the line anyway, using her photograph on my phone to interview each clerk.

Half of them were high. None of them were helpful. I reached the motel I'd stayed at the night before and confirmed a new face behind the counter before I approached. It was no use. The guy examined Jacquie's photograph with uncomfortable fascination, but shook his head.

"Ain't seen her before. She one of Kick's girls?"

I ignored the question and returned to the sidewalk. It was nearing three a.m., and my brain was running on fumes. I needed to rest again, but the clock in my head told me I didn't have time.

I had to solve this. I needed a break, *now*. I should fuel up. Hit my veins with some caffeine, maybe some sugar, and then...

I stopped. My gaze caught on a neon sign a half mile down the avenue. Flashing red, displaying the words "fresh and hot" with enough glare to be visible from outer space. I wanted to hit myself.

Of course.

Donuts. Jacquie wouldn't be found without them. She embraced the cop stereotype with zeal, happy to eat them three meals a day, and never putting on a pound. If she was going to pick a hotel, she would pick one close to a donut shop. There was an off-brand hotel situated directly across the street. Three floors tall, all interior access. It was a grungier place than Jacquie might have liked, but conveniently close to her drug of choice.

I broke into a jog. The neon grew brighter as I approached, and I noted an "Open 24hrs" sign posted beneath it. Another promising indicator.

Turning in at the hotel, I scanned the parking lot for vehicles flagged by towing notices. Very likely, Jacquie's car had already been towed. That could be another lead. For now, I wanted to speak to the manager.

The hotel interior hung with "pardon our progress" signs, masking tape and raw sheetrock everywhere. I reached the desk and smacked the bell.

The clerk appeared with a yawn, taking her chair and asking for my last name.

"I'm not here to check in. I'm looking for somebody."

I presented the picture. She barely gave it a glance.

"Haven't seen her."

"Please, this is important. She's missing."

The clerk rubbed her dull eyes. She took the phone and squinted. Then something like vague recognition crossed her face.

"How long ago?"

"Four days. Maybe you towed her car."

"Yeah...last Friday, right? Black Ford. She abandoned it. Just disappeared right after that other guy came looking for her."

"What other guy?"

The clerk looked up, sudden suspicion crinkling her face. "You a jealous husband?"

"No, nothing like that. She's in trouble."

"Yeah...that's what the other guy said."

"*What* other guy?"

"The military guy."

"Military guy?"

"Sure seemed like it. He had that look, you know. Tall, muscular. That high and tight haircut. Kinda handsome, actually. But real abrupt."

Shiver.

I was sure of it. I pictured him standing outside the Pontiac. Tall, muscular. Scarred but not ugly. A high and tight haircut. A military stance.

But if it was Shiver, I needed more than a name. I needed a way to find him.

"Did you get his name? Did he speak to her?"

"Dude, I don't know. He didn't leave a card or nothing."

"What about security cameras? Do you have a recording?"

Another hesitation. I produced the last of Edwin Schwartz's money and began dumping bills on the counter. The clerk held up a hand.

"Okay, okay. Let me pull it up..."

She took the money and commenced to clicking with her computer mouse. It took a while. She didn't seem to know how to work the system. At last she produced a black and white video. She spun the monitor around. I leaned down as she smacked the play button.

The automatic doors opened in the grainy footage. A tall guy stepped in. He wore a tight shirt, and from the back of his head I noted a cropped haircut. He approached the desk. I recognized the clerk behind the counter. They held an exchange. The security camera feed kept rotating between angles, but none of them displayed his face. He extended something across the counter—a cell phone, it seemed. A picture.

"Don't you have an angle of his face?" I pressed. The clerk shrugged. I leaned farther in. The camera switched again...

And the man at the counter looked up, dead into the lens, and my heart slammed into my ribcage.

It wasn't Shiver. It wasn't any member of the Brotherhood at all, and this man wasn't ex-military.

He was *active* military. It was Captain Thornton.

45

The revelation hit me like a bat in the face. A cold, obvious question that I hadn't invested nearly enough attention in.

Who was the inside man? Who was supplying Hoffman with his weapons?

It was Thornton, that same unassuming Army captain who accosted me on my way out of the MP station. He had been here, in this same hotel lobby, looking for Jacquie.

And the time stamp on the security displayed only three minutes after Jacquie sent her SOS email.

He took her.

I pushed off from the counter, already contemplating my next step. A stolen vehicle and a maddened drive to Missouri. Locate Thornton's private residence. Teach him a definition of combat I could guarantee he had never experienced.

But I never made it to the door. I made it only halfway before the low growl of Detroit muscle tore across the parking lot. A flash of black appeared beneath the portico, gleaming chrome and polished wheels. It was a 1970 Pontiac GTO, and the passenger's window was wound down. The automatic hotel doors rolled back in front of me, and a gust of hot night air tainted by gasoline fumes rushed in.

Shiver sat behind a wood-wrapped steering wheel. Next to him was another familiar face framed by a tan uniform with a gold star stitched above the breast pocket.

It was Sheriff Conroy himself, and long before he managed to get his door open I knew beyond any doubt—he wasn't here to prosecute any legal authority.

"Get him!" Shiver shouted, and Conroy exploded from the side of the Pontiac. I spun on my heel and sprinted past the reception desk just as the first gunshot cracked behind me. A bullet whizzed past my ear and smacked into the wall. I slid around the corner into a hallway lined by rooms. Many of those doors stood open, sleepy-eyed heads poking out to investigate the gunshot.

"*Police!*" Conroy shouted. "Stop where you are, Sharpe!"

I didn't stop. I reached the first open door and barged inside long before the occupant with bags under his eyes could stop me. Slamming the door behind, I slapped the security latch closed and turned to sweep the room.

An open suitcase lay spread across a dresser. Socks on the floor. Scattered shoes. An empty pizza box and a bed tangled with used sheets.

And one shirtless, potbellied man in his fifties with disheveled hair sticking out like the needles of a porcupine.

"What the—"

"Gun!" I snapped. "You got a gun?"

He blinked and shook his head. I shoved past him into the room, ripping through the dresser drawers and the open suitcase.

I found a computer charger and a Gideon's Bible. An electric razor.

Nothing even remotely approaching the category of *weapon*.

"Where is he?" From the hallway Conway bellowed. Voices mixed into an unintelligible murmur of confusion and fear, but I knew the other occupants would rat me out. Conroy was a man in uniform. I was just some random guy.

"What are you doing?" Potbelly asked. "Are you running from the police?"

"Shut up!" I hissed. "Get behind the bed and lie down on your stomach."

He did what he was told. I reached the room's wardrobe and dug past suit jackets and dress shirts. An ironing board stood in the back...and an electric iron. A big one.

"He's in there! Room one-oh-seven."

Here it comes.

I took the iron in my right hand and moved back to the door. The bathroom lay just inside the room, to the right of the door as a person walked in. The light was off. I disengaged the auxiliary door lock and backed into the bathroom, the iron held in my right fist as I wrapped up the trailing cable with my left hand.

Outside Conroy barked at the clerk, demanding a master key. Feet pounded. He called for me to come out with my hands up.

I didn't answer. From beyond the bed Potbelly prayed.

"Stay down," I repeated. "No matter what."

The clerk arrived. The master key was deployed, and the electronic lock actuated. I braced myself, knowing that Conroy would lead with his pistol. He'd look dead ahead.

The door exploded open all at once, driven by a heavy

boot. Light spilled across the carpet and Conroy appeared in the gap, skinny arms supporting the mass of a Smith and Wesson Model 686 revolver. Arms and elbows followed the gun. I waited until his right foot landed inside the room.

"Hands up, Sharpe!"

I sprang out of the bathroom, left hand shooting forward and grabbing Conroy by his exposed right shoulder. I yanked him toward me and swung my right arm in a curve— a punishing right hook, leading with the iron. Aimed straight for his face. Plowing past his gun.

Landing dead on his nose.

The metal face of the iron shattered bone and collided with his forehead. Conroy shrieked and stumbled back, blood spraying across the carpet. The Smith cracked, spitting a round into the TV cabinet. I twisted on my heel and yanked with my left arm, drawing Conroy off balance. His forehead collided with the opposite side of the bathroom door frame and his eyes rolled back in his head. His body went limp.

I dropped the iron and let him fall, scooping up the Smith as I lunged across his limp body. From behind me Potbelly shouted. From ahead the clerk screamed. Doors slammed and a fire alarm wailed for no reason at all. I swept the Smith up and to the right, clearing the hallway in the direction of the lobby. I didn't see Shiver. The blink of the fire alarm flashed in my eyes, disorienting me. Fifty yards ahead a stairwell burst open and sleepy hotel occupants poured out, no doubt responding to the fire alarm.

Then glass shattered. I recognized the undeniable signature of a boot crashing through a windowpane and looked to my left—down the hall to an auxiliary exit. Shiver stood there, and it was his boot that had just crashed through the door's glass panel. A split second later his silhouette twisted, and a gun appeared. I engaged with the Smith—not thinking, not aiming, just acting on years of training and muscle memory. Firing double action and moving backwards, rushing for the cover of the lobby.

Shiver responded just as quickly. He never got off a shot. He dove for cover behind the door jamb as I reached the lobby. Pivoting around I found a crowd of travelers gathered in night robes and pajamas, wide eyed with terror and fighting toward the exit.

"Down!" I shouted. "Everybody get on the ground!"

I raised the Smith toward the ceiling, but there was no need to fire. Petrified bodies hit the floor as directed, hands covering heads as I hurtled for the automatic doors. Outside the Pontiac snarled. I reached the portico just as the car appeared around the end of the hotel, hurtling toward me. Front bumper rising, motor thundering. Shiver sat behind the wheel, his left hand jammed out the window, a handgun pointed at me. The gun fired at random, spitting rounds over my head and across each shoulder.

He expected me to move—to dive for cover while he split away from the hotel and escaped onto dark county roads. But I wasn't diving for cover. I wasn't moving at all. I simply raised the Smith and pressed the trigger—one easy, fluid movement. Not really aiming, just waiting for that split second when my front sight post crossed over Shiver's forehead.

The revolver bucked, and one-hundred twenty-five grains of copper-jacketed lead broke through the windshield and blew off the top of his skull. Just like that.

I stepped to the side as Shiver collapsed behind the wheel. His foot slipped off the clutch and the car choked out, jerking to a stop as the transmission held it in place. From somewhere down the highway, sirens howled. Both police cars and fire engines.

I ignored it all and rushed for the Pontiac, shoving the revolver into my waistband as I reached the driver's side door. Shiver lay sideways over the console, head hanging suspended over the passenger seat. Blood pooled over black leather. His mouth hung open, his eyes wide.

He was stone-cold deceased.

Yanking the door open, I grabbed Shiver by the belt and heaved—not out of the car, but farther into it. I threw his body over the console, then jerked his legs out of the floorboard and folded them at the knees until he was wadded up into a fetal position in the passenger seat.

Then I was diving in. Left hand slamming the door, right hand closing around a cue-ball floor shifter. I found first gear. I pumped the clutch and twisted the key. The old engine whined and coughed, then thundered with that now familiar rumble of throaty exhaust. I dumped the clutch and pulled a hard right toward the four-lane. The engine whistled with the signature whir of a supercharger, and my shoulders slammed into the seat. I raced past fire engines and police cars. Shiver's body flopped next to me. I reached third gear and seventy miles per hour as the Evergreen city limit sign appeared to my right.

Then I was back in the dark. Back on a rural highway. Turning north.

Headed for Fort Crowder, Missouri.

46

I was thirty miles down the road before my thundering heart began to calm. I checked the rearview mirrors every few seconds but saw no sign of pursuing police officers. I no longer heard their sirens.

Somehow, I had slipped away. Right in the nick of time. But the hounds were there, and they would follow me eventually. I'd left an unconscious—but not dead—Sheriff Conroy at that hotel. He would awaken. He would know exactly what story to tell.

Everybody would believe him, too. Unless I uncovered the truth first.

Sixteen miles south of Whitford I pulled the Pontiac off the road and dragged Shiver's body into a cluster of brambles well off the road. I searched his pockets and found three hundred bucks in cash, a folding knife, and a cell phone. Nothing else of use. I dumped those items into the Pontiac's back seat, then used the keys to unlock the trunk. There was no light mounted to the underside of the hatch—I had to use my MacroStream to illuminate the contents.

And the contents did not disappoint. Shiver was loaded for war. Two M4A1 rifles lay beneath a blanket, both equipped with Aimpoint optics complete with rocking magnifiers, rail-mounted flashlights, telescoping stocks, and aftermarket grips. One of the rifles also featured an M203 grenade launcher with a corresponding swivel red dot sight, and stacked next to the rifles were a collection of fully loaded thirty-round magazines and a bandolier loaded with forty-millimeter fragmentation grenades.

Two handguns. Two hundred rounds of nine-millimeter ammunition. A med kit with tourniquets and trauma gear loaded at the top. A KA-BAR knife, razor sharp and well worn. Spare boots, fresh water, and power bars.

Shiver had been a soldier. Judging by the choice in knife he had likely been a Marine, and judging by the care and attention invested into each item, he'd been a good one.

Yet he had died with one bullet to the brain, all thanks to a single moment of overconfident recklessness. I had indulged in a few such moments myself over the past several days, and they had won me almost nothing.

It was time to tighten up. It was time to nail Captain Thornton to the wall and *find Jacquie.*

My burner phone fit into a mount attached to the Pontiac's dash. The interior of the car—save for the blood in the passenger floorboard—was immaculate. No hint of fast food stench. No dirt in the floorboards. The gauge cluster was stock, but air conditioning had been added, along with a modern stereo system. Bolted to the underside of the dash was a CB radio, its display glowing orange. When I hit the key, the engine fired right up and the fuel gauge displayed half a tank. The transmission slid easily into gear.

I turned the car north for Missouri and I dumped on the gas.

47

I reached the town of Gates an hour before sunrise, and I already had a pretty good idea where to look for the distinguished Captain Thornton. He wouldn't live on post. The Army provides a generous housing allowance for its service members if they choose to rent or purchase a home outside of standard-issue base housing, and officers usually do. Base housing is often old and poorly maintained. Small town homes within miles of the fort's gates are often reasonably priced and offer better amenities. Officers with families enjoy living in the civilian world.

I didn't recall Thornton wearing a wedding ring, but even if he was unmarried, he wouldn't stay on post. Not if he was neck-deep in a criminal conspiracy to steal from the US taxpayer while arming violent extremists. He'd want to live outside the gates, where he had a better chance of fleeing if necessary. He'd want someplace quiet where he could make private phone calls.

Maybe even a place to hold a kidnapped Arizona cop hostage while he scrambled for a next step.

The only question was how to find his address. Gates was a small town, but it was too big for me to go door to door searching for Thornton. I didn't even know what sort of vehicle he drove. I would need a hard address, and I could call Feldon to get it, but I didn't trust him. So much as possible, I didn't want him tracking my exact movements.

So I thought of another way.

Parking in the Pontiac at a fast food restaurant not yet open for business, I used my phone's map to locate the name of a street deep inside the on-post housing district of Fort Crowder. Then I looked up the fort's website and found the phone number for Morale, Welfare, and Recreation—the entertainment wing of any Army base, dedicated to keeping bored soldiers out of trouble. MWR installations provide a plethora of services and amenities, ranging from camping gear rentals and golf courses to resort hotels and wedding venues. Nothing they do is exactly premium. Most of their gear is outdated and well worn.

But they're dedicated, and in my experience MWR posts are usually run by the more personable, accommodating sorts of soldiers.

The MWR office didn't open for another two hours, but I dialed anyway, hoping for there to be somebody on site prepping for an early morning golf tournament or a weekend family block party. I wasn't disappointed.

"MWR, Sergeant Fields." The voice was female and sleepy.

"Good morning, Sergeant. This is Corporal Smith. I was supposed to pick up some rental kayaks this morning, but I think I've got the address wrong. The renter was a...uh... Captain Thornton?"

I waited. The phone clicked and a chair groaned.

Sergeant Fields rattled a password into a computer keyboard.

"Thornton?"

"Yeah."

Don't ask me for a first name...

"You say you're picking up a kayak? Don't they usually return those themselves?"

"Not when they bust them on river rocks."

"Oh, dang. No kidding?" She chuckled. "What address did you have?"

"One-twenty-one Colby Street," I said, shooting off a random address from the base housing district.

"Captain Greg Thornton?"

Sure, why not.

"That's right."

"Yeah, he's not on Colby Street. He lives off base. Two-thirteen Parker dr—" She stopped. "Hey, do you mind if I get that ticket number? For the kayak rental."

"No problem. Let me grab it..."

I leaned across the Pontiac. I opened the glovebox and located a vehicle registration slip. I lifted the phone and crinkled the paper near the microphone.

"Looks like I've got—"

Then I hung up, tossing the registration into the seat and jabbing the street address into my phone. I drove slowly to keep the RPMs low to minimize the obnoxious note of the car's exhaust. The closer I drew to Thornton's house the tighter my chest became. My hands began to sweat.

I'd held it back for four days—the increasingly likely reality that my old partner lay rotting in a shallow grave nobody would ever find. Murdered, all alone. Left hanging without backup. *My* fault.

I'd barricaded that fear behind a dam of blind faith, but now the uncertainty leaked through. I knew I was about to hit the truth for better or for worse. If Thornton was Hoffman's inside man, and Thornton had been discovered by Jacquie, he might have kidnapped her instead of killing her. That could explain why Sid and Bucky knew nothing about her fate.

But how long would he hold her? Days? Weeks?

Maybe only hours.

I turned onto Parker Drive and allowed the car to coast down a gentle hill toward a cul-de-sac. I passed minivans and front yards littered with toys. A few jacked-up pickup trucks parked in the streets. A pair of young Army officers departing their homes for six a.m. shifts on post. A dog barking at the newspaper carrier.

It was a quaint place. Exactly the sort of spot where kids could be happy while Daddy or Mommy put on the uniform every day. Not really the sort of neighborhood where a single Army officer would live.

And yet I knew a single Army officer lived at house number 213 the moment I laid eyes on it. I also knew it was a man, not a woman. The property sat at the back of the cul-de-sac, and there were absolutely *no* customizations or outdoor decor items. The porch was bare and dusty. The yard slightly overgrown, leading into a forest. Blinds hung over the windows. There was a two-car garage that I could tell was only ever used by one vehicle—there were grimy tire marks only on the left side.

I might have thought the house was vacant, but a pizza box stuck out of the half-closed lid of a trash can, and behind one of the blind-covered windows a dim blue light gleamed. Maybe the running light on a computer or a web modem.

I stopped the Pontiac across the mouth of the driveway and cut the engine. Looking through the spiderweb cracks left in the windshield by my kill shot, I surveyed the house and thought quickly. I checked both mirrors for any nosy neighbors and didn't see anybody. I press-checked one of the pistols from the Pontiac's trunk before tucking it into my waistband. The weapon appeared brand new, and it wasn't Army surplus. It was a SIG Sauer P365XL. Twelve rounds of nine-millimeter, easily concealed beneath my t-shirt.

Time's up, Captain.

I skipped the front door and slipped down the driveway, listening for any indicator of a dog. A jangle of a collar or a chain. The self-important *woof* that often precedes a louder bark.

There was nothing. I circled the trash can and glanced down at the pizza box. It wasn't old. I could still smell pepperoni. The grease stains appeared damp. Easing up to the gate, I found it latched but not locked.

The back yard was even less maintained than the front. Grass reached up to my knees, littered with sticks and pine needles. I pressed my shoulder against the back wall of the garage and put one hand on the SIG. Then I made the turn.

The rear patio was vacant. Two worn camping chairs, concrete in desperate need of a pressure washing, and several empty beer bottles. I fast-walked to the back door, finding another pair of windows covered by blinds. A bedroom window to my right, also covered by blinds. The ground dropped off sharply, rolling to the fence. There was an AC unit and a smaller window that may have opened into a basement.

I tested the doorknob. It was locked. I didn't have any lock picks with me.

And I didn't need them. My mental clock was ticking too quickly. I scooped my Victorinox from my pocket, driving the butt through a window pane next to the deadbolt.

Glass shattered, raining over what sounded like carpet. I rammed my hand through and found the interior lock. The deadbolt featured a simple lever. In two seconds I was inside, the SIG rising to eye level. I crossed onto dirty carpet and smelled dirtier shoes. The house was dead quiet and the air tasted stale. All the lights were off. I cleared a living room strewn with dirty dishes and more beer bottles. In the kitchen I found the same. The door to the garage was unlocked, and the garage itself stood empty. There were tire marks and a small oil stain on the far side, corresponding roughly to the size of an SUV.

But no SUV was present.

I kept the gun up and swiveled down the hallway. The house was a three-bedroom, two-bathroom. I cleared the spares first. One was empty, the other featured a desk and a computer. The closet was full of hiking gear. The bathroom was dirty and unkempt.

I advanced to the master, kicking the door open instead of pushing it. I already expected it to be empty, and I was right. There was one bed, unmade. A TV coated in dust...and a dresser with all the drawers ripped open. Clothes hung out. I advanced to the closet and found hangers stripped bare, shoes thrown around. I searched the shelves and ducked under the bed but couldn't find any manner of luggage.

No. Please, no.

"Jacquie!" I risked a call down the hallway, returning to

the kitchen. Real panic edged into my system. I could *feel* that I was close. More than instinct, this was practiced skill. The talents of homicide investigation and terrorist hunting blended into one. I was *so* close.

The basement.

I remembered how the ground dropped off on the right-hand side of the house. How there was a small window, just above the AC unit. But I hadn't found a door or a stairwell providing access. I double-checked just to be sure, inspecting each room.

Nothing.

Bolting out the rear door, I stepped through waist-high grass, moving down the hillside. Beyond the AC unit I reached the corner of the house. The privacy fence connected with the home about five yards beyond the turn. There were no windows, just slimy green vinyl siding.

But there was a door. Not a basement door, but a storm shelter door built of steel. There was a padlock...but it wasn't fastened.

I yanked the MacroStream out of my pocket and snapped it on. I tore the lock out and stood at an angle as I threw the door open. It landed with a bang, but I didn't care. I crossed my wrists, pointing the SIG with my left hand while the MacroStream rode beneath it, shining at full blast. It cut a path of illumination eight feet down a ladder. The floor beyond was concrete and dusty. I couldn't see more than a yard beneath the house.

"Jacquie?"

No answer. No sound at all.

And no other option. I had to descend into the dark, exposing myself to open fire. It was the only way forward.

I walked down the ladder instead of turning around and

descending it the ordinary way. That left me a micron of a chance of returning fire if I was engaged, but no gunfire ever erupted. I reached the concrete, dropping the final two feet and scanning the interior with the MacroStream.

Then my blood ran cold. It was a storm shelter, just like I expected. Blank concrete walls and a flat concrete floor. One overhead bulb turned off. A stack of random camping gear stored in one corner. A few jugs of water.

Typical emergency gear. But the back right corner wasn't typical at all. Dangling from the overhead floor joists was a thick chain. There was a blanket tangled up on the floor. The space smelled of urine and body odor, and staining the floor was a wide patch of crimson.

Dried blood.

48

I rushed to the corner, keeping the pistol up, but there were no invisible threats hidden in the shadows, and there was no Jacquie. The spot on the floor bore all the marks of a makeshift prison. In addition to the chain and the blanket, there was a half-empty jug of water, some snack bar wrappers, and a camp toilet. Shreds of duct tape and a dirty gag joined the dried blood as confirmation of what happened in this place. I knelt and sifted through the blanket.

The panic inside of me had built into a tidal wave. I was ready to ram my own head against the block wall. I called out Jacquie's name instead, even though I knew it wasn't rational to do so.

"*Jacquie!*"

My voice reverberated in the small room. I ran a hand through my hair, mind spinning.

The ABA claimed not to know where Jacquie was. Thornton had, presumably, kidnapped her without their knowledge. Whatever his reasoning, she had stayed here for a while. Likely the entire time I had been bumbling around Mullins County looking for her.

But now she was gone. *Recently*, she was gone. The fresh pizza box indicated that Thornton was here the previous night. The disheveled room and strewn clothes indicated a hasty departure. Presumably, he'd taken Jacquie with him.

But where would Thornton have gone? Back to Mullins County? Would he give Jacquie over to the ABA? Maybe the ABA had discovered Thornton's prisoner. Maybe they had demanded her to be turned over.

Perhaps they had even come here and taken her by force. Thornton could be dead.

No. Be rational.

There were no signs of combat. The ABA had their hands full over the previous night. Thornton was acting on his own, but that didn't give me any better idea where he might have gone. He could be halfway to Mexico by now.

Think, Mason. Slow down. Unpack this.

I closed my eyes. I breathed deep. I took myself out of the worn boots of a homeless drifter and plugged myself back into the crisp suit and tie of a decorated homicide detective. A professional.

Examine the evidence. Detach yourself from the situation. What do you see?

I surveyed the room, fixating on the chains for a moment, and instantly generating a picture of Jacquie hanging helplessly from them. I drove the image away, refocusing on the hard evidence.

A blanket, water, and snacks. She'd been fed. That was a good sign. This guy might not be completely insane. The camp toilet was a good thing also. It was indicative of some level of intentionality. Thornton had a plan, and that plan obviously involved keeping Jacquie alive. If this were random, he would have just thrown her down here. Left Jacquie to pee on the floor—

My mind stopped cold. My nose flexed, and I smelled urine again. I frowned, glancing back to the toilet.

I shouldn't be smelling urine. Not out of the toilet. Camp toilets are designed to suppress odor. I toed it with my boot and heard a slosh, but the toilet shifted easily. It wasn't overflowing.

Why was I smelling urine?

I blinked. I saw the dumpster behind the truck stop. The prostitute case.

No way.

Shoving the flashlight into my mouth, I dug frantically through my pocket, sifting past my wallet and the Pontiac keys. My Victorinox, the captured cash, and a hotel card key.

Then I found it. A small black cylinder, roughly the size of my MacroStream, but made of molded plastic instead of machined aluminum. It was the blacklight I'd used to search Cyrus Richardson's murder scene. I depressed the button, desperately hoping that the battery hadn't expired.

The light flashed on, flooding the storm shelter with bright purple. I cut the MacroStream off. I swept the concrete floor and revealed small splash patterns near the toilet. The bloody patch lit up like a spotlight. The blanket was filthy with body fluids.

But it wasn't until I moved the light up to the wall that the panic in my body gave way to a maddened dump of adrenaline. There were marks on the concrete. Invisible to the naked eye but lit up like neon when the blacklight hit them. Scrawled in irregular urine letters with drip marks draining beneath them.

The letters spelled a single word:

Branson.

49

I sprinted out of the storm shelter and back to the street. By the time I reached the Pontiac I already knew everything I needed to know about what the word *Branson* was likely to mean. A single Google search told the story.

It was a city—population, thirteen thousand. Nestled in the Ozark mountains in southwestern Missouri, it was a vacation destination. A resort town, popular with family vacationers...and stocked with rural cabin homes.

The Pontiac roared. I threw it into gear, spinning out of the cul-de-sac with one hand while I dialed Feldon's cell phone number with the other. Concerns of trust were no longer a factor. I needed intel—immediately.

"Sharpe?"

"Branson, Missouri!" I shouted over the thunder of the car. "I need property listings for a *Greg Thornton*, captain in the US Army. Rentals, leases, family vacation homes. Whatever you can find, ASAP."

"Wait—what? What are you doing?"

"Find the listings, Feldon. Do it now!" I hung up and tabbed quickly to my GPS app. I was already back on the highway, roaring out of Gates. The GPS displayed an ETA of one hour, forty minutes.

I dumped on the gas and cut the time down to ninety minutes flat.

I CALLED Feldon twice more along the drive—both times I was bumped to voicemail. He finally called back when I was twenty miles outside of Branson. The sun was hot in my rearview. The fuel gauge on the Pontiac dipped beneath an eighth tank.

But I wasn't easing up, and I wasn't stopping for gas. Long experience as both a soldier and a cop had taught me a crucial lesson about hunting the enemy—escalation is *never* a good thing. Jacquie had been imprisoned for days, and yet quite recently she'd been removed. Thornton had decided to alter the status quo. To abandon his job and move his hostage.

Something had pressured him. Likely, it was the violence and persistence of my own investigation. Whatever happened next, the odds were not in Jacquie's favor.

"Gregory Richland Thornton," Feldon said, his voice monotone. "Thirteen years in the US Army. Thirty-five-year-old white male, five-foot-ten, one-hundred-thirty pounds."

"That's him. What have you got?"

"His only listed property is the lease of a house on Parker Drive in Gates—"

"Did I ask you about Gates? I asked you about Branson. What do you have in *Branson?*"

Feldon now sounded as though he were speaking through his teeth. "He doesn't *own* any property in Branson."

"Family property. An ex-girlfriend's property. A friend of a friend—"

"Will you let me finish? *He doesn't own any property*, but his grandfather did. It's a cabin in the mountains, about twelve miles outside of town. It's stuck in probate. I guess the old man kicked the bucket and now there's an argument about who gets—"

"Text me the address," I snapped.

"What are you doing, Sharpe?"

"Just text it to me!"

I hung up, forced to downshift as the speed limit plummeted near Branson. My body felt as taut as a violin string. I reviewed Feldon's intel on Thornton and knew it was all a bad sign—every bit of it.

Thirteen years in the US Army reflected dedication. Yet Thornton was only a captain. He should have been a major. He was running two or three years behind pace, which could indicate any number of hangups. Maybe the Army had plenty of white majors and was looking for a Hispanic one. Maybe Thornton was comfortable in Missouri and didn't want to be transferred to take a promotion.

Or maybe he was a troublemaker. Unreliable. Lazy. Dishonest. Whatever the case, even if Thornton's career in the Army had experienced difficulties, it was still a serious step for him to walk away from it. More than a speed bump, closer to career derailment.

Yes, Greg Thornton was escalating. Hard.

The GPS routed me around Branson and straight into the foothills of the Ozarks. Convenience stores and restaurants quickly faded, giving way to thick trees and steep mountainsides not so different from those in Mullins County.

The air thinned. The traffic faded. I was alone, passing only occasional mailboxes. Driveways were dirt and ditches filled with leaves. The spot the GPS led me to was completely unmarked—no street number, no mailbox, no visible structure beyond the trees. Just a dirt turnoff passing over a culvert clogged with trash.

But there were tire marks in the soft clay—fresh tire marks. They stamped through ruts and vanished into the trees.

I pulled the Pontiac onto the driveway. Steep inclines rose on both sides with trees leaning low, some of their branches scraping the car's roof. The route was clearly unmanaged, with a substantial tree limb lying across my path just as the two-lane faded behind me. I stepped on the brake and cut the engine. Sliding out of the car, I surveyed the path ahead.

The branch was six inches thick. There was no way I could cross it with the low-slung Pontiac without risking tearing an oil pan loose, but somebody had crossed it. Recently. Bark was scraped away, revealing white wood marred by tire marks.

I shut the Pontiac's door and hurried to the trunk. The woods around me were alive with the soft whisper of wind and the occasional chirp of songbirds. They were all very natural sounds, the standard rhythm of undisturbed forest.

I heard no voices. No crunch of footfalls. No rumble of a heavy engine.

Lifting the trunk, I kept my head up as I dipped my hand inside. The first rifle I found was the M4A1 with the M203 grenade launcher. It was already loaded with a thirty-round

GI magazine. I pulled the charging handle and shut the trunk. Blowing dust off the lens of the Aimpoint, I found the red dot already illuminated.

Shiver had kept it running, ready for immediate action. It was further confirmation of his military training, and reassurance that the rifle should be reliable.

I couldn't afford to risk any test shots, regardless.

Leaving the Pontiac, I stepped across the fallen limb and jogged up the edge of the road. It curved a hundred yards ahead, and I waded through the ditch before fading into the woods. The terrain was uncertain. It sloped and escalated at random, with plenty of rotten logs and invisible holes hidden by dead leaves. I slowed to a steady stalk, the rifle held into my shoulder as I followed the roadbed.

It climbed for two hundred yards, then curved to the west. I was over half a mile from the two-lane, and still the driveway continued. I quickened my pace, sweat running down my face and stinging my eyes. I navigated around a bramble thicket and turned a final corner before, at last, sunlight broke through the trees from almost directly ahead. It glinted off metal, reflecting into my eyes. I slipped behind a tree, stopping to focus and listen.

It was a metal roof. A small house—or a cabin, rather. Situated alone at the end of the drive, with darkened windows. A gunmetal gray Toyota 4Runner sat next to it, mud caking its wheels. I couldn't read the Toyota's license plate, but I thought it was a Missouri plate. I thought I saw a sticker in the back window, also.

An Army decal.

Raising the rifle until I looked through the Aimpoint, I started ahead again. Slower this time, not making a sound as my boots found purchase amid the leaves. I measured my breaths, forcing my body into a rhythm of calm. I closed to within fifty yards of the house.

Then I heard the sound—a steady, muddy scrape. Metal on dirt. A slice and a crunch.

My breath quickened. I circled to the right. A clearing stretched out behind the cabin, overgrown with unmanaged grass. I worked the tree line and saw a slouched back porch slowly rotting away. A path trampled through the grass. Sunlight blazing down on the mini meadow.

But no people. The grass was too tall to see the back of the yard. I thought I heard a human whimper, but I couldn't be sure. The sound was muffled.

The next sound wasn't muffled. It was clear as crystal.

"*Shut up.* Just shut up. Do you think I want to do this?"

It was Thornton's voice. My gaze snapped left toward the cabin. If I circled that way and ascended the deck, I would be able to see over the chest-high grass. I'd have a clean shot.

I'd also be fully exposed to the cabin...and whatever occupants it contained.

The next panicked cry was enough to seal my decision. Muffled by a gag. Escalated by terror. Followed by the meaty thump of flesh landing on packed dirt.

"*Thirteen years!* I gave my life to my country. My marriage. My youth. One dead-end post after another, always pushed aside in favor of wetbacks and women—there's no room for a white American anymore. I've got to *take* what I need!"

Thornton's voice trembled, choking with emotion. I sprinted from the trees and toward the deck, the snap of a hammer being cocked cracking across the meadow like a gunshot of its own. The female voice fell silent. I thought I heard Thornton sobbing. Then: "I tried to save you. I really did. If I don't do this...they will."

My boot struck the porch steps. I leapt the final two feet and landed on sagging, creaking boards. The meadow fell out like a canvas before me, tall grass bending in the wind. I looked fifty yards toward the tree line to see Thornton standing next to a mound of fresh dirt, a shovel jammed into its top. He held a revolver in one shaking hand. His finger fell over the trigger, and his lips moved in a final statement.

"I'm sorry."

50

I pressed the trigger and the M4 bucked in my hands, buffer spring crunching in my ear. The Aimpoint's holographic dot snapped upward, and a red mist sprayed across the trees beyond Thornton. I fought to reacquire, unfettered desperation overcoming my brain. I swept the optic across the mound of dirt, searching. Ready to fire again.

But Thornton was already down. His body lay splayed across the dirt, the polished chrome of the revolver reflecting sunlight next to him.

His head shattered by the impact of a steel-core round.

I flung myself off the deck and ran through the grass, breathing hard and no longer fighting it. I kept the rifle up and swept the tree line by default, but no other movement caught my eye. No further gunshots broke the stillness. I reached the mound of dirt and circled around it, rifle covering Thornton's lifeless, slack-jawed face and passing down his body. Past the revolver, its muzzle blackened by a recent discharge of gunpowder. Right to the edge of a grave, torn bits of roots reaching out like claws over the gaping hole.

And stopping over Jacquie.

She lay at the bottom of the hole, bound hand and foot, gagged and blindfolded, her skin caked with both fresh mud and dried blood. The path of Thornton's shot was marked by a furrow in the Missouri clay, leaving a hole drilled in the side of the grave. It had missed Jacquie's head by mere inches, and she now lay trembling in the dirt, choking around the gag.

"Jacquie!" I tossed the rifle down and dropped into the grave. It rose to my waist, a deep hole carved with the intention of permanence. The Victorinox snapped open, and the razor blade tore through duct tape and cloth. Jacquie kicked her legs, fighting away from me. I put a hand on her arm and squeezed.

"Jacquie! It's me. You're okay."

I traced her arm up to her head and tugged the blindfold off. It left behind a cloud of dark curly hair stiff with dried sweat. Jacquie's eyes were wide and bloodshot, breath rushing through her teeth in ragged gasps. She trembled. Our gazes locked. She started to sob.

Then she threw herself into my arms. I caught her at the bottom of the grave, the knife falling from my fingers as I wrapped her into a hug. Jacquie shook, face buried in my shoulder. Her heart thundered against my chest, and I blinked hard.

I was crying too.

SHE CALMED IN TIME, her sobs growing softer, her breath not as hot against my neck. When at last she pushed away from me, there was something in her eyes I'd never before seen. A deep, passionate gratitude. An appreciation that verged beyond the thrill of survival and edged into something more foundational. She blinked, but didn't look away. Her lips trembled.

Then she hit me in the chest, hard enough to send me reeling into the bottom of the grave.

"What took you so long?" she barked.

I landed on my ass, and I couldn't resist a grin. Jacquie was *back*.

"After-party," I said. "We won."

That brought on a bit of a smile. She scrubbed dirt and sweat from her face, then peered around herself for the first time, taking in the mound of dirt. The dead body. The rifle.

"Branson?" she asked.

"Just outside of it."

"So you found my message."

"How could I miss it? Smelled like a urinal."

A scowl. I stood and offered my hand. "Wanna get out of your grave?"

I hauled her back onto solid ground. Jacquie stopped alongside Thornton, inspecting the body with that same critical, searching eye I had so often admired during our homicide cases. The eye that missed nothing.

But there was something else in her face, now. Vague shock. A personalized, visceral terror. She began to shake and blink. Her breathing grew rapid. I caught her by the arm and she buried her face in my chest again. I gave her a few minutes to gradually calm while I stared at the corpse.

I felt no such horror. Simply unimaginable relief.

"You should wait by the house," I said, giving her arm a squeeze. "I'll only be a minute."

She looked up. "What are you doing?"

"I'm going to bury him. Thornton thought this was a good place to hide a body. I'll take his word on it."

"Wait. You're not gonna call the police?"

The surprise in Jacquie's tone jarred me a little. Not because her reaction was illogical, but because it highlighted just how much I had changed since leaving Phoenix two years prior. I'd come a long, long way from the heritage of a law-abiding soldier and homicide detective. I'd learned to carve my own path.

I'd learned just what a messy world I lived it.

"I shot him with a stolen firearm," I said, gesturing to the M4A1. "Besides that, we've got about a dozen problems to unravel and I don't have time to deal with interview rooms. Wait by the house."

Jacquie complied—which was unusual for her. I thought it was a testament to how badly she was shaken. I pushed Thornton's body into the grave and shoveled enough dirt over it to keep the scavengers away. His wide, horrified eyes gazed up at a clear blue sky in the moments before Missouri clay covered them.

I didn't feel sorry for him. I didn't wonder what his motivations were or what his story was or how he had migrated from arms smuggler to kidnapper to would-be murderer. The spiel about losing his marriage and being passed up for promotions in favor of minorities might explain something of the hate boiling inside of him. The fact that he'd apologized to one of those minorities for dragging her into a grave told a slightly more complex story.

Whatever the answer to the riddle, I simply didn't care. I'd protected mine. That was enough.

Back at the house I found Jacquie washing her face under a spigot mounted on the outside wall. She was still shaking, and now that some of the dirt was scrubbed away I detected bruising on her arms from the bonds Thornton had used.

"Are you okay?" My voice was gentle but somewhat awkward. Jacquie twisted the nozzle closed and squatted behind the cabin, eyes closed, just breathing.

I cradled the M4 and waited. There were next steps formulating in my mind, but my initial goal had been realized. Jacquie was alive and safe. That was a win worth celebrating.

"It was...so much worse than I imagined." Jacquie's voice was dry. "Being alone in the dark. Day after day. Not knowing. Not being able to measure the passage of time, or see the sun..."

She trailed off and I put one knee in the mud next to her. Giving her elbow a gentle squeeze, I looked back into those dark eyes. I saw pain, as before. But now it was joined by anger. A *lot* of anger.

"There's a smuggling ring," she said.

"I know."

"Thornton was moving rifles off Fort Crowder. Selling them to neo-Nazi thugs in the woods."

"I know."

"*Hundreds* of rifles. Maybe a thousand. My uncle was investigating. The skinheads killed him."

"I know."

"Yeah?" Jacquie's voice snapped. "What else do you know?"

I stood. I rested the rifle in the crook of my left arm and extended a hand to Jacquie.

"I know that we're going to smoke them out of their holes, no matter what it takes. And when we're finished, they'll curse the day they ever met a Richardson."

51

I led Jacquie back to the Pontiac. It rested right where I'd left it, the gunshot windshield reflecting midday sun. The moment Jacquie saw it I felt the edgy nervousness radiating off her like heat waves.

"Where did you get this?"

"From a dead man," I said. "Hop in."

I tossed the M4 in the back seat and fired up the big engine. Jacquie made no comment about the blood on the floorboard, and we rode in silence back to Branson. I pulled off at a gas station for fuel—both for us and the Pontiac. Jacquie guzzled Gatorades and crammed candy bars down her throat as though she hadn't eaten in days. With each bite a little more of her personality returned, that fiery but didactic blend of a hot-blooded woman restrained by the bounds of professional dedication.

"Local sheriff said my uncle was mugged. Blamed it on Memphis gangs." Jacquie shook her head and cracked open another Gatorade.

"I spoke with the distinguished Sheriff Conroy when I

arrived," I said, avoiding another use of the phrase *I know*. "He's an idiot, and so are his deputies. The investigation file was a complete slop job."

"You got a look at the file? Perks of being white. He wouldn't give me a copy."

"He wouldn't give it to me either. I had Jeremiah steal it."

Jacquie's gaze snapped toward me, a cutting question in her eyes. I held up a hand.

"He's fine. He and Lucile both. I kept them out of the action."

We reached the highway and I turned southeast for Arkansas. As we returned to farmland planes I pushed the GTO to eighty miles per hour, enjoying the smooth roar of the engine accentuated by a whistle from the bullet hole in the windshield.

I didn't mind the whistle. I was a long way from finished drilling bullet holes.

"I retraced your investigation the best I could," I said. "I got hung up assuming the Brotherhood had taken you. That distracted me from Thornton."

"Brotherhood?"

"The Aryans. Neo-Nazis. We had a few...conversations."

Another sharp look, this time less questioning and more satisfied.

"I got hung up on them too," Jacquie said. "But I never got that close. I was running plates with my partner back in Phoenix, assembling a list of names and addresses. People of interest. That's how I found Thornton. I was headed up to Fort Crowder the next day...before he snagged me."

Jacquie's voice turned cold. I picked my way through her timeline and quickly identified a hole.

"You never found your uncle's notes."

"What notes?"

"He hid notes in the church bell tower. That's how I unlocked the arms-dealing angle. But if you never found them, how did you know this was a smuggling operation?"

"Oh, right. There's an ATF guy. Somebody Uncle Cyrus was reporting to before he was killed. I met him at the funeral. He found out I was looking around. We talked. He clued me in on what was happening."

I yanked the car across the righthand lane and into the emergency shoulder, blood already boiling as gravel popped and Jacquie shouted. We ground to a halt, dust clouding the air behind us.

"What are you doing?"

"Name," I said.

"Whose name?"

"The ATF guy. What's his name?"

I already knew. I already pictured his smug sneer. The mind of a ruthless three-letter agent. A man who would finish the job at any cost.

"Feldon," Jacquie said. "Mark Feldon. Special Agent in Charge—"

"Of Field Division, Little Rock," I finished.

"You know him?"

I didn't answer. It was all I could do not to put my fist through the dash.

He *lied* to me. Right to my face. Not only had Feldon slow-walked the investigation, refusing to act on Cyrus's reports until Cyrus was murdered, he'd also proceeded to recruit Jacquie. To drop her into the jaws of the same beast that swallowed Cyrus. To use her for his dirty work.

And when she went missing? He'd made zero effort to

recover her. He'd simply moved right on to me. The next pawn in his game. Another puppet on strings.

A completely pragmatic SOB.

"Mason," Jacquie said. "What's the deal with Feldon?"

"He's still in one piece," I said, shifting back to first. "And he shouldn't be."

We returned to the highway and Jacquie didn't ask any further questions. Maybe old habits were kicking in—she could sense that I was unpacking the problem, and she was giving me space to do so.

I drilled down. Beneath the basic premise of Thornton's illegal activities. Beneath Feldon's despicable investigatory methods and the still worse corruption of the Mullins County Sheriff's Office.

There was a question at the bottom. Something that manifested itself more as a feeling than a fact. A sixth sense —the voice of my old investigative instinct awakened from dormancy.

"The Nazis didn't want the guns," I said. "Not for themselves."

"What do you mean?"

"I mean they were wholesaling them," I said. "Just another link in a chain. I think the final consumer lies south of the border. A cartel, likely."

"How do you know?"

"I observed a meeting between the Brotherhood and some Hispanic guys down in Little Rock. It was very clearly a show-and-tell sort of event. A product demonstration."

"So...it's all just a cash grab?"

"Apparently. That makes sense, anyway. Beyond the novelty of incinerating beer cans at nine hundred rounds per minute, there's not much use in owning a thousand fully automatic rifles. Not unless you plan to go to war."

"Maybe they do. They're radicals."

"Academically, they are. I doubt they have the guts to risk their own lives. They're making money and spending it on cars."

I gestured dismissively toward the dash. Jacquie squinted. I could sense that she was feeling out a plot hole. Struggling with something.

"What?" I said.

"I don't know if you'd understand."

"What's that supposed to mean?"

Jacquie shook her head. Looked out the window. I twisted in my seat.

"Hey. Spit it out."

"It's hate, Mason. Hate like you can't imagine. I'm not talking about prejudiced morons slinging racial slurs. I'm talking about the real deal. Deep, ugly, consuming hatred. It's why I left my hometown in the first place. These aren't just a bunch of rednecks with muscle car fetishes. I can feel it. There's something darker here."

The conviction in Jacquie's tone was overwhelming. I looked into her eyes and knew she believed every word.

"Watch the road, Mason."

I turned back to the windshield and we drove in silence for a while longer. Then I nodded.

"Okay. So we'll treat this like a mission overseas. We run down the enemy, whatever it takes. And we burn their world to the ground."

"Every square inch of it," Jacquie said. "They'll curse the day they ever met a Richardson."

I lifted a fist. Our knuckles touched. Jacquie settled into her seat with sudden calm.

A relentless professional.

"How do we find them?" she said.

It was the question already on my mind. Hoffman and his thugs had eluded me for days, easily fading into the Mullins County wilderness whenever they wanted to disappear. Finding their outposts, such as the bar, was easy enough. But if Jacquie was right, torching a random bar would never suffice. We needed to torch the heart of the hornets' nest.

"There's got to be a warehouse," I said. "Some kind of operational headquarters where they're storing the rifles."

"I thought so, too."

"Did you find anything?"

"No. Mullins County is a morass. Like a haystack, and we're looking for a needle. So many back roads, hollows, and miles of empty forest. It could be anywhere."

"Did you trail anybody?"

"I tried. It's tough to do on backroads with so many turns and so little traffic. If you don't stay close you lose them."

"And if you stay close, they make you," I said.

"Exactly. Plus, everybody is on their side. Nobody will talk."

I chewed my lip, putting myself in Hoffman's bloody boots. Asking myself how I would organize my own little army in a place so rural. As I turned the problem over in my mind, my gaze drifted down to the CB radio mounted beneath the Pontiac's dash. I squinted, remembering all those winding back roads with no cell phone signal. Yet these people coordinated, deploying out of the shadows right on command. I pictured the bar in the woods again, and examined each car, truck, and motorcycle parked out front.

What did they all have in common?

Radio antennas.

"I think I have something."

"A hideout?" Jacquie asked.

"No. Not directly. But maybe a way to find the hideout."

"What did you have in mind?"

I flicked my turn signal and glided into the fast lane. The speedometer spiked. I settled in.

"We're gonna arrange a religious experience," I said. "We're going to church."

52

W e stopped at an electronics store on the way back to Arkansas, then breezed through a fast food drive-through where Jacquie ordered enough food for six and Shiver footed the bill. The sun was just beginning to fade behind the Boston Mountains when I used a single bar of cell service to make a call on Shiver's phone. The phone was locked, of course, but still allowed for an emergency call, which was all I needed.

The conversation was short. My voice was muffled by my shirt. I got the point across, then hung up.

With our plan in motion I took the Pontiac down a washed-out dirt road, winding all the way to a little grave-yard built along the crest of a hill two hundred yards removed from Pleasant Hill Baptist Church.

Reverend Polk waited at the chain-link gate. He admitted us without questions, then enveloped Jacquie in a bear hug. I parked the Pontiac between two rows of headstones and killed the lights. From the edge of the cemetery, I had a partial view of the churchyard some fifty yards beneath my current elevation. There were trees in the way, and a lot of undergrowth. Enough to conceal the low-slung Pontiac, but standing alongside the open driver's door I maintained a clear shot. What was more, I could easily reach the CB radio mounted beneath the GTO's dash.

"You better get a move on, Reverend," I said. "It's about to get dicey around here."

Polk eyeballed me with one arm still wrapped around Jacquie's shoulders. Then he gave her a squeeze and turned for the gate.

"Don't do nothing you'll regret, son. Don't do nothing Cyrus wouldn't do."

I made no comment as he disappeared. A moment later his old pickup howled. Then he was gone around the bend in the county road, leaving the church building silent...but not dark.

The lights were on, spilling through the windows. I raised Shiver's M4 and swept it from tree to tree, estimating distance. Inside of two hundred yards the rifle would be lethal, but there would still be plenty of places for Hoffman's men to take cover if things went sideways. Still so much that could go wrong.

"I should go," I said. "You take overwatch."

I extended the weapon toward Jacquie. She ignored it, dipping through the open driver's door to retrieve a plastic bag from the electronics store.

"We covered this, Mason. I'll do the sneaking."

"Jacquie..."

Dark eyes snapped toward me. "What? You're gonna tell me what to do? They *murdered* him, Mason. My family. This is my fight more than anybody's."

My shoulders slumped. I was exhausted again. I'd missed

298   LOGAN RYLES

a full night's sleep. I also knew from long experience how pointless it can be to argue with Jacquie.

"Just don't die."

Jacquie grinned. "I'm great at sneaking. You're in for a show."

TWO MINUTES later Jacquie slipped into the darkness. By the time she reached the bottom of the hill I'd lost her entirely, despite my best efforts to track her progress with the soft glow of the M4's Aimpoint optic.

It was two minutes past seven, and full darkness had consumed the churchyard. The yellow light shining from the rows of tall windows looked warm and inviting. The premises were almost perfectly silent, and that would play perfectly into my plan.

My phone call to the corrupt Mullins County Sheriff's Department detailed Shiver's narrow escape from death, and his certain knowledge that Jacquie Richardson had not only been located by the troublesome Mason Sharpe, but also "knew things". Even now she was headed to that little church, planning to rendezvous with federal agents. *Legitimate* officers of the law.

It was bait I knew Hoffman couldn't resist, and he proved me right at seven fifteen when the rumble of his big Dodge broke the stillness. It appeared like a black cloud, roaring into the lot with headlights blazing. The 1970 Boss Mustang I'd witnessed at the roadside bar joined it, followed by the '69 Cougar Eliminator. All three vehicles fanned out in front of the church. I tracked the appearance of one skinhead after another using the Aimpoint's magnifier. There were six in total, all stomping directly toward the church as though they feared neither man nor law in all of Arkansas.

I picked out Hoffman leading the lot. He ascended the church's front steps and tried the door. It was locked, and he pressed an ear to the outside. Then he gestured, and the others circled the building. I swept my point of aim back to the parking lot.

Jacquie appeared as a shadow, circling quickly behind the Cougar. She knelt at the rear bumper and leaned beneath the car. Her left arm moved, slapping something onto the undercarriage. Then she was moving again, headed for the Dodge.

Hoffman and his men gained view of the church through the windows and found it empty. They searched the picnic area and eventually returned to the parking lot. I could feel the frustration radiating off them. Hoffman marched straight for his truck, and I snatched the rifle back toward it.

Jacquie was still bent beneath the rear bumper. She seemed to be fighting with something. She didn't respond to the approaching men. I knew she couldn't hear their footsteps over the steady chug of three oversized engines. My finger curled around the trigger, and I kept the red dot hovering over Hoffman's chest. One flick and he'd go down like a tree.

Hurry, Jacquie.

She finally emerged just as Hoffman was circling around the front bumper. He would see her in another two seconds. I tracked his ugly face as Hoffman looked back over one shoulder, shouting at his men. He twisted toward me. My finger constricted.

Then Jacquie dove beneath the truck, as quick and

graceful as a cat. One second she was visible, the next she was swallowed by darkness.

Yet still only feet away from Hoffman. He stopped, one hand on the open door of his truck. His face contorted into a frown, and alarm bells clanged in my head. Hoffman started to turn, started to stoop.

I reached into the Pontiac and snatched up the CB radio handset. "Breaker one-nine. Any skinheads? Copy?"

I knew they heard me. I had left Shiver's radio tuned into channel 19, the channel I assumed he used most frequently. It was a good bet. Hoffman's face snapped toward his truck. He dipped inside. I waited. The volume on the Pontiac's CB was turned down, just loud enough for me to hear.

Then Hoffman's voice rumbled through the speakers. "Who's this?"

I couldn't resist a smile. "It's Shiver, Hoffman. Don't I sound like Shiver?"

Slight pause. Hoffman reappeared from the cab of his truck. He looked to his men. They were all crowded around their cars, listening the way he was listening. Hoffman raised a handset to his lips.

"You think this is funny, Sharpe?"

"I'm laughing like a schoolgirl."

"You have no idea what you've stepped into."

"On the contrary, I have a very good idea. You're a third-rate backwoods thug saturated in all kinds of radical ideology you picked up off the internet. Probably inbred. Probably with an IQ of about fifty, but that's okay, I'll speak slowly. You've picked up a pile of retired rifles from Fort Crowder. You're selling them to a Mexican cartel, making a nice little pile of cash and willing to kill to protect it. You killed Cyrus Richardson. You killed Sage Fuller. You tried to kill Jacquie Richardson, but she slipped away. Now you're gonna contend with me—and buddy, that's more than you can handle."

I watched through the optic. Hoffman held the radio near his face, but he didn't answer. I thought I saw a flash of white across his mouth, reflecting the headlights of the nearby Cougar.

I thought I saw him smile.

"Wow," Hoffman said. "You really have no idea."

The voice was calm—unthreatened.

It was *amused*.

"You can't talk your way out of this one, Hoffman. By sunrise this is all gonna be over. Take my word on it."

Now I knew he was smiling. No, he was *laughing*.

"No. Take *mine*."

Hoffman threw the handset back into his truck. He jerked his head and his men piled into their cars. As I watched, tires spun. All three vehicles raced onto the road and disappeared in a thunder of exhaust.

Jacquie picked herself up from beneath where the Dodge had sat. Ninety seconds later she was back in the graveyard, panting from her jog up the hill.

"Well?" I asked.

Jacquie grinned. She extended her palm, offering me my burner phone. There was an app loaded onto it, displaying a GPS screen with a web of winding Arkansas roads stretching between the mountains.

Blipping along one of those roads were two blue dots. Tracking beacons.

A forest-green Mercury Cougar and a jet-black Dodge one-ton. Headed back to base.

53

"You heard what he said." Jacquie's tone crackled as she climbed into the Pontiac. "*We have no idea.*"

"I heard him."

"There's more, Mason. A lot more."

"Or maybe he's bluffing. Our plan remains the same, regardless. We trail them back to base. Scope out what they're up to."

"Then call the feds?"

I didn't answer. We were back on the winding two-lane, the Pontiac running hard. Jacquie looked up from the burner phone.

"We call the feds, right?"

"We can't call the feds," I said. "Not immediately."

"Why not?"

I didn't answer. Jacquie lowered the phone. "What did you do, Mason?"

"I kidnapped some people. Busted some shin bones. That ATF guy, Feldon, holds a grudge against me for an incident in Atlanta."

"Wait. You met him before?"

"Unfortunately. He doesn't remember me kindly. He'll be more than happy to burn us both while he takes all the credit."

Jacquie considered, using casual flicks of her hand to direct my turns at each intersection.

At last: "So how do we handle this?"

"Feldon is playing chess. We make that chess three-dimensional. We unpack this mess on our own terms."

I glanced toward her. "He could have moved sooner, Jacquie. Cyrus had the details. Feldon stalled. Cyrus paid the price."

Jacquie's gaze turned hard. "I know."

The tracking beacons led us deep into Mullins County, far from civilization, where the roads were so rough that I was forced to creep along them. I was worried about the crackling exhaust of the GTO. Sound carries amid hills and valleys. Shiver's car made a distinct growl. When the two blips stopped three miles ahead, I stopped also. We waited until they began moving again, off road this time, into a wide cross-section of forest.

"That's it," I said.

"Do we park?"

I considered, remembering the third car that had accompanied the Dodge and the Cougar. That Mustang could have doubled back to check for a tail, or might have parked at the end of the driveway to serve as a lookout.

"We close to a mile, then we hoof it. You feel good for some hiking?"

"Ten-four."

I shook my head.

"What?"

"You and your codes."

Jacquie grinned.

I PARKED a mile from the turnoff. The blipping dots on the burner phone were now way back in the sticks. The terrain was aggressive, with foothills looking more like small mountains. Undergrowth clogged the gaps between towering hardwoods and scrawny mountain pines. The best place I could find to conceal the car was a shallow spot in the ditch. While I circled to the trunk Jacquie went automatically into the woods, returning with fallen branches and tangles of torn vines. It was an imperfect disguise for the car, but it would have to suffice.

"Fun switch on the receiver," I said, handing Jacquie the second M4A1. "I recommend semi-automatic mode. The muzzle rise is aggressive in full auto."

Jacquie broke the receiver open, inspecting the chamber and bolt-carrier group before locking it closed again and snatching the charging handle. She tapped the Aimpoint.

"On zero?"

I shrugged. "Mine was."

I shut the trunk and took inventory of my own equipment. One thirty-round magazine locked into the M4, with twenty-nine rounds remaining. A spare mag in my left pocket, the SIG P365XL jammed into the small of my back. My Victorinox, the MacroStream, and two forty-millimeter grenades packed into my right pocket.

I desperately needed a full chest rig. Accessing my gear from jean pockets would be difficult, but I couldn't help that. It was time to move.

"Let's roll."

We proceeded into the brush. Jacquie's tactical training consisted of urban, SWAT type skills. Teamwork, specifically, on concrete, not in the woods. She was highly competent with a rifle, but she made a lot of noise out in the sticks. She didn't know how to avoid low spots and piles of the dryer leaves. I took point and kept my shoulders low, gliding along like a Ranger student back at Camp Merrill, taking Mountain Phase. Learning the techniques that I would soon apply on the other side of the world, with real weapons pointed back at me. It was all so natural it almost concerned me how quickly I fell back into the mindset of a calibrated hunter.

I had to remind myself that these were American mountains, with American citizens hiding amongst them. Then again, if they shot first...all bets were off.

We crept through the woods for half an hour, only making about a mile of progress amid the brambles. They served as a natural barrier that somehow felt very intentional, as though whatever operational base lay beyond the next ridge had been deliberately surrounded by them. There was a roadbed about a hundred yards to our left. Along it I noted two cattle gates, both closed. Reflective KEEP OUT and PRIVATE PROPERTY signs hung on them. On at least two occasions I spotted what I thought to be security cameras.

But there were no people. All was deathly quiet. It wasn't until we topped a jagged ridge and looked down into a valley that we finally reached our target.

It was a compound, plain and simple. Wafting with Waco vibes, the large building that dominated the center of the complex might once have been a house, but it had been added onto so many times by slipshod carpenters that it was now impossible to tell what the original structure had looked like. The complex sprawled at least five thousand square feet, with a slouching front porch and a dirt drive.

The cars were all there. The Cougar, the Boss Mustang, a couple of the other muscle cars I recognized from the bar, along with Hoffman's Dodge. A fence ran around the perimeter of the valley, ten feet high and topped with razor wire. A metal pole barn stood behind the compound with a truck parked in front of it—a day cab semi with a short box trailer. Security lights glared down over a dusty gravel lot, and half a dozen men were gathered near the box trailer smoking cigarettes.

Flapping atop a thirty-foot pole and illuminated by spotlights was a flag. Bright red with a black symbol embroidered over a white circle—an eagle holding a horizontal cross with swastika legs.

I settled onto one knee and deployed the Aimpoint's magnifier for a better look. With three-times zoom I captured details of the parked cars. License plate numbers, weapons stacked in their back seats. Racist bumper stickers and supremacist window decals. My line of sight swept over the house, and then the gravel lot. The meeting was breaking up. One man climbed into the driver's seat of the semi-truck and the engine rumbled to life. The others moved back into the pole barn.

"There are no known white supremacist groups in Arkansas," I muttered, parroting what the FBI PAO had told me. Jacquie tugged on my sleeve, pointing as the truck pulled away. It exposed a clear view into the metal building beyond, illuminated by bright fluorescents. I didn't even need the magnifier to identify what lay inside.

They were crates. Dozens of them, stacked in a heap. Each stamped with bold, black ink.

UNITED STATES ARMY. M4A1 RIFLES.

54

"That's it," Jacquie said. "Let's call the feds."

I held up a hand, watching the men now scurrying across the gravel lot. Some headed into the pole barn. Some headed back toward the house. Hoffman remained by the flag, lighting up a new cigarette.

Something was wrong. The body language, the organized chaos. It all spoke to impending action. Even as the truck disappeared down the roadbed, it seemed that the mission was just beginning. The ABA soldiers gathered in the valley were animated.

"Mason. We gotta call Feldon."

"Not yet," I said. "Wait a moment."

I guided the muzzle of the M4 across the gravel lot, tracing a thickset skinhead who hobbled on one leg. It was Bucky. He handed Hoffman a black object, roughly the size of a brick. Hoffman extended an antenna, and then I recognized the device as a radio handset. CB, perhaps?

Hoffman spoke into it. Waited. Spoke again.

Then he jerked his head and Bucky hobbled after him

toward the back of a parked SUV. It was situated next to the pole barn, inky-black windows reflecting the gleam of the security lights.

My spine tingled with sudden electricity as alarm bells rang in my mind. I wasn't sure why, but my every instinct was on fire.

"Come on," I said. "We're closing in. Move quietly."

I took point, quickly leaving Jacquie behind as she picked her way amid dry sticks and brambles. The hillside sloped down to the edge of the valley, with trees and undergrowth providing cover all the way to the fence.

I made it only halfway before a shrill cry broke through the stillness. Feminine and laced with panic, I recognized the voice long before my mind could make sense of the babbled words.

Lucile.

"Please! Don't hurt him. He don't—"

A meaty thud of fist on flesh. Lucile went silent. I threw myself through the brush, still moving with care but not as quietly as before. I circled along the fence line until the flagpole came into view, then the gravel lot. I saw the pole barn and the SUV with tinted windows. Its rear hatch was open. Hoffman and his men stood outside it, encircling two figures thrown onto the gravel.

Lucile and Jeremiah. Both bound. Jeremiah gagged. One of Hoffman's men was raining kicks down on him. I could hear the shouts. They were laced with racial slurs, punctuated by Jeremiah's muffled cries. Hoffman stood back and held the radio over his victims, face stretched into a grin. He drew the device back to his face, and this time I was close enough to hear the words.

"You hear that, Sharpe? You recognize that squeal? Gonna get a whole lot worse if you don't pick up the radio."

My blood surged hot. I sighted through the Aimpoint and painted a point of impact on Hoffman's skull. I rested a finger over the trigger, but I didn't fire.

I would give away my position if I did. With a hillside at my back and a fence blocking my path forward, I would be a sitting duck. I would wait for Jacquie, unless and until the beatings turned lethal.

Jacquie must have heard the cries also. She rushed in behind me, sliding to her knees and snatching up the rifle.

"*Hold*," I hissed. "Don't fire!"

"They're gonna kill them!"

"No they're not. They're hostages. They're trying to flush us out."

"That's my *aunt*, Mason!"

I yanked Jacquie's muzzle down. She fought me, but I had all the leverage. I knocked her off balance, pushing her behind a tree just as Hoffman turned our way. I didn't think he had heard us. Jeremiah's cries were too loud. Hoffman paced, his face now twisted into a nasty snarl.

"You better pick up the radio, you spineless swine."

"Mason!" Jacquie said. "Let me go!"

I shook Jacquie by one arm, hard enough to arrest her attention from the broken sobs of her aunt and cousin.

"*Look at me.*"

Jacquie finally did. I kept my voice low. "There's a fence, Jacquie. We're pinned in here. We've got to circle and find an opening, establish the high ground. Then we take them. Okay?"

"We've got surprise!"

"And they've got numbers. It's three to one. You really want to risk Lucile and Jeremiah's life to those odds?"

Jacquie breathed heavily, her bruised and dirty skin gleaming with sweat. She looked like she was about to explode as her wide eyes darted toward the compound.

But she didn't spring out from behind the tree. She trusted me.

"We circle right," I said. "Get behind the barn. We get through the fence and take them from the flanks. Okay?"

"Okay."

"Stay focused, Jacquie. This is just another investigation, okay? You're a professional."

Another nod from Jacquie. Her body calmed. She shouldered the rifle and stepped in behind me.

With a belt of underbrush shielding our position, we circled toward the pole barn while the beating at the flagpole persisted. Lucile seemed to be the focus of violence. She pleaded while the pejoratives continued in a steady stream. Despite what I'd told Jacquie I knew Hoffman would absolutely kill his prisoners before this was over.

He wanted to lure me out, yes. But only to tie up the last loose ends. Cyrus Richardson and Sage Fuller were already dead—Jacquie would have been also if Thornton hadn't protected her by holding her hostage. The Brotherhood had no problem with wholesale slaughter. They had a corrupt sheriff's department and sprawling wilderness on their side.

Lucile and Jeremiah would never leave this place. Not unless Jacquie and I arrived first.

We reached the backside of the pole barn. There were empty beer kegs, broken shipping crates, and piles of trash heaped against sheet metal walls. The fence stood just behind the barn, the curled razor wire littered with fallen branches and pine needles, but still an efficient obstacle to anyone attempting to climb over. I leaned my rifle against a tree and dug past the forty-millimeter grenades into my pocket.

"Cover me," I said.

Jacquie fell into a kneel and swept her rifle along the length of the barn. I produced the Victorinox from my pocket and snapped open the metal saw from the lineup of compact tools. It was three inches long, built of tempered steel, with a fine cutting edge. I tested the tension on the chain link. Whoever erected the fence had done a good job —the chain was tight.

From the far side of the pole barn a bloodcurdling shriek was followed by Hoffman barking into his radio.

"You hear that? I'm gonna kill this whore! *Where are you?*"

"Mason..."

"Hold," I snapped.

I selected a fence wire about four feet off the ground and went to work, pumping with the Victorinox. The tempered blade tore through the relatively soft steel in barely three seconds, and then I was on to the next wire, using the post to brace myself.

"Hurry," Jacquie hissed.

From the gravel lot the cries of abused hostages had grown dim, likely because I had failed to answer Hoffman's radio calls. The skinheads would be reevaluating, now. Potentially moving their prisoners inside the house.

I didn't want that. Things would be much easier if this remained a battlefield instead of a house clearing.

I'd cut a two-foot line through the fence but it wasn't nearly enough to squeeze through. I needed to reach the bottom so that we could peel up a section to wriggle through. I pumped my arms harder, listening as Hoffman shouted again. Not to his radio. To his men. The saw blade had grown hot. It cut a little more slowly. Each section of wire bent under the pressure of my arms. From beyond the pole barn feet pounded across gravel. Jeremiah must have worked his gag free because he was now dog-cussing his captors. Jacquie left her post and closed to my left side, pointing her rifle to the nearest corner of the pole barn. I would have preferred she remained behind me, sheltered amongst the trees.

It no longer mattered. I had two wires to go. I reached the bottom of the fence just as an engine whined to life. Not the heavy chug of Hoffman's truck or the rumble of a modified muscle car, but the smooth whir of a modern four-cylinder.

The SUV.

My arms worked like hydraulic cylinders. Muscles burned and breath whistled between my teeth. I didn't let up. The final wire snapped. I pocketed the knife and grabbed the bottom edge of the fence. Jacquie ducked right through. She turned automatically and held the fence in the opposite direction while I fought my large frame through the gap.

No sooner had I reached the other side than Jacquie was slapping my shoulder.

"I'm going left!" she said.

It wasn't a question. I didn't argue. I swung to the right, breaking for the end of the pole barn. The M4 rode at eye level, red dot shuddering with every step, my finger closing over the trigger.

I made it all the way to the corner and was just turning toward the gravel lot when I collided headlong with the first of Hoffman's men. It was Bucky, headed for a piss. I knew because his fly was already open. His lips parted in the first notes of a panicked cry.

The butt stock of my rifle silenced him, landing between his eyes and knocking him out cold at the same moment as Jacquie's rifle opened fire with a throaty snarl.

Contact.

55

I reached the face of the pole barn just as World War Three erupted in the gravel lot. Jacquie's storm of gunfire was nothing short of apocalyptic. She'd ignored my recommendations of semi-automatic and switched straight to full auto, spraying lead toward the nose of the SUV as it raced for the drive. Tires blew and the windshield shattered. All of the Aryans still in there were headed for the house, scurrying like cockroaches when the kitchen light is flicked on. Jacquie stepped out of the shadows, still engaging them, but the spray and pray method loses its luster after thirty yards. Bullets zipped into the exposed plywood walls of the house to no harm of the fleeing skinheads.

I fired twice into the spine of the nearest guy. He pitched forward with a scream, and then I was forced to duck behind the barn as handgun fire rained toward me. It wasn't coming from the fleeing men, it was coming from the second story of the house.

Muzzle flash marked the shooter's location, dug in behind a window. I lifted the M4 and unleashed half a dozen rounds through the glass, silencing the handgun. Long before I could leave cover another window flashed with orange, this time both louder and faster than the handgun. A hail of zipping lead slammed into the metal walls and I was forced to scramble back as dirt and rocks exploded on all sides. I choked, rolling the M4 over in my lap.

The M203 grenade launcher slid open on greased rails. A forty-millimeter fragmentation grenade fit into the chamber. The holographic grenade sight was set for two hundred meters. I only needed fifty. I rotated the swivel to shorten the distance and returned to my feet.

The rifle on the second floor had adjusted fire to Jacquie's position. Her angle on the shooter rendered her near helpless, while it was easy for him to keep her pinned down.

Easy...so long as he remained in one piece.

I swung out from behind the pole barn and squeezed the trigger on the grenade launcher in one motion. It was an action I'd practiced a few thousand times before and had learned to master. I love a grenade. I love the way the launcher pops. That smooth, flashing arc of death racing through the air.

The crash of thunder when it lands.

The second floor of the house shook as blood and smoke erupted through the window. The rifle went silent. I leapt out from behind the pole barn and made for my next point of cover—the disabled SUV. From inside the vehicle Jeremiah shouted and Lucile screamed. I circled to the driver's side door where I found a skinhead writhing in the front seat. He was gut-shot, reaching for a pistol. Three quick rounds from my M4 silenced him forever.

"Mason!" Lucile shrieked.

"*Stay down!* This isn't over."

Hoffman was gone. His compatriots were gone. Two lay dead in the gravel beneath their bloody red banner, but the rest had disappeared into the house. Maybe they planned to flee in the cars out front...or maybe they planned to stand and fight.

My question was answered by a hellish storm of gunfire erupting through every orifice of the house's rear wall. I recognized the snarl of M4s, the chug of AK-47s, and the hiss of what may have been an Uzi. Bullets rained over the nose of the SUV and I dove for cover behind the engine block. Jacquie shouted and I looked to find her still dug in behind the corner of the pole barn. She was trying to return fire but couldn't lean out without drawing enough hot lead to eviscerate an elephant.

From the back of the SUV Jeremiah screamed in wrenching pain. I imagined a jagged slug ripping through the vehicle's thin body panels and zipping into his leg—or worse, chest. I had to draw fire away from the SUV. I had to *move.*

Loading my second grenade, I swung out from the front of the SUV. I wasn't aiming. I simply pointed the launcher toward a first-floor window and pulled the trigger. The launcher popped and glass shattered. A thunderclap was matched by an unearthly shriek, loud enough to draw the attention of the gunmen on the second floor.

It was just enough time. I sprinted to the back corner of the house. The nearest door stood open, three steps leading to the threshold. Halfway up them a shout rang from the second floor of the building, but it was quickly silenced by a burst of cover fire from Jacquie.

Inside I smelled blood and gunpowder. Bare plywood creaked under my boots as I circled left. The victim of my latest grenade lay jerking like an earthworm dropped on hot asphalt. The grenade had blown away most of one leg. He would bleed out soon.

I never gave him the chance. Kill shots to the chest and face. Then I was headed through a dining room cluttered with empty pizza boxes and beer cans. Every wall was hung with neo-Nazi propaganda. Swastikas, posters written in German. Photographs of Hitler, Heinrich Himmler, and Adolph Eichmann plastered in fancy frames like the esteemed portraits of hospital benefactors. A hand-painted canvas depicted the ghastly front entrance of Auschwitz with the phrase "Death to the Jews" scrawled beneath.

I crashed through it all with barely a thought, clearing a kitchen and then a mudroom. Still no sign of Hoffman and his men.

Second floor.

It's what I would have done. They could barricade them-selves up there, forcing me to advance up the stairs, fully exposed.

As if on cue, a confirmation of my theory came in the form of a chugging AK-47. It blasted down on me, 7.62 millimeter rounds ripping out of the ceiling and zipping into the floor as I danced backward. I tipped my M4 upward and squeezed the trigger, spraying a plywood ceiling with half a magazine of hot lead. My return shots were nearly useless— they broke through three-quarter-inch plywood with ease, but I knew they weren't reaching the second floor. Joists, insulation, and another layer of plywood fouled the light 5.56 rounds while heavy AK slugs ripped right through.

I had to keep moving.

Racing out of the mudroom, I located a hallway. Bedrooms opened on either side, but I still didn't see a stairwell. The bullets followed me, obliterating a light fixture and shredding linoleum flooring. I dropped the exhausted mag on my rifle and slammed in my spare, moving on the balls of my feet as shots from the AK became increasingly sporadic and farther off target.

They'd lost me—for the moment, anyway. I listened to growling voices from overhead and tried to estimate how many combatants remained. At least three, including Hoffman.

Where were the stairs?

The house was like a maze. Hallway after crooked hallway connected to narrow, smelly bedrooms. I wound through an entire wing of the house before finally approaching the bottom of a stairwell. The door hung half open. All was dark beyond. Sweat streamed down my face as I approached. I barely realized it, but I wasn't thinking in terms of neo-Nazis or rural Arkansas anymore. The target didn't matter. The context was no longer relevant.

Only one thought rang over and over in my head: *Complete the objective—don't die.*

I listened at the bottom of the stairs. Voices were too faint to discern words. I thought I heard a pained groan. It was impossible to pinpoint where the sounds originated.

I gritted my teeth and faced the inevitable. I had to storm those stairs. There was no other way. Not unless—

Jacquie's attack on the front porch came as a crash of glass. She'd thrown something, and it landed with a slam on plywood. The response from the second level was instantaneous. Pounding boots and thundering rifles—Hoffman calling orders, all attention fixated on this new threat.

Jacquie had given me an opening, and I took it. Blasting through the half-open door, I hit a flight of pinewood steps and hurtled toward the second level.

56

The stairwell switched back on itself halfway up. I thundered over abandoned beer cans before reaching the top. A standard bedroom door blocked my path—possibly locked. I didn't wait to find out. I kicked it open, and then I was in.

It was one big room—the entire second floor. Windows on front and back, a sloping roof overhead. A giant conference table capped on either end by two-foot square columns. A giant projector screen on one wall. Racks of long guns hung between the windows. A kitchenette in one corner. The floor covered in plywood. One giant blood-red flag suspended by all four corners over the table.

I saw it all in a split second, but none of the landscape really mattered. The only thing that did matter were the occupants—six of them. One was dead, the victim of my forty-millimeter grenade. Another lay propped against a computer desk, bleeding and shrieking while his comrades ignored him.

The remaining four men were gathered near the front of

the house, to my right. Two knelt with their rifles poking through windows, engaging Jacquie. One stood with a smoking AK-47, fighting to lock in a fresh magazine.

The fourth and final man—Hoffman himself—stood behind the kitchenette counter. He and the skinhead with the AK saw me first. The guy snatched the rifle toward me.

I beat him to the punch by a lifetime, drilling four neat holes into his sternum. Hoffman shouted and dove behind the kitchenette counter. The two men at the windows jerked toward me. The gunshot guy to my left shouted and clawed for a pistol.

I calculated the odds in a split second and knew I could never shoot them all before one of them got a shot at me. I broke for cover instead, slinging myself out of the doorway and hurtling straight for the nearest column—the one at my end of the conference table. It was encased in three-quarter-inch plywood and just big enough to fit behind. As I slid behind it two things happened at once—the guys at the windows opened fire on the column, and the injured skinhead got a hand around his pistol.

I shot from the hip with the M4, eviscerating the guy with the pistol. He crumpled sideways as bullets blasted away chunks of the column, zipping only inches from my shoulders. I clutched the rifle and smacked my right pocket, searching for another forty-millimeter grenade. It wasn't an ideal application, bottled up in a room like this, but it would be seconds, not minutes, before the hillbillies behind me wised up and started spreading apart to take me from my sides.

I couldn't shoot in two directions at once. One of them would get me. But there was no grenade in my pocket. I'd only brought two, and they were both expended.

A lucky shot burst through the framed edge of the column and cut over my left shoulder, slicing flesh. I grunted and ducked. From across the room, Hoffman yelled at his men.

"Spread out! Get to his flanks!"

Time's up.

I thought quickly and ratcheted the grenade launcher open anyway. The empty casing from my last discharge fell into my left hand. Manhandling the rifle with my right, I shouted to nobody in particular: *"Frag out!"*

The empty grenade casing flew out of my hand, around the column and over the conference table. Straight between the two skinheads dug in behind me. The metal casing struck the floor with a dull *ping* and a split second passed in slow motion. I thought the ruse had failed.

Then a panicked shout erupted from behind the column. *"Grenade!"*

The two gunmen split, one of them dashing for the stairwell. It was the logical direction to flee the alleged explosive, but the worst possible direction to flee my rifle. I cut him down with a stream of gunshots to his spine, and he dropped like a tree. Then I was circling the column in the opposite direction, keeping the conference table between myself and my last two targets.

Hoffman was still hiding behind the kitchenette. His last soldier sprinted toward him with his rifle clutched against his chest, but Hoffman was smarter. He rose from behind the counter, unimpressed by the empty grenade casing, rotating an M4 toward me even as his man dove for cover.

I dropped to my knees, landing beneath the table just as that last soldier slid for shelter inside the kitchenette. He never made it. I riddled his exposed side with three rounds while Hoffman dumped fire into the top of the conference table. It wasn't a cheap table—not a box store special, but a custom piece constructed out of a heavy oak. There was no chance those light 5.56 rounds would penetrate, but it wouldn't be long before Hoffman decided to swing out of the kitchenette and shoot beneath the table.

I rolled onto my back, placing both boots beneath the edge of the table. Just as a heavy thump signaled Hoffman's drop to the floor, I shoved upward with everything I had. It was like a giant leg press, a few hundred pounds of weight balanced on thick table legs. The left side of the table lifted. I shoved until my knees locked.

The table fell sideways onto its edge just as Hoffman opened fire again. Bullets slammed into the table top and I scrambled to my knees, dropping the mag on my M4 to check the load.

Only five or six rounds remained, counting the one in the chamber. Plus the SIG in my waistband.

I wiped sweat from my face. Hoffman's rifle fell silent, and a split second later I heard the familiar smack and click of a fresh magazine locking into place.

We both breathed hard. I knew his ears must be ringing as badly as mine. The battlefield buzz would have set in. He would be so high on adrenaline that he could barely process a clear thought. Instinct was taking over.

Judging by the quickness with which he'd loaded a new magazine, I guessed those instincts to have been honed by a little training. Maybe a lot of it.

"What branch?" I called.

Hoffman spat. "Does it matter?"

No. It didn't matter. A traitor from one branch was no different than a traitor from any other branch. But I wanted him talking while I gave Jacquie time to find us. To tilt the status quo in my favor.

"I was Army," I said. "They sent me to Afghanistan. You ever go overseas?"

A snort of a laugh, but no answer. I looked left toward the entrance of the stairwell. I didn't see Jacquie. I couldn't hear her, either.

"You expecting that colored whore to save you?" Hoffman said.

"Actually, I was giving you a chance to save yourself."

"Oh really?"

"It's the last chance you'll ever get."

Another pause. I grew still, listening for any creak of plywood. Any hint of Hoffman moving from behind the kitchenette.

There was nothing. He just panted. I wondered if I'd winged him.

Then he said: "Iraq."

"How many tours?"

"Enough."

Enough. I knew what that meant. I'd hit that number myself.

"So you know how this ends," I said. "People die. Nobody wins."

"That's where you're missing the forest for the trees, Sharpe. Sheep like you always do. You think this is about some dumb black toilet wiper? A few worn-out rifles?"

From someplace beneath me I detected the dullest creak of wood. A footfall, maybe. My ears rang so loudly I couldn't be sure.

I decided to keep Hoffman talking.

"So educate me, then. What's the forest look like?"

"It looks like two hundred bloody years of Jews and coloreds—sucking this country dry one conniving financial scheme and civil rights march at a time. Flooding our borders. Eroding our wealth like locusts. Taking *everything*."

I laughed. I couldn't help it. I knew it would infuriate him, but what was he gonna do? Pull a gun on me?

"You can't honestly believe that swill."

"*Believe?*" Hoffman seemed to choke on the word. "I'll tell you what I *believed*, Sharpe. I believed the sales pitch. I believed I wanted to *be an American hero*. To defend a country that needed me. But you know what I learned? It's all about money in the end. Always has been. They sent me over there to shoot one brown person in the defense of another while Jews at the top of the food chain and the wetbacks at the bottom sucked away everything my family ever had. I came home to a bankrupt family business, a father who committed suicide, a mother so drowned in alcohol she could barely stand, a shrinking middle class, a country overrun by—"

The thunder of an AK-47 silenced Hoffman in mid-sentence. I automatically dove into a fetal position, covering my head. The noise came from the other side of the table, beneath the floor. Splinters of plywood ricocheted off the ceiling and landed on my side of the table while the rifle just kept going. Fully automatic. A total mag dump.

When at last the Kalashnikov fell silent I lay at the bottom of the conference table, not moving. Footsteps struck the floor from below me, and I pivoted toward the stairwell. I held the rifle at eye level as those footsteps proceeded up the pinewood.

I laid a finger over the trigger. Waiting.

And then Jacquie appeared in the doorframe, wielding a

smoking AK-47 in one hand, her face filthy, her right arm bleeding from a bullet graze. She looked like something out of a nightmare, her upper lip curled in a frozen snarl of disgust.

I stood slowly, keeping the M4 clamped into my shoulder as I pivoted to look over the upturned table—already knowing what I would find.

Hoffman lay spreadeagled on the floor, half his body hanging out from behind the kitchenette. Absolutely riddled with 7.62 slugs.

Jacquie said, "Man, I was sick of hearing him talk."

57

As soon as my senses returned, I moved to the windows overlooking the front yard and swept the muzzle of my M4 across the parked cars. The Boss Mustang leaned to one side, the tires flattened and the windshield blown out. The Dodge's bed was bullet ridden also. The Mercury seemed okay.

I detected no sign of human life.

"Your family?" I asked, looking over my shoulder.

"They're fine," Jacquie said. "Jeremiah took a bullet to his calf. I've already stopped the bleeding. He'll make it."

Her gaze broke from mine and drifted back to Hoffman. She stared at the body with a lifeless emptiness in her eyes that I'd seen so many times before—a dull sort of shock mixed with stunned acceptance.

I knew what that look meant. Jacquie had crossed a threshold. She'd killed people before, sure. But always under the umbrella of a badge and a uniform. She'd never spilled blood in the capacity of a civilian...or a vigilante...or whatever we were.

For myself, I'd crossed that threshold years ago, and it wasn't as glamorous as it looks in the movies. In real life it tastes as bitter as it feels.

"Good job, Jacquie," I said. She turned away and wiped her eyes. I departed the window and surveyed a pile of fallen books, laptops, and documents spread across the floor. They'd spilled off the table when I tipped it over. Many of them were soaked in blood or blown apart by bullets. The electronics would be locked, no doubt. The notepads and books told the story, however. Alt right material, all of it. Litanies of manifestos written by crazed extremists from half a dozen countries. The works of Adolf Hitler himself.

Madness.

I kicked through the mess, thinking what a treasure trove it would be for Feldon. More than enough to shoot him back to the top. Maybe enough to catapult him onto every talk show and news room in America.

Perhaps that was a good thing. Maybe Feldon's glory could be my exit. But something still didn't feel right. Something about the hate-saturated tirade, the extremist paraphernalia, and Hoffman's scoffing didn't mesh with the picture as I knew it.

I was starting to think that Jacquie had been right. There was a bigger picture here. Something *else.*

But what?

"Let's search the place before we call Feldon," I said. "You dig through this slop. I'll take the pole barn."

Jacquie nodded a little dumbly. I thought she was still in some level of shock, which was why I wanted her inside. There were bodies, sure, but I wasn't worried about booby traps.

I had no idea what to expect in the pole barn.

"One piece at a time, right?" I offered a smile.

Jacquie seemed to collect herself, pushing sweaty hair out of her face. Then she started toward the pile of documents spilled off the table. I took the stairs, M4 riding at my side, a fresh mag collected from a body along the way. Switching my weapon light on, I found Jeremiah and Lucile seated next to the bullet-ridden SUV. Jacquie had done a nice job with Jeremiah's leg, but the agony in his face was evident.

"What happened to your heater?" I asked, a little humor in my tone.

Jeremiah's eyes dropped. "I forgot to load it."

I gave his shoulder a squeeze. Lucile's face was still damp with tears, but she'd stopped crying. She whispered a nearly silent "Thank you," and I simply nodded.

Then I was headed into the pole barn through the open rolling door. The stacks of crates I'd seen before, each stamped with *US Army,* remained just inside, although many of them were now splintered by bullets. One had slid off the stack and landed on its end. The lid had come off.

The inside was...empty.

I used the weapon light to illuminate the interior. All the hallmarks of small-arms shipping were there. Dirty wood shavings. The smell of gun oil. But not the rifles themselves.

I approached another crate. The lid lifted easily, the nails already removed. The interior was empty. So was the third crate. And the fourth. I worked all the way to number ten before giving up, and I had yet to locate a single M4 rifle. I thought back to the truck departing the pole barn and could only think of one possible solution.

The rifles had just left. They were en route to rendezvous with the cartel. That would be another nugget to pass off to

Feldon just as soon as I figured out how to wriggle my way out of his grasp.

Turning away from the crates, I felt my nostrils flex as an acrid odor flooded them. It was faint at first but grew stronger as I journeyed deeper into the barn. It was...acidic. A little like ammonia. It smelled like...

Urine. Like the storm shelter where Jacquie had been kept. I attempted to hold my breath as the weapon light passed across an open concrete space coated in a fine dust, like orange snow. I kicked the toe of my boot through it, squinting again. Confused.

The rest of the room was nearly empty, except for a giant fuel tank parked against the back wall. The tank was marked as diesel fuel, which was also confusing, because other than Hoffman's truck, none of the ABA vehicles I'd seen burned diesel.

I glanced over my shoulder to the opening of the barn. Nobody was there, but a cold tingle ran up my spine. I squinted back at the floor, studying that fine orange powder. I knelt and the smell of urine intensified. Dipping a hand, I scooped up a little of the powder and ground it between my fingers. A faint cut running the length of my trigger finger burned immediately. I lifted the hand to my nostrils and sniffed.

Reality struck the moment that acrid odor flooded my nostrils. The memory, recently confused by the urine smell in the storm shelter, finally clicked. I blinked and I was back in Afghanistan. Deep in the mountains. Kneeling on the floor of a Taliban bomb facility where IEDs that sent soldiers home in body bags were manufactured by the dozens.

I'd smelled the same odor then. Not urine. Not ammonia —at least, not raw ammonia. It was ammonium nitrate, a common agricultural fertilizer, and when mixed with fuel oil...

My gaze snapped to the diesel drum parked against the wall. My blood ran cold. I rushed to the drum, rapping against its side with one hand.

The drum rang hollow, not a hint of liquid sloshing inside. Three, maybe four hundred gallons in size. And it was bone dry.

No.

"Mason!" Jacquie's voice broke from the back door of the house. I met her at the entrance of the barn, right at the pile of empty rifle crates. Suddenly, they made perfect sense— and so did the truck.

"*Fort Smith,*" Jacquie gasped. "The migrant camp the feds built! There are notebooks chock-full of details about it. News stories. Maps. Look at this."

Jacquie shoved a document into my hands. It was a map, drawn in crude pencil by an unsteady hand. What exactly it depicted might have been a mystery. It could have been a rough sketch of a corn field or an amusement park or a zoo. Random circles, dashed lines, little squares.

But the label at the bottom gave reality to the entire picture. It read *MIGRANT CAMP*, and circled in bold lines was a large X. Right at the heart near a notation that read *LOADING DOCK*.

My gaze snapped up. Jacquie's eyes were wide.

"You don't think..." she said.

I didn't answer. I simply ran past her, headed for the front of the house.

"Come on!" I shouted.

"Wait. What about them?"

"We'll call an ambulance," I said. "Let's move!"

Jacquie followed me to the front yard. I selected the Cougar because it was the least banged up. The keys hung from the ignition and the engine howled to life with the whine of a supercharger. It was modified. The gas tank was half full. I grabbed a T-handle shifter and ratcheted it into first gear as Jacquie slammed her door.

"Where are we going?" she demanded. "What did I miss?"

"The *truck*, Jacquie. The one that left here just as we arrived."

"What about it?"

I found the washed-out roadbed and stomped the gas. The Cougar surged, rocks and dirt pinging against the wheel wells.

"That pole barn was full of ammonium nitrate fertilizer," I said. "And *diesel fuel*."

Jacquie squinted. Then her mouth fell open. "Oklahoma City."

I nodded. "There was something else, just like you said. They used the rifle sales to fund a fuel oil bomb—a giant one. They loaded it into that truck."

Jacquie finished my thought: "And it's headed for the migrant camp."

58

I had no cell signal as we returned to the two-lane. The CB radio mounted beneath the dash of the Cougar matched that in the Pontiac, and it would be useless in radioing any help. The only people likely to hear us would be more skinheads, or possibly some corrupt cops. We needed the feds—all of them, as fast as possible.

"How far to Fort Smith?" I said.

Jacquie clung to her arm rest as I powered the car around tight curves in the mountain roads. The digital compass built into the Mercury's aftermarket rearview mirror pointed in a generally westward direction. I knew that Fort Smith lay on the Arkansas/Oklahoma border, which meant we must be headed toward it.

But I couldn't be sure how much time had passed between the departure of the truck and the moment when I realized what that truck contained. How much of a lead the Aryans already had.

"Two hundred miles?" Jacquie said. "I don't know."

An edge of desperation coursed through Jacquie's voice as she answered. I pulled into another corner and was forced to slam on the brakes as an oncoming car laid on its horn. I was riding the double yellow line, swinging wide. I yanked the Cougar back onto my side, losing my lefthand mirror against the edge of the oncoming truck. I punched the gas and kept going.

"Get directions," I said.

"I'm still waiting for sig—wait. I've got some bars!"

Jacquie punched at the burner phone, fighting with the GPS. She input the address and waited for it to load. The icon spun and spun. I tracked it out of the corner of my eye.

At last a route was generated. Jacquie sat bolt upright.

"You want Highway 62 to Mountain Home. Right in half a mile!"

I dumped on my accelerator and the nose of the Cougar rose off the pavement. The car ran hard, supercharger whining, wind blasting through the gun-shot passenger-side window. Signs displayed the oncoming intersection with US Highway 62. I guided the car down the hill as Jacquie completed an emergency call for Lucile and Jeremiah's ambulance.

"Call Feldon!" I said. "His number is—"

"I know his number," Jacquie growled. She punched into the phone. We hit the highway and the Cougar howled like the big cat it was named for.

"Feldon?" Jacquie shouted. "It's Jacquie Richardson. *Remember me?*"

There was more than a little venom in her voice. Feldon must have remembered her. Jacquie cut him off.

"Shut up and listen. These skinheads built a *bomb*. They

—" Jacquie gritted her teeth. "Don't worry about how I know. *Do your job* for once. They've loaded it into a truck and they're carting it to Fort Smith as we speak...yes. Fort Smith, Arkansas, where they built that migrant camp. We're talking two hours tops before this thing arrives. It's just like the Oklahoma City bomb, ammonium nitrate fertilizer and diesel fuel. Enough to kill a few thousand people."

Jacquie looked at me as she said it, and the words sank in.

A *few thousand people.* But not just any people. Some of the people Hoffman professed to hate the most. Some of those thousands streaming across the southern border, fleeing collapsing economies in hope of a better life. Men out of work. Women with small children.

Families.

Feldon must have repeated a question because Jacquie sat up. She squinted. Shook her head.

"I'm not...I don't know." She looked to me. "Do you remember what kind of truck it was?"

I thought back to the moment the truck had left the compound. It was dark, only illuminated by the overhead security lights mounted outside the pole barn. I couldn't be sure, but I thought the truck was white. I knew it was old. A day cab, used for local deliveries.

I focused on the image and thought I saw a bar crossing the grill of the truck, top right to bottom left.

"It was a Volvo day cab," I said. "Short trailer. Like one of those tandem trailers a shipping company uses, but only one of them."

Jacquie relayed the information to Feldon. A brief pause. Then: "Are you kidding me? We'll stand down when this is finished. Put a chopper in the air!"

She hung up. "Swine!"

"He wants the glory," I said. "All of it."

I swerved into the fast lane and found forth gear. The accelerator bottomed out against the floorboard. The tachometer spiked. We hit one hundred miles per hour and screamed west toward Fort Smith.

59

Traffic along US 62 was sparse. Gentle hills rose and fell, driving the air from my lungs each time we crested a rise, but there were few curves. Few trucks. Few causes for me to decrease speed at all.

I've never been particularly good at math, but this math was simple. The truck had a forty-five-minute head start. Call it an hour for simple numbers. Assuming a speed of sixty miles per hour, that gave the bomb crew a sixty-mile lead, give or take.

At one hundred miles per hour our differential was forty miles per hour. So, we needed exactly one and a half hours to overtake it.

Assuming they didn't increase speed, select an alternate route, or pull off the highway altogether for a midnight meal, allowing us to blaze past. There was one differential but a thousand possible variables. None of them mattered. I kept my foot on the floor and burned rubber toward Fort Smith.

Feldon called back twenty minutes later. He was deploying one ground team out of Little Rock and a secondary team out of Tulsa. Each team was about two hours out, meaning their chances of reaching the migrant camp ahead of the truck were roughly equal to the flip of a coin. Meanwhile a separate bomb crew would be circling in from the northeast, driving more directly toward the camp. Giving them a slight edge.

"What about helicopters?" Jacquie demanded. "Where are your birds?"

Brief pause. Jacquie's face contorted into a scowl. "Are you kidding me?"

She hung up. "They can't find their pilots."

Of course they can't.

"What about the state troopers? They should have a chopper."

"He's working on it."

Not fast enough.

With a crisis like this Feldon should be ringing every phone of every law enforcement and military agency across the region. Not just police and three-letter colleagues, but the National Guard. A truckload of fuel oil explosives would be no match for an Army AH-64 loaded with hellfire rockets, or an Air National Guard F-16 with an air-to-ground missile.

But Feldon wouldn't call the National Guard. Not only because it would be almost impossible to convince them to fire on a civilian vehicle based on the word of unproven intelligence, but because a split mission meant split glory.

No. The troopers might provide a chopper or they might not. Regardless, two vigilantes in an antique Mercury were still the best shot at overtaking that truck.

Jacquie was better at math than me. She tracked the shrinking gap between the Cougar and its prey in real time, counting down the miles. Wind beat through her shattered window, but she didn't seem to notice. I hauled us around another bend and roared through a rural intersection, narrowly avoiding a collision with a passing van.

"We're down to ten miles," Jacquie reported. "Check every truck."

I didn't need to be told. With each semi-truck we passed I relaxed off the gas just long enough to inspect the make and model. A couple were Volvos. One hauled a flatbed and the other a car hauler. Both were too new to be the truck from the compound, and neither of them were day cabs. I punched the gas and hurtled over the next rise. We had just cleared the town of Harrison and were passing north of the Boston Mountains. The terrain was so dark I couldn't see more than a few yards off the highway, but I thought it consisted of fields leading gradually into foothills. I slowed to take a sweeping turn toward Alpena. The car chugged and the fuel gauge bobbed just above empty.

We'd blown through gas exactly as quickly as I would have expected driving a modified, oversized engine at three-digit speeds. If we didn't overtake the truck soon, we'd be forced to pull off for fuel.

Please, not now.

The dim headlights of the old car paved a path ahead—fifty yards, not more. Open blackness spilled beneath the crest of the hill. The pavement rose, and the Cougar powered up it.

We reached the top at a hundred miles per hour. My stomach convulsed. We nosed down again and screamed into the next valley. I could see for a mile ahead, nothing but an empty expanse of four-lane with fields stretching to either side.

And four red dots outlining the taillights of a semi-truck

trailer chugging directly ahead. I knew it was our target even with half a mile of space between us. Call it instinct, or just raw intuition. I slammed on the accelerator to squeeze another ten miles per hour out of the car, knowing we were ready to pounce. Jacquie knew it also—she reached for her rifle. The gap between us shrank. I identified an orange logo on the rolling back door of the truck. A gleaming white license plate that was still too far away to read, but I knew. This was it.

I looked to the Mercury's dash. The fuel gauge rested fully on E.

60

"Call it in!"

I downshifted and swerved into the left lane. One steady yard at a time, we closed on the truck. Jacquie placed the call to Feldon and notified him of the mile marker. She hung up and replaced the phone with the rifle.

"They've got a chopper, but it's twenty minutes out."

Of course it is.

The truck was barely a quarter-mile distant. It vanished for a moment beyond a hill, and my headlights flashed over a green sign that read:

ALPENA — 7 MILES.

"We've got to take it before it reaches the next town," I said. "We can't risk a vengeful detonation if this guy gets backed into a corner. I'll get in close on the lefthand side. We'll aim for the driver."

Jacquie shouldered the rifle. Then she looked back at

me. "Wait. Is a fuel oil bomb a high explosive or a low explosive?"

I gripped the wheel, knowing what Jacquie was thinking.

"Low explosive," I said. "Aim carefully."

Jacquie's lips pressed into a hard line. She poked the M4 through her window and leaned her head into the stock. I focused on the truck, rehearsing in my mind everything I'd ever learned about improvised explosives—mostly in Afghanistan.

People think that the term "high explosive" has to do with the destructive potential of a given bomb, but that's not the case. A high explosive is an explosive that requires a detonator to be set off. Their destructive potential is extreme, but without the detonator they're usually stable. You can hurl a wad of C4. You can set it on fire with a cigarette lighter. It won't explode.

Low explosives are entirely different. They don't detonate, they deflagrate. They burn, very rapidly, producing copious amounts of expanding gas. They can be just as destructive as high explosives, and they aren't nearly as stable. A spark from grinding metal, muzzle flash from a nearby weapon, a sudden crash as the truck veered off the highway...

Any of those things might set the bomb off. It wasn't predictable. It wasn't safe.

It was one giant improvised explosive device.

"Whatever happens we've got to keep that truck on the road," I said. "There's no telling what happens if it hits the ditch. Don't fire until I give the signal!"

Jacquie settled in behind her rifle's Aimpoint. I mashed the gas and closed to within a hundred yards of the trailer. I could see the license plate. It was an Arkansas commercial plate. The rear bumper of the trailer was rusted and mangled. The tires sung and the trailer shuddered.

The driver had accelerated. Had he seen us?

He would soon enough.

I pulled alongside and noted how the trailer shuddered over every bump in the road. It moved heavily, like an overloaded car. The bare walls of the box bore half of a shipping company logo, faded and ripped. The truck itself surged at nearly seventy miles per hour, engine straining as we hit the bottom of the next hill.

"Here we go!" I said.

Scooping the CB radio from beneath the dash, I hit the call button.

"Breaker, breaker, this is the Arkansas State Police hailing white van body Volvo. Pick up!"

The radio crackled and fell silent. I'd relaxed off the accelerator, gaining on the truck by a yard every five or six seconds. I could see the sideview mirrors but couldn't see a face. Everything was black. I hit the call button again and waited. I thought I saw movement in the mirror.

Still, no answer. Maybe I had the wrong channel. I looked to the dash and noted the fuel needle resting on its lower peg. There was no low fuel light—not on a car this old. I didn't need one. I knew I had minutes. Maybe seconds.

"I'm pulling alongside." I slung the radio down and hit the gas. We closed on the truck's cab just as we topped the hill. Looking through the busted window I saw faded white paint and the peeling sticker of an Arkansas trucking company.

Then I saw the driver. He was white and heavy set. Middle aged, a ball cap kicked back on his head. He looked down at the muzzle of the M4 staring up at him and didn't so much as flinch—he actually hardened, face pinching into a scowl.

I keyed the CB handset. The trucker's ceiling-mounted radio flashed as soon as my transmission began. I knew he heard me.

"Stop the truck or we will fire on you!"

The trucker snatched up his handset and barked, *"Get back!"*

"We're not going anywhere. Stop the truck or we'll shoot!"

He didn't stop the truck. Instead, he swerved. The nose of the heavy day cab shot toward us and my reflexes kicked in. I yanked the Mercury to the left on instinct, smashing the brake and only narrowly missing a collision with his whirring front wheel. We dropped back fifty feet before I could find the gas pedal, and when I punched it I thought I felt a cough in the engine. A slight hesitation.

No. Not now.

"Get me close!" Jacquie shouted. "I'm going out!"

"What?" I turned to see Jacquie pulling herself through the blown-out passenger's window, rifle grasped in one hand, her other gripping the car's roof. She sat on the door frame even as I accelerated. I grabbed her leg and tugged.

"Get back in here! We'll blow his tires!"

"If we blow those tires we'll blow everything! Shut up and get me to the running boards."

I knew she was right. Even now, the deadly concoction of diesel fuel and ammonium fertilizer could be sloshing inside the back of the truck. Heating up. One spark away from complete detonation.

Looking ahead, I saw a dull glow about three miles away, just over the next hill. Soft yellow illumination reflected by dark clouds—the ambient light of a city, drawing ever nearer.

No other choice.

I released Jacquie's leg and floored the Mercury. It coughed again but it surged ahead.

One final sprint.

61

W e reached the day cab's running boards just as the Mercury finally ran out of gas. There was a chrome handrail mounted just behind the Volvo's door, running vertically along the exhaust manifold. Jacquie released the hood of the Mercury and grabbed the railing just as the nose of the car slumped. The engine coughed and the tachometer died. In a flash we dropped from seventy miles per hour to under sixty, and Jacquie's legs vanished through the shattered window as though she'd been yanked out by a giant. The truck raced ahead. The trailer flashed by. I saw the M4 fly out of Jacquie's grip as she fought to find a foothold on the truck's running board.

Then I saw muzzle flash. Blazing from the truck's window, three quick shots. We reached the crest of a hill and the truck raced into the valley while the Mercury simply stopped.

Maddened adrenaline pumped into my veins and I pounded my foot against the accelerator. Three plunges to prime the carburetor, then I hit the ignition.

"Come on, baby. *Run!*"

The Mercury didn't run. It threatened to start, then simply went silent. I yanked the door handle and erupted onto the blacktop. The Cougar sat balanced right at the top of a hill, and with the aid of the Aimpoint magnifier I looked into the valley below. The glow of Alpena lit the sky, maybe two miles distant.

And the truck hurtled on, tail lights bouncing as it swerved. I thought I saw muzzle flash again, but I couldn't be sure. I couldn't see Jacquie or the driver. I couldn't tell if the truck had slowed. I couldn't hear its engine through my still-ringing ears.

But I could hear a siren. It screamed from someplace behind me, and when I turned I saw blue lights racing toward me.

I stepped automatically into the middle of the road and clicked my weapon light into strobe mode. It flashed into the eyes of the oncoming cop—I couldn't tell whether it was a trooper or a sheriff's deputy or Mark Feldon himself. The car laid on both its horn and its brakes. I moved to the side just as the vehicle screamed to a stop. It was a white Dodge Challenger with a blue star on the door—an Arkansas State Trooper. I advanced to the passenger door, rifle pointed at the ground, and snatched it open.

Inside the patrol car a single cop flailed for his sidearm. He couldn't reach it around his seatbelt. I ignored him, piling in and slamming the door.

"What the—"

"*Drive!*" I shouted. "Bomb is that way!"

The trooper's face washed white, and I smacked him on the arm. "*Go!*"

That shook him out of it. The back tires of the Charger

spun. Then we were hurtling down the hill. Engine surging. Cop panting. His radio barking as dispatch updated him on the ETA of an approaching helicopter—coordination with the ATF.

All things that wouldn't matter in the next five minutes if that truck reached civilization and the driver chose violence.

"Who are you?" the trooper choked. His voice was young and shrill. I looked his way and found a pimply face that I would have carded if I were a cashier at a liquor store. He couldn't be more than twenty-two. Fresh out of the academy. His uniform was crisp and perfectly pressed. Sweat streamed down his face. His pistol hung halfway out of its holster.

He was brand spanking new—and a good thing, too. A veteran cop would have had his doors locked. He wouldn't have stopped, either. Not for a random guy with a rifle.

"You see that truck?" I shouted. "That's a *bomb.*"

He paled. I ran the passenger's side window down. The rifle banged into the glovebox as I lifted it toward the roaring wind outside the car.

"Get us close!" I said.

The trooper seemed to have descended into mental deadlock. He was overwhelmed. I couldn't blame him. I was overwhelmed also.

But I was zeroed in on the truck, half a mile ahead. A mile outside of the glow of Alpena. Taillights marked its path as the rear end jerked sideways. It was swerving again. I thought I heard a gunshot. The trooper was barking into his radio. The Charger had reached ninety miles an hour and was still gaining speed.

I braced the M4 over the car's sideview mirror. "Left lane!" I shouted.

"What?"

"*Move left!*"

He moved. I pressed my cheek against the stock and clamped my left eye closed. The Aimpoint magnifier painted a clear view of the truck, now five, maybe six hundred yards distant. A half mile from the outskirts of Alpena. I saw a truck stop sign and motel neon.

I was officially out of time.

Centering the red dot over the rear tires, I rested my finger over the trigger. I thought of Jacquie, and I almost couldn't press. I didn't want to press. I didn't have any other choice *but* to press.

Next to me, the trooper prayed out loud. I stopped breathing. The world stopped spinning. I began the squeeze.

Then the truck jerked. Not a swerve, not a jolt, but a hard jackknife. The nose of the Volvo swerved into the lefthand lane, but the trailer hurtled onward. Tires screamed and brakes locked. The trailer fishtailed and I relaxed off the trigger.

No, no, no...

It was too late. The truck flipped. The trailer tore the semi cab sideways and the whole unit slammed into the asphalt, still hurtling onward. Sparks exploded from the roadbed and the back doors of the box trailer burst open. Barrels came tumbling out. I grabbed the trooper by the arm.

"*Brakes!*"

He didn't need to be told. The nose of the Charger dove.

Then the truck went up. One white-hot flash of fire, followed by a thunderclap so loud I felt the concussion in my chest. The horizon illuminated in brilliant red fire and the shockwave ripped down the highway like a nuclear blast.

The front of the Charger lifted straight off the road and then we were spinning like a child's toy, headed straight into the ditch.

62

The patrol car bit Arkansas soil with a crunch of metal and an explosion of glass. All the airbags detonated. I face-planted into the one shooting out of the glovebox, then I was slamming backward into the seat. We rolled. Dirt blasted through the windows and I choked. The M4 dug into my ribcage and the trooper shouted.

Somehow, right amid the chaos, I heard dispatch radioing an update on the chopper—five minutes out. SWAT team on board.

The Charger landed on its wheels with a thud, a cloud of dirt illuminated by bright orange flame. I was trapped between airbags and a semi-collapsed roof. Everything was hazy. My mind buzzed.

I swept my arm across the dash and collided with my rifle. The muzzle was bent like a soda straw. Then I felt fabric. An arm.

And lots of blood.

"Can you hear me?" I choked on the words and clawed the airbag away from my face. I found the trooper resting in his seat, panting and streaming blood from his right arm. It was riddled with glass, but I could already tell that no artery had been cut. Blood was seeping, not spurting.

"Hey!" I grabbed his shoulder. The trooper looked toward me, mouth hanging open.

"You good?" I asked.

He blinked. Looked to his arm. Then he nodded.

"I...I think so."

Jacquie.

It was the only thought left. The only thing that mattered.

I fought with my seatbelt for only a moment before digging my hand into the trooper's glovebox in search of a seatbelt cutter. I found a box cutter first, and that was good enough. I sliced the belt and slammed my elbow into the Charger's door. It took effort to force it open. The whole body was crunched together. Hinges groaned and I managed only an eighteen-inch gap.

I fought my way through, staggering out and almost toppling. I steadied myself against the roof of the car and turned to look.

It was fire. Nothing but fire. It burned across what once had been a four-lane highway. Now there was a crater a hundred yards wide and stocked with chunks of busted asphalt and shredded metal. Flames gathered near the cab of the semi-truck, which was little more than a hulk of obliterated metal. The trailer was absolutely gone. I tasted ammonia and diesel fuel, a smog so thick it burned my throat.

And I didn't see Jacquie—not anywhere.

"*Jacquie!*" I nearly fell climbing out of the ditch. I regained my footing and forced myself onward, screaming again. My vision blurred and hot tears dripped down my cheeks. The desperation was all there, but it was aimless. I could hurtle ahead and throw myself into the fire, and it wouldn't mean anything. If Jacquie had been on that truck when the bomb detonated...

No.

I threw myself ahead anyway. I broke into an unstable run toward the crater, closing a five-hundred-yard gap like a snail fighting its way up a hill. Everything was slow motion. The heat grew on my face but I didn't seem any closer. I drew to within a hundred yards of the bomb site and heard the pound of a helicopter from someplace behind me, closing fast.

It was too hot to go any farther. The hair on my arms singed and I staggered to a stop. I could see into the bottom of the crater and there was...nothing. Just dirt, ash, and obliterated asphalt. Emptiness.

No Jacquie.

I choked, a slow, aching misery descending through my chest worse than anything I'd felt since the last time I'd stood in this position. Just moments too late. Watching somebody I treasured snatched away—

"Mason!"

The voice coughed, so soft I thought I imagined it. I blinked and squinted into the smoke. I wanted to answer but was unable to voice a shout beyond the lump in my throat.

It was just a hallucination. A desperate trick of my shattered mind.

"Behind you, idiot!"

I looked over my shoulder. Now I was sure I wasn't imagining it. The space behind me was clogged by smoke too dense to see. But I heard the breathing. I knew that voice.

I hurried back the way I'd come. Through the smoke and to the edge of the highway, even as the helicopter hovered overhead and blue lights appeared from every side. Sirens screaming. A bullhorn blaring.

But there was only one sound I cared about. That rasping breath, that weakened voice. I broke through the smoke and found Jacquie lying on her back in the ditch, one arm held over her lap, one side of her face swollen with an ugly burn. Tears streamed from her eyes and half of her hair was singed away. Her shirt was torn. Her mouth was full of grit, blood streaming from a jagged bullet graze on her neck.

Yet she was alive. I struck the mud on both knees and scooped her little body off the ground. My vision blurred as hot tears bubbled from my eyes. I didn't care. I barely even noticed. I clung to her and squeezed until Jacquie coughed. She shoved me with the palm of her good hand.

"Enough already!"

I relaxed, giving her room to breathe. Jacquie's dark eyes were rimmed by red, but she was smiling. A beautiful, filthy smile.

"Are you okay?" I managed.

Jacquie laughed. "Pretty sure I busted my ass."

63

It turned out that Jacquie had busted her ass—quite literally. Her tail bone was broken, the result of flying off the truck and landing on the pavement only moments before the driver lost complete control. Jacquie's right arm was broken also, in two places. She'd lost blood from the bullet graze and she had a concussion.

But she was alive, having just reached shelter in the highway ditch before the truck detonated three hundred yards away. Even the brand-new pair of silver bracelets affixed to my wrists couldn't shake the joy of that reality. I was bottled up into the back of a state trooper car while Jacquie was carted away in an ambulance, and I didn't even care. I fell contentedly asleep while first responders scurried around like ants out of a smashed anthill. There were sirens. There were flashing lights and multiple helicopters.

I tuned it all out and didn't awake until they hauled me out of the car and into the police station at Harrison, Arkansas—the nearest city on our side of the bomb crater. There I was processed, put into a holding cell, offered medical and water. I declined a lawyer, but I took my phone call. It was a long call. Nearly ten minutes. When I hung up, I knew I was likely in just as much trouble as before I dialed. I was going out on a limb—rolling the dice with my life on the line. If my mental math was off, even by a degree, I was very likely headed to jail for kidnapping, murder, vehicle theft, and assault of a law enforcement officer. Plus whatever other high crimes and misdemeanors I'd already dismissed from my memory.

But I didn't think I was wrong. The more I considered it, the better I liked my odds.

Special Agent Mark Feldon visited me seven hours after my arrival at Harrison. The local moved me into an interview room upon his arrival. It wasn't like a room in the movies. There was no two-way mirror or steel table. Just a pair of metal chairs, and a single folding plastic table.

I sipped water with cuffed hands for another half an hour. Then, at last, Feldon appeared. He was dirty and smelled of smoke. His face was smudged with soot. He looked like he hadn't slept in weeks.

But despite all that, he was smiling. It wasn't a kind smile.

Feldon settled into the seat opposite me and cracked open a can of Coca-Cola. He slurped a long swallow and sighed with the theatric satisfaction of a soft drink salesman. Then Feldon dug into a briefcase. He produced a digital voice recorder and turned it on, but didn't mash the record button. He spread out a legal pad and produced a pen. The pen clicked open, then closed. Clicked open, then closed.

Feldon kept smiling. But he didn't speak.

I smiled back—not only because I was familiar with this

game, but because it worked both ways. After five long minutes Feldon finally broke, just the way I knew he would.

"We'll dig into the sordid history of your vigilante behavior in just a moment, Mr. Sharpe. But before I turn on that recorder...I've just got to say. *Thank you.*"

With that Feldon commenced to slow-clap like a true cartoon villain, grinning ear to ear. I remained silent and drank my water, indulging in a satisfied sigh of my own.

"I guess I can assume you're going to renege on our bargain," I said.

"Bargain?"

"You know, the deal we made where I bring you this mess on a silver platter, and you whitewash my legal difficulties."

"Oh, right." Feldon tapped his chin with the pen. Squinted. Then shook his head. "You know, I feel like we made that deal before. The deal where I take the glory and you walk away, and it didn't work out for me. Kinda left me holding the bag, as it were. Pretty much got me fired."

"But now you're back on top," I said. "A rocket-ship ride to whatever job you want. After all, you just foiled a terrorist attack. Saved a few hundred, maybe a few thousand lives."

"Ah, that I did. Just in the nick of time, too. But the thing is, Mr. Sharpe...that's a flexible narrative. The what, when, and where of it all are a little...vague. I wouldn't want any confusion. And frankly, the only thing that would make me happier than a cushy job way up the food chain is knowing that you're bottled up in some bleak hole alongside toothless drug smackers and child predators for the next decade. So... yeah. I'm gonna renege."

The grin returned. The pen clicked. I said nothing. I didn't stop smiling. I waited, knowing Feldon would break again. This time it took a lot less than five minutes. His grin melted and he mashed the record button.

"Okay, champ. Let's cut to the chase. There's a dead man in Evergreen and witnesses report that his killer subsequently stole his vehicle. Did you kill Wesley Shiver?"

I didn't answer. Feldon marched on.

"Sheriff Conroy of the Mullins County Sheriff's Department reports that he was assaulted by a clothes iron. He accuses you. What do you have to say about that?"

No answer. A vein flexed in Feldon's neck. His voice dropped in irritation.

"You won't help yourself by playing hardball. I've got enough to bury you. You better start talking."

This time I chuckled—because Feldon had used the exact same threat in Atlanta. What was more, I knew by the flush rising slowly up his neck that emotions were getting the best of him.

It was time.

"You know," I said. "It's funny you mention the business at the hotel. That thing with Shiver and Conroy. It's a crazy coincidence, wouldn't you say? Having them find me so quickly. It's almost as if somebody told them were I was."

Feldon leaned back. He folded his arms. His face was perfectly blank, but I knew it was a façade.

"I guess it leaves me thinking," I continued. "There's still a piece missing."

I waited, and Feldon's curiosity merged with his irritation to generate a bad decision. He surrendered the initiative.

"And what's that, Mr. Sharpe?"

"It's just this whole business of the arms deal. All those rifles flowing out of Fort Crowder. According to you, the first tip-off of a smuggling operation came through Cyrus

Richardson. I guess he saw rifles disappearing off base and put two and two together. Thought something might be up."

Feldon squinted. He didn't answer.

"But how could that happen?" I continued. "I spoke with the MP commander at Crowder, and he said that Cyrus never cleaned the warehouses facilities where the guns were broken down. Contractors did that—for security. Cyrus only cleaned offices, and it wasn't like he was poking around on any computers. Even if he saw a truckload of rifles headed for the gate...why should he think twice? It's a military base. Guns are everywhere."

Feldon's body tensed—just a little. I detected it in his next breath, which was shallower than the last.

I kept going.

"It just got me thinking. The machinations of a military base are complicated. Even for a guy like me, with a long Army career. I needed to ask an MP just to understand what Crowder's mission was. I can't imagine that a guy like Cyrus, smart as he was, would have known what to look for...unless, of course, *somebody told him*."

Feldon didn't budge. I leaned across the table and lowered my voice.

"It was you, wasn't it? From the very start. You didn't just connect Cyrus with Captain Thornton, you connected Thornton with the Aryan Brotherhood Army. With that many rifles being shipped into Fort Crowder to be destroyed, there's *no way* the local ATF office wasn't notified. It's standard procedure. Weapons have gone missing before. So you knew about the potential for a massive smuggling operation—the kind of thing that could restore a career. With a little sniffing around, you also found yourself a local criminal organization who might be interested in participating. I'm guessing you dropped them some tips. Maybe you pulled some personnel files from Fort Crowder and found yourself a weak link. A guy like Greg Thornton who was way overdue for a promotion, and angry about it. Disillusioned with military service and sympathetic to alt-right extremism. So you passed Thornton's name along to the ABA...anonymously, of course. A chance encounter at a coffee shop was arranged. The wheels were in motion. Pretty soon, the rifles were moving. You had your dream scenario in the making...the ultimate bust. Career rocket fuel."

I stopped. Feldon hadn't so much as blinked during my entire monologue. He was rock still.

I leaned back. nodding. "Yeah...that's what you did. But of course, you couldn't report your own crime. You needed a hapless third party to do that for you. Somebody who could feed you intelligence without stealing any of the credit for the eventual bust. Somebody like...a janitor, say. Like Cyrus Richardson. So you got him on the phone. You told him his country needed him. That if he poked around for you, he could be a national hero. You told him where to look and what to document, and he got it done. But you didn't act on the intelligence. Not yet. That's because at some point along the way, you discovered that the ABA was stockpiling the rifles, planning for a big sale to a Mexican cartel. Why not wait until the sale was primed and ready to go? I mean, a bust like *that*...talk about a headline. So you stalled. Cyrus was killed. You needed another pawn. Jacquie turned up at the funeral. You used her. Then she disappeared and you were up the creek without a paddle again. But then I showed up. Like a golden ticket falling right into your crosshairs. An even better tool than the first two."

I shook my head, almost as though I were impressed.

Feldon finally blinked but he didn't look away, and he still didn't speak. I was fully in charge of the conversation, and it was time for the kill shot.

"You had me arrested in Little Rock so that you could bring me into your circle. Then you tipped off Shiver and Conroy right after you dropped me in Evergreen because you figured I'd string Shiver up by his thumbs. Find your pie the brutal way."

Feldon's lips pursed. I leaned close and nodded encouragement.

"Come on, Mark. You've landed on top. I screwed up your career and now you're about to screw up the rest of my life. Give me something to keep me awake at night. Tell me what a mastermind you really are."

Feldon's teeth clenched. His facial muscles constricted. I could feel it boiling inside of him, pressing against the limits of his willpower. The desire to disclose his true genius. His checkmate move.

"Tell me," I urged. "You did it, didn't you?"

Feldon reached forward and mashed the power button on the recorder, cutting the device off. His face closed to within inches of mine. His lips spread into a wolfish grin.

"You better believe it."

I laughed. "Just the way I said?"

"Right down to the coffee shop rendezvous. It was a Dunkin' Donuts, actually. I guess you're one heck of an investigator, Mr. Sharpe. Too bad you'll spend the rest of your life rotting in a concrete closet."

"Too bad indeed. But hey...maybe we can be cell mates."

Feldon snorted a laugh. He pocketed his recorder and stood. He turned for the door.

"Oh, Feldon. One other thing."

Feldon stopped. He turned back with the transparent irritation of a father dealing with an attention-hungry child.

"*What?*"

I reached up with my cuffed hands and tugged down the neck of my t-shirt...revealing the microphone taped to my chest.

"State your name for the record?" I asked.

Feldon's face washed pale. The door behind him burst open and two men in cheap government suits marched in. One grabbed him by the elbow and wrenched him around, shoving him against the wall. Before Feldon could say a word his sidearm was removed from his hip. His hands were behind his back. The second agent was looking at me, shaking his head in something between disbelief and admiration.

I rose from the table. The grin faded from my face, the heat returning to my blood. I spoke through my teeth.

"You got a good man killed, you scum. You put a good cop in danger. Risked the lives of a few thousand destitute migrants. Empowered a band of militant thugs. For the rest of your life, every time that door slams behind you, I want you to remember...that's *me*."

Feldon's face flushed, but he didn't answer. He'd already said too much. The government guys spun him around, and then he was gone.

64

I remained an incarcerated guest of the state of Arkansas for the next ten days—first in Harrison, then in Little Rock. Eventually I was transferred to federal custody. They fed me well and gave me a crisp white jumpsuit to wear. I slept a lot and had my injuries tended too. Most were bruises and strained muscles...issues only time would heal.

I wasn't subjected to any further interviews. I didn't consult a lawyer or volunteer any testimony. I simply waited to see what Special Agent Matthews—the FBI agent I contacted with my free phone call—would do next. I estimated that it would take some time before he reached the bottom of Feldon's escapade as the hero of his own villainy. I was right.

On the tenth day Matthews finally arrived. I was transferred out of my cell to an interview room, where I relaxed in an uncomfortable chair and waited for Matthews to arrive.

When he did, he smiled. Not in an approving sort of way, or even in an amused way. It was more like a smile of disbelief—the proverbial "I'm laughing so I don't cry" sort of smile.

The special agent took his chair, dropping a portfolio of documents on the table between us. He loosened his tie and didn't say anything for a while. I waited, prepared for my fate no matter what it might be.

Jacquie was safe. It was worth it.

"I tell you what, Sharpe," Matthews said at last. "You made one unbelievable mess."

I made no comment. Matthews called for coffee, and coffee arrived. He requested the cameras to be turned off. We drank in silence.

At last he said, "As of this morning I'm officially recommending a US attorney to charge Special Agent Feldon," Matthews said. "The list of offenses is as long as my arm. I won't bore you with the details."

"So you found evidence?" I asked.

Matthews and I both knew that Feldon's manipulated confession would hardly stick in a court of law. Feldon could claim that he was being sarcastic. Yanking my chain. With a veritable circus of bad guys to prosecute, Feldon would likely slip away.

But what the confession *could do*—what I desperately needed it to do, if I had any shot at freedom—was incite a hungry dog like Matthews to start digging. Apparently, it had.

"For such a clever guy Feldon was kind of an idiot," Matthews said. "We found emails linking him to both Captain Thornton and the Aryan Brotherhood Army. Anonymous emails, of course. Feldon successfully convinced the ABA that he was Thornton, and Thornton that he was the ABA. He arranged the whole thing without

alerting either one of them to the existence of a third party...
but there was an IP address for those emails. Traced right
back to Feldon's apartment. Then there were communica-
tions he transmitted to Cyrus Richardson. Details that he
couldn't possibly know without being on the inside. Several
other circumstantial things, and we expect to obtain more
hard evidence from Thornton's digital records. It's going to
be a haul."

"You expect to convict?" I asked.

"Absolutely. And I'll crack a beer the day we do. I hate
dirty cops."

I nodded. Drank coffee. My body tensed as the next
logical question boiled in my gut.

"So where does that leave me?"

Matthews sighed, not looking at me. He tapped the
portfolio.

"You, Mr. Sharpe, just might be the luckiest joker I've
ever met. I've got you flagged for half a dozen potential
felonies, but I don't know if I can convict you of any of
them."

"Is that right?"

"Well, let's start with Wesley Shiver—the man you shot
outside that hotel."

"I admitted as much. He was trying to kill me."

"So you say—and so the hotel cameras confirm. We've
already recovered his body from where you left it, and the
forensics all match your narrative. The primary witness to
the crime, Sheriff Conroy, claims that Shiver was a deputy
acting with official police authority, but there's no record of
Shiver ever being formally deputized, so his use of lethal
force was provocative and illegal. That brings us back to the
good sheriff himself, whose nose you flattened with a clothes

iron. It turns out that Conroy is every bit as crooked as Mark Feldon, and even more intertwined with the ABA. The bulk of his department is, as a matter of fact. So we can hardly accept his testimony of your alleged crimes as a kidnapper to hold any water in court."

"What a shame."

"Like I said before. I *hate* dirty cops. So that brings us to the question of the cars you stole—all from criminals who aren't available to press charges. Or the bodies you stacked at that ABA compound in Mullins County. Seven men dead, in total, but I have two credible witnesses who claim to have been held hostage. They state that you and Ms. Richardson killed those men while saving their lives. There's a reasonable argument to be made that their deaths were justifiable."

"A reasonable argument is a powerful thing."

"A jury might think so. I have a similar problem with the death of Captain Thornton. Jacquie Richardson willingly admits that you shot him. But because he held her hostage —and was apparently about to execute her—that shooting was justifiable as well. Curious as it may be that you proceeded to bury the body."

"There are scavengers in Missouri."

"Of all sorts. So at last we come to the matter of the Arkansas State Trooper you manhandled while pursuing that bomb. And let me tell you, I *really* want to charge you for that."

"But you're not going to," I guessed.

"Unfortunately not. It seems that Trooper Allen's testimony is foggy. He's having trouble remembering exactly what happened."

"Stressful situations can be that way."

"They certainly can. As can embarrassing situations.

Allen is a brand-new trooper with a young wife to impress. It's not very impressive to be manhandled by a stranger, or to admit to stopping his car and leaving his doors unlocked."

"Young cops make mistakes."

"And hopefully they never make them again."

Matthews fingered his cup and stared hard at me. I couldn't tell if he was angry or just perplexed. Maybe a mixture of both. I got tired of waiting and went for the throat.

"So what are you going to do, Matthews?"

The special agent flipped the portfolio open. A stapled document lay inside. The seal printed at its top was that of a United States attorney out of Memphis.

"I've spoken with the US attorney in charge of this circus," Matthews said. "He's willing to overlook your questionable actions given the circumstances of your military and police service, and the end result of this investigation. Lives were saved. He has bigger fish to fry. You sign this and you get to walk."

I studied the document. I wasn't fooled. There's always a *but* with attorneys.

"What's the catch?"

"The catch is you must agree to testify, should we wish to call you as a witness. You will promise to stay out of the media limelight. You will fade quietly into the dark and leave us to do our job."

I rocked my head as if I were considering. Matthews breathed a curse and threw me a pen.

"Good grief, Sharpe. Just sign."

65

J acquie picked me up outside the jail in a rental car. She didn't get out. She just sat behind the wheel with one arm in a cast, a burn salve coating her face, and multi-colored bruises covering every square inch of visible skin. When I settled into the passenger seat, she shook her head.

"What?" I said after a few seconds of silence.

"Five days," Jacquie said. "I left you unsupervised in my hometown for five stinking days, and you nearly burned the state down."

I shrugged. "You called for backup."

That brought out the smile. Jacquie slapped the shifter into gear and we hit a donut shop on the way north. We rode in silence, just enjoying the relative calm of being off duty for a change. My body still ached. My head still pounded.

But I'd done a lot of thinking during my time in the slammer. I'd unpacked the puzzle of Feldon, the ABA, and Captain Thornton, identifying two key truths that required my attention.

The first was Jacquie.

"Thank you," I said.

Jacquie was polishing off her third jelly-filled. She wiped her mouth with her good hand and slurped coffee.

"For what?"

"For getting me out of this mess. I know you had a hand in it."

Jacquie shrugged. "I made some phone calls. There *are* good people in the FBI, believe it or not."

"Oh, I believe it. We just don't get along."

"Maybe that's because you're always blowing stuff up."

"No, see, the bomb was *your* fault."

"My fault?" Jacquie's voice cracked in indignation.

"You were the last one on the truck before it toppled."

"So we're just gonna dismiss the culpability of a dozen skinheads?"

"It's a thin blue line, Detective."

Jacquie snorted. I relaxed in my seat. My eyes were half open. I felt a nap coming on and estimated that we had about three hours of drive time remaining.

"So...back to your truck?" Jacquie asked.

"No. We're going to Branson."

"Missouri?" Jacquie's voice edged with surprise.

"One and the same."

"Why on earth?"

"Because Captain Greg Thornton didn't work for free, and somebody owes me for the damage to my truck."

WE REACHED the cabin and were forced to park on the street. The mouth of the winding driveway was blocked with yellow crime scene tape, but there hadn't been any cops on site for a few days. I could tell by the condition of the tire prints in the soft clay, washed out by a recent rainstorm.

Ducking beneath the tape, I enjoyed the crisp mountain air as we started toward the cabin. Jacquie didn't ask any questions. I didn't volunteer any information. My theories about Captain Thornton's payment—that other key observation which required my attention—were paper thin. For all I knew, Thornton had been paid in gold, or with a wire transfer to a Cayman Islands account, or with Bitcoin.

But I didn't think so. This was an old-fashioned deal, conducted by men who appreciated the simplicity of a bygone muscle car era. Those didn't sound like the kind of men who knew anything about Bitcoin.

The cabin itself was also roped off with police tape. So was the now-empty grave at the back of the overgrown yard, which I ignored.

I was interested in the house.

Reaching into our pockets, Jacquie and I produced rubber gloves we'd purchased from a hardware store on the way up. Jacquie only needed one, and she required my help to get it on. I used the butt of my Victorinox to knock the glass out of the back door before reaching through to flip the lock.

It was dark inside. It smelled of mold. I tried the lights, but they didn't work, so I resorted to my MacroStream. The first room was a mudroom, followed by a kitchen and a dining room. The decor was decades old. The dishes faded and dirty. I could tell by the disturbed dust on the floor that the cops had made a passing inspection, but they hadn't honestly searched the house.

Why should they? The body was out back. The story of

how it got there was plainly explained. There was nothing else to look for.

Except, maybe there was.

We split off automatically, fanning around each room with the same practiced rhythm we'd learned as partners back at the PPD. Inspecting furniture, floorboards, and wall panels. Everything was so dusty that it wasn't difficult to dismiss one section after another, tracing the footprints into the largest bedroom at the back of the house where we finally identified marks on the floor at the foot of a queen-sized bed. The large swath of displaced dust could have been caused by a duffel bag, or grocery sacks.

Any of the things Captain Thornton may have stacked here in preparation for a lengthy stay. All that material was already removed, no doubt taken into evidence by the investigators. So what remained?

I checked the closet. Jacquie checked the chest of drawers. We rapped our knuckles against wall panels, but none sounded more hollow than their counterparts. The ceiling was constructed of popcorn drywall, and I detected no cracks, nor fresh spackling. We searched the single bathroom and found the second bedroom completely empty.

I returned to the master bedroom, sweeping the flashlight across it. I could *feel* that I was close, like sonar on a submarine reporting vague but definite contacts from the far side of an underwater mountain range.

Jacquie and I thought of it at the same moment.

"He moved the nightstand," she said.

I focused the MacroStream and noted fresh scuff marks on the hardwood floor. Stepping alongside the chunky piece of furniture, I pushed it with my knee.

It was heavy. It didn't budge. I put the flashlight between my teeth and heaved.

The nightstand scraped back. Even before it was fully out of the way, I felt the shifting floorboards under my feet. I hit my knees and Jacquie closed in next to me. The Victorinox snapped open, and I jammed the blade into a gap between the floorboards.

A single plank popped out. Dust exploded off the floor. The MacroStream blazed into the cavity beneath...

And exposed *stacks* of American currency. Tens of thousands of dollars of it.

It was Captain Greg Thornton's price of betrayal.

66

We unpacked banded stacks of ten thousand dollars, all in US one-hundred-dollar bills, and trucked them onto the rear deck. There was nobody around to watch us. The beer in the fridge was old and warm, but still beer. We cracked open two cans and sat cross-legged, counting the loot one band at a time.

There were twenty-five hundred bills in total—two hundred and fifty thousand dollars. Divided by one thousand rifles provided to the ABA, that was a sale price of two hundred and fifty dollars per unit. A pretty good haul for Thornton. Enough to make himself a handsome little retirement in some southeast Asian country without extradition.

"If they had this much money I don't know why they bothered with the rifle thing," Jacquie said. "There's more than enough money here to build a fuel oil bomb."

"This wasn't their cash," I said, sniffing a stack of bills. It smelled like laundry soap and yellow mustard, common substances employed by Mexican cartels to smuggle drugs and money past border patrol dogs. "This was cartel money.

An advance payment. I'm guessing the ABA was selling those rifles for a thousand dollars a pop."

"Pennies for a cartel," Jacquie said.

"And enough money for Hoffman to disappear if things went sideways."

Jacquie's brow furrowed. I knew what she was thinking.

"There's more money," she said. "The cartel took delivery. There's another three quarters of a million dollars piled up someplace."

"Likely in the compound," I said. "The FBI will find it, but they won't find this. They won't even be looking for it."

Licking my thumb, I commenced to counting out fifteen thousand dollars, roughly what I'd held in my pickup truck's lockbox before Hoffman and his thugs mugged me and stole it. I estimated the cost to fully repair my truck, and then decided I may as well purchase a complete restoration. I counted out another twenty grand.

Lastly, I remembered Tally, my accommodating used-car salesman. According to his rental policy I had to purchase the vehicle if I wrecked it, which I had. I closed my eyes and tried to remember the bright yellow numbers affixed to the SUV's windshield when I had rented it.

Ten grand? Maybe twelve?

He'd been a champ. I'd give him twenty.

I piled my fifty-five grand next to me, added another ten for pain and suffering, then pushed the remaining stack toward Jacquie.

She breathed a little laugh. "What do you expect me to do with this?"

"I don't know. Buy Suns tickets."

Jacquie stared at the cash for a long moment, and her gaze turned hard. She shook her head.

"I don't want a dime of their filthy money."

She dropped her legs off the edge of the deck. There was a tension in her shoulders that quaked like the tremors of an earthquake ready to erupt. I settled down next to her, resting my beer on one knee. For a while we enjoyed the quiet. I knew Jacquie was crying, but I didn't look. I gave her time, sipping warm beer and enjoying the glow of the sun on my face.

I was tired. My body hurt. I had that vague sort of after-action buzz that I'd only ever felt overseas after a good fire-fight. Sometimes, it lasts for weeks. A mix of survival elation and vague regret at the necessity of violence.

Most of all, I felt profoundly grateful. Grateful to be alive. Grateful to have stopped that truck. Grateful to have been given the opportunity to destroy the ABA.

Most of all...grateful that Jacquie was still alive. Just feeling her warmth next to me was the most calming, reassuring feeling I'd experienced in...years.

"I never got to thank you," I said.

"Sure you did," Jacquie said. "In the car."

"I'm not talking about the US attorney. I'm talking about you...for trusting me. You could have called anybody. Maybe Dallas. I hear he's your new partner."

Jacquie rolled her eyes. "What an idiot. He's almost useless."

"I'm a hard man to replace."

Jacquie looked at me. She didn't blink. Her smiled faded. Then she said, "Yes, you are."

I looked away, suddenly uncomfortable. We both chugged beer. Jacquie burped. We laughed. Then she jabbed a thumb over her shoulder.

"So what? Do we bury it?"

I looked back, swishing my beer can. Thinking back over the case. To all the people the ABA owed restitution to. All the pain and the suffering that no dollar amount could assuage.

And the legacy that one great man left behind.

"I have an idea," I said. "Come with me."

We reached the Richardson home at dinner time. Lucile had a feast prepared—pot roast, potatoes, beans, and cornbread washed down with sweet iced tea. There was "nanner puddin" for desert. I didn't hesitate to stuff my face while Jeremiah exclaimed about how Jacquie and I "wasted them dudes".

Lucile scolded him. Jacquie winked. We finished the pudding and Jacquie suggested that Jeremiah help her with the dishes. From the end of the table Lucile wiped her mouth and stared into her tea. She'd been quiet for most of the meal. Despite Jacquie's survival and the satisfactory destruction of those responsible for Cyrus's death, she wasn't jubilant.

I thought I understood why.

"Lucile, would you care for some coffee? Maybe on the back porch?"

Lucile forced a smile. I went to the kitchen for the coffee, then joined her in a pair of rocking chairs facing a manicured back yard. I couldn't help but think that I was sitting in Cyrus's old chair. It was worn.

Loved.

I sipped coffee and the two of us enjoyed the calm for a long while. Then I faced Lucile.

She was crying. Very quietly, but not ashamedly.

"Her name was Mia," I said. "We were planning our wedding when it happened. School shooting...senseless thing. I've missed her every day since."

"Jacquie told me," Lucile whispered. "She said you understood."

"I do...and I don't. I knew Mia for nine miraculous months. I can't imagine what years would do. How long were you married?"

"Twenty-nine years," Lucile said. "And twenty-six of them were good years."

I cocked an eyebrow. Lucile laughed, the tears still in her eyes. "Takes a while for a girl to whip a man into shape, Mason."

I joined in her laugh and sipped my coffee. There was a pit in my stomach that I'd been fighting all day. Actually, I'd been fighting it since that moment in the woods when the bat swung and bones broke. When I felt myself becoming something else. Something I didn't recognize and didn't like.

"I wanted to ask you something," I said.

Lucile cocked her head.

"It's about Cyrus," I clarified.

She blinked but didn't object. I pressed ahead.

"You called him a man of God. So did the reverend."

"That I did. And so he was...sure as any man could be."

"Right. I was just wondering..."

"What that means?" Lucile asked. Suddenly her eyes were dry. She looked very focused.

"Yes, actually."

"I felt it when I first met you, Mason. I knew."

"Knew what?"

"Knew Jesus had his hand on you. Was working on you. There's a feeling you get. You'll understand one day."

I swallowed. The pit in my stomach felt more like a chasm. "I guess that's where I'm confused. I've felt something, too. Things I can't explain. There was this lightning in New Orleans, and here in Arkansas there were dreams. Random memories that helped me find Jacquie. I just..."

Lucile didn't interject. She waited, looking like she had all the time in the world.

"I just don't understand what He wants with me," I finished.

"God?"

"Right." I thought again of Sid and Bucky. Of their screams. "I'm not a good person, Lucile. Not even close."

Lucile laughed. It was a smooth sound, very pleasant, and not at all condescending.

"What's funny?" I asked.

"You said you're not a good person."

"I'm not."

"Neither was Cyrus...not till God got ahold of him."

It wasn't the answer I expected. I sat a little stunned, just staring.

Lucile filled the silence. "We can't change ourselves, Mason. If you wanna belong to God, He's a'waitin'. All you gotta do is ask."

"Ask what?"

"Ask for Him to take over. Ask Him to make you a man of His own."

I nodded, but I was still confused. I squinted into my coffee.

"And...how do I do that?"

"Talk to Him, child. Talk to Him just like you're talkin' to me. He's listening."

Lucile went back to her coffee. I let the confusion swirl, too tired to unravel it. Too totally spent. From the back yard crickets chirped and an owl hooted. Lucile leaned back in her chair and closed her eyes.

It was the most peaceful moment I could remember in forever. I decided to let the questions hang for a while longer, and I reached next to the rocking chair to lift the duffel bag I'd hauled in when Jacquie and I arrived. I set it between us.

"I brought you something."

Lucile's eyes opened. She frowned at the bag.

"What's this?"

"Open it."

Lucile did. She peeled back the top to reveal one-hundred eighty-five thousand dollars in cartel cash. She blinked, then frowned.

"What in the world, child?"

"It's a gift."

"From who?"

"People who no longer need it."

She looked up. "Is this blood money? Don't you bring no blood money into this house, Mason Sharpe. We don't want nothing—"

I held up a hand. "It's not blood money. It was going to be, but it's not. It doesn't belong to anybody, and nobody is looking for it, honest. Jacquie and I want you to have it...to help with the bills and things. Maybe put Jeremiah through college. Whatever you need."

Lucile's lip trembled. She shook her head. "Mason, I can't take this."

I leaned across the gap and wrapped her in a hug. Lucile hugged back. Her tears dampened my neck, but I didn't mind. I finally released her, and again she shook her head.

"It's so much more than we need."

"I thought you might say that. I had a suggestion for whatever's left over. Something Cyrus would approve of."

"Yes?"

"I understand there's a local church in need of restoration."

That brought the smile back to Lucile's face, wide and sweet. I raised my coffee cup in salute and leaned back in the chair. We drank in silence, just enjoying the calm while Jacquie and Jeremiah swapped jokes and the Arkansas moon rose slowly out of the horizon.

It was a perfect night.

67

It was harder to say goodbye to Jacquie than I thought it would be. In the end we kept things simple. She punched me in the gut and told me not to be a stranger. Then she dropped me off at Tally's place to collect my truck and roared away in her rental car.

She didn't wave. She pushed her glasses high up her nose and was gone in a flash. I wondered if her eyes were moist like mine.

Then I heard the bell mounted to Tally's office door and turned to see him shuffling out, hands in the pockets of his camouflage pants, a semi-amused smirk on his face.

"I don't see my Traverse," he said.

"Yeah...well. How about cash?" I dropped two banded stacks of ten grand onto the hood of a Mustang. Tally eyeballed it a moment, then nodded.

"Fair enough. I'll get your keys."

My pickup was every bit as beat up as I remembered, baseball bat dings in the body panels and headlights hanging out by their wires. The driver's door only half-shut, and there was nothing to do about the busted windshield except enjoy the breeze. All my stuff was there—my camping gear, my violin. Tally had even spread a tarp over the truck to keep the seat dry in the event of a thunderstorm.

I fired up the engine and waited for it to warm, watching Tally as he changed oil on one of his used cars, whistling while he worked. He didn't seem the least perturbed by the vague conclusion of our rental arrangement. There was a vague sort of peace about him, as though neither the loss of the Traverse nor the subsequent cash payment altered his life in any way.

I thought of Lucile and her comments about sensing the hand of Jesus. I wondered if Tally was like Cyrus—a man of God. The question brought on a smile.

Once the engine was warm I shot Tally a two-finger wave and eased out of the parking lot. I sat a moment at the edge of the road, thinking about Jacquie again. My stomach was still sore from her punch. Maybe that wasn't all that hurt.

I could turn west, I realized. I could rumble all the way back to Phoenix. Call up the chief and ask for my old job back. Put on a uniform and turn up for third shift on Monday. Wheel out my old murder board and unpack the latest body in a south Phoenix ditch, listening to Jacquie whine about the Suns while we drove to a seedy bar to track down a witness...

It was all so easy to picture that it almost felt real. Like it was happening right before my eyes.

But it wasn't right. Not because it wasn't a good life, but because it wasn't the life I wanted. I'd become too addicted to the open road. Too curious for what lay around the next bend.

And what bend would that be?

I tugged the burner phone out of my pocket and found a message from Jacquie. Four short words, no punctuation or emojis. Just *"Call me sometime jackass"*.

I grinned. I tabbed to my maps and typed in an address. I'd found a classic vehicle restoration shop in Saint Louis. It was a four-hour drive. I'd never been to Saint Louis before. I knew there was an arch, maybe some good barbecue.

A good place to call home for a while. Maybe I would call Jacquie when I arrived.

ABOUT THE AUTHOR

Logan Ryles was born in small town USA and knew from an early age he wanted to be a writer. After working as a pizza delivery driver, sawmill operator, and banker, he finally embraced the dream and has been writing ever since. With a passion for action-packed and mystery-laced stories, Logan's work has ranged from global-scale political thrillers to small town vigilante hero fiction.

Beyond writing, Logan enjoys saltwater fishing, road trips, sports, and fast cars. He lives with his wife and three fun-loving dogs in Alabama.

Did you enjoy *Strike Back*? Please consider leaving a review on Amazon to help other readers discover the book.

www.loganryles.com

ALSO BY LOGAN RYLES

Mason Sharpe Thriller Series

Point Blank

Take Down

End Game

Fire Team

Flash Point

Storm Surge

Strike Back

Knock Out

Made in United States
North Haven, CT
13 November 2024

60229908R00236